I0583863

THE RUE OF HOPE

JASON R. KOIVU

Black Rose Writing | Texas

©2020 by Jason R. Koivu

All rights reserved. No part of this book may be reproduced, stored in a retrieval system or transmitted in any form or by any means without the prior written permission of the publishers, except by a reviewer who may quote brief passages in a review to be printed in a newspaper, magazine or journal.

The author grants the final approval for this literary material.

First printing

This is a work of fiction. Names, characters, businesses, places, events, and incidents are either the products of the author's imagination or used in a fictitious manner. Any resemblance to actual persons, living or dead, or actual events is purely coincidental.

ISBN: 978-1-68433-436-0
PUBLISHED BY BLACK ROSE WRITING
www.blackrosewriting.com

Printed in the United States of America
Suggested Retail Price (SRP) $19.95

The Rue of Hope is printed in Caslon

*As a planet-friendly publisher, Black Rose Writing does its best to eliminate unnecessary waste to reduce paper usage and energy costs, while never compromising the reading experience. As a result, the final word count vs. page count may not meet common expectations.

For Emma

The fierce little thief of my heart

THE RUE OF HOPE

CONTENTS

Chapter 1
The Gamble

In a city divided by more than the river running through it, the Harbormaster of Port Morton cast his weary gaze over the scant shipping in the sluggish water and sighed. The day had been typically long and trying for this uniquely important man entrusted with much of the city's prosperity. His ingenious ability to turn a profit was greatly valued by his lord, Faella Middlefield the Iarl of Port Morton, but maneuvering deep-draft ships and organizing a fleet of barges had not been easy during this years-long crippling drought.

As evening fell, the lighthouse beacon on the far point down in the bay flared up and warming fires showed as auburn squares in the open windows of riverside taverns. The harbormaster's comfortable abode across the Aed River in Brynseht, the hilly western side of town still clinging to its wealth, might as well have been on the far side of the world for all the time he spent there. He wished he didn't have to leave his home and family to cross the river every day for his work in Eastfeld, where slums were overtaking this lowland east of the river. However, Eastfeld had the warehouses and docks to accommodate shipping, so it had become his home away from home.

A quick and diligent, but distressingly pimpled assistant brought a lantern and hurried off to complete the last of his duties before going home. With his quill tucked behind an ear, the harbormaster held the light close to a cargo list and went over quantities with the captain of the eminently seaworthy Swiftwind.

"And finally the rice," he said a quarter of an hour later. "By your count, you unloaded how many sacks?"

"Twenty and five in all, and all of equal weight and dry," said the proud grizzle-bearded captain.

"Such a paltry shipment hardly seems worth the bother," sighed the harbormaster. "But our figures agree. Very well. That's all present and accounted for, Pool. And yes, quite bone dry as always." He smiled and patted the captain's back. The stoic Captain Pool nodded, allowed himself the slightest of smiles in appreciation of the compliment and took his leave, climbing aboard once more and disappearing into the depths of the hold with his first mate and a harbor carpenter to inspect his ship's seams.

The harbormaster rolled up his list, stowed it in an inner pocket of his fur-lined long-coat, and drew in a deep breath. The salty air coming off the brackish water might have been an unpleasant scent to most, but to him it signified another day on the job, and while there were certain aspects of it he could do without, he did love his work. Attending to the minutiae of the shipping trade could be a bore and an assistant could manage it for him, but he would have it no other way. With his day done, he cast one last look over the moored ships a mile off in the bay, cleared his mind and turned on his heel for home.

Hovering by a towering stack of empty crates not far along the wharf was a slender woman in a dark cloak that subtly changed color with the slightest movements to blend in with the browns and grays of the drab, decrepit waterfront buildings. Her hood remained up as she advanced upon the man with the sort of lively skip in her step of one who has spotted the person they had been searching for all along. The tread of her boots caught the harbormaster's attention and after a quick glance, a moment's confusion gave way to elation.

"Sister!" he cried. "I was thinking of you not but this very day! What brings you to Port Morton?"

As they came together, a slaughterhouse odor and some exotic scent sourly unpleasant but too elusive to pinpoint, radiated from her, yet he joyously threw open his arms and wrapped her in a loving embrace. She did not return his affection in the least, but rather stabbed him just below the heart and jerked the blade up. A perplexed shock and horror contorted his face as he sought for the source of the pain and then the reason for the betrayal in her eyes just inches from his own. Inhuman eyes, he thought as the lantern dropped from his hand with a clatter. With him still impaled upon the blade and blood and entrails sloshing down between them, she walked him toward the water and let him drop lifeless into the river, where he disappeared between the wharf and the hull of the Swiftwind. Above the lap of water and creaking wood, footsteps thumped down the wharf from behind her. In an instant, she turned upon her heel and faded into a dark corner.

The heavy-booted tread of the tall and broad-shouldered Ford Barlow stomped upon the worn planks with a steady, determined beat. Much about his build and appearance, even the way he moved, reminded people of a young bear who had learned to walk on his hind legs and to shave all but his straggly beard, as well as an ever-growing mop of dark, shoulder-length hair. A heavy brow and frowning, square-set jaw-grinding away at strong teeth at the moment could just as easily break into a laugh, but not today. Though young and strong, today he walked hunched as if shouldering a wearisome burden. It wasn't the work he had done as a porter on the docks for the last year and more that had put the bend in his back so much as the troubling thoughts weighing upon a simple man who preferred a clear mind. His hand rubbed against a bulge in his pocket, and he dug out one of Xalen's Luckstones, a robin's egg blue winkle known to give the bearer luck as long as the whelk living within the shell remained alive. Ford's winkle had died a long time ago, but he had kept it in hopes that some luck might still be gained from it.

"Lot of good it's done me," he said, tossing away the shell. It bounced off the side of the Swiftwind and came back to clip the very end of one of his fingers, sending a twinge of pain up through his hand. He swore, threw a shoulder into the towering stack of crates as he passed and toppled them with a resounding crash, then walked on with a bowed head, letting his hair fall over his eyes as a kind of shield against the attacks of the world. The outburst might have sufficiently released his tension for he was not a particularly vindictive man, but his foot hit a slick patch and slid out from under him. He growled, spat down at the puddle of gore upon the planks, and remained sullen. His nose filled with a strange, unpleasant smell beyond the familiar blood and guts, an odor unknown to him in its entirety, yet vaguely reminiscent of wet dog mixed with the stench of burning flesh with its peculiar sweet notes that tug upon the consciousness as it battles nausea. He waved away the air before his nose and dismissed it as one more disagreeable thing added to his already miserable day.

One more miserable day added to a life that had not gone as planned. After an accidental death by his hand had exiled him to a bandit's life from which he had then escaped to the city, he had come to Port Morton for a purpose thus far unfulfilled. "Not even close," so he thought.

Out of the shadows of his wake emerged a short, slender woman in a dark cloak with its hood drawn up. She glanced about to see that no eyes were upon them, then like a darting spider, a spasmodic spring sent her skittering from around a corner to slide silently up behind Ford.

"You will die," she said, the words slipping from her like a shiver from a crypt, and then she smiled.

"Gods and demons below, don't do that! You'll scare the life out of me one of these days!"

"Someday you will die, yes, if not for me." Her speech was awkward, a product of an uprooted childhood in which multiple dialects and languages had been thrust at her ever since she could remember.

"Probably because of you." Normally Ford would have been glad to stop for an amiable chat with his friend Elle. After all, they had a mutually beneficial scheme to discuss. However, today he barely let up his pace, which forced his diminutive fellow conspirator into a double-time race to keep up. As they left the docks, the seamstress-turned-thief with the slight, lithe frame hurried alongside, occasionally skipping over a mud puddle and dung piles to keep her knee-high leather boots and embroidered hose clean, without so much as raising the slightest perspiration or quickening her pulse. "What do you want?" Ford eventually grumbled.

From beneath her hood and a mane of shiny, black hair, Elle's round eyes, which could be quite beguiling at times, carried the baggage of mistrust. A past cut deep by violence witnessed at too young an age had fostered that mistrust and edged her eyes in suspicion, which the young woman masked in black makeup made fashionable by the influx of Amita women immigrating from over the sea. Those eyes now registered a degree of hurt. The little innate levity Elle possessed vanished in the face of Ford's frosty gruffness, and so she delivered the information she had come to relay in her common, cold reserve. "I come with your orders."

"Come on, say it. Which is it?"

"Loose."

"Lose, you mean."

"Yes. You fall."

"Fine! Just fine," he said by way of brushing aside her words as she repeated them with insistence. After they parted, the words stuck with him down a rutted lane and into an even narrower side street, subjecting his other thoughts with the persistence of an endless echo.

Ford was fighting for a prize that night and the odds-maker and fight-fixer he should care most about, a thug turned businessman named Barker, had decided Ford was to throw the fight. If he didn't play along, there would be severe repercussions, and yet Ford was actually considering disobeying the order. He told himself that he belonged to no man and would not be used as a puppet, but in all honesty, Ford needed a victory at this moment to make himself feel like he truly was his own master. And besides, he reasoned, the people coming to see him were his friends, and they wanted to see him win. In fact, they expected him to win, because he generally did. They would be counting on it, laying down hard-earned coin in the certainty of increasing their meager wealth. Barker recognized the worth in Ford's reputation as a reliable fighter and planned to milk what he could from it. If Ford went along with the scheme, he too would profit from his friends.

A cool peck upon his forehead, like the rebound of an errant fly, went unheeded. When a second landed on his considerable nose, he saw that it was rain. "Great. Just what I need." After such a long drought, he knew he should be happy. The people needed rain, but right now he didn't care what the people needed. The droplets irritated him. He wanted to be dry on the outside and wet on the inside. He wanted a drink. "That'll mend my fence."

From the moment he stormed away from his boss, his intended destination had been his favorite watering hole The Bald Man and the Barrel, or Baldy's as it was lovingly nicknamed by its patrons. At this former monastery converted into a tavern much frequented by dockworkers, he was guaranteed to meet his friends, and they would help him drown some of his sorrows in cheap ale for a time.

Moments before, the door at Baldy's had been shoved open and in the frame stood two mammoth-like figures, a father and son straight from the country, or so it appeared from their heavy wool coats worn over billowy smock-frocks, a fashion people of the city had given up years prior for tighter fitting garb. The pure white fabric, ruffled at the neck and laced down the front spoke as much to their wealth as did the heavy jowls on the father and the baby fat still clinging to the son, more excess weight than seen on most souls within the city for some time. The pair surveyed the establishment with sour and apprehensive expressions, expressions that sank into a curdling disapproval.

"Shut the damn door!" shouted half the patrons at the two newcomers, who shuffled in a few feet farther.

The father gathered up his voice in an affected bellow meant to carry his importance right across the room while jamming his stubby thumb into his chest and nodding to his son, an even more substantial version of his father, "My boy and me have come all the way in from Ashby."

"And wherein all of Dan O'dan is that?" someone shouted. At this a derisive jeer from the patrons shook the man's concentration and drove some red into his wide white face. His son had walked in this shade.

"My son here, they call him the Ashby Masher!" Pride swelled the man as he spoke.

"Looks like he's been mashing a whole lot o' potatoes into his gob," someone fired in from deep in the crowd.

"Listen now, all I want to know is, is this where the prize fight's a takin' pla--" He was cut short by a sharp hissing and Frid, Baldy's humpbacked landlord with a long ponytail and nothing much on top, waved his hands about as he wobbled over on tired legs supported by increasingly precarious knees and ankles.

"Hush there! Come along," Frid called to the newcomers, gesturing them over to the bar. In the city, there were rules about gambling, written and unwritten, and Baldy's followed some and forgot about the others. Keeping the tavern's extracurricular activities concealed was in its landlord's best interest.

"Is that who's gonna fight Ford?" shouted Owen, Ford's dopey-eyed friend. He yelled over the mild buzz of the patrons much louder than necessary as he always did since falling from a roof on to his head. Kind folk called him "dim-witted," while the hurtful taunted him with "sap-brained" and worse. At Baldy's, Owen was one of Ford's beloved tablemates along with Dunn, Stocky, Fingers, and Dunstan, whom they called Stan to distinguish him from the various Duns and Dunns about the city.

"Country boys," mocked Dunn, a sturdy young man from a well-to-do family. He stood like a newly-hewn oak mast, a build fostered by a doting mother who had fed him up proper since he was a sapling. Dunn lacked natural ambition, so to satisfy his insistent father, he made a very small profit by renting out a bed in his room to Ford. "Just look at them nice, new clothes," he went on, though he was himself always the best-dressed person at Baldy's. "They got all fancy to come up to the big city." He punctuated this last remark with a barked, mocking laugh directed at the two men from Ashby.

"He's a big boy, that one," said Stocky while sizing up the competition and guessing the lad to be about as tall as Ford with a frame as wide as his own, the rather squat Stocky being built like a tree stump. Ugly and brutish as he may have appeared on the outside, Dunn said he had a pile of ham for a face, Stocky was a pot of honey at heart and a man who had recently been like a father to Ford.

"Like a barrel of butter and beer!" shot out from another friend, a dark beanpole with a wiry bush of hair perched atop his head. He was a dyer of wool whom his friends had dubbed Fingers for his colorfully stained fingertips because it was easy to remember and they had forgotten his real name. A fawning slattern of indeterminate age wrapped around Finger's waist was still laughing at his coarse jest as uproariously as a drunkard, though she had not been drinking.

Stan, who upon the death of his father had inherited the spot at the end of the bench where he leaned his mounded girth against the wall, brought one rock of a hand crashing down upon the table and muttered a spiteful muddle of words about well-fed country folk as the two Ashby men huddled close to the hearth where the landlord had left them. Stan rarely spoke and since understanding him could be an elusive game and an often fruitless ordeal, all of his friends simply nodded in agreement as usual and added their own irritated grumbles, all but Owen, who smiled at the newcomers as he did at everyone.

The door crashed open again, and the patrons called out, "Porter!" as Ford barged in.

"It's Porter no more," he said while taking a few pats to the back as he made his way across the room. "They quit me. It's back to plain old Barlow."

"Sorry son," said Stocky sliding over to make room at the table. Over the past two years, Stocky had made more room in his life for Ford than anyone else the young man had met since coming to Port Morton.

"Bah, it's nothing this can't fix." Ford reached for the beer a barmaid was pouring out in front of him, but no sooner had she finished than it was snatched away by the landlord, and the barmaid was driven off.

"Not yet," Frid said nodding to the two men in from the country sitting by the hearth. "You've got work to do."

Ford fought with his instinct to layout the man who dared take away his beer. Besides, most of the room had their eyes upon him, viewing him with the pleased anticipation of making money on him. They wanted him to be in the best possible condition. Disappointing them would be painful.

"Hurry up then," said Ford. "Let's get this over with!"

"This way, gentlemen! And the rest of ya," called the landlord eliciting some good-natured grumbles from his standard joke.

"They call me the Ashby Masher," said the young man jostling Ford at the top of the stairs. The false depth he forced into his voice didn't suit the baby fat about his jowls or the fuzz upon his pink cheeks.

"Don't care," said Ford as he elbowed his way past the Masher.

"Knock his corn-fed face back outta town!" cried Dunn at the head of the crowd shoving around behind the bar and tumbling down the stairs into the cellar. This was the old monastery's former catacombs where the dead had once been housed, most of their miseries long since put to rest. Now the dank crypt-like space stored other kinds of spirits, namely Baldy's dwindling stock and the yeasty fumes from emptied barrels. The landlord locked away the whiskey and rum in a cabon, a sturdy white-oak cabinet left behind by the monks, who had used it to store their precious relics and treasured artifacts.

The patrons helped roll and shuffle barrels around the room and out of the way. Two lanterns were hung from the ceiling, casting an insufficient light that threw contrasting shadows against the illuminated walls, the support beams and the faces of impatient, mostly bearded spectators crowded together on the uneven floor where creepers crawled up here and there from between the flagstones. The cobwebs drooping from above were wiped away by the greasy hats and heads. The dusty, stagnant air remained unpleasant as ever, and Ford breathed in sparingly, for he hated it here. There was a hole at the bottom of two rickety flights of wooden stairs and then a poorly spaced half flight of loosening stone, leading into the chilled cellar that would soon be as hot as a blacksmith's forge.

The Masher, stripped to the waist as he swung his right arm about to loosen it up, already had steam rising off of his thick chest and round shoulders. Ford hadn't fought anyone quite as large as this in some time. Throwing the fight and making it look real would be easy, he imagined.

The cramped space, low ceiling and even lower ceiling beams forced Ford into a crouch; bent at the waist, head jammed down between his shoulders, and his long arms tucked against his body with his fists up at chest height. It was awkward, but he had grown used to it. The Masher, however, scraped his head along the ceiling, inadvertently elbowed his own father and bumped into one of the beams before they even began.

The crowd was a mixed bag. A few on hand weren't necessarily there to cheer on the Masher, so much as to jeer at Ford for having beaten them in a previous fight. Many were loyal to Ford and wanted to see their favorite local boy win. Some were more serious gamblers and had laid substantial wagers on the fight with a man paid off by Barker to do so. This confidant was slipped a few extra coins to sit in on these fights and report back the results. That unassuming man had long since infiltrated Baldy's crowd quite seamlessly.

Frid, the landlord, rapidly beat two mash paddles together three times in quick succession. At the signal, the two fighters began wheeling around one another, cautiously sizing each other up. "Solid lad," Ford thought as he watched the Masher duck under a beam. It was true, his father had worked him hard in the fields. Though no great lover of labor himself, Ford had done his fair share of hard work, hulling a cart loaded with filled trunks, sacks or barrels through the rutted streets to and from the dockyards all day long for the last few years until bulging muscles ran down his back and into his legs like wound ship cordage.

"Throw a fucking punch already!" The spit-filled shout blasted the side of Ford's face. He blinked and turned away into a fist that slammed against his ear, sending his head reeling in a disorienting half-silence that gradually gave way to a ringing. His hands must have gone up instinctively, he guessed, because a crushing blow caught him on the arm, followed by another just under the elbow. Sharp pain in the ribs and the tremendous force sent him stumbling sideways. Spinning back just in time to face the Masher coming on, Ford blocked a shot to his head and caught the next two aimed for his gut on his forearms.

The crowd threw their own fists and leapt over one another for a better look. Suddenly the room was aglow in a wavering orange as a fire spread upon the floor where one of the lanterns had been knocked down. Some drunken fool fell to the ground and rolled over the fire to put it out, while another pissed on it, both of them whooping and laughing.

Once it was out and the only remaining lantern hung directly behind the Masher, the singular light transformed the big farm boy into a polymorphous shadow in Ford's eyes and disguised his opponent's hands. The buzzing in his ear was dying away, only to be replaced by the crowd's din, amid which could be heard the father bellowing, "Y'all shoulda bet on my boy! I told ya he was good! I told ya!"

If a punch was coming, Ford couldn't tell, and he realized he might not have any say in going down. They would say this Masher fellow caught him one unawares right at the get-go and then it was all over after that. Letting it happen might be the smart thing to do.

Ford took a long step back, let his hands droop, and Ashby's Masher came on with a bull-rush. Ford stabbed out with an ineffectual right jab at the lunging shadow. The Masher dodged to his right directly into Ford's left, a left that sent a shock of pain tearing across his own bruised ribs. The blow rocked his opponent backward, where he cracked the back of his head on a beam with a sickening thud. Ford had done the same thing more than once before, but not with the same force. The Masher was out on his feet. Ford, holding his throbbing side, heard his friends urging him on, the crowd begging for blood.

Pouring on the hyperbole with the storyteller's flourish they loved so well, those who were there would later attest to witnessing the dismantling of one man by another with the ferocity of a hurricane laying out a great oak, its limbs waving about as the immense trunk crashed to the ground, its roots splayed in the air. The utter finish of a seemingly indomitable entity.

Amid the cheers and curses of the jostling crowd, the landlord tucked a small pouch of coins into Ford's pocket and began the laborious process of herding people back up the stairs. They were already replaying the best moments, relaying the details to their companions with joy and relish, as if the person walking back up the steps with them had missed the fight. There were a few sour faces, but more were happy than not. As he sat on a barrel resting, Ford took a barrage of slaps on the shoulder with shouted congratulations in his recovering ears until the room finally cleared of spectators.

"It's a damn fraud," shouted the father from the ground with his unconscious son cradled in his arms. The natural vitality of this robust man visibly drained from him like sand from an hourglass, all but for a beet red mask of anger and frustration. "This place is…"

He struggled through grief, gritting teeth, and a straining voice to find the right words. "This place ain't proper! Not by half! My boy didn't know he was to fight in a damned cave!" A ghostly pallor overtook him as he tried to revive his son with trembling hands. He called out his boy's name, shouting it into the young man's bloodied face and hesitantly slapped him where it looked least damaged in hopes of reviving him.

Ford got up and then leaned against a beam, while heaving in a lungful of the mildewed air. He wiped away the blood, running down his neck and watched the boy for signs of life as the father withered. He wanted to tell the man not to bring his son to places like this, not if he truly cared for him. As winded as he was, all he could manage was to wipe the pink spittle from his lip and say, "Go home." The man looked up at Ford and Ford looked away. He did not want to see a father's tears, but if he had looked he would have seen the boiling rage within.

"We're going to wipe out your sort, you worthless city scum! Clean off the land! Clean off the land!" he roared after the disappearing form of Ford crawling up the stairs with painful, tentative steps. Only when he reached the top did he feel the hand of Stocky supporting him from behind.

"Good show, son, good show!" Stocky strained to reached Ford's head and muss his hair. "You had us all worried, but you put him away! Boy, you put him away!"

Ford tried to lay a hand on his friend's shoulder in thanks, but jerked it back and grimaced as a bolt of agony ripped across his chest. He turned away and spat to hide his discomfort and watering eyes.

When they reached the top, Baldy's was strangely empty aside from the resolute drunkards, who never left their seats. The two stepped into the chilly street to find everyone outside, where a steady rain fell on amazed, uplifted faces. An elated Owen danced a bouncy jig of his own devising to music only he heard. "Is it raining or is it a dream?" he asked in his optimistic way, each word rising in glee along with his open palms.

"No dream," replied Ford. He took deep, labored breaths of the cool air and lifted his bruised face to let the refreshing water wash over it and revive his spirits. "It's not much, but more than I can remember since I got here."

"That's right," said Dunn. "It pretty much stopped raining when you arrived."

"You saying I'm to blame?" There was little recrimination in Ford's question, mostly a mild concern, for he was superstitious enough to jump to just about any conclusion.

"It's raining now, and you're still here," said Stocky. "Stands to reason it's got nothing to do with you."

"I suppose," said Ford. "Yeah, stands to reason."

In darkness broken only by the weak light from the window by Baldy's door, the tavern's patrons lingered in the rain, congratulated Ford once more and wished their friends a good night. Then some wandered off home, and others went back inside for a final drink for the night. Eventually, only Ford and his good friend were left in the subsiding rain.

"Here. I still got a little left." Stocky pulled a pouch from his pocket and held it open for Ford, who took from it a small wad of what they called demon's weed. Depositing the bitter leaf between his cheek and gum, he sucked contentedly and soon felt its soothing effect descend upon him.

"Thanks," said Ford. Being nearly spent and manners never having been drilled into him, it was as much gratitude as he could manage in the moment. There was a whole lot more to be grateful to Stocky for. His friend never left without saying goodbye or wishing him well and was forever checking up on him, making sure he was doing all right. Ford had no words for such kindness. However, he also knew Stocky would stay if he felt he was needed, and his friend had a family waiting for him. "Off for home?"

"Suppose I ought to be." Stocky spat brown juice wiped his lips on his sleeve and looked about him at nothing in particular.

"Suppose I'll head home, too."

"You'll be all right?"

"Yeah, I'm fine." Ford dropped the hand he was running tenderly over his ribs. "Go on."

"All right then. Suppose I ought to. Wynna's a great one for thinking up all kinds of stories for why I'm late." Again, Stocky spat and did not move. Finally, he got around to the question he really wanted to ask. "You'll be all right? I mean, after tonight? You got enough to go on?"

"Oh. Yeah, I'll be fine for a while." Ford held up the small purse of coins he had won, and he expected more once his friend Elle delivered what she reluctantly made on side bets for him, but he kept that to himself.

"All the same, I'll ask around, see if I can find something for you."

"Don't put yourself out for me."

It had been Stocky who had found Ford the porter job in the first place. His motives for helping the young man were more than just kindness, but Ford knew nothing of that. They locked arms in farewell without the usual clutching and jerking, then parted ways in opposite directions.

Each of his feet hit the wet ground like canoe paddles slapping water as Ford hurried away. Once Stocky was out of sight, he leaned against the nearest wall with his head lifted, letting raindrops sprinkle his face and licking those that hit his lips. As the rain came on heavier, he held an arm protectively tucked at his side and shuffled off.

The clouds blocking out the moon and stars forced Ford to grope along a lane of two-story, tumbledown buildings on either side of him vaguely outlined in these claustrophobically tight streets. Eventually, a light coming from a corner window ahead provided a familiar beacon to guide him.

More loud than visible, a man stomped his way, clinging to the overhanging buildings like a barnacle in order to keep out of the rain. Wall-hugger was the name for those stubborn sorts that hogged the outside of the roads, forcing all others regardless of age or frailty out into the filthy gutter in the middle. Ford didn't care how much wetter he got and usually would have surrendered the wall out of politeness for most people, but the fight was still in him. That thumping pulse and flush of hot blood was coursing through his body, and he was in no mood to move for this ill-mannered, neckless man obstinately plodding forward with an irritating arrogance.

From a few feet away, Ford recognized the sour face of Kearney, a hopelessly crude and ignorant man-child he had fought months ago in the street because, as he explained later to friends, "the stupid bastard was so eager to get his nose bashed into his ugly face he couldn't wait for the proper fight." Not only had he made nothing on the fight, but Ford busted his hand up that night and couldn't fight for months.

"What a waste," Ford recollected as they came together.

"What you call me, Porter?" growled Kearney through a sneer Ford found oddly confident considering the beating he had given him not that long ago. Then again, it was likely Kearney had forgotten all about it already. They met head-on and neither budged. Another few inches and Kearney's chin would have been buried in Ford's chest.

"Watch yourself Kearney, it's bad manners--"

"You oughta watch you -- yourself an'… an' where you're goin'," Kearney shouted, clenching his fists and reddening as he blundered over his words. "An' what ya sayin'!"

Ford steeled himself for the inevitable clash. Splattering footsteps in the mud raced up from behind. He turned, and something like a dull hammer smacked into the side of his skull, sending a blinding flash and an explosion of pain through his head. Distant distorted voices in Ford's ears called to one another as he verged on collapse, stumbled sideways into Kearney's vice-like grip and was dragged into the narrow gap between an abandoned import merchant's warehouse and Lightermen's Hall, its faded paint and cracked or missing siding much the same as all the buildings in the area.

The warehouse leaned dangerously to one side, and its eaves met its neighbor's in a crumbling kiss. In the cave-like atmosphere of the alley below the reek of urine hung in the motionless air. A firelight shone through the gaping holes in the abandoned warehouse, brightening the night enough for Ford to make out the shapes of those working him over with a flurry of fists and knees. More splashing footsteps, more voices, more fists. Someone had his tunic up over his head, holding him down after a blow to the belly bent him double. An elbow jabbed at his head and neck, knees dug into his sides, while hands tore through his clothes seeking valuables.

"Got it!" one of them shouted, plucking out the pouch containing the coins he had won in the fight.

"There's probably more! Look again!"

There were five or more of them, and Ford guessed they were young by the way he was able to throw them off and because the voice belonging to the one kicking at his groin rose high in a giddy, shrill laugh. "Keep your feet. Keep your feet," Ford kept telling himself; otherwise those boots would all rain down upon him relentlessly and cause far more damage than they were doing now. He thrashed out at the one holding his head down, and the boy crumpled under an elbow to the nose and fell away, but the others dove on him, gripping his arms, rendering him defenseless. His head came up in time to see Kearney's determined scowl as he threw a low punch that sent Ford to the ground gasping.

"Come on, Porter," said Kearney, bending over to holler in his ear, "thought you could take a punch!" The fists flew and then again, the boots. Ford rolled about trying to escape the kicks and cried out when one landed on his ribs. His attackers hooted in derision, but then the laughter died away.

"Hey," Kearney shouted. "Hey, you! Fuck off!"

Lifting his head with an effort, Ford made out the silhouette of a man blocking the far end of the alley. Down the other end, there were two more bulky figures. Ford's whole body slumped. These two were as familiar to him as was the labored breathing coming from the lone man at the other end of the alley.

Though they were only three, the hefty men stood like behemoths compared to the reedy lads surrounding Ford. Yet, outsized or not, Kearney's gang had the confidence of youth. They stood their ground, high on the ecstasy of their victory. The youngest of them wailed an improvised war cry as he whipped his fist about in the air with the coin purse clutched in his fingers.

"I said, *fuck off*." Kearney stepped forward, but already his resolve had taken a step back. Waning confidence infected each new word. "You hear me? This one's ours."

"Hand over that purse, boy," snarled the silhouetted man in a parched rasp that battled its way up a throat scoured of any fine, gentle qualities and leaving little more than dry edges. Ford knew that stripped voice well. It belonged to Cuthberht Barker, who was called Berht or just Barker by everyone unless they wanted to get hurt. A former butcher's boy known for a bellowing call in his younger days eventually lost his voice and his job and turned his massive forearms and wide fists to prizefighting. His new profession had netted him a flattened nose, a punctured tongue, missing teeth, a cracked rib that never quite healed and hardly enough money to make it all worthwhile, an embittering fact that still gnawed at him. After a particularly bloody battle that nearly killed him and his opponent, he had taken what remained of his winnings and parlayed it into a somewhat successful career as a fight fixer and minor racketeer in dockyard affairs. Bribes, deals, threats, and more, he would use whatever it took to get someone else's money into his own pocket, and through his own convoluted logic, he considered himself honest, because as he said in his own words, "I never stole nothing that weren't due me."

Kearney came from the same mold, but without the same ingenuity. Clever or not, he had plenty of ambition and burgeoning designs on Barker's fertile racket.

"You don't listen, old man," he said. "I told you--"

Behind him, Ford heard a struggle, and then a brawl broke out on all sides. Punches, kicks, wood cracking on bones, and bodies hitting the ground, accompanied by grunts, cries, and running feet. The other two men with Barker, his current lackeys Grady and Keene, were still there, while most of Kearney's gang were not. Holding over his head a two-foot-long broken board in one hand, Barker straddled Kearney's body lying face down in the dirt. The board cracked as it connected with the back of his skull and broke into two stumpy pieces. Barker pushed Kearney's head to one side, looked into his face and let out a satisfied grunt. The boy with the giddy laugh dodged away from Grady and Keene.

"Grab him. He's got the purse," Barker commanded. The boy danced nervously about the alley, not sure which way to run. He darted for Barker's end and was caught by a shoulder that slammed him into the wall with a thud and a tinkling of coins. "Oh, that lovely jingle!" Barker smiled broadly as he reached down, gripped the boy around the neck with one hand while searching him with the other. He held up the purse, drove the boy's head into the ground, and stood up with a satisfied sigh.

Ford blew a slug of blood from his nose and took shallow breaths as he struggled to stand. He faced Barker and received a crippling dig to his lower back that sent him stumbling forward, hunched over with a hand stretched out to stop himself from falling. It landed on Barker's chest, and he leaned on him for support as he sucked in air like a man suffocating.

"Throwin' it in so soon, Porter?" snorted Barker. "Little late now for takin' a dive, what you shoulda done back at that miserable hole with them pitiful wretches you call friends. Wouldn't wanna let them down, eh? But you go and let down your old buddy Berht?"

Ford's fingers tightened around the cloth of Barker's long-coat. With its deep indigo hue produced far away in the southern tropics, and the golden buttons and fine stitching bunched in this sweating fighter's paws, it was a coat made for a man of wealth and refinement, as well as one a good deal thinner. Ford thought had might take him down with one solid headbutt and make an escape down the alley, but his head sank deep into excruciating, pounding waves and swam in a languid mist of slow contemplation that only hazily comprehended the club slipping under his chin. When it clamped down upon his windpipe, he immediately leaped back into the present and concentrated on what needed to be done: relax and breathe, relax, and breathe.

"In there," said Barker tearing away a flimsy door midway down the alley. "And take that bit of snot, too." Grady, a mound of muscle and little else, threw on to one shoulder the limp body of the barely conscious boy with the giddy laugh.

Inside the abandoned warehouse, the smoke of a cookfire smoldering on the dirt floor stifled the air within the gutted building. Amongst the stripped interior and what remained of the blackened walls three forms vaguely distinguishable as men huddled together. One lay snoring, but the other two peered warily at Barker's crew from under bundles of ratty blankets, assessing the danger.

One of the three, a man looking twice his thirty years in his gnarled beard and wild hair, climbed to his feet, bent almost doubled over from having sat crouched for countless hours, and pulled a red-hot tipped iron poker out of the fire by its leather-wrapped handle. "Leave us be," he screeched, mania permeating every part of him as he waved the poker at the intruders. Ford and the boy were shoved down on their knees in front of the fire, and Barker's men moved to flank the man with the poker. He swung at the nearest. Grady threw up a hand to deflect it, caught the tip on his wrist and howled as the skin singed with a sizzle.

"Get out!" cried the man. The lanky form of Keene loomed behind him and caught his attention, while a furious Grady grabbed him by the rumpled clothes about the neck with one fist, then pulled him in and knocked him out with the other. The unconscious body was tossed into a corner like a loose bundle of sticks. His companions let out a collective groan, both quite fully awake now. The boy with the giddy laugh tried to flee, but Barker horse-collared him and threw him to his knees beside Ford. The boy choked and grasped at his throat.

"Don't nobody move," said Barker while casually walking around the fire.

"Stay down, boy," said Ford. He shut his sore, dry eyes to the smoke choking the room and heard sniffling and felt the shaking beside him. Barker stepped up to them, and the boy let out a whimper.

"I'll get to you right quick," he said and passed around behind him to stand in front of Ford. "But first, you–." Once more, the boy scurried for the door, this time on his hands and knees. "Grab him!" Barker shouted. As if wrangling a wild boar, Grady chased and pinned the boy against the wall by the door, lifted him upside down all thrashing and squealing, and dragged him back to the fire. Barker might have been more annoyed if not for his love of making someone squirm.

"Don't shit yourself, boy," he said, picking up the poker where it had fallen and replacing it tip first back in the fire. He still held the handle and leaned on it, precariously over the flames. "You ain't going down to the Old Hole tonight. I still got use for you. No boy, you're walking outta here on your own legs for one reason."

Ford opened one eye a sliver and searched the smoky room for another way out. There appeared to be a hole in a far wall. He couldn't be sure. All he knew for certain was that right now the attention of Barker and his men wasn't on him. He shifted his weight to get his legs under him more. If this jumpy child caused another distraction, he would be ready to bolt.

"You go back and tell your friends to stay off my patch from now on. You got that?" The boy's wobbly head bobbed up and down. "Let me hear it!"

"Stay off your patch."

"That's right. Think you can remember that?" The boy nodded vigorously. "To make sure you don't forget," Barker said, taking up the poker, "hold him good."

Grady clasped one of the boy's arms, Keene the other, while Barker grabbed him by the hair and stuck the poker into one of his eye sockets. The boy flopped about on the ground like a fish and screeched like nothing Ford had ever heard. He was so shocked that he forgot to run and just sat there watching horrorstruck along with Grady and Keene, who were standing by dumb and useless. Barker grimaced as if disgusted by the sight and annoyed by the sound.

"Fuck!" he yelled when the hysterical shrieking seemed like it would never end. "Shut him up, or half the town will be in here!" No amount of shouting at him would quiet the boy. They took to kicking him, striking at his floundering body harder and faster until a frustrated Grady kicked his head so hard it flew back and cracked against a wall. The body flopped on the ground and blood spilled from it in a swiftly widening pool.

Barker gritted his teeth, sneered and spat in the direction of the boy's body. A hand stuffed into his coat and scratched at the lice bites under his armpit. He took a few steps around the fire, absentmindedly kicking up the sooty dirt while thinking things over. The beggar who had been knocked out came to, and now four of them huddled in the dark corners, moving away whenever Barker neared.

"Was a nasty stunt you pulled back there, Porter," he said coming back to Ford and stooping so that their eyes met. His wheezing voice rose and sped up as he went on, while his face grew ever closer to Ford's until he was spitting on him with every word. "What you think was gonna happen? You just gonna take the money and run? Or'd you think, well now, Barker's a good friend, it won't trouble him none?" Keene held Ford steady with the club shoved under his chin. "You lost your mind? You got to be mad thinkin' you could pull that and walk away! Thought I made myself clear before! This ain't no fucking *game!*" He butted his head up against Ford's to punctuate the last word, then leaned back and glared down his nose at him before turning away to catch his breath, along with a lungful of smoke. A rough coughing fit had him more annoyed than before, and he broke into a bitter, malicious smile that he directed back at Ford. "You make me come down here to a godforsaken hole like this? That's a cruel way to treat a friend." He snorted and wiped his mouth on the sleeve of his coat. "I got this," he said shaking the coin purse in Ford's face, "but you lost me a damn sight more." He seemed upset in the way one might be when wronged by a sibling. "You fucking whoreson, you couldn't just lay the fuck down?"

Ford wanted nothing more than to lie down right there and then and go to sleep, but he knew it would only lead to a beating, and he wasn't sure he could endure much more. His head throbbed, and his chest felt like it was tearing apart.

"You're gonna wish you had when I'm through with you. Get ahold o' him good!" Keene yanked Ford back and held him firm and steady. Barker spun around and drove the hot poker into Ford's chest. Ford jerked violently back. Smoke from his burning tunic **was** sucked into his lungs as he gasped from the searing pain. Barker pulled off the poker and Ford floundered from Keene's grasp on to his hands and knees. He clutched at his chest, pulling away at the smoldering clothes as if he might jettison the inferno at his core. Barker turned back to the fire, pushed the poker tip into the coals, and stirred it around. "Let's get it nice and hot this time. We'll get a nice, clean burn straight through."

"No. Stop," Ford gasped.

"You ain't got the coin to stop me." As Barker spoke, he eyed the fire for the hottest embers. "We been to your squalid little hovel and you ain't got shit."

"Berht," said Keene. Barker ignored him. "Berht! We got a problem here."

Barker turned around to find a woman wrapped around Keene's torso. A threadbare and filthy beggar's blanket slid from her shoulders to the floor, revealing a dark cloak, a slim figure and the angular face of Ford's friend Elle. Her thin legs were wound around Keene's arms, pinning them to his side, while her ankles locked together and her heels dug into his abdomen. Sinewy muscles showed through her tight hose. Keene might have thrown her off, but he dared not move with the point of the needle-like blade she held in his ear. Barker and Grady moved toward them.

"No," shrieked Keene as the blade pricked his inner lobe.

"Don' not be the stupid ones," said Elle. Barker and Grady backed down. Ford stumbled to his feet and snatched up Keene's club. The three cowering beggars escaped out the door. Elle looked Barker in the eye. "Get out."

"I'm not going nowheres until I get what's owed me," said Barker.

"I kill him then."

"I'll get another."

"Bad loyalty costs."

"So, we got ourselves a logjam here. What's your move?"

"Give Ford a fight again. Another. And this time," her inflection and eyes darted at Ford, "he goes down as you say." Barker paced about, grunting and huffing, overwrought with irritation, while Elle held firm to the shaking Keene.

Barker whipped around and pointed at Ford as he shouted, "Don't fuck with me this time! One more fight, one more chance!"

Chapter 2
Seer, Seeker, Speaker

"What you seek may never be found, if what you seek seeks never to be found."

Ford stood before the weather-stained, cracked and rotten timbers of the dingy and disreputable Seer's Door listening to one of the greasiest men he had ever laid eyes upon. Had this man never washed in his life or was his oily hair and skin an intentional affectation? Ford couldn't guess. Mokaenyn the Seer ran his house as a brothel and a place of "spiritual refuge," where for the right price one might discover happiness in knowledge of the future or a woman. What Ford was after confused Mokaenyn, so he fell back on generalities as he did when he mistrusted a mark.

"What?" asked Ford in a wash of incredulity and confusion.

"That is what the cards say." Mokaenyn waved a hand over a few cards laid upon the rickety table perched in front of his house and at which he sat everyday. From there, he did his best to drum up business, from clients who sought either his fortune-telling services or the pleasure of the company of the ladies within. Because the house was located so far from the center of the city, married men like Ford's friend Stocky preferred it.

"They don't say much."

"Well," said Mokaenyn with the mysticism evaporating from his voice and manner, "if you gave me more to go on."

"I already gave you more than I could afford."

"I mean particulars. Your birth, anything. Give me something to go on."

"I told you, I don't know when I was born," said Ford, whose ill-temper was not subsiding as quickly as his bruises from a few days prior.

"Not even the month?"

"Not even the year."

In the doorway behind Mokaenyn, two haggard and middle-aged women worked what they had left of their alluring charms. Neither interested Ford. The one leaning on the left side of the door pulled back a sheer wrap to reveal deflated breasts dangling loose and lifeless like her drowsy eyes. In stark contrast, the particularly tall one on the right wielded an almost frightening stare framed by deepening facial lines and black, wiry hair streaked with gray. Her stare stayed fixed on Ford to the point of unnerving him. He was sure he had offended her by his indifference toward the women. However, the working women who took to drink often had peculiar or plain vacant expressions, as if they had drunk their own souls dry. Ford preferred the livelier girls, not these old husks. The one on the left kept at it though, pulling apart the slit up the side of her soiled skirt. Her pale and blue-veined legs did not help her cause.

"Don't even know his own age," said the seer turning to show his amazement to the women, who went on ignoring him.

"Never mind, just…if you see someone from out Lewiston way, tell her Ford of Barlow is looking for her."

"Ford? What, were you born in the middle of a river?"

Only tall jokes had grown more wearisome to Ford than this sort. He turned to go but stopped after a few steps when a thought struck him. "Tell her my father's name is Myer."

"I'm not your messenger boy," Mokaenyn called after him. The wiry-haired starer slipped inside, and the other followed out of boredom. Mokaenyn had no intention of keeping a watchful eye and Ford couldn't blame him. What was all this nonsense to him? Unfortunately, Ford couldn't afford to part with coin enough to pique his interest. And why bother? The seer obviously didn't recall, but Ford had been to this establishment before, with no results then either. None of the brothels he had been to within Port Morton had turned anything up, and he was pretty sure he had been to them all.

Here on the outskirts of the city, the air felt fresher, more alive and reminiscent of his former home in the country. Still, this was a far cry from his wooded hamlet. The shack of a brothel sat like a toad amongst frogs between clustered houses in Tilden, a somewhat new settlement that was already on the road to ruin. So far out on the eastern edge of Port Morton did the little settlement lie that many, if not all, of its citizens, felt no loyalty to the lord of the city, Iarl Middlefield, the wife of their lost Iarl. Instead, they sought protection and guidance from Pennaeth Brastersceatt, a minor lord whose family's vast holdings and wealth did not match his ambition for power.

Ford got an earful from the local folk in the Two Oaks Inn when he stopped to suck down a bowl of thin soup that hardly touched his nagging hunger. They were farmers and sniffed him out as a city-dweller right off. They didn't think much of the Iarl and her city folk. They backed Pennaeth Brastersceatt to the hilt. The Pennaeth would do this, they said, and the Pennaeth would do that. If only the Pennaeth had control over the city, "he'd whip it into shape! Perfect rows all around!" There would be beer and bread enough for all they assured those within earshot.

After the noonday crowd filtered out and the farmers went back to their fields, Ford sat alone on a sagging bench seat by a window, peeking through the shutter now and then to see if the rain was letting up. Outside in the rutted track leading out of town, a bar stretched over the road. It was only a plank resting on a pair of trestles, nothing that was going to stop anyone from coming or going. Its presence merely indicated a symbolic border, the Port Morton limits. It was where Ford had first entered the city after his long walk across the countryside from his home away east.

In a precariously leaning tumbledown guardhouse next to the bar, two ancient toll men sat dozing as they waited to extract fees from travelers, mostly merchants, looking to enter or leave the city. These two wizened men were meant to stop trespassers, toll-runners and other miscreants, while also warding off bandits and acting as an early warning to the rest of the city in case of attack. There was no great stone wall protecting them here in Eastfeld like the one surrounding the western side of town known as Brynseht, just two sleeping old men to save the city in a time of crisis.

Ford snorted at the thought and closed the shutter. He decided he wouldn't bother seeking employment as a tollman. Those jobs didn't pay well and always went to old folk or cripples. Anyhow, it felt too close to the law, and the law wasn't for him. He told himself that bossing people about wasn't his thing, and besides, forcing others to follow the letter of the law when he was so poor at it himself seemed a touch hypocritical.

As the rain eased off, Ford turned back toward town, passing through the stockyards, once alive with bellowing cows and bleating sheep, now silent and absent of pungent animal musk and endless dung. By whichever gates were open, he was funneled through the empty corrals, by the killing field, and into Butchers Lane.

The beef trade had not fared well through the drought. First, the grass and grain had dried up, then the cattle had disappeared, and finally, the price of bread and meat had risen, and with it the animosity between the producers and consumers. Tradesmen everywhere were closing up shop to wait out the calamity.

So little trade took place that Ford despaired of finding a shop open, never mind actually finding work within. Up and down the lane, shops were closed, boarded up or abandoned entirely. All but one, where he found a group gathered about a butcher as she dissected every ounce off a slender calf hanging from a beam at the front of her shop. A stream of steaming blood drained from the animal's neck into a bowl, where the butcher's beloved and territorial cat licked it up. Some leaked from a crack in the bowl and oozed down into the gutter, where a half-naked and fearful-eyed boy crouched on filthy hands and knees, and an alert dog with a wrinkled, twitching muzzle both lapped up the red-brown sludge.

"Nothing here," said a man Ford had crossed paths with over the past few days during their mutual and desperate search for work. Ford looked over his shoulder with some dread down Old Tannery Row. "Save your shoes. There's only one tanner left, and that's him." The man nodded at the youngish lad leaning against a wall. In his leather apron, Ford mistook him for the butcher's assistant, but he was waiting for his turn at the calf's hide. The relief of avoiding the tannery stench blended with the discouragement mounting within him due to his inability to find work.

Futile days hanging around the docks with the older men who had precedence over him waiting for any jobs that inevitably never came, drove Ford to seek out work in any profession that could use his services. Everywhere he looked, it was the same story as the docks.

All was quiet even by the riverside timber yard and wood mills, where an impasse over northern forest rights had stopped the flow of logs floating down the Aed and ground the wheels, gears, and shafts of the industry to a halt. At Fuller's sawmill, the squinting owner with three missing fingers joked that they could have used Ford's big feet years ago when the family had started in the textile industry and still beat out the cloth by foot. That was the most encouraging word he received all day. Even when there was a whiff of work to be had, Ford found more discouragement. Either he was too old to begin an apprenticeship, or he was not qualified and never would be.

He tried to shed the melancholia setting in after yet another miserable day by walking along a dammed canal and occasionally kicking rocks into its dried bottom where a multitude of refuse was piling up. However, the relative silence and solitude only gave him more time to regret his lack of education and wasted youth.

"That's enough of that," he declared, as he turned on his heel and headed back toward the more prosperous part of town. Full of determination to find work at one of the shops, he did his best to strap on a winning smile as he rounded a corner into a crowded street. The first thing he did there was to tread squarely upon a pile of dung.

As it turned out, it didn't matter what he looked or smelled like. There was no work there, so he left and passed on to the narrow, centuries-old and mostly forgotten market at Issinari Square. Shops and housing towering dangerously high above pressed in on all sides and echoed with the shouting of children and jobless men and women kicking a worn cow's bladder up and down the scalloped flagstones. No bellowing merchants called out to the haggling customers who had once filled the square in years past. Only a single and somewhat disgusted oil merchant prodded a dithering, old woman.

"Closin' up shop. What's yer pleasure?"

Ford's tired legs and sore feet vanished at the sight of his friend Dunn amidst the players, happily shoving people around. Ford loved a good game and dove right in, pushing his friend about and taking wild hacks at the bladder. Normally he would end up bruised and bloodied, but today he threw fewer elbows, no shoulders to the chin, and not once did Dunn end up on the ground because of Ford throwing around his size advantage. Consciously or unconsciously, Ford lost his individual battles with Dunn.

"You're getting soft!" shouted Dunn. The fact was, Ford couldn't bring himself to batter a friend whose help he needed so desperately.

"You find something?"

"No," Ford admitted.

Perhaps Dunn understood. After a while, even Ford suspected his friend was playing two games at once and knew that Ford was taking it easy on him because he was chasing after something besides the bladder. This made Ford try harder than ever, and he was on the verge of breaking his friend's skull and swearing off his generosity even if he did offer it when Dunn dodged Ford's driving shoulder and slapped him on the back.

"Hey, don't worry about it. I'll keep you afloat until you get back on your feet."

"Thanks, brother."

"It's nothing!"

It was as simple as that. Simple and surprising, thought Ford while passing the Issinari family hall on the way out of the square. How fortunate one was to have such friends. Everything seemed brighter and better as he turned on to New Market Street, the main road that curved its way through an increasingly prosperous neighborhood before sloping slightly down to the wide sunken grounds of Brastersceatt Square.

Easily the cleanest and airiest space east of the river, the square housed a few wealthy families alongside the Brastersceatts' townhouse, among other middling yet well-off personages in relatively tall, terraced dwellings. The market, a few profitable shops and the unfinished temple project alongside the Aed rounded out an area still spacious enough to be a natural meeting place for the masses. On certain days of the week, merchants handpicked by the

Brastersceatts were allowed to set up orderly stalls to sell their select wares here. Their voices rang out clear across the broad square:

"Whadda'ya'lack?! Whadda'ya'lack?!"

"New shoes sold! New soled shoes!"

"Lowest prices on only the best merchandise!"

"Boxes, baskets, baby caskets!"

Colorful awnings pitched over sturdy carts, and jealously guarded crate-covered spaces drew crowds of bargain hunters from Brynseht, people with the money to purchase new clothes or the odd luxury item, but who still felt the economic hardships that had long since crippled most Eastfelders. However, many simply came from all over the city to gossip, as this was nearly the geographic center of the city.

Ford aimlessly wandered through the stalls until he stopped by the temple construction site where Dab Yankin, a chunky man with a small head sitting on mounded shoulders like an egg in a nest, spoke from atop one of the foundation stones piled about the area. In front of a handful of drunkards and wastrels, Yankin stumbled through platitudes regarding the city's corrupt souls, often losing his train of thought and relying on humming drones to fill in the gaps. One of his few sober listeners was a fool, but an engaged fool, and so he directed much of his speech toward him.

Ford stood at the back listening for a while, but the speaker was so poor it was difficult to follow his tenuous thread. The only thing interesting that came of it was when a man near the front got sick and splattered his neighbor's leg with vomit. Both men swayed about and looked down at the mess in mild, almost careless disbelief. The sick man let out a pathetic moan and apologized.

"It's nothing," replied the other with a sincere though crooked smile and an exaggerated bow. The fool in the crowd immediately leapt forward, wiping away the mess from the man's leg and cleaning the surrounding the ground until the area looked nearly as it had before. He shot back up, hands coated in dirt and bile, and dutifully continued listening to Yankin, whose speech had completely fallen apart. He struggled to begin again.

"Ex...exsuvive...exsivsive? I, huh, ummm." Yankin's body drooped. He wanted with all his heart to impress his audience with the flowery oratory of more proficient speakers, but those words would not come to him when called for. He studied his shoes and lifted his head again. "It's too much drink what will do the good man in." The racking cough of a terminally consumptive case in the audience drowned out his last few words and drew attention away from him once more.

Ford took a sharp elbow in the side, as did the many others around him when a short, dusky man built like an autumn sapling pushed through the crowd to the front. His name was Tintot Song and he was a Weaverite lay preacher absolutely devoted to the relatively new religious sect, which took its name from its founder, Haccom Weaver, a virtue-obsessed boy from a weaver's family that was broken up by a father who would take their wares to town and spend half the earnings at a whorehouse. The way it tore apart his family and destroyed his mother made a lasting impression upon the boy. Soon after she took her own life, the young Haccom declared that he had had a visitation from the gods, who told him whores were the spawn of the most lascivious of demons. He took to the streets, and as a handsome young man preaching against whoredom, he found a fast following amongst housewives with his family-first message. After Haccom's death, the message was taken up by other preachers with their own ideas and agendas, which eventually warped the movement into a man-first, woman-second message with so gradual a shift that many female followers didn't notice the change.

Though Song was a foreign-born half-breed, the locals looked past that when they heard him speak, for his sermons and streetcorner speeches were more colorful even than the peculiarly brilliant blue eyes beneath his light, fuzzy eyebrows.

Once beside the fumbling Yankin, Song laid a gentle hand upon the much bigger man's shoulder and whispered something inaudibly soft and apparently soothing, because Yankin looked relieved and at peace as he relinquished the high ground and slipped in amongst the people, ready to add an enthusiastic voice in favor of Song.

Knowing they were in for a show, the various loiterers who had ignored Yankin now packed in. Market patrons and even the stall workers they left behind, turned their attention his way. Those with time to kill were happy to kill it watching the antics of this particular raving fanatic.

Even the mere sight of him was entertaining to them. In keeping with the attire of the typical preacher of the Weaverite Word, he wore a waistcoat jacket with old-fashioned, purely ornamental buttons – Ford never did see the purpose of buttons that didn't button – and a broad-rimmed wicker hat. Whether or not Haccom had ever wore a woven wicker hat was in doubt, but it was in keeping with the dress they believed had been made popular by their savior.

Though lax in his outward devotions, Ford's faith remained rooted in Hau, often referred to as the old religion. Still, he enjoyed a spectacle as much as anyone, and so he settled in with the rest.

Song filled his narrow chest and drove as much depth into his piping voice as he could muster. "Advocates and admirers, disciples and devotees of the true seers of the path to The Beyond…" Each word he pronounced with a serious, surgical exactitude. When he finished, however, he raised one eyebrow, and his stern façade broke into a devilish smirk. "I hope you've all paid your taxes."

He knew full well that this sensitive subject would get a good deal of the audience on his side. The road taxes imposed by Iarl Middlefield would have been imposed by any lord of the city for the upkeep of the town-to-town highways, yet it remained a sore subject with the merchants who paid this tax every time they entered the city, and not a few of them stood before him now. The crowd grumbled with mounting vehemence against the perceived injustice, and a few raised a cheer when Song claimed that his patron the Pennaeth would never levy such a tax.

"Only because he can't," taunted a mildly defiant tailor, who had been reduced to nothing more than an old clothes mender. He took a moment's pride in bringing about a chorus of cheers and a response of jeers. Song ignored the interruption, sucked in a chestful of air again and pushed on.

"The tyrannical powers that be in this town," he exclaimed, pointing across the river toward Bowen Dome, the Iarl's squat stone castle topping the craggier of the two hills west of the river, "they would take away your right to bear arms!" Cries against such an injustice shot up from various points in the audience. "But yes," Song nodded gravely, pushing the advantage of this bipartisan rallying point further than he ever had before. "It's true, she wishes to remove arms from the people so that only her own guard may hold them and hold dominion over you! Yes! It's already happening! The very rights that protect you!" Only recently had Song and others like him introduced these strident politics into their religious agenda.

"And not only that! She would let run riot about the city those purveyors of the dark arts! She would have magicians among us, free among us to conjure at will and at their whim turn you or I into a gelatinous worm or worse, disappear us! I'm sure you are, as I am, all for the healing arts, but those most holy of arts, they be no base magic." He spat out the last as if he could not get it off his tongue and away from him soon enough.

Shouts of distress shot out from various points in the crowd. These were points most could rally behind, especially if worded the right way. Though Ford was sure he didn't like this man, he found himself agreeing. He didn't want to be a worm.

Yankin quietly moved about the audience soliciting donations for the new temple while Song continued, touching upon a wide range of topics. Some were relatable and made sense, while others were far-flung and as incendiary as blaming the drought on the Iarl's seeming inaction. Whether you sided with the man or not, everyone agreed that Song was an entertaining spectacle.

With a wide, commanding stance atop the stone block, Song's ever-contorting features and acrobatic voice carried to all within the square, so that he would have to be willfully ignored, which few managed. His hands, now hidden safely behind his back, couldn't help but catch the notice of those watching him when his fingers curled in and out. His digits disappeared into sweating fists, only to reappear like spidery, flailing legs that crawled together over an imaginary web up to his chin from where they would threaten to take flight and flutter away like bats before being tucked and stowed again.

"Women, loose of nature, swarm the streets!" This didn't sound so bad to most of the men listening, but Song was delving into one of his most passionate beliefs, and a rush of blood-streaked his copper cheekbones with an umber swath when his emotions flooded his very soul and gushed out upon the crowd like a torrent of fire. His tongue licked at his lips as if to savor particular words and phrases, tasting the sweet essence of his convictions.

"The Iarl allows whores among us. Whores among you and I! I tell you, one and all, she has lost all moral standing!" He withdrew from within an inner pocket a short-handled iron brand with a crosshatch design. "There is nothing for it, but to brand all loose women and outlaw women to hinder them from taking part in such vile a practice." As his rant continued, he explained the necessity of simple identification of the diseased and degraded. A few didn't understand his meaning, others couldn't fathom that he might be serious, and many grumbled. The brand quickly disappeared.

"You Weaverite fanatics!" shouted someone. Emboldened by this, others shouted, "Braying braiders!"

The powerful combination of adrenaline from when all was going his way and the nerves infecting Song when things suddenly turned sour dared him to dive headlong into the dangerous waters of the religious divide. "No true believer believes in a dead god," Song cried out in hopes of heading off this heckler. Such a blatant attack upon the Hau religion infuriated many in the audience, who shouted insults and hurled curses at him, wishing him dead and on his way to the Deep Beyond, to Dan O'dan, that underworld where resided the god he had insulted. But Song took heart in the congregation of satisfied, nodding adherents of the Weaverite sect who smiled broadly back at him. Perhaps the seemingly indestructible spell he had woven at the start had broken down somewhat, but he felt sure he could gather the whole flock back into his favor.

But before he could accomplish this, mummers and a few exclamations from the back drew the crowd's attention. Song's resolute voice died away. His hands fell to his sides, and he stood vaguely staring over the turned heads of the people.

Ford was confused until his neighbor nudged him and pointed across the square to a brilliantly armor-bedecked warrior on a gorgeous warhorse. Everyone left the unfinished temple and hurried across the square, some unhinged souls out and out running, while others were tentative and merely amusedly curious. Regardless of their excitement or interest, soon all had gathered about the exotic warrior and his retinue of gaily-attired attendants trailing in his wake.

Though the throng made it difficult to see, it was hard to miss the radiant gleam of his flawless, shining full suit of armor. With a head above the rest, Ford could make out no less than a half dozen separate weapons, including ornamental blades, an over-sized mace, and a lance from which hung a banner. Though the warrior kept his jutting jaw stiff and his gaze remained rigid, he could not keep the jolts of his mammoth steed from shaking the various feathers affixed to his helmet. Snowy owl wings on each side and an albino peacock's plume running along the top all swayed like Okonkwon flesh dancers.

The warhorse itself, holding up very well under the weight of all this showy armor and heavy weaponry, was quite the spectacle itself. A rainbow-colored mane flowed out from under a helm capped with a single horn at the forehead, giving it the appearance of a metal-headed unicorn. The plate that held the helm and weighty horn generally in place must have blocked the horse's view for it had to be constantly reined in as it veered left and right. Its trimmed hoofs and braided tail and mane must have taken the warrior's attendants hours to prepare, thought Ford, but that's where his sympathies ended. He could think of far worse occupations than grooming a horse for half of the day.

And as for the warrior's attendants, even they wore attire outstripping that of the Port Morton inhabitants by far. Vibrant hues, plumage, and furs for mere servants! Such excessive grandeur had seldom been seen this side of the city. This warrior and his people came from the Forest of a Thousand Names, a land so distant as to be considered little more than legend by local inhabitants.

"What a gaggle of odd geese," said Ford, and though one man nearby told him to "stuff it," he wasn't alone in his opinion. Amid the overjoyed and overawed crowd, some laughed and mocked, waving their fingers back and forth atop their heads. That said, the majority of the people had fallen in love with Forest culture these days. Children wore fake elf ears made of paper or hog's ears. Even though the people of the Forest weren't actually elves, those who lived outside of the Forest could not be convinced of it. And it didn't help that Forest folk were more fairy-like in some ways compared to the people of Port Morton, who were much more stout than their shorter and more slender neighbors in the faraway northern lands.

However, this warrior and his attendants were as human as any of the folks surrounding them, many of whom boldly stood before them and said hello in the Forest language before running away laughing with their friends. Those were mostly children, though even a few adults were making fools of themselves. A disheveled fellow with patchy hair followed behind the horse on his knees with his trembling hands clasped and tears streaming down his face as he called out beseechingly to the warrior. His random pleas for assistance either went unnoticed or were disregarded.

All this fluttering worship was quite ridiculous to Ford, who had seen true fairies with his own eyes. It was clear to him that these Forest folk were as human as the next man. There was nothing special about them and yet he couldn't help but look on with some measure of interest. The warrior and his attendants halted a short distance from Pennaeth Brastersceatt's door, and while two of the attendants kept the horse calm and the crowd at bay, the third ran up the stairs to knock.

"He won't find nobody home," came a slow, methodical drone from somewhere below Ford. He looked down to find the familiar frowning face of Daellyn "Ratty" Hallofford by his elbow. The stunted little man in the tattered rat-catcher britches was an occasional patron at Baldy's, who had gotten the nickname from his job, as well as from his rodent-like shape and appearance.

"They won't, eh?"

"No," said Ratty, shaking his head with a solemn gravity. "Brastersceatt's man has me in once a week and he ain't there at present." The warrior would not be pleased. In a token gesture of service to his lord, he had floated on a boat down the Aed along with the first log drive in years, and now he felt it his due to be accepted into the great houses of Port Morton, regardless of whether or not an invitation had been extended. Ratty went into a more detailed account of his mundane work, which Ford mostly ignored until his interest was once more piqued. "You know what's funny?"

"No, what?" Always ready for a good joke, Ford momentarily forgot he was speaking with one of the least humorous people he knew.

"I wasn't allowed in the cellar this last time."

"How's that funny?"

"How's that funny? Cellar's where you find all the rats. There and the pantry, of course. Why would they not want a rat-catcher in the cellar? Makes no sense." They stood there watching Forest folk along with everyone else for the longest time and then Ratty broke the silence between them with a dreamy question. "Have you seen any rat-faced people lately?"

Ford had seen only the one standing beside him, but it seemed cruel to say so. "No. You?"

"Yes. Just yesterday and not far from here. They looked like real rats, I swear to you."

"Maybe you just got rats on the brain."

"Maybe."

Behind them, Tintot Song tried to begin anew by railing against the money being spent upon trivial entertainments and lavish feasts for the visiting delegation from the Forest of a Thousand Names. Hosting the weeks-long diplomatic mission meant to bring an accord between the people of Aelwyd, specifically the city of Port Morton, and the people of the Forest would indeed be costly, but no one wanted to hear it. A party was a party after all and there promised to be free entertainments brought all the way from that distant and fantastical land, the likes of which were seldom seen in Aelwyd, and the people couldn't wait.

Song consoled himself with the observation that the warrior and his retinue would eventually leave. It was merely a matter of waiting out the distraction and then recapturing his listeners. But just then a flash of blue light lit a puff of smoke rising up from a small group of children gathered at a corner on the far end of the square. Away went the crowd to see what new entertainment might be afoot.

"A magic show!" Ratty's dull eyes popped like full moons, and his face became a mask of joy twenty years younger. Ford had never seen him so excited. When Ratty skittered off, Ford followed with a hop in his step to keep up.

The two of them stood behind the children all crammed into the "magic circle," a five by five-foot square marked in charcoal upon the flagstones in front of a makeshift stage. Those within the designated area were submitting themselves to any magic done to them without recourse to prosecution against the magician, barring death or irreparable disfigurement.

From behind the small stage, the mage manipulated through levitation a pair of puppets, which he used to tell a well-known moral tale about a warrior fulfilling all of his clan chief's wishes time and again regardless of their mounting difficulty and unreasonableness. Though loosely based on a true story, the part about the many-headed giant who swallowed a mountain whole seemed a dubiously tall tale.

The mage's wrinkled eyelids drooped, and he hardly took notice of the puppets hovering beneath each hand, twitching ever so slightly with the old man's involuntary shaking as he dragged them about and went through the motions in an almost entirely silent retelling of the story. The children soon grew impatient.

"Make me big!" and "Light my brother on fire!" some began shouting.

Awaking to his audience's agitation, the mage cut the story short, and the puppets flopped to the ground. His assistant, a lanky teenager standing stock still beside the stage for most of the show with lowered eyes and long reddening cheeks, grabbed the puppets just before the children did.

The mage hobbled around to the front of the stage and stuck a wooden rod a yard long into the ground. He then cast a yellow orb onto the top end of the rod, set it to spinning, and went to work setting up the next part of his act while the crowd remained mesmerized by the whirling ball of light. Most of the children were delighted just to gaze at it, but one entranced boy with a gleam of greed in his dark eyes reached out, wavered for only a moment, then cupped his palms under the orb, which burst and vanished all but for an oily film dripping from his hands. This had the audience in stitches, especially at seeing the boy fighting to keep the oil from slipping away between his fingers.

The mage came back around and without the least look of surprise that his magic had been disrupted, plucked the rod from the ground and commenced the next act. The children groaned as one when they saw that it would be another puppet show. This one told an old story of ambition gone too far and power corrupted, though interjected with new characters, characters that drew a striking resemblance to leaders of the community, most notably Pennaeth Brastersceatt. The jab was lost on no one, especially not Tintot Song, whose person full of disapprobation infiltrated the mage's audience like a plague permeating the populace.

However, the old chestnut of a tale was chosen not so much for its political agenda as for its almost total lack of magic. The old mage looked worn and levitating the puppets appeared to be all he was up for at the moment. The children became restless, the assistant turned redder, and the conversation of two Hilmarsan men standing in the middle of the crowd grew louder.

"Listen ta story," said Stan, one of Ford's drinking companions at Baldy's. The gruff, no-nonsense tone surprised the men into silence. Ford almost called out to his friend, but the menace in Stan's voice made him hold his tongue as well. The old mage pushed on. He had to, if his faded robe and the holes in his shoes were any indications of how much he needed the extra money, he might get by putting on a good show. Unfortunately, he no longer had the energy to make up for his lack of natural showmanship, and so the tired performance had the children sulking and whining for "real magic". Eventually, the two men of Hilmars resumed their conversation.

"Listen ta story!" shouted Stan into the face of the loudest of the two men just before head-butting him on the nose and knocking him over backward with blood spurted and flowed over his mouth and chin. That brought the crowd to life. Some cheered for a fight. Fearing the gathering might disperse, the mage dug into a pocket within his robe, pulled out a handful of colorful dust, muttered a few archaic words and whipped out his hand. A dazzling prismatic spray of light shot from his fingertips, the air filled with the scent of flowers, and instantly the audience turned docile, even some of the people standing outside of the designated magic circle. After the spell was cast the mage leant on his assistant's shoulder with his mouth hanging open as he took a few deep breaths. His spell had not been cast wide enough to quell the outermost members of the audience amongst whom Stan and the two Hilmarsans tumbled about.

"This is illegal witchcraft," cried Tintot Song repeatedly as he shoved his way toward the old mage. "It's heresy! Evoking demons! Unnatural acts and worse! I'll have you arrested and thrown in a dungeon where you belong!" He had plenty more to say on the matter, but it only gurgled from him as he was elbowed out of the way by Ford, who cleared a path through the people to get to Stan.

While Ford dodged punches and pulled bodies apart, behind him, Song madly sputtered away after catching his breath, and the old mage and his assistant packed up and slipped off as inconspicuously as possible.

"Let's go," Ford pleaded with Stan. "We got to go. Don't want to get arrested, do you?" Nothing was getting through. Stan thrashed about and swung wildly at the Hilmarsans while Ford held him about the waist. "Stan! Stan, let's go get a drink!" Only then did Stan reawaken to the present world and allow Ford to lead him away from the square.

Chapter 3
A Mage's Proposition

"I swear to you, I stuck my hand in that hole and when I pulled it out it was covered in slime." Ford put down the knife he was using to carve pieces to the game Strategaeth and wiggled the fingers of his raised hand. It was the following day, and the two companions to whom he was relating the story leaned even further forward and let out small gasps of intrigue and astonishment. "And that's not the odd bit!" Ford went on to describe an encounter he had had years before in which he fell into a ravine and saw "some weird looking little people."

Whether the story was true or not didn't matter to his friend, Alan o' Tilbury, a scribe whose youth was disguised by a studious nature, bags under the eyes and a habitual slouch like that of the willowy quill he used to hurriedly scribble down the essence of Ford's tale. Alan collected any and all of Ford's tales in hopes of turning a small profit from them by way of a book of legends or lore he was compiling in his free time. Ford was paid in ale and mutton chops, which he thought quite a fine trade. Since Alan hoped to pocket a few coins in the transaction, Ford felt he could trust such motives and was willing to tell his tales of fairies, tales he never would have told his friends at Baldy's for fear of being belittled. That would not happen with this pair of eager listeners.

Alan's friend Adeline Lighterman, a music teacher who looked like a blanched stalk of wheat perpetually blowing in the breeze, listened with rapt attention for the story and the storyteller. Her upbringing had created a wall of the reserve, and yet she found herself unable to take her eyes off his expansive frame, his solid chin, and even his long, strong nose with its slight bump along the bridge from the time it broke. She was still trying to get used to the overall length of him. Aelwyd men were a bit taller than the other races on the whole and Ford had a head more height than most of them. She liked a tall man, one who would at least match her own lanky form. Finally, her eyes rested upon his as she tried to capture their true color in a moment when they were averted in the midst of a deep conversation. A while later, she went back to them for a second gaze but didn't notice that he had since stopped talking.

"What do you want?" Ford asked with a slight air of irritation.

"I'm sorry?" said Alan looking quizzically to Adeline, who looked just as flustered by Ford's sudden, inhospitable turn. "I don't understand. Have we done something wrong?"

Ford gave no response, but rather stared, somewhat annoyed, just above their heads. They followed his sightline and gave a little start when they found someone standing directly behind them in an otherwise empty tavern.

"What is it?" asked Ford. He was not fond of Elle tracking him down like this. It felt too much like an invasion of privacy. Besides, he couldn't figure out how she so often appeared out of thin air, and that vexed him as much as anything. Getting a better look at her flushed cheeks, his irritation evaporated. "Have you been running?"

Elle eyed Alan and Adeline, and leaned between them to get as near to Ford as she could in order to whisper, "There are men come for you."

Ford overturned a chair and knocked aside a table as he thundered across the room. His face paled as he eased back the shutter and peered through the window up and down the muddy street where a gaining drizzle rippled the myriad of puddles. Worried though he was, his body heaved and tensed, and to his friends watching on it was apparent he was ready to take on whatever was coming for him.

The fear was for Barker. They had a deal, but Ford couldn't be sure Barker wouldn't change his mind. Perhaps he decided he wanted his money now. Ford leaned as far to either side as he could to see without sticking his head through the window. The street was empty of all but washerwomen.

"They are gone," said Elle at his elbow. "I sent them off to…" she searched her mind for the phrase, "to chase the mild goose."

Ford breathed easier but drew her a few steps farther from Alan and Adeline. "Who were they?"

"Magi or I think. They come to the Baldy Mens[RF1]. The chubby one with a silly hat said he is…" At a loss for the right words, she entwined her fingers, thrusting them together repeatedly in a way that brought to mind coupling and intimacy. "You cause and a Dan?"

"My cousin Aedann? Why didn't you say so? I haven't seen him in ages," mused Ford the color returning to his cheeks along with an enlivening smile. "What did he want?"

"You. I say this before."

"Do you think you can find them again? It must be important if that slug got off his lazy ass to come all the way over the river. Must be damn important." If his cousin had been looking for him, it then dawned on Ford that it could only mean he came to relay some bad news he had received from back home, perhaps a death.

"I think it will not be hard for to find a slow fat man and a tall skinny boy both in magi robes," said Elle, admirably injecting sarcasm into a language she was still mastering, but Ford caught none of it.

"Great. That's real good," he said, grabbing her by the shoulder and inadvertently jostling her about as he stared out the nearest window with a suddenly dreamy contemplation. "It'll be good to see family again, eh?"

"Listen," she said, prying away his hand and lowering her voice again as she tried in vain to move him farther from the table where his friends sat. "It is set. It is set, you understand?" She poked his chest and punched him in the stomach until he noticed and focused on her face. "Two weeks of today at…maybe a banyon barn?"

"A banyon? Oh, abandoned. Hmm, it'll do, I guess. Where?"

"He do not say. But maybe also at the Horseshoe. The place it is not set in…in rock. I will find the fat man and boy, and I will return later and to tell more about--" Instead of saying it, she stopped and, looking him purposefully in the eye, inclined her head slightly to one side as if to say, *you know what.* Then Elle slipped from the tavern like a cross-current breeze.

"Your friend--" began Adeline, but she stopped, pausing to allow Ford to correct her if he wished. He did not, which pleased her, and so she went on, gayer and quite charitable. "She has lovely eyes."

Ford gave a noncommittal smile and scratched behind his ear, keeping mum as he reflected upon his friend's natural beauty. He was on the verge of admitting what most men and some women felt about Elle, that the gods had put in a good day's work when they created her. However, Alan cleared his throat and began reciting verse to a serpentine playing piece held before him.

"River drake, river drake! Vile sneaking snake--"

"Oh, that's good!" put in Ford.

"Serpent of the night. Take flight, take flight! Its deathly poisoned bite. Son of water, slippery daughter. Roiling coils drag deep the slaughter."

Adeline gave a melodramatic shudder and clutched her shoulders. "You give me the chills!"

"This is a work of art," said Alan squinting at the playing piece held close to his nose. Its intended serpentine shape was a touch angular, but Ford redeemed himself with tidy marks upon its sides indicating legs, the small fins of the drake where such a dragon might have wings, and the perfect little pockmarks for eyes and nostrils at the end of its snout.

As an amateur carver, it was Ford's best attempt at the Drake of Dynwyllae, the legendary beast that had once terrorized villages about the sodden swamps of Maccon until slain by Loegaere and Laytha of Mudfeld, legends themselves, this shieldman and his spearwife. Ford's best work it may have been, but it had only come after much trial and a great deal of error.

"I tried one all coiled up," he admitted, "but it looked more a turd than a drake."

"Well, this one is no turd," said Alan as he placed the piece on the table amongst the others. "All the same, I'm afraid I can't afford the whole, not its true value, I mean." Both he and Adeline had spent the time during Ford and Elle's private talk admiring the craftsmanship that went into the Strategaeth set. Adeline ran a graceful finger, long and thin like herself, down the length of a miniature tree.

"Exquisite," she said. "You show a promising artistic aptitude." Drunk on the compliments, Ford blushed, and a cockeyed smile crept up one side of his face. Even though he didn't understand what she had said, she said it with the kind of warmth that could only be complimentary in his experience. And though Ford denied his creation's worth, he was inwardly pleased. Never had he received so much attention for what he considered to be nothing more than a hobby. In his mind his father and brother were far superior in the craft. Placed against his skewed memory of their ability, the measure of his own talents always came up short.

When he had brought the set to the Three Sheets, a Wash Lane tavern south of the docks with spongy floors that attracted launderers by day and lovers of music and dance by night, he wasn't expecting to get much for his carved creation. When he first met Alan, it was obvious by the young man's tunic with the worn elbows, as well as the toe poking from one of his shoes, that this scribe was not weighed down by coin. However, Alan's enthusiasm and usual generosity assured Ford he would get a reasonable price, perhaps more if Adeline's will prevailed

"You'd better buy this beautiful piece of art before I snatch it up," she goaded Alan. "And don't be your usual stingy self! Ford…May I call you Ford?"

"Sure," said Ford with some spirited nodding.

"We've known each other only a short while, but you have a way of putting one at ease." It had been months since their first meeting, and although they had only seen each other twice in the intervening time, by now Ford would have been on a first name basis with most others he would call friends. This woman was different, however, and so he simply gave a bow of his head. "Ford deserves the best, the fairest, the most advantageous price!" As she said this, she placed one of her boney, white hands upon Ford's forearm almost absentmindedly. A woman laying hands upon him was something Ford had grown accustomed to since moving to the city. However, he had not paid for her and further, this was a lady from the western side of the river. It gave him a little unexpected thrill. Alan's glances, the silence that descended upon the group, and Adeline's suddenly retracted hand all went unnoticed by Ford, who sat there emitting happy, embarrassed mumbles.

"More ale," Alan called across the room, though he wasn't the shouting kind. The scene was more than he could bear as the extra wheel of this awkward cart.

"Cheers to you, brother!" Ford called, returning to his old self as the drinks were poured out. "I don't like to beg, but I won't turn down a drink!"

Alan then launched into the topic of music, a subject guaranteed to distract Adeline and interest Ford, who loved a good tune. Seldom was a good tune played well at Baldy's. Better entertainment was the reason he came to the Three Sheets on occasion. A more boisterous entertainment was the reason Alan and Adeline traversed the river to be here. Adeline could hear more refined music in houses about her own neighborhood. In fact, she even played such music for wealthy individuals and taught it to their children. But as she explained, the attraction of Eastfeld music for her lay in the way it was played with joyous abandon and for the simple love of song.

"One does not get that same passion when teaching the harp to boys who would rather be chasing girls." Ford agreed wholeheartedly. Whenever his brother had tried to teach him something, he'd often drifted off into a daydream about girls.

The conversation still had legs when the door opened and in walked a short, double-chinned, round man wrapped tightly in a tattered cloak. The head of a teenaged boy stuck out from behind him like a spotted, white oval plate with a wobbly pair of olives rolling back and forth upon it.

"Danny!" shouted Ford as he bounded up and across the floor like a shaggy dog excited to see its master return after a long separation.

"You may declare it impossible. You may even laugh at the very idea it being so utterly implausible. However, I believe the rain has never been wetter," pronounced Aedann Goldsmith, while shaking off droplets that splattered everyone around him.

"Wetter than ever, cousin! Couldn't agree more!" Ford hardly knew his uncle's son, but that wouldn't stop him from referring to him by the familiar

"Danny." Having not seen a single relation in years, he would have been glad even for a reunion with his stepsister Tilda, the least favorite of all his relations. Danny was beloved by few. In fact, some tax collectors had a more sympathetic, lovable nature than he. And so he stood stiff and miserable while enduring the jostling Ford gave him about the shoulders. "It's great to see you!"

"Bellowing demon's bawls, you have a field hand's carrying voice," Danny sniped while removing his tall acorn hat, spanking in vain at an unruly wave of springy hair, and making Ford help peel off his soaked cloak, which did nothing to reduce his rotund figure.

"You've lost weight," exclaimed Ford.

"The food at the school is execrable. Tasteless when not disgusting and never enough of it," replied Danny as he succumbed to the pressure of Ford's hand on his shoulders and flopped down upon the last remaining seat at the table with a great blustering sigh. This left his companion, fully visible for the first time, standing slump-shouldered and vaguely forlorn. Ford leapt up again, introduced himself and the table while jerking the boy's arm half out of its socket. The gangly, long-faced teenager with close-cropped hair peeking from under a boxy calotte, his school's official headwear, mumbled a greeting and murmured that his name was Yonn. Then his eyes promptly dropped to his tall-heeled shoes that kept most of the mud from the ends of his thick robe. Ford blinked at Yonn's face. "Oh say, you're that boy I saw at the magic show!" Yonn reddened somewhat as he considered lying, but as far as he could tell, Ford was not about to make fun of him, so he nodded. Ford did not mock him for playing toady to a haggard and desperately poor mage, but rather he lifted a bench from an empty table over everyone's head and seated Yonn on it, then planted himself beside him and told the table about the scuffle in the square the day before where he had seen the boy.

"So, it was our Ford who saved Instructor Walader," said Danny.

"Me? I didn't save nobody," protested Ford, but the boy nodded.

"No doubt the instructor would wish to show his gratitude to the one who extricated him from the indignation and prohibitive cost of prosecution. Yes." Danny's gazed drifted, and his speech trailed off almost to an inner monologue. "Yes, that could come in handy. Possibly quite useful."

A *quiet* consumed the table so quickly and completely that the bored barmaid listening in, felt conspicuous, and moved away to busy herself at the unoccupied far end of the tavern. After the general pleasantries were dispatched and fresh rounds were ordered, Ford let loose a few of the questions begging to leap from his lips.

"Have you heard from home? Is everyone all right?"

"Everyone is fine," said Danny.

"My folk at Barlow as well?"

"Them as well."

Ford wondered how much his cousin knew about the accidental death of his stepmother and what Danny thought of the part Ford had played in it. He decided his cousin couldn't think him a murderer and still show up here to meet him of his own accord and with relatively good humor.

After the most pressing questions had gotten answers, Ford let up and found interest in his cousin's time in the city, where Danny had been for a long time, now attempting to cultivate a budding capacity for magic that had revealed itself in years past when sparks fired from his young fingertips like a tiny blast of lightning.

"How's school?"

"Every day spent there plummets me deeper into ruin."

"I hear you, brother." Ford gave a brief rundown of his own monetary woes.

"Well then, I have come at an opportune moment it would seem." A satisfied gleam came into Danny's eyes like a predator with its prey firmly under claw. "I have a small piece of business to discuss with you." He leaned back from the table, though his belly still pressed against it, and cast a singularly icy expression at Alan and Adeline, who—having been lulled into the role of passive listeners—gaped a moment before starting at the abrupt turn in the conversation.

"Um, I ah," stammered Alan withdrawing a rolled parchment from the inner pocket of a flimsy robe. "Adeline, my dear, let's move over to that table by the window. I have a new poem I'd like to try on your ear."

"I suppose, as long as you promise it's better than the last," said Adeline smiling through an embellished sigh.

"That's for you to judge."

"Lucky me!" she said and gave an airy laugh back toward the table as she was led away by the elbow.

"Quite the girl," said Ford following the retreating Adeline with an appreciative eye. "She says what's on her mind. I like that."

"She cannot honestly be called a *girl* anymore than could I and probably not for some twenty years now," said Danny after a moment's honest examination of the subject. "However, I suppose the odd gentleman might find some form of attraction about her person." He continued to squint across the room, and his furrowed brow displayed his struggle to see in her what others might. Ford had forgotten Danny's innate ability to deflate a good mood. This pricking reminder pushed Ford to move things along.

"So, what's this you wanted to talk to me about?"

Danny perked up, and his whole demeanor became instantly more pleasing as he dove into the details of a scheme he had been developing when he'd seen how recently his fellow students had been in dire need of supplies.

"Potion ingredients and spell components are often hard to come by, and the cost is through the roof of a hundred-foot tower!" However, he claimed, owing to his study of flora—a subject he found nearly as enthralling as that of insects—he had discovered the possible location of various uncommon, even rare herbs and other useful plants.

"Plants," slipped from Ford's doubt-laden frown. He had still not wholly grasped Danny's scheme, but what he gathered didn't sound promising.

"Yes. Now just listen to me. There was a holy man, one of those hermit sorts that casts away his worldly possessions and shuns society and its comforts in favor of some dank hole in the ground away in some godforsaken backwoods land. The loon I refer to found a cave or more likely an exaggerated fissure from the sounds of it, in just such a place." Yonn unexpectedly excused himself into the conversation with a tiny throat-clearing cough.

"It's at the site of an-an…" He swallowed hard. "An old castle or um, tower or something, I think."

"Yes," said Danny. "As I was saying, this…what was his name?" Yonn whispered to him. "Right, Larkwine. Perhaps you have heard of him, Ford; you always went in for devotion more than I. At any rate, he was a great breeder of infinitely useful flora. Some fantastically rare species for these parts, if what I have read is in the least partially true. Well, the old relic kicked off some many years ago and from what I gather, his gardens were left untended and grew quite wild. There could be hillsides or even mountainsides of the stuff up there by now just waiting for us to pluck them from the ground!"

"As simple as that?" questioned Ford with heavy suspicion.

"Well, there is a short walk involved. Some hills…" Danny's voice trailed off, and he waved an airy hand as if to brush aside such trifles.

"Rogues of the road at every turn," said Ford. Danny leaned back and looked evasively about as if the floor and ceiling suddenly interested him.

"Potentially."

"And that's where I come in?"

"You have the gist of it, yes."

"And what makes you think someone else hasn't already thought of this and grabbed up the stuff already?" Ford was leaning back now, proud to have come up with such a thoughtful question on the fly.

"Our school is the only one of its kind in the vicinity. The location is remote and uninhabited, no doubt. Even if it were, I hardly think the locals would be aware enough to know the true value of the commodity lying in their own backyard."

"You'd be surprised," said Ford remembering how resourceful his stepmother had been with the weeds, bushes, and roots around the village where he'd grown up. Unimpressed and still a touch skeptical, Ford sighed, rapped his fingers on the table and gave it some thought.

"You would receive a full share in the profits, after expenditures."

"A full share, you say? So the same as everyone else? And what if we come up empty-handed? And what if I find work in the meanwhile? I wouldn't be about to leave after I finally found something."

"Very well. Quite understandable." Danny's short, quick answer said he was anything but understanding. "And you are quite correct, I cannot guarantee anything. I can, however, tell you, that at worst the trip will put a few weeks' worth of pay in your pocket, *at worst.*"

"At best?"

"Oh, I could not say. Perhaps a year's worth…two possibly." Ford's eyebrows shot up, and he let out a low whistle. "What do you say?"

"When do we leave?" Ford jumped up, grasped Danny by the wrist and pumped his arm. Their goodwill filled the room and lightened everyone's faces.

"There are some matters with the school that must be settled before we take our leave, but it would not be long."

"The sooner, the better," said Ford thinking that it might be smart get away from the volatile Barker for the time being.

A somewhat unsocial and assiduous worker, Danny was careful with his time and seldom willingly wasted it idly with people whose association would bring him no gain, so once through transacting business, he was prepared to break up the little gathering. Conversely, Ford had grown to relish camaraderie, and he did his utmost to keep the party together by blocking the door, corralling Danny and Yonn in his big arms, and talking them into another round. He even convinced them to stay for a bit of music. However, soon enough he grew drunk and was too caught up in his off-key singing to notice when Alan suggested taking Adeline home and Danny and Yonn followed suit.

It only made sense they should walk together since they were all headed back over the river, but it was an awkward and mostly silent procession of four strangers to Brynseht. Eventually, Adeline's curiosity to know more about Ford's past prodded Danny into conversation about his relationship with his cousin, reminiscences the two shared and what they had been like as children.

"I confess, I know very little of my cousin. The distance between us, in age and our physical localities, not to mention temperament, made interaction infrequent, to say the least. I do know that there was some, oh, let us call them difficulties. He is a bastard, did you know?" He didn't wait for answer. He seldom did. "Given up by his mother eventually, he was. She handed him off to his estranged father, my uncle Myer. And then it is quite safe to say Ford did not get along with his father's new wife. Resulting difficulties made it impossible for him to remain with the family. Eventually he ended up here." They were crossing Weald Bridge when Danny went silent again for a brief moment before letting slip a mildly sardonic cackle.

"What is it," wondered Adeline. "What makes you laugh so?"

"Do you know, giving it some thought just now, I believe our friend Ford may have travelled all the way to Port Morton in search of his mother. Would you believe that? Why a man would trouble himself to travel unheard of miles in search of someone who abandoned him as a child is beyond me, but there you have it. Human nature! What a mystery!"

CHAPTER 4
A ZEALOT'S SALVATION

"The House of Haccom is closed! We are closed," the aging yet elegant, dignified and precise High Priest of the Weaverite Order called down the temple's nave. The holy houses of the Weaverites held specific devotional hours, and this was the high priest's hour of private prayer. "How did you get in here? The door is bar--Bless my soul!" He saw before him the spare and lively figure of Madame Ribi, the bronze-skinned proprietress of one of the city's most popular brothels.

Born Ribiane Qisette in distant Mane over the southern seas, she came to Port Morton a lost and troubled young woman, whom the high priest longed for and longed to welcome into his flock. However, the desires of the flesh being intrinsic to the way of life of many Manerds, she soon turned to prostitution. The desires of many Aelwyd men for her meant that in no time, she had been able to establish her own operation. Importing as many Manerd women as she could find who matched her own style of beauty, she rapidly flourished. Through it all, Ribiane and the priest had maintained a friendship, a mutually beneficial bond in which she felt a sense of salvation, and he had kept up the hope that one day he might truly save her. If he might also savage her, all the better.

The high priest's robes swished over the smooth stones, the embroidered trim sweeping the edges of the pews, as he rushed toward the slight woman in a dark cloak. Intermingling thoughts of conversion and sex-filled him with urges almost beyond bearing.

"I have been praying for this day for quite some time! It has been so long I feared never seeing you, here again, my dear, my child!" His cry echoed in the vaulted ceiling, and joy spread through him as wide as the arms he flung open to take her to his bosom. As they came together, his bosom received her dagger. The blade plunged in and came out with a rush of blood. He shoved her back in shock. Like cold water to the face, he awoke to the fact that this was not Ribiane. Seeing the blood and blade, he twisted away making for the dais and the door to his chambers beyond. She leapt upon his back and continually drove the blade in until he dropped to his knees, gave his last gasp and fell to the floor with his arms outstretched, one hand reaching for the heavy scepter leaning against the altar.

From a hidden pocket within her cloak, she drew forth a brightly colored strip of cloth and dropped it near the body of the priest. It was the Bond of Dilys Caru, a decorative ribbon used in Haunan ritual to bind the hands of participants in marriage. Though an important, distinctly Haunan symbol, the ribbon might be found upon the person of the lowliest ranking priests ordained to perform such rites. These priests were often tasked with carrying out the order's menial labor. The dirty work, some called it. There was little work dirtier than murder.

Pulling her cloak from around her back and gathering it about her to cover the blood-splattered from her chest to her knees, the assassin slipped out the side door by which she had entered and disappeared into the night.

Heading away from the House of Haccom, Ford walked over the bridge and into Eastfeld. The strolling unwed couples and their trailing families who had filled the rain-cleansed cobblestones of Brastersceatt's Square to enjoy an evening out in the cool, crisp air were now mostly dispersed by the vanquished sun. Ford looked kindly upon the few who remained. A lightheaded joy that he would have thought silly if he'd recognized it in himself had sneaked up on him after having walked Adeline home with Alan upon the conclusion of a most memorable early evening.

Having finally finished his pieces for the Strategaeth game and delivered it to Alan, he had been paid, and quite generously. It seemed Alan had come into funds lately, and that was reason to celebrate. They had more than a few drinks, and at one point Ford felt Adeline's leg against his under the table. She couldn't have mistaken what she was about, because after Ford initially moved his leg, hers found its way back against his, and for the longest of moments. She even slid it back and forth on occasion, leaving Ford more than a little aroused. Nothing more had come of it, and Ford was left wanting.

Beyond the carnal, Ford felt a growing fondness for Adeline in a way he had not felt for a woman in years. To be honest, he had never felt like this toward any woman. His experiences had been confined to a kind of puppy love in his youth. Was this love, he wondered? Or had it been too long since he had lain with a woman? All he knew for certain was that he wanted her and wanted to be with her, but as a man without prospects, and he didn't feel he could propose to a woman like Adeline. He needed work and fast.

The footfalls and shadowy figures of a group of men fell in behind him. One called out to him. "Porter!" Dunn strode forward with arms spread wide like his foolish grin and a bit of a stagger in his swagger. "Come on Porter, we're on our way to, ah, to a sort of..."

"A party!" offered one of his companions.

"Yes, a party!" said Dunn louder than necessary. "Come with us!"

It wasn't an invitation so much as an abduction. Dunn and his friends engulfed Ford within their group and rambled off through the streets in rollicking high spirits. From the little he knew of them, Ford wasn't especially fond of Dunn's friends, these callously carefree and somewhat coddled offspring of the merchant class. However, after a few swigs from a bottle of something sour and strong being passed around, Ford became more pliable, more willing to be cajoled into whatever idea of fun they might have in mind.

They hobbled down one lane and stumbled down the next singing "Milly of the Sweet Brown Brew," while rattling window shutters and scaring off urchins and a lone watchman, indulging themselves in harmless yet cruel joys stolen from the comfort of the community. Their thoughtless pranks annoyed Ford, but tonight he endured their foolishness and stuck with the group, quite close to the group because for some time now trailing not far behind were Barker and his thugs.

Ford first caught sight of the surly trio two blocks back, and since then any effect the alcohol had on him had dried up. While the others continued on oblivious, he became ultra-alert and wondered how drunk Dunn's friends were. Barker wondered the same and was content to linger in the background surveying the situation and hoping Ford was foolish enough to wander away from the pack. He wanted to squeeze what he could out of Ford now, if he could get the chance. Shake him down, quite literally if need be, but mainly he wished to put a bit of fear into him before his next fight. He wasn't happy with the way their last meeting had resolved. Barker and his mates would have been happy for the opportunity to rough him up. After all, Ford was meant to lose the next fight, so it didn't much matter what shape he was in.

Dunn caught Ford looking over his shoulder and turned to see what the problem was. "What is this? What've we got here, Ford? You know these old hens?" Loud and defiant, Dunn made himself and the four friends with him seem as imposing as possible. Though he was tipsy, he knew trouble when it followed him down dark streets.

Barker and his two toadies halted a half-block behind. The two groups stood stubbornly eyeing one another. Drunk or not, Dunn's friends would present more of a challenge than Barker cared for, so he turned with his men and disappeared into an alley.

"What was that about," Dunn wondered aloud. Ford shrugged, and no one else had any clue.

In no time Dunn's friends regained their festive jollity. They were hooting up a storm as they turned into a narrow lane and passed under the bent tin archway sign for the Temple of Bliss. Tripping down a narrow flight of trash-strewn steps, they all held back, crowded together around a corner, while one stood by the entrance to a kind of former rectory cast in the red glow of a tinted lantern hanging overhead. A knock brought a swift response: a chest-level peephole slid open, and a darting eye appeared. Dunn's friend at the door jingled a pouch before the peephole. The door opened and in rushed the entire group.

Inside, the low-ceilinged, close and warm antechamber was lavish with the décor of many lands. This was called the Manerd-style, for those brown-skinned people sailed the sun-drenched seas of the known world and traded in the wares of myriad cultures. Inhaling a long satisfying lungful of rich tobacco smoke and catching a whiff of some pungently sweet aroma Ford couldn't place, he could see beyond the gray sheets of air into two adjacent rooms off to either side, each decked out in thick carpets with strange patterns, soft silks draped over low chairs, the flickering light of overtly phallic oil lamps shining off the gilt-worked legs of oval tables stretching out before plump couches, glass vases and goblets half-filled with blood-red wine on polished metal trays, and ceiling-to-floor tapestries portraying various acts of copulation.

What appeared at first to be girls or young boys, turned out to be Manerd men. All the Manerds were of slight build, but the males tended toward the effeminate, at least from what the people of Port Morton knew of them. When Dunn's friends first entered, these lithe bodies had been lying about in various states of undress or curled upon vast velvety cushions at the feet of male patrons, Aelwyd men decked out in decorative robes from foreign lands. At the sight and sound of drunkards tumbling in, both the Manerds and their patrons sat upright. Dunn, with his friends filtering in behind him, passed through the rooms, spreading out among the uneasy Manerds, who beamed back automatic, caressing smiles. Dunn tousled the hair of a long-lashed, bronze-skinned and ludicrously beautiful individual of quite deceptive ambiguity.

"It's time to party, lads!" shouted Dunn, slamming the beautiful head in his hands on to a table. The violent crack shocked the flabby Aelwydan on the couch before them, who squirmed and let out a cry that gurgled in his throat. Dunn's friends stormed through the rooms, knocking over tables and chairs, tearing the silks and ripping down the tapestries, grappling with whatever soft flesh fell within their grasp. Half-naked bodies flew in all directions, some ran upstairs or disappeared down a hallway to the back, but some were tossed against walls or crumpled under boots. One was grabbed by the throat, lifted off the ground and thrust up so that his head crashed into the ceiling. Dunn held in his stomach and laughed heartily at the sight of the body flopping limply to the floor. A slender flash of flesh making for a doorway was grabbed and thrown across the room, smashing into a table and sending a shower of glass shattering to the floor.

Dunn's friends laughed like it was a holiday celebration while the miserable panic-stricken Manerds screamed and begged for mercy in their mother tongue. The patrons were covering their faces and fleeing out the front door. One stood in the middle of a room complaining bitterly. Another sat froze and pop-eyed upon a couch. Both took thrashing blows before being driven out. A sunken-chested and manic-eyed Manerd pulled a knife and slashed the hand of one of Dunn's friends, then held off another attacker until subdued from behind and pummeled until he stopped moving.

Ford had passed by the lane leading to the Temple of Bliss from time to time, but being discretely tucked away, it had gone unnoticed by him. Tonight when he first entered, he couldn't believe its opulence. Now he stood stock-still watching the anarchy unfold and shocked by the brutality. He had known Dunn and his friends had a vein of disdain running through them for anything foreign to them, but he had not realized how deep it ran or that they would act upon it like vicious beasts. It all happened so quickly and seemed so unreal.

Dunn marched down the hallway toward the back after a retreating Manerd. Ford snapped to and ran after him, rounding a corner in time to see Dunn kick in a door. Inside the room, Tintot Song, the zealous lay preacher and a half-Manerd himself, was hurriedly pulling on the last of his clothes with a mostly naked, smooth-skinned and rounded-cheeked young Manerd cowering behind him on a bed grasping at a fur blanket.

"Fucking disgusting," Dunn shouted as he stomped into the room and planted his boot on Song's chest. Song landed hard upon his back and Dunn spit on him with the force of one trying to rid himself of poison upon his lips.

"Dunn!" Ford shouted. The Manerd prostitute slipped by him out the door. "What are you doing? Let's get out of here!" He grabbed Dunn by the shoulder and pulled him back. Dunn jerked free. Song scrambled to his feet and made a dash for the door, but Dunn caught him against the doorframe and shoved him back into the room. Song stumbled to one knee, and Dunn kicked him over on to his back. "Stop!" Dunn raised a boot over the fallen man. Ford dragged him back. "Why are you doing this?"

Dunn turned on Ford with anger and questioning in his eyes. "These animals need to know we don't put up with this sort of filth!"

While they argued, a trembling Song crawled on his knees to the closest wall, got to his feet and dashed for the door. Dunn caught him by the neck and swung him around, slamming him into the wall where he fell motionless on the floor.

"Leave them alone!" Ford roared. He grabbed Dunn by the shoulders, pulled him back out into the hall and pinned him against the wall with his forearm on Dunn's throat. Ford had no love for these people, but seeing such diminutive beings being thrown about and beaten senseless brought flooding back the essence of his father's maxim. *Defend the defenseless.* It was one of the few moral lessons Ford ever remembered his father imparting to him. The whole scene filled Ford with anger, confusion, and repulsion, so much so that he found himself speechless and only able to stare at a snorting, gasping figment of his friend, whose whole body directed the concentrated fury within toward Ford. Dunn swung a free fist, kicked and even bit until Ford finally let him go. Dunn coughed, sucked in air and shoved Ford hard in the chest. Ford stood his ground and, though the manic scene drove him all but senseless, he still cut a menacing figure that Dunn did not challenge. Nor did he back down. Ford's hearing, muted by the thrum of blood in his ears, was coming swiftly back and the place seemed oddly quiet.

"What is wrong with you?" shouted Dunn.

"What's wrong with *you*? What is going on here?"

Dunn cleared his throat, but the anger and indignation remained. "We got to show them this shit don't happen in this town. We don't want their kind here!" His eyes sharpened with hate and looked upon Ford like a stranger, like the enemy. There was only revulsion, an absence of reason.

Ford wanted no part of this and pushed past Dunn, who took a swipe at him. Ford ignored it and turned to go, but when a shove in the back sent him stumbling forward, he spun around and squared off with Dunn in the hall. They eyed one another, their heavy breathing intermingling. Dunn looked away first, dabbing at a cut on his lip. Ford turned his back on him and walked into the front rooms, passing through a stand-off between Dunn's friends and a group of half-naked Manerds holding them at bay with gleaming, sharp knives. He shoved aside the man at the door, and as he was plodding back up the stairs to the street, he heard Dunn's voice behind him livid and taunting.

"You're either with us or against us! Which side are you on, boy? Which side are you on?"

CHAPTER 5
THE FOUR LOVES

A fiddler plucked with wild, flying fingers. A horn blared away like a rutting elk. A blacksmith's apprentice rapped a thoroughly battered tin bowl with red knuckles. A young woman choked a bladder until it hummed high like a lamb. Those with lips free for singing matched the tone in a rough attempt to mimic the flighty-voiced daughters of the droning throat singers of Findun.

A good time, this was what Ford had come to the Three Sheets for. That and a place to stay. For a fair price and at the landlord's discretion, the tavern would allow patrons to sleep the night on the common room floor. He couldn't go back to the room he shared with Dunn, not for a while at any rate, though the room was likely empty. Lately, Dunn had been spending his nights with his "honey pot." Ford was hoping for a bit of the same. After the encounter with Adeline's leg, he had been in an almost constant state of arousal. Tonight he thought he stood a good chance of getting that taken care of.

The musicians downed their drinks and pressed on, filling the room with a rolling, hopping tune that brought the tavern alive once more and drove Ford's bemused thoughts clear away. A haggard old regular who didn't care what people thought of her sagging breasts and near-toothless grin, got him to his feet and he danced in the humid room amongst the floundering, sweat-soaked folk of the docklands.

During one of his dangerous, whirling spins in which someone usually got hurt, or something was broken by his gigantic stomping feet or his inadvertent ramming elbows, Ford caught the eye of the boy Yonn, who stood by the door looking every bit as insecure and out of place in his mage's robes as the insecure he felt within.

"You come to tell me Addy ain't comin'? 'Cause I figured as much already," slurred Ford with a wave about the room to show no Adeline as the two sat at a table together to share some ale paid for by Yonn. He meant to include Alan's name, but he was only thinking of Adeline. His heart had already sunk along with the sun since he knew there was no chance of seeing her here this late in the day.

But no, Yonn knew nothing of them and couldn't give the reason they hadn't come, no matter how many times he was asked. This confused Ford. Why had the boy-mage come all this way then? Shouldn't he be at school? It hardly mattered, he decided as he continued drinking away the coins Alan had given him, a bout supplemented greatly by Yonn's liberal hand dipping into his own purse.

Though Ford thought him a nice enough lad, Yonn was far too shy to provide good company. When it seemed they had talked themselves dry, Ford was up dancing again. He had hardly drunk half his usual, and yet the insistent rhythm of the music had wrapped about his head, tearing away his inhibitions more than any amount of drink. After three hard, fast songs he flung himself backward, down on to a bench, giving his legs a much-needed rest. The music would not leave him in peace though. With each downward pitch of the swaying of his head back and forth, like a ship rocking over rolling waves, he brought his heel down with a thud, keeping a rough beat with the crashing rhythm, along with everyone else there who could still lift a foot or clap their hands together.

"One more song and I'll go," he said as the time flew toward midnight. An hour or so later he had made new friends, whose names he had already forgotten, but whom he could not leave. Red-faced and jolly, they were the good kind of friends who always made sure you had got a full mug in front of you at all times. They withstood his sincerest backslapping thanks until they had to move out of reach for their own wellbeing.

Yonn, too, found himself a safer spot. Though he had had only half as much to drink as Ford, he was twice as drunk, and he found himself agreeing with the voice in his head telling him the floor was likely cooler. So, he stopped trying to hold himself upright and finally let his body slid under the table. "Where it wants ta be anyhows," he muttered to any of the friendly folk about him, none of whom noticed him disappear.

"I'll go," began Ford stifling a belch. "Just after thish…after this one."

And then Genevieve blew in.

The whole ample and ever so limber body of this devotee of life's pleasures swung and gyrated with the cyclical thump, hum, and jangle of the music. Her arms soared into the air as if that strange vocal droning levitated them irrepressibly from her sides. The gray sleeves of her once-white dress slid from her wrists down to the elbow, and Ford's eyes fixed on the soft, white skin he had kissed and bitten not so long ago. He watched her twist those alluring wrists and loved the way her hands flopped this way and that in the smoke, her fingernails occasionally scratching across the sooty ceiling. Around and around she twirled amongst the drunkards with dopey, crooked grins who tripped about her for a step or two before falling into the arms of their laughing friends, themselves too wasted to stand up now. And when the strings of the fiddle really started to jump, she absolutely pranced. The loose threads at the ends of her sleeves flew around, one by one sticking to those moistening arms. A stilt-legged lecher made a sloppy grab at her waist. She laughed, pushed him wobbling back and spun away, sweat catching at her dress so that it clung to her thick thighs no matter how hard she swung herself around the room.

Ford's head came to rest on one side as he followed her round and round with one half-lidded eye, the other being so sore and dry from the smoke that he gave up trying to coax it open any longer.

"Are you giving me the eye?" she asked him on one of her passes. He wanted to say something, something clever perhaps about "giving," but he couldn't bring his mind around to it before she bounded away again. He ran his tongue along the back of his lips. They seemed glued together. Even if they had parted, he wondered what in the world he might say with this great lump of a tongue gumming up the whole inside of his mouth.

With mind and mouth failing him, he lifted himself and the table half up before both came thumping back down into place, drawing as many laughs as reproachful glares from his tablemates. Genevieve's head fell back, and her smile spread wrinkles at the corners of her eyes.

"Oof," he groaned from the pain of landing on his pouch of coins. He dragged it out from under his thigh and held it up for recrimination. Not only had it attacked him unprovoked, it was far too light. He jigged it about to force a jingle into the few remaining coins then stashed it away again and made another attempt at standing. Simple enough, it had seemed not just a moment ago, and yet he could not get his legs to work in concert. The right was doing all the heavy lifting, while the left lazed about. An ancient, walking scaffold covered in gray skin called Sunny saw what Ford was at and hobbled to his feet, making an earnest attempt to lift the younger and much heavier man to his feet.

"Come on lad, up! Up!" Sunny croaked through his gums. Ford didn't budge. He slumped back with both eyes clamped shut.

"Come on, Ford." He heard this once and then again repeated, but who said it and where exactly the speaker was he couldn't tell. A mumble and a groan was all he could manage as he watched the ground and saw one of his feet shuffle forward followed by the other some time afterward. A cool night breeze licked his face. How he had gotten outside was another mystery. This neighborhood of century-old, single-story houses lined by rickety garden fences seemed vaguely familiar. Under the fingers of his left hand he felt Genevieve's capable shoulder, and he lurched to his left.

"Steady! Steady now." Sturdy though she was, carting him about like this was too much to ask of her, and so he thought he would just slip his arm from hers. The next thing he knew, he was tripping over a fence and falling headlong into the muddy remains of a tenant's garden. Though nearly exhausted, she couldn't help but laugh.

"Oh no..." he said.

"What?"

"Ish...it's wet. I'm all wet," he said. She snorted.

"Yer soaked in sweat and drenched in filth, I don't think a little wet'll hurt."

He opened and closed his mouth, then opened it again to catch the rain.

"They's...they's so mush mud...everywhere." The soft caress of the mud soothed him, and he began slowly flapping his arms by his sides like wings. "Oh Genny, have a feel. Is won'erful."

He had never felt quite so coddled, caressed and effeminate, and he laughed for the thoughts of the men at the Tower of Bliss. "So like women," he murmured. Genevieve ignored him and his incessant nonsense. Yes, she was annoyed, he could see that, but he knew she didn't truly mind. She was a good person, after all. It was she who had softened his heart toward the idea of men loving men in that way. *There's so little love in the world, it seems a shame to say no to it when it comes along, whatever it looks like*, she had once told him, and it seemed sound enough.

Genevieve. Such a big girl. Plenty of meat on her bones, just the way he liked them. A big, hardy girl. With a little assistance, she got him up out of the mud and into a water trough. That was someone he could see himself marrying.

"Come on, we gotta get you outta there," she said between grunts and gasps while pulling at one of his arms. "Help us out love, use your legs."

"Wait, wait," he said, staggering his feet and standing amazed for a moment as a torrent of water drained from his relatively clean clothes.

"A few more steps and we're there." They had taken more steps, he was surprised to see. When this had happened, he could not have said.

"Now hold up, just hold up." He stopped to show his insistence.

"What now?" she asked, her flagging energy, sapping her last ounce of enthusiasm.

"I loves..." He leaned closer. "I loves...love...I love yo--" He stammered on until she clasped an arm around one of his shoulders and slapped a hand over his mouth.

"Your breath stinks. Come on, this way, my love." She threw his arm over her shoulder. A warmth flamed within him and blotted out the cold of his damp clothes. They passed along Lower Common Street, so well-traveled by day. Now, as the garrisoned buildings leaned in over them, they happened upon only one person, a night watchman happy to turn a blind eye upon them as they passed and made their way to the free-standing, three-story monument to debauchery known as Madame Callistra's House.

Genevieve rapped upon the door, but it was the rhythmic taps on the shuttered window that brought Nileechi, a pitch-black and pie-faced girl, one of the few southern imports Madame Callistra had managed to retain. Most foreign girls either escaped back to their homelands or obtained work at Madame Ribi's. Others found husbands amongst the clients as quickly as possible. And recently three had died at the hand of an insane man with an unhealthy fixation for exotic women. That frightened many away. These days most of the girls of the House were the same white, drab, wide-hipped Aelwydian women attempting to create the illusion of overt femininity with heavy scents and make-up. They tried for glamor, missed, and went straight into the glaring. But the fact of the matter was that they were among the few who were still willing to work for the disagreeable Madame Callistra and her deplorable wages.

Among the lace draperies, once a shimmering gold and now drab yellow, the dusty red satin furnishings, and the matted fur carpet with the footpath worn through the middle of its orange and black striped pattern, a pale blond woman sat peering at Ford with forlorn hope through black smears about her eyes. The soaked giant swayed about the entryway staring into the slightly warped mirror by the teakwood table with the giant wooden fork and spoon hanging above it. She was not surprised when he took a step and caught his head in a spindly chandelier of wood and chipped shell; the shocked expression she wore came from the old Southern Isles custom of shaving off one's eyebrows and painting on false ones about an inch higher with striking angles that resulted in a perpetual look of wonderment.

After faltering backward, Ford tried again, giving the chandelier a wide berth and keeping his palms raised toward it, as if ready to catch it should the tricky thing mess about again. He followed Genevieve to the stairway, where he crashed through the first step. She pulled him loose and lugged this anchor of a man up two flights of stairs, leaving him balancing precariously in the middle of her room. She roused him a bit with a splash to the face with a handful of cold water from a small basin on a bedside table. She took a belt of gin from a bottle tucked behind a box of powders and creams and then undressed both of them. As she peeled away the layers of clothing, he played with the hair falling about her face.

"If I could, I'd take ya," he said pausing to concentrate his thoughts, "take ya away, all away from all thish."

"Don't say ridiculous things. Now lift. Lift!" she grunted until he picked up one of his feet enough for her to slip off his pant leg. Shifting to the other leg, he lost balance, and they both toppled back onto her bed, which cracked as it bent nearly to the floor under the weight.

"You're crushing me! I can't breathe!" she gasped.

He braced himself above her as best as his tired limbs could manage and grinned down at her with leering bleary eyes.

"Phew! That's better."

"I love you, Genny. Do you...do you love me?"

"How can I love a man who sleeps with whores?" She laughed. He was confused but started laughing along with her anyway until he caught the irony and then the real laughter came in heaving spasms that thwarted her efforts to get the job started. Ford had heard her motto *the sooner begun, the sooner done* many times. "Ow! Hold on," she said, reaching for the basin, wetting her hand with more gin and slipping it down between her thighs. "There, that's better," she said as he moved up inside her.

His repetitive plodding thrust mounted to a steady rocking rhythm like a loaded barge on a heavy swell. He pulled both her hands up by the wrist above her head and when his meaty, sweating palms pressed her's flat and spread her fingers out, her nails scraped the tips of his fingers. He let out a murmur of pleasant recollection and drove plunging forward in a pulsing brusque sprint to the finish, collapsing on top of her moments later.

"Honey, honey," she fought for breath and pushed against his shoulder, eventually rolling him off her. Leaning over him, she took another sip from the bottle just as his long rumbling snore, the evening's death knell, reverberated throughout the room.

A horrible nightmare of screeching, like an enraged bird gone hoarse, rattled Ford awake. He pried one of his dry eyes open enough to make out a blur of red, white and blue. It was the made-up and scornfully twisted face of Madame Callistra.

"Turn out your pockets! Now, you son dogs bitch! Turn dem out!" she screeched, poking and prodding him with her stubby fingers, while he gripped on to the blanket and pulled it up around him like a shield, his mind slowly coming to grips with the situation. He caught a glimpse of Genevieve behind the madam, scrubbing the make-up off her face in the basin.

"You owe bunches coin! You pay, or I call *protesshin!*" She hissed the last word through the gaps in her brown teeth. Ford knew she meant "protection," her personal collection of patrons who vowed to safeguard the House from deadbeats and any other miscreants. In return they received services on the house. These steadfast customers weren't chosen for their kind manners. They were large and leathery. Ford had fought two of them, but could only remember one. A blow to the head had wiped the other from memory.

"All right, all right," Ford acquiesced and reached for his pants under the frame of the bed. Madame Callistra snatched them up first and shook them upside down. His pouch fell free and flopped to the floor without so much as a tinkle of coin. The madame sucked an admonishing mouthful of air through her teeth. Ford threw up his hands. There was nothing else he could do. As he lay back, his body spent, icy prodding fingers greedily dug into the folds of bedding and all areas of his person with workmanlike precision and without modesty.

"It's here," said Genevieve and stopped drying her face long enough to point out a stack of coins by the basin.

"That's all I got! That's everything," said Ford.

"You owe more! Bunches more for whole one night," screamed the madam as she delved into his boots, her small round face pruning in disgust. Finding nothing doubled the disgust and she pointed to the door.

"You get out!"

"Genny," said Ford while slipping on his clothes. What he wanted to say to her he couldn't be sure. He wanted to offer something of himself, but what he didn't know.

"Out!" The madam's voice broke in indignation. That someone would have the audacity to spend the entire night with one of her girls and not have the money to pay for a single hour was an assault upon her trade and might lead to others taking such advantages, in essence ruining her.

"Genevieve," Ford croaked out and took hold of her hand with his fingertips. She immediately withdrew it and watched without emotion as Madame Callistra drove him from the room with pokes and pinches. The remainder of his damp clothes flew down the stairs after him, and he finished dressing in the dark of the second-floor landing in the otherwise dormant house.

In the dull light of morning he sat between two puddles in the lane behind Madame Callistra's House and closed his eyes. An hour later, a cart rolling by his head barely made a dent in the pinging and dinging of the tiny smith he was sure was working at a tinny piece of metal within his brain. People walked over and around him on their way to work. An ancient and bent man opened a nearby door a crack to peer at him out of mistrust and boredom.

Another hour later, groggy and parched, he sat up and meant to get to his feet, but a wave of nausea swept over him. He vomited, felt refreshed, and stretched out upon his back to rest. Having only ever visited her at the House after dark, he couldn't be sure, but he thought he knew which window on the top floor was Genevieve's.

Such a lovely girl, he reflected, and solidly built. Out of all the working women he had been with over the past year or so, she was his favorite. Funnily, he thought, she reminded him of his mother. Not that he knew what his mother looked like, but he had conjured his ideal and could just recall the exasperatingly indefinable shadow of her leaning over him and the caress of her thick hair brushing his cheeks. The recollection was one of the only memories he had of her. He hated not knowing what she looked like and regretted his failure to find her, perhaps more so than his failure to make something of himself since arriving in the city.

His fingers ran over the ground beside him and found a stone here and there that had resurfaced after the recent rains. He plucked a few out so that he could roll over on his side comfortably to give his back a rest. The lane was quiet now. Even the old man had left the doorway. Eventually he sat up, mastered the dizziness and suppressed the nausea. He gathered up the stones before him and began hurling them one by one at Genevieve's window. Most hit the side of the house and bounced back. One caromed off her windowsill, and another went through the window, but she never showed her face. If he could only speak with her and get out what was within, she would understand his heart. And if he could only get work and make something of himself, she would see his worth.

"Genny! Genny!" Without thinking it through, he found himself at the front of the House with the design that if she would not come to him, he would go to her. He would show her his love. Stomping through the door, he shouted up the stairwell, "Genny! Genny! Come down!" Madame Callistra's shrill voice echoed from somewhere deep inside the house. There wouldn't be much time. "Genevieve, come down straight away! I want to talk to you!" Certain she was up there, he bounded up the first flight of stairs. It dawned on him that she might be with another man. His shouts became louder, more insistent. Perhaps she was sleeping. Yes, she was probably sleeping off the late-night they'd had together. It had been a rough night of drinking and dancing, but a fun night nonetheless, and they had spent it together.

"You big, stinking louse, no coin, shit-boots!" Madame Callistra's enraged yell gather Ford little time to avoid her bulldog rush; she barreled into his chest with both hands, poking and prodding him more vehemently than before. "Get out, you! Get out!"

The more he persisted, the more the madam shrieked and shoved. Her girls peeked from the doorways and laughed, throwing Madame Callistra into a deeper rage until finally, Genevieve stumped down the stairs.

"I'll deal with this." She grabbed Ford by the arm and led him out into the street. "Go on, you! Go stare at the sea!" she shouted at the gawking neighbors and the girls gathering in the windows. "Or jump off a pier!" This was the best entertainment most would see all day. They weren't going anywhere. She turned on Ford. "You got nothing. Nothing, am I right?" Ford had nothing to say to that. "So why are you here?"

"I want to be with you, my girl," he said, grabbing her arms and meaning to massage them the way she had done to him in the past.

"Don't." She batted his hands away. Seeing he wasn't leaving, Madame Callistra began shouting from the door. Her bombarding insults angered him, and Genevieve's rebuff surprised him, but he wasn't put off. He grabbed again for the woman he was sure was the one for him. Suddenly, the madam was between them like a gadfly. Genevieve backed away. He tossed the madam aside and came on. Genevieve pushed him back, and he hardly noticed. She slapped at him, and he grabbed her more forcefully than intended. Her fingernails flew. She cried out. There was blood. Then men were about, seemingly from nowhere, pulling him off, tearing away with her face twisted in fear and fury. He didn't understand what was going on. He only wanted to talk.

The strong hands of stalwart House patrons escorted Ford mercilessly toward Stanrocc Hold, a former keep converted into cells for petty criminals awaiting judgment and the payment of fines levied against them. But it was a long way, and before the mob got anywhere near it, half of them left with better things to do and the determination of the final two melted away when an acquaintance from Ford's days as a porter happened upon them and promised to lead him the rest of the way. This acquaintance took him to the nearest tavern for a drink to calm him, but when he saw that Ford had no coin he left him there.

"What was I thinking?" he wondered aloud with his head hanging, and his thoughts miles away from the stones he kicked at on his way from the tavern.

That night, lying outside, staring up at a strip of pure blackness between overhanging roofs, he let doubt consume his confidence at the realization of unfulfilled expectations and errant conclusions. Voracious negativity revolved, turned back upon itself, manifested in a sapping pain in his chest that burned and chilled in alternating waves that left him as profoundly empty as the starless sky.

The sounds of fornication coming from the candlelit windows of Madame Callistra's House stirred nothing within him but pitifully sad loneliness. Like a fool, he had come back after dark to the lane behind the house for a second chance, even though Genevieve had made it clear where they stood. Replaying the scene and running over the whole situation again and again throughout the day, he knew now that he was in the wrong.

"I'm sorry, Genny!" He shouted it once, only once, and that was the last of it. Timeless seemed the void within him until a temple bell rang, and the gray light of morning set him on weak legs to stumble blinking into a new day.

"Still no work?" No work and completely broke, Ford might have replied to Alan and the equally curious Adeline sitting across from him at the Three Sheets late that afternoon. Embarrassed and not wanting to burden them with his woes, he merely shook his bowed head.

"That's a pity," mused Alan and Ford felt he meant it. On the other hand, Alan couldn't repress his joy as much he tried to stifle it. "I've had a bit of luck, though."

"None for me," said Ford setting a hand over his mug. Alan had paid for the first round and as much as Ford wished to return the favor, he couldn't. The musicians wandered in in high spirits, and he was glad for the distraction.

"Ford," said Adeline pointedly looking toward the barmaid. Ford looked up and found Elle there instead. A hint of pride lit up her face ever so slightly. As an orphaned immigrant child, she had been so devalued and ignored in Port Morton that she cherished even these simple moments when she could surprise Ford and display her cunning.

"Oh, it's you. What do you want?" The question barked from him inadvertently, partly due to the noise of the rowdy musicians and partly out of annoyance. He was feeling prickly and didn't need someone sneaking up on him. Somewhat blind to others at the moment, he nearly let his rudeness pass before catching himself. "Sit. Please."

"I come with words."

"Go ahead." He waited for her to deliver her message, and when she only stood there somewhat embarrassed and silent, he got impatient. "Is everything a damn secret? Just say it." Elle's eyes flitted to Alan and Adeline. "These are my friends. Nothing you got to tell me is nothing they can't hear. Spit it out."

"A man you know, he asks around for you. He looks for you to give him..." She couldn't bring herself to give out any more details so freely in front of people she did not know.

"You mean Barker? I know about Barker." Ford turned from her to his other two companions. "A friend of sorts after something. It's nothing."

Even without actually seeing Elle's thin frame collapse, he knew her well enough to realize that he had just burst her bubble. She loved to bear him intelligence from the secretive network of informers she had fallen in with after getting out from under the thumb of a militant seamstress and escaping the forced servitude imposed on some orphaned children. So much loss and upheaval in such a short lifetime had created an antisocial creature. Ford understood little of the reasons, but he knew her nature and bypassed the cajoling he might have used on others by taking her by the arm and guiding her down to the seat beside him.

"You were talking about being lucky, I believe," said Adeline to Alan after some uncomfortable, dithering conversation. Sensing there was plenty of room in this awkward group for a long explanation, Alan backed up and gave a full account of his recent work as a scribe.

"Iarl Middlefield's late husband was a bit of an adventurer, as I'm sure you know. But what you may *not* know is that he kept a journal of his journeys. Well, they were notes really. I'm helping to tidy them up. The late Iarl's hand...well, he scrawled more than he wrote. But then, he would be in a dank cave somewhere with only a lantern or maybe just a candle for light and no place to write. No flat surface, I mean, perhaps just his knee to scribble out the barest of details. Some of it was written on his ship's rail as he and his crew set off on some new adventure."

"What a life," groaned Adeline shooting a conspiratorial smirk at Ford that missed its mark.

"What a life indeed," Ford sighed as he slipped into remembrances of his own adventures.

"You should wait to hear it when it's finished," went on Alan with a glimmer in his wide eyes and a flourish of his hands that came dangerously close to toppling his full mug. "Such fantastic tales!" said Alan "And the maps! You should see the maps! They tell a tale all their own! He, the deceased Iarl that is, he always brought along a cartographer with him. Or I should say as many as three or maybe four were employed over the years for they would be killed, yes killed, on the various expeditions, you see. I'm forgetting, one of them was a woman. Very clear hand and apparently accurate. But the important thing is the hand, you see. The individual's hand is as apparent and obvious as a scribe's,

I dare say. But I'm wandering. The maps, as I say, you should see them. They are wondrous! Such far off places as you could imagine. And detailed, minutely detailed. There are even illustrations in the margins of beasts rare and magical that they encountered along the way! And treasures, too!"

"Treasures?" interjected Elle. Up to that point, she had been sitting like a scolded child plaintively listening to a conversation that hardly held her interest. Now she came alive with a penetrating, quite disarming gaze aimed at Alan's eyes and lips.

"Oh yes! They collected such rare and valuable wealth!"

"What? Name?" Elle's aggressive eagerness only encouraged Alan.

"Oh, let's see, gems and gold ingots. Coins of all manner imaginable. Ah! A scepter of silver so heavy I doubt any of us, but Ford could lift it. And magic, as well! I don't understand nearly enough to explain even a portion of what I read, but I know they found this bracelet or armband that sings!"

"Sings?" wondered Ford and Adeline together.

"No, *hums* I should have said. It hums. How or to what purpose I could not say. I'm not sure the late Iarl could either, nor the wisest of his sages."

"Truly fantastic," muttered Ford, quite in awe.

"Yes, they brought back some fantastic items indeed and loaded barrels of gold and silver, all they could, all that was obtainable, that is."

"What is *obtainal?*" asked Elle. This whole time she had been on the edge of her seat, her face a sharp tool of intense interest, working to chisel out all of the information Alan possessed.

"What I mean is that some of the treasure could not be found or dug up or brought back, and so they had to leave it there."

"These maps, they show the treasures they leave there?" Elle all but leapt out of her seat in anticipation of the answer.

"The maps show the locations, sure. Where they are and all, but it's the journal that's the interesting thing. The descriptions are fantastic!" While Alan went on praising the journals, both Elle and Ford were lost in daydreams of riches. "The Iarl, Lady Middlefield, intends on making a book out of them, you see. So she wants to keep it all under wraps until it's finished. If the stories get out and the storytellers get ahold of them, well, soon everyone will have heard the stories and no one will buy the book."

"She's selling the book?" asked a surprised Ford.

"Yes."

"But if she sells it,"-Ford paused here to turn the notion over in his mind before continuing-"she won't have it anymore."

"Oh no, I see. That's where I come in. I and other scribes are making copies of the stories, and so there will be many books, not just the one. Perhaps as many as a dozen. Those will be sold off to interested buyers. She'll keep the original. Am I making it clear?"

Ford had no concept of the finer points of the arts, never mind reproduction, but he nodded at what little he had grasped.

"Where is the book?" Elle asked in a slower, more measured tone than before. She had become cognizant of her own eagerness, and now she leaned back, broke eye contact and sighed as if bored. The sigh was one step too far, she realized, sensing Ford turn her way.

"Right now it's all under lock and key in Middlefield House. That's where I have to go to do my work. Sadly, I was turned away today. None of us were allowed in today. I believe it's something to do with the death of that priest. Did you hear of it?" They all nodded solemnly, even though none of them followed the Weaver faith. News of the horrible deed had been passed from mouth to mouth, spreading around the entire city like wildfire and there was little else anyone talked about since the priest's body had been discovered in a wide pool of blood on the temple floor.

A noisy pack of sailmakers, pushing through the door, half blustering and half arguing the outcome of some contest, drowned out Alan's conjectures on the possible identity of the killer. The conversation was dying anyhow. Ford, whose short but regular deep-throated interjections had given tempo to their talks, was no longer attending. He was thinking of how his daydreams of the Iarl's treasure were just dreams, and he worried that Elle might have been thinking of how to make the dream a reality. If she wasn't devising ways to get her hands upon the journal and maps, then he didn't know her as well as he was sure he did. Ever since they'd first become acquainted, Elle had shown a desire to step up the petty theft in which they both engaged. Those journals and maps held the key to wealth for whoever was daring enough to take it and so getting hold of them would be anyone's natural desire, but it took someone like Elle to consider stealing something like that out of a well-guarded lord's house. It would be an incredibly dangerous undertaking. If she got caught, she might be hanged for even making the attempt. A tightness gripped Ford's chest at the thought of her dangling from the end of a rope, and a shiver ran up his spine. Certainly of late he had been indifferent to her company, but losing her would break his heart. He jumped when her voice broke into his private contemplations.

"That boy, your Danny's friend, the boy he is come."

"Yohan?"

"Yonn, I think it was," put in Adeline.

"Right, Yonn. Yonn's coming?"

"He is come."

"How can you possibly know? You've been sitting right here with us this whole time." Elle merely nodded toward the front window where Yonn bobbed, ducked and craned as he peered in like a moth drawn to light, but one that had found a conscience filled with apprehension.

"Why doesn't he just come in, the odd duck?" Ford gave a welcoming wave, and the boy smiled and made for the door, stumbling into a group entering at the same instant. They all shot Yonn an evil eye and shoved him aside. But as they passed into the tavern they found themselves tossed left and right like dolls by Ford, who casually threw his shoulders about as forcefully as he could without it seeming obvious on his way to greet Yonn and draw him to their table. "So, that slug of a cousin of mine has finally set a day, eh?" Ford asked of Yonn as they sat down together.

"No." Yonn gave a short shake of the head.

"No?" Why then, Ford wondered, had the boy come all this way? He looked Yonn over in hopes an answer might be sought somewhere upon his person. Yonn merely shook his hand again and offered nothing more. Ford was considering pursuing the subject, but right then the musicians launched into an old crowd-pleaser, and so he jumped up to drag benches and tables aside, scattering the few patrons that littered the place. "Who's up for a dance? Come on! Where's Elle?"

"Strike me blind, but she was just here," exclaimed Alan with a look left and right and back again. "She was right here."

"Not much of a dancer, that one," said Ford. "No bother, Addy will dance with me!" He extended his hand to her. She begged off, but he got down on one knee and pleaded with her, keeping at it until the attention threw her into little nervous exaltations she tried to hide: folding and unfolding her arms, rubbing them unconsciously; turning this way and that to avoid his gaze, while allowing her long hair to fall over her flitting eyes. She was in no hurry to brush it aside, but when she did, she also slid her hands up the back of her neck to fluff the strands out and let them fall full upon her shoulders. Alan watched her from the corner of his eyes and suddenly stood up.

"It's getting late. We should be going."

"No, come, stay!" said Ford his paw-like hand on Alan's shoulder, inadvertently shoving the insubstantial scribe back into his seat.

"Yes, let's stay just a little while longer," said Adeline. "They've only just begun, and I would so much love to hear music tonight. Don't you love music, Ford?"

"Sure do!"

"What do you love about it?"

"Oh, I don't know," said Ford resigning himself to a seat beside her. He was on unsure footing, having never given music much thought beyond the pleasure he derived from it. "Everything, I guess."

"What is your favorite instrument? I love the systole," she said. Ford only nodded while she expounded upon the nuanced usage of the fiddle-like instrument. To the common folk, stringed instruments were still considered a foreigner's delight. Drums, horns and a booming voice was what warmed an old fashioned Aelwydian heart.

"That's enough stalling! Come on!" Ford cried, taking Adeline by the hand and swinging her into the middle of the floor. After a twirl about the room in which Adeline hung on to her wild dance partner like a cat dangled over water, Ford bobbed up and down, thumping the floor with his heel and occasionally clapping in time. Not knowing what to do, she stood stiff at his side clapping along with him. The song ended to whoops and cheers, none louder than Ford's.

"Damn good music, eh?" he shouted as the pair swung back around to the table all smiles and laughter, and trying to catch their breath, while the musicians dove right into the next tune. Ford's head throbbed with the beginnings of a headache, and his knees trembled. Never had he felt so tired so fast.

"You dance well," said Adeline and then repeated it louder.

"Bah, I stomp around some," shouted Ford. No longer bothering to compete with the rowdy music, they merely smiled at one another, nodded or tapped fingers upon the table and were happy to listen and watch others dance. During a quieter song, Adeline started in again on her love of stringed instruments, especially the harp, expounding on their different sounds, body shapes and styles of play.

Ford grunted in affirmation, but nothing more. Such fancy music was fine for the cultured classes, and he was happy to sneak away to the Three Sheets for a slice of variety now and then, but he wondered what his friends at Baldy's would make of it all. And he wondered how things stood between him and Dunn now that a few days had passed. They hadn't seen one another since the incident at the Temple of Bliss. Certainly they could patch things up. They needed to. Ford was sick of sleeping outside and waking up wet.

"Then he finally let go of me," Adeline was saying when the music stopped. Ford's attention came flying back to the table. "It was unpleasant obviously, but I got over it, and now I'm not afraid of strings at all." She lifted her head with an almost haughty air, a pose that might have made her appear as triumphantly proud as she intended, but for a childish tittering giggle and a too-intense flare of the eyes.

The ghost of mortification passed over Alan's face before he folded his hands and locked on to a fixed point in the distance. Ford forced his mind back in an effort to piece together what he had missed, but he could make neither heads nor tails of it. Adeline ducked from his blank gaze, hung her head, and went a shade pink.

"A thought has just occurred to me," said Alan hoping his attempt to change the subject wasn't too obvious. "Why don't you look for work over on the other side of the river, right now, with us? Gods know, there are plenty of moneyed merchants over there. Trade is still going on, better than over here."

Ford had sought work along the Brynseht hills. Days ago, walking along the promenade stretching along the western embankment between the city's two bridges where inns and taverns had overtaken the glaziers, he had passed by ship's captains hobnobbing with merchants at tables along the water's edge. They were killing time more than transacting trade, but Ford had called out to them regardless, "Any work?" There was either nothing to be had or no reply. At a rug merchant's he had tried to display his strength, only to realize how much strength he had lost when he attempted to heft one of the long and surprisingly heavy rolled rugs on to his shoulder. One of his knees buckled, so he quickly dropped the roll with a thunderous thud to save face. "Impressive, but what do I need with rugs being lifted when no one's buying?" asked the merchant as he showed Ford the door. Ford had also tried Mrs. Bakerbywell to whom he had delivered countless sacks of flour. Kind when she could afford to be, the baker took care of those around her as if they were her own children. She was the kind of person one went to when a helping hand was needed. He chided himself for not thinking of her sooner and ventured forth on a day when even an unrelenting languorous drizzle could not dampen his confidence. Huddled under the baker's raised shutter were two old biddies and a perturbed cat, all complaining bitterly in their own way of the weather. The elderly women declared it the condemnation of the gods for the people's sins, not an uncommon refrain to be heard throughout the city and the surrounding countryside. "I'm sorry, my boy. You see how it is," said the baker waving a hand through the empty air in front of her shop. "Flour's hard to come by, and when there's no flour, there's no bread." And then, not long after losing his job as a porter, Ford had found himself on the north side of town where a strong woodworkers' trade had developed around old Ox Bridge upriver. The artisans there received the choicest pieces of lumber from the mills over the water and fashioned the city's finest wares: high-backed chairs, chests, jewelry boxes, picture frames, idols, most all of which were heavily adorned with the Haunan tree motif. But here too, Ford had received nothing but rejection.

"A splendid idea, Alan!" interjected Adeline with a hop in her seat and a clap of her hands. Ford tried to beg off. He wasn't thrilled about the idea of seeking employment with an audience in tow. Begging for work was embarrassing enough. He didn't think he could do it with friends witnessing his humiliation.

"It's a long ways," he said before realizing how silly that sounded and trying another tack. "Folks there, they take one look at me," he held up a frayed cuff, "and they don't give a second."

"Nonsense!" This was as demonstrative as ever Ford had heard Adeline, and he thought she might be drunk. She definitely seemed high-strung.

Alan was also taking her measure, and he suddenly cried out, "What am I thinking? It's far too late. Shops will be closed before we could make it over the bridge." It was true, the evening was long in the tooth. With Ford's willing assistance, they were able to convince Adeline to give it up. Soon after, Alan took her firmly by the hand, pulled her from her grasp upon Ford's arm and bustled her out the door with a hurried goodbye and a sad lament from her.

"Odd," said Ford and leapt somewhat when Yonn, still sitting quite quietly on his far side, peeped in agreement. "Demons below!"

Ford made his way home, eventually shedding the boy-mage along the way. While he liked having the company of such smart friends who were good enough not to rub their superiority in his face, and he was grateful that they had his interests at heart, his embarrassment over the situation threw a pall over his appreciation and he wished to slink back home alone.

"Now we see, brothers! Now we see, don't we? The evil hand of the Iarl and her dark desires! Her evil priests!" The vehement shouts came from a wild-eyed man stripped to the waist standing atop a block at the temple construction site in Brastersceatt Square. In one hand he held a lantern aloft and in the other a short cat o' nine tails with which he habitually punctuated his declarations and denunciations by striking his chest or back. By this he claimed to be cleansing the land of its sin, and as his profoundly vitriolic rants intensified against certain Haunan sects for their apparent hand in the vile murder of the Weaverite high priest, so did his self-flagellation. "Now our eyes are open! Now we see!" A few listened intently, and some shook their heads, but more shook their fists and shouted along with him.

Sole-sore and leg-weary, Ford began the climb up to the small, third-floor room he shared with Dunn and it felt as if he were ascending a mountain. If Dunn wasn't there, so much the better. A good night's rest was in order. Tomorrow he would get back to it. He would find work. He had to, for he assumed this must be the bottom and there was nothing left to do but pull himself back up. At the top of the stairs he found a board nailed across the door to his room.

"I been barred?" He stared at the door, blinked at it vacantly a few times and then knocked on it. He tried again, pounding hard until the neighbors complained. For a moment, he didn't know what to do, and then he clomped back down the stairs to see his landlord, Master Mapleby. He called him Master Mapleby because Master Mapleby called him Goodman Porter.

"The dues on the room have not been paid. Not been paid in weeks," said the landlord in his soft yet insistent and hasty speech like the patter of rain on the roof.

"But that's my home!"

"The room is no longer yours, Goodman Porter. It is late now. Good evening."

With disbelief and despair clouding his mind until it refused all other thoughts, Ford hardly noticed that the door had been slammed in his face. "Where will I go?" he murmured at the door.

CHAPTER 6
A NEW HOME

The wind and rain drove all of the city's inhabitants toward any shelter they could find; this included Ford, who sneaked into the only place he could think to go that night. Some time in the early hours he heard the creak of floorboards and sensed someone stepping over him where he lay cramped and sore upon a stairwell landing. Not long after he heard another set of footsteps approach.

"Goodman Porter," the voice of Master Mapleby echoed in the stairwell quite shrill and far louder than Ford ever remembered hearing. "What do you think you are doing? Get out! Get out immediately, or I shall have you clapped in irons and brought up on charges! And indeed I shall do if ever I find you here again!"

Hurrying away, Ford made for Ox Bridge. He wasn't running away from Master Mapleby, so much as running toward the Armory of Academia. During the many hours he had lain awake the night before uncomfortable and unable to stop his mind turning over the troubles weighing upon him, he had come to the conclusion that there was only one thing left to do. He had to see his cousin Danny and insist that they set this scheme of his in motion at once. For Ford, there seemed to be nothing else to do. No work would come his way. This morning, like countless mornings before, as he made his way through the streets he passed men and women everywhere, even children, looking for work. Others sat about with pools of hopelessness for eyes, having given up the prospect.

Sitting like a ponderous beast at the end of a square, the stony square mountain that was the Armory of Academia dwarfed the wooden buildings around it. After a new armory had been built within the walls of the new castle, Bowen Dome, the old armory was left abandoned for years until eventually a wealthy and aging mage bought it for a song and opened the Academia, a school teaching the rudiments of magic to the sons and daughters of the rich. With a low enrollment to start, the location amply suited their needs at the time. The thick, windowless walls kept out nosey neighbors and kept in errant magic. As the school expanded, with laboratories and dormitories absorbing surrounding buildings, and students without an ounce of magic ability were admitted, the old armory was converted into storage and an antechamber, a place to kick the mud off one's shoes or hang up a damp cloak. A new façade went up to make the whole appear as one gigantic edifice.

Ford stood in front of the giant building's stout double doors staring up into the beady eyes of a vampire bat. Just above the door and glaring down at visitors hung its remarkably-crafted protruding head with a sharp-toothed jaw all sculpted from a single piece of smooth and shiny black obsidian with a touch of gray about the ears to indicate fur. The leering creature held him enthralled and made him hesitate before finally knocking. Nothing. He tried again. Still nothing. He waited, looked around, and when after some time there was still no response, he considered knocking on the bat's forehead. Doorknockers were, after all, becoming quite popular on the west side of town. Ford thought perhaps the bat might be something as mundane as that, though it hung above the door to a school of magic and looked as evil a thing as he could imagine at the moment.

Banging with all his might upon the door, he got no answer but stares from passersby. No one came to the door, but he did draw the attention of one of Brynseht's plentiful watchmen. "Go on and leave alone those that wish to be left alone." Ford insisted that he knew someone within and was expected. The watchman would have none of it. "Go on, back over the river with you." The watchman didn't know him personally but could size him up easily enough by his clothes, since his were as torn and filthy as any of the city's other poor souls with their sack shirts, cloth-wrapped shoes, and patchwork trousers.

Ford gave up on the Armory and on work as well. He wasn't going to find anything looking the way he did. And to top it off, now he had no place to stay.

"But maybe…" he murmured as an idea cropped up on his way back to Eastfeld.

"Ain't seen him in a good long while," said Frid, the landlord at Baldy's when Ford inquired about Dunn. If only he could patch things up with his friend he might at least have a roof over his head again. But it appeared that Dunn had abandoned him. He flopped down at a table, allowing his sinking spirits to drag him down with them. "Stocky's been asking for you, though!"

"Well, that's something," Ford muttered mostly to himself. There nearly was only himself at the tavern, aside from one other patron sleeping at a table in a far corner. Ford was terribly tired and felt he could have nodded off as well, but for an aching head full of worry and thoughts of hunger. There was nothing for him at Baldy's as far as he could see, so he got up to go but immediately crashed back down when a spell of dizziness overtook him. He laid his head down upon his arm on the table to steady himself. When the waves within subsided, he closed his eyes and was soon asleep.

A grumbling gibberish woke him, and he found Stan sitting at the table. Though his flabby and thoroughly ugly friend looked no worse than his usual slovenly self, he too had been out of work for a while now. A good number of depressed and downtrodden people had filtered into the tavern in the middle of the day, either to drink or pass the time until they could go home and lie to their families about having looked for work.

Ford thought he might slip out before more friends arrived, but Stan's rambling nonsense kept him seated until Fingers showed up with a woman attached at the hip and Owen trailing merrily behind. At the sight of Ford, Owen slapped the table, let out a gurgling cry of joy and came around to shake Ford vigorously by the shoulders and slap his back. After that, it wasn't long before others arrived.

"What do you get when you butcher a pig with an ax?" Stocky asked the moment he walked in and plunked himself down at the table in the darkened tavern where candles and lanterns were no longer being lit by the landlord. "Pork chops!" After an explanation so that everyone but Owen got it, they all laughed until their sides hurt, including Owen. "Dropped off a load at the stockyards this morning when I heard that—," Stocky's eyes shot open upon finally spotting Ford slumped against the wall at the far end of the table. "Where in Dan O'dan have you been?" Ford only smiled and nodded, but Stocky jumped up and came down to his end of the table to sit beside him.

"I been around," Ford offered after some prodding.

"But not around here that's for sure. You nor Dunn."

At the mention of his former friend's name, Ford let loose his feelings about being left high and dry by Dunn, and before he knew what he was saying, he had admitted to being homeless. A full mug slid down the table to him. He pushed it back, saying, "If I can't buy, I won't borrow, not from you all." That's when they knew he was truly destitute.

The next thing Ford knew, he was on all fours with girls hanging off him as they wrestled before the hearth at Stocky's one-room home. He had hardly resisted when Stocky told him he was taking him home. How could he turn down a solid meal and a place to stay? He would be looked after and cared for by Stocky's wife Blodwyn, and this, perhaps more than anything, was what he yearned for.

Everyone who knew her affectionately called her Wynna, and in return, she was affectionate to most. For all the hardnosed toughness she used to keep control of her household, she was warmth personified and caring to a fault.

Hard-luck cases like Ford were guaranteed her generosity. Wynna was all one could wish for in a friend, mother, and wife.

The excited screams of the youngest girls met his ears, and they ran to greet him as soon as he passed through the door. A half dozen questions assaulted his ears, followed by a sound scolding for not visiting more often. Then Ford was stripped naked and made to wait for the kettle to heat, so he could scrub up while Wynna worked her magic on his dirty clothes.

Standing behind a hanging sheet, he felt highly self-conscious and for good reason. Their oldest daughter Wylla had a covert eye upon him the whole time. He pretended not to notice and hoped nothing would come of it. She was a lovely girl, cobbled together from the best features of her parents, but she was also only twelve. Her fixed gaze made him shrink within himself and notice, when he wrapped his arms abashedly around himself, the high definition of his ribs and how the muscles in his shoulders and arms had gone soft or completely disappeared. As he stood washing his chest and running his hands over what had been a monument of strength not so long ago, he knew his fighting days were through if he couldn't regain what had once been.

Though it meant no fire tomorrow, a good blaze was kicked up to dry his wrung-out clothes, and soon Ford was succumbing to the second youngest daughter Burra's demands to "Lift me up!" So up she went, spinning around in his arms so that she could walk upon the ceiling upside down to the wild giggles of the other girls, who wanted a turn. Sapped of energy, he made up an excuse. The girls cried "No fair!" and pounced upon him. Somehow during the screeching, flailing melee Wylla managed to slither under him so that he was straddling her.

"Dinner!" called Wynna and Ford couldn't have been more relieved. "Stop your horsing and tuck in!" The saying was purely figurative since the family had no tablecloth to tuck in to. Having to provide for so many mouths, Stocky's table had never been bountiful, but now it was conspicuously sparse. Without much to stuff their mouths with, the girls were soon back at their play. Burra rhymed random words and sounds in a rising sing-song; Aedelfyn, the ten-year-old tomboy of the lot, who they called Fyn, regaled them with the story about the farting mule which she'd heard that morning; and all the while Stocky's elderly father Anno slurped away at an impressive volume.

With all the commotion at the table, Ford never noticed the beggar enter, but there he was just off to the side at Wynna's end of the table. At the shouting of "Pass bowls!" the table fell to an unnatural quiet. Ford looked round at the bowls being handed up, each with at least a spoonful of the pallid pottage or soggy piece of cabbage at the bottom. Ford looked at his drained bowl and the kind of intensifying shame he had not experienced since he was a boy swept over him. He passed it up and watched with dread as it reached Wynna, who was scraping out the left-overs of each bowl into the greasy-handed beggar's own bowl. "Whose—" she blurted out with a disapproving glare around the table before she could cut herself short.

"That's Ford's," accused Burra.

"Hush!" shouted her mother and eldest sister simultaneously.

"It's not polite to talk with your mouth full," chided Wynna.

"It's not!" complained Burra, opening her mouth and poking out her tongue as proof.

"Keep your tongue in your mouth," said Wynna, and Fyn gave the girl a light smack on the back of the head. In the ensuing argument, Burra's defense broke down into wailing protests nearly drowned out by the suppressing din of her mother and oldest sister, as well as the nonsensical squawking of the others. "If you girls don't behave," Wynna finally hissed low and dangerous, "the Sever Man will come and get you and sell you as slave girls. They'll take you off to some cold, dark place and you'll be beaten and have to scrub floors for the rest of your life!"

"That shut them up," said Anno, giving out a satisfied guffaw as he eased himself into his special chair by the dying fire. Stocky motioned Ford to follow him, and they too sat by the fire upon a low bench seat made from wood found discarded upon the docks, sticking their toes nearly on top of the remaining embers. Fyn appeared, throwing herself on Ford's back.

"Where's Bobo?" Ford asked Stocky as he hoisted the girl over his head and on to his knee to her great delight.

"Where's Bobo?" Burra asked her father while pulling at Ford's arm and begging to be lifted to the ceiling again.

"Wee-ha Boobo?" repeated their youngest, Nae, from where she toddled about across the room. "Wee-ha Boobo?"

"Honey, run along and help Mother. Go on!" Stocky tried to shoo Burra away, but it was Fyn who finally dragged her little sister off. Once they were far enough removed, Stocky leaned in to Ford and lowered his voice. "He had to go, few days ago."

"Sorry, I didn't know." Stocky waved it off, but Ford was still embarrassed. Getting rid of the dog meant they couldn't afford him. Likely he had been sold for meat or even eaten by the family themselves, which was becoming common throughout the city where the scarcity of pets was markedly noticeable these days. Ford looked around the room at all the mouths they had to feed and wished he hadn't imposed upon them. As his eye cast about, it rested upon Fyn wrestling Burra to the floor over by the sheet screening the far corner. The older girl sat on top of the younger and threatened to drool on her. Burra's screams, mostly ignored anyhow, melted into the general noise of the tiny abode. She thrashed about, and the spittle fell in a glop upon her eyelid, after which Fyn laughed and let her sister go. No one else had seen this besides Ford, who smirked and looked the other way. It reminded him of things he had done to his own younger sister.

"There's something I've been meaning to tell you." Stocky was about to go on, but not having found the sympathy she wanted from her busy mother, a tearful Burra nuzzled her way under her father's arm and tucked herself into his chest. He stroked her head and whispered into her ear soothing words only she could hear, even in this tightly packed room. Ford picked up the least chipped of the clay dolls littering the floor and danced it upon his knee, pretending it was tottering on the edge of a great cliff about to fall off. Burra sucked up a sniffle and grinned at his silliness.

"No," she admonished with a giggle before taking the doll from him and crawling back into her father's arms. The girl turned the doll about in her hand and began tentatively playing with it as if it was the first time she had laid eyes upon it, and became so engrossed that she hardly noticed when Stocky passed her off to her grandfather.

"Hullo! Who are you now?" said Anno cradling the drowsy girl in the crook of one of his hairy, broad arms and stretching his stumpy legs out toward the hearth, lounging as comfortably as possible in the only chair in the house to have a backing. Stocky elbowed Ford and nodded at the door.

They hadn't taken a few steps into the street when they came upon the beggar the family had just fed slouching against a wall dragging his finger along the bottom of his bowl and licking it clean. Catching sight of Stocky, the man murmured blessings for his family.

"Sorry about that," said Ford as they walked away. "Didn't know you kept a man at your table."

"Think nothin' of it," Stocky said with an airy wave.

"That's awful generous."

"We do what we can."

"But it's gotta be tough. Always knew Wynna could stretch a coin, but that's generous, that is."

"Oh we manage, we manage. Father's getting to be a handful, but we manage."

"Anno not getting any better?"

"Worse," said Stocky and chewed at his inner lip rather than spew the unkind things he might have said about his ailing father, whose mental faculties seemed to decay daily. "He gets angry over nothing. Took a swing at me the other day!"

"Over what?"

"Nothing! He got it in his head I stole his trousers. He was wearing them! And did I tell ya 'bout the time he wandered off? Took Wynna half a day to find him. And her havin' to watch over him and the girls, tires her out somethin' terrible, it does."

As they turned from the back lane to a more well-traveled street, Stocky bowed his head and went silent, thinking how best to phrase what he wanted to say next. Thinking he had more to tell about Anno, Ford waited and watched as his friend appeared to begin saying something, only to close his mouth. He started and stopped again, then opened his mouth one final time when a shove to the back drove him headlong into the muck.

"Step aside!" shouted a wall of a man armored in mail and armed with a halberd, who grinned with relish at having had the chance to knock someone down. Custom called for a warning to clear the way ahead, but in the busy street, neither Ford nor Stocky had heard a call or even noticed the retinue of guards and bearers accompanying the ornate litter of Barwnig Corradin, a cousin of Pennaeth Brastersceatt and a universally disliked minor tyrant of Lower Eastfeld. A man with more money than actual power, the barwnig liked to dress himself and his servants as regally as he could afford. Their sashes and plumes brought them in for ridicule, and so his guards liked to get theirs back when the opportunity arose, which was why Stocky now found himself in the muddy street.

As if daring this peasant to carry his insolence further, the guard stepped forward just as Stocky climbed to his feet. The inevitable clash guaranteed the provocation the guard sought, and when Stocky stumbled into him, the guard brought a gauntleted fist down upon the bridge of Stocky's nose, knocking him down a second time. Ford had not been prepared for the unexpected attack, and at first he simply stood in place mutely witnessing it all unfold. But finally he lunged forward. The blades of this guard and another immediately swung about with their newly-sharpened tips trained upon him. If he moved one step in the wrong direction they would skewer him.

"Back down scum, or I'll stick a hole in you!" barked the one who had knocked down Stocky. Ford looked each guard in the eye in turn and gathered himself up. The blades pressed in on him, and Stocky pulled him back by the pant leg.

"Know your place!" shouted the other guard and off went the litter with the guard who caused the scuffle keeping a vigilant eye upon the two commoners until they passed around a corner and lost sight of them.

While Ford did his best to help staunch the flow of blood from Stocky's nose, a ragged street sweeper, of the kind sometimes referred to as dungmen for the refuse they swept into guts and canals, pushed his broom by them while speaking in the direction in which the barwnig and his men had gone. "If the Pennaeth gets ahold of this town, we're in for it. High and mighty like them wouldn't stop pissing on the likes of you and me." No one paid him much mind, and he passed on.

"Not as quick as I used to be," said Stocky through the blood running over his mouth. By the time Ford got him back home, dizzy but recovering, the blood had caked upon his chin and all over the front of his tunic.

"Dear gods!" cried Wynna when they stumbled through the door.

"I'm fine," said Stocky dabbing at his face absentmindedly. The house, which had been in a tumult when they walked in, went silent a moment before exploding anew.

"Why are you bleeding, Puppa?"

"What's happened?"

"Is Puppa gonna die?"

"What's wrong? What's going on," begged Anno half in worry, half in agitation. Ford let go of his friend, and Stocky took a couple wobbly steps amid a swarm of women before planting himself on a stool.

"I'm fine, fine." He tried to wipe his sleeve across his mouth, but the arm was weighed down by the girls hanging from him in their paroxysm of grief. "Probably looks worse than it feels."

Amid the continued barrage of questions, attempted explanations tumbling over one another, and Burra standing in a corner wailing with her fingers in her mouth staring through frightened, watery eyes at her bloodied father, Ford slipped back out the door unnoticed.

A miserable night was spent mostly in wandering and wondering what to do, feeling like a wounded animal seeking a hole to hide in, to avoid being seen in his weakened, vulnerable state. "Pathetic," he murmured. It was a word he'd picked up from his stepmother. Later Alan had rounded out its meaning for him. "It's a good word. Suits me. And now I'm talking to myself." When finally finding a back-alley with a discreet corner to curl up in, he had terrible trouble falling asleep. His future, or lack thereof, ran through his mind in an unstoppable loop of failures revisited.

The following day, overcome by a listlessness he blamed on a chokingly thick mist, he didn't have it in him to go looking for work. More and more, he was convinced there was no work to be found, and there never would be. Instead, he loitered here and there, wading deep in self-contempt and prayer, or more precisely, desperate wishes for the easiest answers of whatever powers that be. Though, at this point he doubted anyone was listening.

At a corner in a vacated blacksmith's yard, he leaned against a post and picked at his teeth in an attempt to look casual, while impatiently waiting for a few people to pass him. Three elderly men shuffled by, too caught up in their own friendly argument to take heed of a lay-about with darting eyes. Ford stepped back into the street and followed behind them for a few foot-dragging yards. Their conversation was loud, but even so, they held their heads close together to hear one another. Ford could see how easy it would be to grab the two outer men by the ears and smack all three of those ancient and wrinkled heads together at once. Then it would be a simple matter of snatching purses and taking a moment to search for further valuables. He picked up his pace and just one stride behind them he noticed that there were no purses, nor concealed bulges that might indicate a pouch of coin. In fact, their clothes were not in much better shape than his own. One of the old men took notice of him hovering just behind and stopped. The other two stopped with him, and Ford tumbled into them.

"Pardon yourself!" cried one of the old men and "Watch it, you!" complained another.

"Oh, go bury yourselves," grumbled Ford in a huff as he pushed through them. What did he need with old men's money? Something to eat was what he really wanted.

For once, his prayers were answered in the form of a dirty child, half-clothed and standing under the garrison overhang of the defunct Anchor Inn chewing on a hairy bit of gristle and pulling away sinewy strings between his teeth. Ford hastened across the street and went down on one knee to seem less threatening while also getting closer to the child, whether boy or girl he couldn't tell. The child edged away.

"Don't be afraid. I just want a little bite. Just a taste. What do you say?" Without knowing what he was doing, he grabbed at the thing in the child's hands. A foolish attempt. The child, born to the streets and fully aware of such tricks, evaded his desperate grasp with a deft lean to one side and stepped back out of reach. No fear or surprise crossed the child's face, only a steady vigilance. Ford's stomach growled. He lunged again. The child backed away, and Ford fell face-first into the mud. He thrust himself up to his feet, and the child scampered away. Casting sour looks all around and knocking the mud clod from his nose, Ford walked off as if nothing had happened.

But something had happened, and it happened to the deepest part of him. Something broke within him, and it could not have been displayed more clearly than when he passed into a fairly busy market lane and trod in yet another pile of filth. Scraping his heel across the dirt a few times, he lifted his foot to see how much of a mess was left and waved off a beggar shoving a hand in his face.

"Got a sliver, master?" croaked the beggar. For a moment he thought that the man had said *silver* and looked at him askance, before realizing he'd said *sliver*, referring to the nickname for copper coins ordered by lords to be beat thin, literally stretching out money in difficult times. The beggar's eyes dragged up from the ground, got a better look at Ford and the condition he was in. "Never you mind," he said and moved on.

While grinding his sole into the ground some more, Ford noticed a slight boy a few feet away, awkwardly posed beside a forager's wobbly cart half-filled with scrap wood and two lumpy burlap sacks. Like the countless other waifs cluttering up the streets, nothing about the boy drew any notice. But Ford saw beyond the clothes so threadbare they weren't likely to last another winter and caught the desperation in the sunken eyes and the survivor's desire from which is born a new thief. He would have laid good odds on the boy stealing something off the cart right then and there, and sure enough, up went a tiny hand slipping into a sack. Out came a handful of acorns, and with a quick glance around, the boy was off running.

"St-st-stop!" sputtered the forager. "Stop! Stop him! Thief! Thief!" Reluctant to leave his cart should more be stolen, the forager drew back his arm to hurl one of his sticks at the fleeing waif, but then thought better of it.

Up went the cry "Clubs! Clubs!" around the streets as the shop boys within earshot poured out into the narrow street wielding clubs, rods, and whatever was at hand. Whether they wore ghoulish grins or serious frowns, all were eager to dole out justice. They pushed aside bystanders and leapt over stacked crates, handcarts, bundled sticks, empty barrels, and the huddled homeless all in the defense of their trade. For in their wisdom, a thief who stole from one stole from all.

If the waif hadn't run, he might have slipped away unnoticed amongst the crowd, but he had run, and now he was a target. Cut off, the agile child skidded a yard's length in the mud and changed direction. Ducking this way and that, he weaved around old women and housewives who made no attempt to grab him, only imploring "Leave the beggar be!" and "The little devil's only just hungry!" Up the street the waif scampered, with every slip and hesitating decision bringing the half dozen pursuing shop boys that much closer.

A pair of idle sailors slurping pints while leaning against a stack of firkins outside of an inn cheered on the chasers and the chased. One of them made a playful grab for the waif, missing the child by a long shot and splashing beer back up into his own face. His companion hadn't been so entertained in a good, long while and hooted with joy. The lunge sent the waif in another direction, straight at an empty handcart. The annoyed sailor went for him again. The waif jumped on to the cart and leapt off the back, the whole thing seesawing and kicking up the handles into the air, which caught the sailor under the chin and knocked him tumbling backward. The sailor's companion couldn't catch his breath.

A cluster of young women snorted and snickered at this, and one pockmarked, and thick-lipped girl blasted a torrent of ridicule at the shop boys, whose faces reddened more from embarrassment than from exertion. They grew decidedly more determined. If they couldn't match the slippery child in speed and agility, they made up for it with experience at the chase. Splitting up, they moved to block off the alleys at each end of the street. The waif, sweating and bug-eyed, saw what was happening and went for the only opening left. With a lanky shop boy just behind, he dove under a mule's belly. The mule jerked its head and kicked high in the air. The hooves flew by the shop boy's long nose. A second kick caught him in the stomach and knocked him hard on to his back. His involuntary gasps, like the bleating of a goat, echoed in the street and brought unbridled laughter from the gathering crowd, most of whom clutched their own stomachs as they bent double and roared.

"Can't breathe. Can't breathe," the stricken shop boy wheezed.

The waif still hadn't escaped. The mule's wild thrashing sent a hen leaping from the arms of one of the girl's and shooting across the road, tripping up the waif and dropping him face-first. Breathless and terrified, he scrambled to his feet, but a fleet-footed shoemaker's assistant caught him by the shirttail, spun the boy around and sent him flying headlong straight back at the shop boys, all of whose cudgels cracked upon his head in quick succession, sending the limp body collapsing on to the street.

The lanky shop boy still clutching his belly stumbled up to the body and kicked at it, sending blood flicking from the head. The girls screamed. The sailors quietly slipped inside. The shop boys, still panting but empty of malice, stood dumbstruck. Most of the remaining onlookers fell silent. The mule brayed on.

"You're all witnesses! You all saw what happened! That thief got what was coming!" cried the forager trying to keep up his indignation. Eventually, the sight of the bloodied body subdued even him.

In former days, Ford had fought for the undesirables of the world such as this boy, but his heart had hardened to such things. An embittered self-preservation was overtaking him gradually. Now he merely turned away and walked on. He walked away from kindly friends offering handouts from their tables as if he were a beggar, walked away from the neighborhoods that might offer temptations to a cutthroat thief, and walked into the most desperate section of Port Morton.

Here could be found vacant homes and gutted shops, decaying and filling with filth; incendiary and indecent charcoal scrawls on the sides of dilapidated buildings; shellfish middens covered in flies; vagrants fighting in the rutted, muddy streets over bones; the emaciated, scurvy-ridden and diseased. A stench hung in the unmoving air of these streets like crustaceans clinging to the bottom of a boat. This was Dwyer's Depression. Even in the best of times, it was a bad place. This maze of dim, dank streets began on Fish Street at a set of broad, grimy stairs leading down into a sunken warren of ever-constricting lanes and dead ends. The rain-darkened planks that remained of the buildings crowding in on either side bit into the street like rotting teeth in the gaping maws of eviscerated skulls. The Depression was the forgotten part of Port Morton, housing only the truly destitute and hiding a criminal underground. The remnants of failed lives and those who wanted to disappear found a home here.

This far from the docks and buried in such ruin, Ford would not be spotted by friends, and although eyes and ears could be bought by people like Barker, he doubted anyone in the Depression had been paid recently. He would find an empty nook somewhere, perhaps a dry corner to call his own where he could sleep undisturbed by the occasional passing watchman.

A pack of nearly feral children threw stones at him as he passed under the overhang of an inn ready to collapse into the street. He tried to ignore them, but the boldest of them came right up to him and spit in his face. He grabbed the boy and threw him through a gaping hole in the side of the inn. Amidst the laughter of the boy's friends, Ford hurried around a corner and away. The straining grunt that slipped from him when he lifted the feather-light boy made him feel every bit of his frailty.

As the sun went down, he crawled into an empty cartwright's shed and lay down, but barely had he relaxed when a scrawny apparition burst in full of rage and shouted him off the spot with accompanying kicks. Ford had never seen someone fight so vehemently for a scrap of ground. It took him off guard, and he scurried away like a dog scared off by a cat. There was no point in risking a rock to the skull in the middle of the night for having bedded down in someone else's sty.

Yet, fatigue had a grip on him, and if he did not find a place of his own soon, he was sure he would drop right where he stood and fall asleep in the middle of the road. The loft of the barn he had slept in for years as a child seemed like a luxury now as he moved deeper into the Depression, pressing on into an existence more bereft of comforts than any he had ever known. Stepping over a gurgling trench of water that cut through the street, he stretched too far and slipped in the mud, falling spread-eagle upon his back on the sodden ground. Aside from his bruised ego, he wasn't hurt, and if it weren't for the chill damp seeping through his pants, he saw little reason to move. Propping himself up on one elbow, he stopped at the sight of a skeleton peering from the dark of a collapsing shop window across the cramped street. Ford blinked hard for a clearer look. There was skin over the bones. The vision disappeared, and a moment later a grayed drapery over brittle bones tottered from the shadow of a nearby doorway. The emaciated figure shambling toward him resembled little that was human, only scant remains withered by time and ravaged by deprivation. Yet, this thing was a man.

The old man's long gray hair and hanging wispy cobweb-covered rags hovered over Ford, while his small, deep-set eyes made a study of him. Suddenly a filthy hand poked out from a crusty sleeve. Ford took it, but using all his own strength and fighting a sudden pain in his groin, he sat up, one hand going deep into the mud before finding solid ground from which to heave himself up. The old man crept back into the shadow of the doorway from where he had come, turned back, and gave a beckoning wave. Tired enough to trust anyone, Ford hobbled through the doorway with reeking chunks of muck falling from his back.

Leading the way with a small fish oil lamp taken from a ledge by the door, the old man took Ford through the wreckage of a building destroyed beyond recognition. Timbers dropping from the ceiling created a labyrinth of diagonal pillars through which the old man deftly climbed and around which Ford struggled. A crumbling gap in a dissolving wall toward the back led to a claustrophobic den furnished with a short table on three legs, a board over rocks for a makeshift bench, a short tripod made from barrel staves, and partially broken crates and boxes without their lids in which various unrecognizable bits and bobs were stowed. Dirty blankets covered some of the ground, and a few were draped over the dangerously leaning beams in order to create a screen around the old man's humble living quarters. Dissolving deep red embers smoldered in a battered tin basin by a wall with a head-sized rent near the top leading to the outside, which drew out enough of the smoke.

The host motioned to his guest to sit. He then grabbed a short length of board from a small pile, stirred the embers and tossed in the board, creating a warming fire. It cast a welcome light into the dark recesses of the dreary place, which helped to diminish Ford's fear that he might be walking into an ambush.

"Name's Ford." The old man nodded. When it was obvious he would say no more, Ford went on. "Just you here on your own?" The old man nodded. "You don't say much, do you?" The old man nodded. From then on to Ford he was known as Nod.

Nod shifted a crate, folded back a sheet, and lifted a tight-wrapped bundle from a hole in what remained of the floor. He turned sharply back to eye Ford with suspicion but seeing he hadn't moved, Nod grinned a rotting bank of gums and brought forth the bundle. Ford watched the unwrapping with great interest and almost as soon as a fish was revealed in the dim light, his stomach began to rumble. Nod tied the fish to the tripod with a short length of wire and positioned it so the fish would cook over the fire.

Over the next hour, Nod cut away pieces and offered them to Ford, who took them gratefully, wolfed them down, and fought the urge to take the rest of the fish and run. A jug of water was passed between them as they ate in relative silence. Nod stared at Ford quite openly, not meaning to be rude, merely out of curiosity, as if he saw in him someone or maybe just something he recognized.

Though not nearly full, Ford found that by the time they were done, he did feel a lot better, so well in fact that he stretched out on the floor to rest as long as Nod would allow it. He hoped it might last, as this would make a good place to rest and recuperate until he could figure something out.

"It's raining again," he said at hearing the distant tinkle of raindrops hitting the puddles in the street. Listening to the rain and watching the embers fade as the fire died away, he felt a heaviness come over him and a desire to simply rest his eyes for a moment. The next thing Ford knew, he was stretching and blinking awake to the morning light slicing through the gaps in the walls of this ruin Nod called home.

"Where is he, anyway?" The lighting was sufficient enough to reveal the hidden nooks and farthest corners, and there was no sign of the old man. "He can't have got too far."

Ford poked his head through the collapsing front window and peered about the street to where two wretched women were fighting over a rat's carcass. There was a rip, and one of the women flopped to the ground, while the other ran off. When the one on the ground saw that she only held the rat's head, she tore off after the other woman. Ford went back inside.

For a moment he had considered scouting about the area, but he didn't want to abandon the place with no one to defend it. It didn't occur to him that prior to his arrival, Nod must have left on a regular basis. To become so territorial so quickly over such a meager piece of property showed a grasping level of desperation that would have surprised him, if not shocked him, had he been more aware of himself. However, self-reflection was not at the forefront of his thoughts at the moment.

In the light of day, a survey of the wreckage that was once someone's shop and home revealed the place to be less unpleasant than it had appeared the night before. "This horrible hole might serve," he muttered. "Might not be so bad with a little work." Shaking out a blanket or two and clearing away some of the rubble helped. Shifting a fallen plank that lay over the main path made the passage in and out easier. Shoving a beam under the sagging ceiling, while not repairing the damage, would at least keep the whole thing from falling on their heads. "Least I hope."

Just as Ford dropped down upon the makeshift bench from the exertion and felt a powerful hunger come on, Nod shuffled in smiling and nodding at the improvements. The recognition made Ford glad to have put forth the effort. He was even happier when the old man withdrew from his tatters a half loaf of bread and offered it to him. Ford took it with hands that trembled under the weight of such kindness.

"This is—" He cleared his throat. "Generous of you. Truly." Tearing the loaf in half yet again, he would not allow Nod to refuse his share. The two ate in companionable silence. Grateful beyond further words, Ford turned away now and then to hide his emotion.

The remainder of the day was spent as Nod spent most of his days. They scrounged about the rocks of the bay. He tended to his frayed hemp line in hopes of tempting the odd fish onto the rusty hook with whatever few grubs they could find under spongy bits of wood or rocks during their achingly slow trek over to the lower, derelict dockyards where a canal emptied into a bay that was becoming silted into uselessness.

The following morning Ford tried to convince Nod that he could to do the fishing for both of them, suggesting that his host might rest instead. But no, the old man insisted on doing his share, and so they shuffled along together, like a pair of tortoises toddling through the narrow lanes. All the while, Ford inwardly lamented every step, which wasted time, time in which the line was not in the water, and the best kelp beds were being picked over by the early birds.

Coming to the bay reminded him of the only other time he had visited the seaside. Only this time experience was on his side, so he jumped from rock to rock seeking and finding edible crabs, mussels, winkles and whatever other shellfish that had washed ashore the night before. Not everything they rustled up and hauled in appealed to Ford's stomach–a bottom-feeding suckerfish had tasted particularly muddy–but they did eat, and he was feeling stronger, more himself.

After a time of no hope, he was once again thinking about the future and concocting ideas of how to get back on his feet while sitting with Nod on the boulders by the water or upon the sparse, rotting boards of the old piers, gray with age, exposure and a consuming mold. They watched their line, prayed for a bite, and stared out at the shipping. Lightermen and fishing boats plied to and fro. A merchant's sloop sailed right up the river on the surging flood. One of the larger trading vessels back from the warmer southern climates slid into its anchorage away down the bay but still within sight. A longboat loaded with prisoners and jailors pulled out from a demasted hulk and sluggishly jerked and glided across the bay into the deep channel to a transport ship bound for Polecat Island, the penal colony where Port Morton and other cities of Aelwyd rid themselves of reoffending petty criminals. An idea hatched by the Iarl and her advisors, this was a new, non-lethal method of dispatching the lawless element infesting the city in ever-increasing numbers.

"An ape!" Ford suddenly shouted, scaring Nod awake from one of his frequent naps. "It's one of them apes! Up in the rigging, see? He's just hanging there from one of them ropes there. See him? Boy, the sights you see in this town!" A wide grin lit up his face and a buoying lightness of being lifted his spirits as they had not been in some time. "Look, he's off!" He pointed, but the old man squinted and saw nothing of the ape's capers: rocking from ratlines, climbing up to the foretop crosstrees and sliding down stays. In a flash he was arm in arm with one of the idle hands along the rail, waving at the land with enthusiasm equal to his only slightly less simian companion when Ford's attention was distracted by a cloaked figure just a few feet away on the remains of the old wharf. Ford threw his head back and laughed so loud it made a ragged little girl scavenging on the rocks below him drop the seaweed she was picking through and run.

Elle stood before him in formfitting leggings and a smart leather bodice over a wine red tunic. Everything about her was dark, even down to her radiance. And she did look radiant, thought Ford. With arms folded and shoulders tense, she frowned at him, perplexed by how he had come to this. He took it for contempt, but couldn't blame her and even felt he deserved her scorn.

"So, you found me. Again. I would not believe it, but there you are." Ford dipped into an almost morose acceptance. His self-imposed exile wasn't going to last forever, but to end, it now felt too soon. "Perhaps not." The slow wheels of his thoughts were turning, and he missed her quizzical look while the gears churned. Over the previous days, grand ideas for the future had floated up like ships from the horizon. The lull in his mood rebounded spectacularly. "Say, listen, I've got a plan!" Like a madman of single-minded insanity, he dove into a rambling description of a scheme entailing his upcoming fight. "If it's still on. Do you know if it's still on?"

Just then he realized he hadn't introduced her to his friend Nod, but when he turned to Nod's accustomed boulder, the old man was nowhere to be seen. There was no way for someone who moved as slow as he did to vanish in such a short amount of time. "There was an old man beside me. He was right here. Did you see him?"

The subtle amusement and pity that cracked the hard-cast mold of her face fostered a nascent notion within Ford that maybe, just maybe she already knew Nod. After all, the desperate people of Dwyer's Depression would be willing to do much for very little, and it was possible that Nod came by the little extras he happened upon, such as the loaf of bread they shared, by providing Elle's guild of thieves with information. It would also explain how she found him so quickly. "Did you...Is the old man--"

She broke into his fumbling questions to deliver her message, one that would deliver him from this wretched place. "Now you go with me."

CHAPTER 7
GOING DOWN

The thrust of a taunt and a sharp jeer stabbed the air above the softer, flowing waves of frivolity rolling down the street to meet Ford's ears long before he reached the wide gate of the courtyard at the Horseshoe Inn. A rambunctious audience, excited and enjoying the fun on this Maradew Day, had packed itself into every available space. People hung from the balcony that surrounded most of the courtyard. They sat on each other's shoulders. A few even made it on to the roof, anything to see into the middle where a square of wooden partitions held in the entertainment.

"Ford! Ford! Ford," came Owen's voice shrill with excitement until Ford spotted him hopping above the crowd some yards off and acknowledged him with a wave. A momentary rent in the crowd revealed Stocky standing beside the feverishly happy Owen. He gave a hearty wave too and shouted something that drowned in one of the random crashes of the unruly sea about him. At least he was smiling, thought Ford, who was glad to see that his friend held no ill will against him for ducking out on him when the man only meant to help. While not noticing anyone else from Baldy's, Ford thought he got a glimpse of the student mage Yonn but figured it for an apparition of the mind.

"Ford! Ford! Ford!" hollered Owen once more. "See the bear? Do you see the bear? See him?"

Though he couldn't get near the center, Ford could see over the heads of most of the crowd and into the partitioned square, where a bear stood on its hind legs waddling back and forth. No dogs, just a dancing bear. The restless audience booed. Those closest rattled the partition. They wanted more action, more excitement. The bear's owner began to sweat. Ford would have liked to watch the show, but he gave another glance around the packed courtyard and drove a shoulder between two men, saying "Pardon! Pardon!" as he pushed through, peeling away the bodies in search of the innkeeper, who oversaw the prizefights held at his establishment. So, although Ford heard the portion of the crowd nearest the ring raising a chant, he missed them placing money into a hat. A jar flew by his nose as it was passed from hand to hand out of the inn and to the square. Everyone took up a rhythmic stomping that rattled loose a balcony rail, which fell and knocked a man on the head. The man twisted about in place to throw a punch at the man behind him, causing a ripple effect of pushing and shoving. The hat full of coins jingled as it was dangled tantalizingly over one of the partitions. Rallying cheers from those around the square extinguished the fighting spirit from the crowd, and they turned their attention to something far more interesting within the square.

The listless bear with heavy eyelids slouched at the end of his leash, looking with only mild interest at his blazingly red-cheeked owner, who succumbed to the demands of the crowd and pulled down his trousers, dipped a hand into the jar and smeared a brown, syrupy dollop on his genitals. A pandemonium of laughter and disgust broke loose throughout the courtyard. The bear sniffed the air, lunged forward and licked its owner clean. Hysteria electrified the crowd. People fell over one another. Someone fainted. Most had trouble catching their breath from the laughter, but others had plenty with which to curse the man for a degenerate and cheer him for his daring and willingness to provide entertainment at any price. The purse and a few small coins were hurled into the square, which the bear's owner scurried to collect while drawing up his trousers.

On his way into the inn, Ford moved with the ebb and flow of the audience. Sometimes they all slid forward, sometimes back a step and occasionally to the side. At one point he was thrust up against a man, who disappeared between him and the brick wall of a man on the other side of him. The ghoulish face of Barker's man Grady, almost unrecognizable in its intense malevolence, jutted sour hatred at Ford. The throng held the three of them pressed together, while Grady pointed at his own squinting eyes before turning his finger around to point at Ford.

"Yeah, I see you too, Grady." An impulse of bodies propelled Ford toward the inn door, and he shouted back, "I'll see you after the fight!"

"Bet on it!" Grady went on shouting, but whatever he said never reached Ford's ear over the frightened screams of the crowd giving way to a pack of howling and snarling dogs being led into the courtyard. A wave of bodies swept Grady away and thrust Ford through the door to the inn.

Once the dogs were securely within the square, the crowd gathered around again, now laughing off their fear with abashed faces and lighthearted airs. Wagers were made on the dogs straining at the end of ropes and chains. The most vicious dogs, the ones clearly ready to rip out a neck, any neck, were heavily backed. Between the sweating men and women leaping for joy, beating the backs in front of them and cheering themselves hoarse, could be made out the low growls of the beasts just before they tore flesh and crunched bone.

After having checked in with the landlord, Ford stood flexing his hands as he waited by the inn door alongside his opponent Nolen Maddock, a round-headed lumpy man he had fought three times over the previous year. Losing the first bout as a young lad new to the game, he'd gotten smarter and knocked Maddock out of the second one, and then threw the last. He knew this man's abilities nearly as well as his own. You could punch his mashed-up face with its flattened nose and protruding cauliflower ears all day long, and it would not faze the man in the least, not if he could see it coming. The trick was to surprise him, and since the man's perpetually vacant stare mirrored the intellect within, taking him unawares wasn't much trouble. No, Maddock was no mystery. The mystery lay within himself. Ford had no idea if he was ready for this if his body could withstand the kind of punishment Maddock could dole out in an appallingly short time.

The partition slid away. A savaged, lifeless dog was carried out of the square, and the fighters passed in. Smears of blood spotted the walls and pooled on the ground. Tufts of fur stuck to the boards here and there. Now that he was within the partition, Ford could see how the people leaned upon it and threatened to collapse the poorly constructed, loosely joined walls under their weight, and possibly fall in on him. There was little time to worry. The fight got underway almost immediately.

Word of a fix was on the wind and some in the audience shouted barely veiled directions in Ford's ear: "Do the right thing!" and "Give us what we come for!" Ford wondered if maybe Maddock was also under orders to go down from some other fight fixer, but that theory got knocked right out of him. From the get-go Maddock plowed ahead, digging down deep to the body with intent. Ford blocked with his elbows and countered with quick, glancing jabs to the head. Maddock brought his hands up to defend, and since he was an unimaginative fighter, Ford knew his opponent would throw to the head now because that's where his hands were and that's where his eyes were pointing. Maddock lashed out, and Ford threw a hammer of a shot into his ribs just under the armpit, where Elle informed him Maddock had been hurt just the week before. Maddock winced and blew out an oath. His arms went down to his sides, opening him up like a morning glory for the blow across the chin that whipped his head around and shut his blank eyes.

Ford watched, waited, and heard the roaring ovation and exuberant huzzahs overriding an undercurrent of slanderous curses, derision and incensed confusion when Maddock did not get back up. The partition slid back, and he stepped into the crowd. Jostled by well-wishers and the embittered alike, Ford searched desperately for blue hats in the jubilant and contemptuous sea of faces. There were none. Plenty of brown hats caught his eye, but there were no obviously blue ones as Elle had said there would be. *The blue hats will make for you the way*, she had claimed.

Instead of a path to freedom, he saw before him Grady. Ford tried to force his way in the opposite direction. He got nowhere. No one wanted to give up a spot so close to the square. If he had only been born a bloodthirsty dog, he thought, and immediately he began snarling and barking, especially at the mean faces looking to vent their rage at him for having lost their money. Something blue flashed a few heads deeper just as his rabid dog act opened a space and he fell into it, sending him further from the blue hat he could now see quite clearly.

"Swindler!" and "Cheat!" stung his ears. Someone spit in his face, and he took a swipe at whoever it was. Hands pushed, punched, patted and grasped. The press of bodies yielded one moment and then held him in check. The only saving grace was that what held him back likewise kept back Grady, who swam against the wild turbulence to get at him, hooking necks and thrusting bodies aside. Ford caught glimpses between the heads of his pursuer's gawping maw growling, frustration reddening his eyes in his yearning to get at Ford clear across the packed courtyard.

A shift in the bodies and his own bullish surge thrust Ford toward the door of the inn, but a sneering face with bulging-veins about its bug-eyes blocked the way. One utterly malignant screech from it complaining of the losing gambler's gripes and Ford palmed the repugnant face and shoved it backward, stepping over the prostrate body and in through the door.

The bar room within the inn was nearly as crowded as the courtyard, but with some weaving and shoving Ford was able to squeeze through to the back door where he crouched to peer through the dirty and warped glass window to the street behind the Horseshoe.

A lanky figure on the other side caught the motion within and turned his face toward the window. Keene squinted and blinked his eyes wide in surprise. Ford jerked back, then reached forward and flicked the bolt home. He ran back through the inn as fast as his tiring legs could carry him into the bar room, where he nearly collided with Grady just blundering through the front door. As they came together, Ford grabbed the back of Grady's neck and swung him over the bar. Glass scattered at the back of the inn. Ford leapt for the stairs as Keene hurtled in. Thundering up to the second floor with the planks of the steps snapping and Keene on his heels, Ford heard the landlord hollering up after him for a moment before being trampled by the trailing Grady.

A rung from the railing at the top of the stairs came away in Ford's hand, and he swung it down hard on top of Keene's head. Keene felt for his forehead and fell back into Grady. Finding the rung cracked in half, Ford whipped the remainder down at them and tore down the hall, punching at some doors and wrenching the handles of others desperately hoping one might be open. None came free, so he ran headlong into the door at the end of the hall, which burst open in a shower of splinters, hinges and handle.

Careening through the room, huffing, and sweating, he plowed through the shutters of the room's only window and fell head over heels into a surprised row of spectators along the balcony. Regaining his feet, he pushed passed them, lumbered along the balcony searching frantically this way and that for the stairs down to the courtyard. If there were stairs, they were obscured by spectators watching the square below. Keene was just stepping through the window with Grady shoving him from behind. Ford threw someone aside, stepped on the balcony railing and leapt.

The people Ford fell upon wheezed grunts like squashed bellows. One of them lost control of his overflowing bladder. Ford hurt in a hundred different places, and when he tried to get up he toppled back into the pile of shouts, elbows and kicking feet. Behind him another crash and crush of bodies preceded exploding anguish and complaint. Through a forest of legs, Ford saw Grady sprawled out on his own pile of writhing limbs and anguished faces. Keene still gauged his jump from the balcony.

Ford's ankle throbbed so much that he could barely stand, but he forced himself to lean on the nearest complainer a moment before hobbling for the gate. To his relief, the crowd parted before him. But it was not for him. A giant cage just lifted off a cart was being carried into the courtyard, and everyone near it was scampering away. Inside the cage an enormous squawking beast snapped at the slats holding it in. It was a cheffyladeryn from the Forest of a Thousand Names, a flightless, horse-faced bird the size of a pony with a long duckbill and extremely fine feathers akin to feline fur. The cheffyladeryn showed its displeasure at being confined by continually tearing at the cage with beak and talon while squawking and lashing out at anyone foolish enough to get too close. By contorting its body and twisting its head, it could slide its beak or a pronged talon through the narrow slats midway along the cage and snatch away clothes and skin.

Whether they were planning to unleash the cheffyladeryn within the partitioned square, Ford couldn't wait around to find out. He thought to slip between the cage and crowd, but the overexcited and skittish people would not give way. Leveraging his one good leg, he pushed into them. Just then, someone panicked and leapt bodily over others to get away from the cage, leaving a gap Ford stumbled into. His ankle gave out, and he fell to the ground, where he was trod upon and kneed in the side by the mindless mass above. The cheffyladeryn's squawking rang out inches from his ear. Instinct made him turn to face the danger, and that was when he saw the space between the carriers' legs. Immediately he scurried under the cage. Once clear, he rose upon his good foot near the gate and hopped out of the courtyard. The crowd closed ranks behind him and the cage, blocking the gate once more, and away he went, limping down the street as fast as he could.

The din of the pandemonium behind him faded with each hobbling step and as it diminished it was replaced by the sound of his name repeatedly shouted with definitive insistence so that it eventually replaced the Horseshoe tumult as the lone voice of the streets. To his hearing, muddied by pounding blood and his labored breath, it could have been anyone calling out, but he did not turn to look. Nor did he slow. His step kept time with his thumping heart, and the protests of his ankle were ignored.

The sun, heading fast for the horizon, flashed between the buildings a half dozen times before he realized he had been running in a straight line. From the street behind him came heavy footfalls, the persistent stomping of pursuit. He dove around the next corner into a maze of short lanes turning this way and that, making for the quickest corner.

The sounds of an approaching mob echoed off the buildings and could have been coming from anywhere. He worried that the furious bettors he thought he had left behind at the inn had caught up with him. Not knowing from which direction they came, he bolted around the nearest corner straight into the menacing teeth and piercing eyes of an undulating serpent. Its lolling, red tongue licked the air before it, and its coiling body filled the street. Fire broke out from behind it, multiple fires, the light of a dozen or more torches. Ford jumped back into an adjacent alleyway as a massive puppet, the people's handmade representation of the Maradew Wyrm, whooshed by in swoops and dives, shaking its wood, paper and canvas head. Ford leapt at a death scream from one of the parade participants pretending to be bitten by the serpent. It scared the youngest of the trailing children and delighted those looking on from their windows and doors.

With a horn missing, chipped paint and mud down one side, this once greatly feared menace was much reduced from the figure of pure fright it represented. Acting as the personification of Raenalf Maradew, the courageous warrior who slew this terror of the wetlands all those years ago, a gangly youth in a plain battered helmet pranced about before the monstrous head taking ineffectual swings at it with a wooden sword. The four men under a long canvas trailing behind the head ran at odds with one another so that the body slithered along the street, while the last man whipped a long tail at those following behind.

Laughter and smiles could be plainly seen under the raised torches. Ford would have loved to join in the frivolity, but on this day he only scanned the parade as it passed by. On the other side of the street, his eyes locked upon Keene's. Keene made for Ford, lunging straight into the center of the serpent. He crouched to go under it, but it ducked. He leapt up to go over, and the body jumped, and the two got twisted together. The serpent kicked and shoved him. Parade goers grabbed him and threw him back, so that by the time he had fought his way to the other side, Ford was gone.

Wide, long avenues funneled him inevitably into the open space of Brastersceatt Square, where bunting fluttered between buildings and fresh flags and brilliant pennants hung from the windows of wealthy home and shop owners. The people milling about, some lighting extra torches in sconces all about the space, might have been enough to deter Barker's men, but Ford pressed on, hopping a sledge and barreling over a cartwheeled into his path.

His ankle still felt weak, but he put it to the test, laying on more weight and relying on it not to give out as he ran on from the square, heading for the warren of narrow streets behind the docks. If he could just get to Baldy's, he thought he might find a friend or two there willing to take a break from celebrating the holiday to back him up and repel his pursuers.

"There!" shouted Keene from two blocks away. Grady appeared from around a corner behind him, and both came racing after Ford. After a few quick turns his wits left him, and he hit a short dead end. Panic gripped his lungs so tightly that he doubted he would ever breathe again and then a hand grabbed his elbow. He jerked it back and swung. Elle ducked his fist, and he nearly fell forward on top of her.

"There you are!"

"Shhh!" She yanked at his arm until, overcoming his moment of uncomprehending stupidity, he followed her through a door that she swiftly yet gently closed behind him.

"What happened to all the blue hats?" wheezed Ford between great heaving gasps. "I nearly got killed back there."

"Shhh!" She swatted at him and held an ear to the door. Plodding footsteps slowed and stopped just outside. Another door creaked open.

"May I help you?" inquired the carpenter whose shop they had invaded. His curiosity took on an edge of annoyance as he called again from atop a flight of stairs across the shop. The two seemingly furtive intruders hunched by the door ignored the question, instantly infuriating the man. He stomped down the stairs and grabbed up a planer, the nearest thing to a weapon at hand, then marched across the sparse room with its neat stack of lumber, woodworking tools hanging from one wall, and a worktable upon which sat a coffin. "I said, may I help you?"

Elle held up a hand to silence him. Though Ford's chest burned to breathe deep, he kept his lips sealed as firmly as Elle's. She felt certain the footsteps had receded but listened all the harder for a moment longer before speaking in a low, but insistent tone. "Fast, go back where you come. When you see iron man go right. No. Other way."

"Left?"

"Yes, left to shoeman's there and then to right down next street."

"If you have no business here, I would ask you to leave!" shouted the carpenter. Elle tried to hush him with impatient gestures.

"Down there is locksmith. Wallace is name."

"I know it."

"Go in, ask for—"

"Leave my shop now, or I will have you arrested!" shouted the carpenter strutting up to them. Elle yanked the planer from his hand and held its blade up to his lips as she drove him stumbling backward to the nearest wall.

"Shut your mouth, or I skin your tongue," she hissed in a completely calm, but utterly serious tone. "I make myself plain?" He chirped a trembling acquiescence. She turned back to Ford. "Ask for Reilly. Tell him Ethel has sent you."

"Ethel?"

"Yes," she said. "Do not use real name." She freed the carpenter, who slid from her, scampered across the room, up the stairs and into his living quarters. The upstairs door slammed, and its bolt went home. Elle poked her head out of the shop door and looked both ways. "He will not know it. Go!"

"Aren't you coming?"

"I go back to the Horseshoe for the purse of coins."

"Oh no, Elle. It's too dangerous back there now." Certainly, he was anxious to get what he was owed for the fight, but the whole idea to scam Barker was his and he wouldn't risk his friend's safety. "I'll get it."

"That is more dangerouser." She shook her head and shoved away the hand he had placed upon her shoulder. "Besides, I do not get it. I have a man do this, and I get it for, from him. Now go!"

Ford followed Elle's directions through the darkening streets with hurried steps and anxious glances that caused him to tread upon a vagrant and nearly fall into a gong cart. The evening light created just enough vagueness in the narrow lanes and alleys under the two and three-story buildings to make every person, every object, even a crooked stack of cut rocks appear to be Grady or Keene. He all but jumped out of his skin when a bent old woman wrapped in a shawl met him at a corner.

Raindrops splatted upon the ground to the rhythm of footfalls. Deep muffled voices around the next corner stopped him in his tracks. Without bothering to chance a look, he backtracked, his feet slapping the wet ground, stumbling in a rut as he crossed a street from one alley to the next. Carefully picking his way around and over heaps of garbage piled in the narrow way, a bump and a sudden scurrying bustle somewhere behind made him bolt.

The exact location of the locksmith was lost in his mind, but eventually he found what he hoped was the cobbler's shop Elle was talking about. Gingerly stepping heel-to-toe and taking great pains to avoid noise, he crept down a lightless side street, reaching up over each door until he came to the one with the dangling knotted length of rope hanging above. Two soft thumps with the side of his fist and almost instantly a ray of dull light shone through a finger-sized hole head-high in the door.

"Wallace's. What is it?" a man asked, curt and tired through the hole.

"Reilly," Ford wheezed out. "I'm looking for Reilly. El-Ethel sent me." The light in the hole disappeared and a multitude of latches and locks lifted and released. "Hurry up," he urged while trying the door again and again until it opened and he pushed his way in, immediately clapping it shut behind him.

"*Hurry up*, says the dawdler himself! I been here, well past closing time, awaiting on you and you say hurry up?" said the pudgy man, whipping the locks and bolts home with a nimbleness that seemed incongruous to his stubby, square-ended fingers.

"You are Reilly?" asked Ford.

"I am."

"I'm For—"

"Don't care, don't want to know. My god, where have you been?" reprimanded Reilly through the least chastising little smirk worn by any taskmaster type Ford had ever known. His hands were propped up on his hips and, although he paused with a head tilting an upraised eyebrow toward Ford in a way that said he expected an answer, the stance did not last, nor could Reilly's true anger. He loved life too much, especially his own life, to burden its beauty with a sourpuss' attitude. A bit of fun was to be had tonight and he was ready to lead Ford to it via the light of a lantern, guiding the way through a shop cluttered with every imaginable variation of skeleton key hanging on the walls, files, a grinding wheel, a few doors, chests, boxes and an endless variety of locks in disrepair. Tight paths wound through the chaos to a set of stairs on the way toward the back that led up to a door to the second floor, much like the carpenter's. A creaking hinge sang out from the top of the stairs.

"What is it, Reilly?" The words croaked out like brittle branches snapping, and autumn leaves falling from an ancient tree.

"It's nothing I can't handle, Mr. Wallace!" shouted Reilly. "The customer only wants a new key!"

"Eh?"

"A new key is needed! Which I will do!" shouted Reilly, projecting a clear, penetrating tone upwards. There was a coarse grumble, and the door slammed. "Don't worry about old Mr. Wallace. He's nearsighted as they come and half deaf. It's the perfect situation really." The locksmith's apprentice's eyes brightened and latched on to Ford's. "Do you have the fee?"

"Do I? No, I—"

"Damn it! I knew it." Reilly's shoulder sagged some and Ford's hopes took a dive, but then Reilly shrugged. "Never mind. They'll get it to me. Let's go."

Hefting his lantern to shoulder-height, he led the way through another door at the back camouflaged by unfinished doors leaning against the wall. It opened onto spongy stairs leading down to a damp unused cellar directly under the shop. Musty air swept up and Ford buried his nose and mouth in his sleeve. They crept crab-wise under the cellar's low ceiling and mold-covered beams across the room to a stack of rotting doors leaning against a wall of smooth, fitted stone. Handing the lantern to Ford, Reilly slid the doors aside, got down on one knee and dug his fingernails into a crack. Eventually, he all but silently pulled back a stumpy, wooden door that looked made for a cabinet.

It had been painted to match the fitted stone on this side and the rough natural stone on the other. Ford stood amazed while Reilly disappeared with the lantern into the secret passage and the cellar went dark. He bent down to peer in and then called, "Hello?" Reilly's head popped back out.

"I almost forgot! Here," he said, handing Ford a vial of clear liquid stoppered with a cork. "Drink that down. Compliments of the house!" To Ford, Reilly's smile seemed more genuine than any tavern's landlord obliged to give away drinks. Again the locksmith's apprentice disappeared, but this time he left the lantern behind in the passage entrance.

While Ford eyed the tiny odd-shaped glass vial, a series of subtle clanks echoed back to him followed by the whispered voices of Reilly and someone else. Ford leaned in closer but could make out nothing more than the vaguely disagreeable tone of the conversation. He uncorked the vial and sniffed. It was a little peculiar, a strange fermented concoction he had not smelled before. Though he wasn't sure how much he trusted Reilly, the man was an acquaintance of Elle's. Ford tilted his head back and drank it down in one quick gulp. The taste was nothing memorable and certainly no worse than some ale he had had. The only effect it seemed to have on him was to arouse his thirst.

"Ill-natured son of a bitch," muttered Reilly, crawling out of the tunnel stoop-shouldered and covered in cobwebs.

"What was that?" asked Ford handing the vial back.

"What did it taste like?"

"Like, I don't know, nothing much. Maybe rotting vegetables?"

"Then that's what it was," said Reilly. He held up a hand to silence Ford, listened a moment and said low and confidential, "You can go through now, but mind your head and watch your step, and be warned. There's a man waiting down there ready to burst. He's got a stick up his backside about the delay and the fee and whatever else under the sky. Don't mind him, he's always a lemon-licking sourpuss." He shook his head, and his face clouded in confusion. "What your friend Ethel sees in him I just don't know. Anyways now, just follow wherever he leads you, and you'll be all right. Go on!"

Reilly gave him a shove, and Ford ducked and squeezed through the secret door, scraping his head on the downward sloping passage. In the fading light of Reilly's receding lantern, he missed the first step of the stairs and only narrowly missed plummeting the remainder of the way when his shoulders got stuck between the narrowing walls. As he turned to ask Reilly for help, the secret door thumped shut, leaving him in complete darkness with only his own rapid breaths of the chill air in and out of his flaring nostrils for company. Beyond the next step, the way ahead of him lay in mystery. He wanted to turn back to the only thing he could be sure of, but it would have been cowardly and served no purpose. His way out of all of this mess had been paved by Elle, and he must have faith in her. There was nothing to do, but to go forward.

The locksmith faded from memory as he twisted free and took the rest of the stairs at a snail's pace with his toe tentatively testing the ground ahead. At what he thought was the bottom, he stretched a hand out in front of him and felt nothing. The cold, damp walls pressing in tight on either side had gone nowhere, and neither had the floor nor the rough ceiling. Beyond the twinge of fear of the nothingness ahead, what really started to bother him was that he was having difficulty remembering how he had even gotten here. He knew *why* he was here to get away from Barker's men. He even recalled Elle directing him here, but from the time of that conversation with her up to this point, he could remember nothing.

"Stop stalling!" cut irate through the void before him and shattered his already tense nerves.

"Who's there?"

"Come on. I haven't got all night." The voice was young, male, and annoyed. The wispy immediate past parted for the memory of Elle telling him to meet someone. This was part of the plan. This must be that someone. A glow formed from around a bend in the tunnel ahead just before a penetrating light from an unveiled lantern hovering a few yards ahead hit him in the eyes. It lit the dusty stone walls squeezing in around him, but the man holding the lantern remained in shadow. Even when the light turned away, it left in its place a white glare burned into Ford's vision so that he could make out little more than the silhouette of the figure ahead of him. Ford turned his lowered head to see from the corner of one eye and followed the shadow blocking the light. They crept through a series of buttressed tunnels dug ages ago that eventually forked off to newer passages of pungent earth where dangling roots clung to Ford's hair.

"Don't make a damn sound," spoke the angry voice for the first time in what seemed like ages. A few yards farther on they came to a section where the ceiling turned into heavy planks. Ford bowed his head, then bent at the waist and finally got down on all fours to crawl through this portion of the tunnel. At one point he even heard footsteps passing upon the planks directly above him.

"Holy—" cried Ford when he dropped over a short ledge into a cooler but more open tunnel where he was able to stand again after finding his feet once more. For balance, he ran his fingers along the knobby wall until a flash of the lantern revealed stacks of bones from floor to ceiling crowding him in on either side.

"Hold your tongue!" hissed the man, twisting back around to face him after an inadvertent outburst. After that, Ford kept at least one hand on the ceiling as a precaution and the other against his chest.

Ford's every utterance and misstep garnered grunts and muttered curses from the annoyed man. Both wished to get this over with as soon as possible. Ford's hope rose when they stopped by a door in a thoroughly damp part of the tunnel with a thin trickle of water running through a groove in the middle of the floor. The man turned abruptly on Ford. His thin lips were tight and colorless. Beneath his hood, worn low over his eyes, poked out a dimpled nose and chin, a chin covered in a soft, patchy beard and spotted with acne.

"Go through," he commanded and shined his lantern on the thick, wooden door bound by iron. "Go on!" The man jerked his thumb at the door and without waiting another instant, grabbed the handle and swung it open wide enough for someone of Ford's size to shuffle through sideways. Ford squinted and tried to peer in, but his eyes had not entirely adjusted, and the door blocked the lantern.

"Shine that light in here. I can't see a thing," he said, leaning in and squinting for a better look. A shove in the back sent him stumbling in, where he rammed his head into a stone wall. The door slammed shut behind him. Bolts slid home as he threw his weight against the solid, immovable door. He kicked, he punched, he shouted. When nothing would prevail, no answer came to his threats and pleas, no amount of leverage with legs and back would budge the door, his heart began to pound. Breath came strained through a tightening chest and sweat beaded upon his brow. Frantically he felt about the walls, floor, and ceiling like a blind man and discovered quite quickly that he had been imprisoned in a cramped and damp cell with no windows and no way out but the immovable door. "Let me out! Let me out now!" His repeated shouts turned hoarse and then wheezed into nothing. He slumped down to the ground and pushed back against the four walls that he was sure were closing in on him as his breathing came fierce and fast. With the will of self-preservation, he forced himself to stop or thought he had, but his head spun until he was dizzy.

Stop. Stop.

As the sweat ran freely from him in this cold cell, he knew he must control his fear. He curled into a ball, wrapped his arms around his chest and pressed his forehead against the ground until he felt its coolness permeate and ease the enflamed whirling within his skull. Slowly everything cleared, and a relative calm returned.

"This was her plan," he said aloud. "She will come for me." Though Elle had never explained in exact detail the assistance her guild would provide in his escape, she had led him to this, so there must be meaning behind it. "Keep faith."

Such thoughts lent him fleeting assurance. All too soon, however, malevolent speculations, such as the needlessness of locking him away in a hole, crept back to poison his heart and mind against his miserable jailor, that dimple-nosed, spotty chinned man, who had left him here to die for all he knew. "I'll rip him apart," he growled toward his stomach as he pulled himself into a tighter ball to fight back the panic.

Time passed in thought of escape and revenge. If he had fallen asleep or not, whether his eyes were actually open or closed, he couldn't tell. Here in the utter darkness, time was meaningless. Hours passed like minutes and then minutes like hours, exhausting hours of racking pain at every point upon which his body touched the hard floor and the gritty, slime-cover walls. A maddening thirst had him licking at those walls for the moisture. Nothing for company and no sound beyond the occasional scratching and squeaking of rats and mice. He floated in a dazed state, unsure of his own waking and dreaming. Imaginings swam and danced in the dark. An army of lean and desperate warriors with him as their leader conquered all before it. Yet, in his hour of glory, victory was torn away by horrid claws that scratched at his vitals. Terrible demons squealed in delight with him watching on as they dismantled his living corpse and stole victory over an underground wasteland of gritty slime. The squeal of the mightiest demon struck the very center of his brain.

A crashing clank like a god's hammer upon an anvil forced open his eyes to a searing light like a merciless sun staring down upon him. He clamped a hand over his tearing eyes. A voice from beyond the light spoke like thunder and Ford was sure he had died. Then a hand shaded the light, and he could make out a vague human form behind a lantern.

Ford lashed out with his legs, landing a foot in something solid but movable. The lantern smashed against the door as the bearer tumbled backward. Part of the door and the ground by it went up in flames, and through the explosive orange glow, Ford saw the warped and bewildered face of Elle.

"Ford!" Elle got to her knees with a hand on her pelvis and confusion in her eyes. She blinked it away and shouted, "Come! Come out!" He fought to stand, but his long-contorted body resisted. It took all he had to crawl and dive through the doorway, while tongues of flame licked at his clothes and face. They lay there tumbled together on the ground, her arms holding him about the shoulders, while someone else smothered the fire. All that remained of the lantern was its base, in which still burned a flickering wick no brighter than a candle.

"That's going to cost you as well!" snarled the man who had locked Ford up. He stamped out what he could of the fire, while the damp of the door and floor extinguished the rest.

Feeling Ford's muscles tensing and his body coiling to lash out again, Elle held on to him and whispered, "Hurt him, and we do not leave this place alive." The man sneered at them both and Elle feared that he would lose his temper or that perhaps that Ford had blown it for them already. But he merely picked up the lantern base, held it like an oil lamp and headed off up the tunnel leading away from the cell. "Come," said Elle plucking at Ford's sleeve and pulling on his arms. "We must not be forgotten behind."

"He don't seem worth troubling over to me," replied Ford as he lumbered behind his friend, who hurried ahead after the dimming light. "Elle, ain't you got nothing to drink? I'm thirsty as a fish."

"No."

"Nothing?"

"Soon." She sped ahead, striding with ease up a lengthy stretch of low-ceilinged slope. Ford crouched to get through the tight, earthen tunnel and fell further behind. His hands stretched out for the ceiling and walls, and his tentative steps dragged slower upon the ground. At an intersection he found both ways equally dark, and his nerves got the better of him.

"Hello?" he cried out. A biting hiss shot back at him. A moment later, the vague image of Elle appeared in the right-hand passage, beckoned to him and disappeared again. As he neared the spot where he had seen her and passed around a gradual corner, the light grew strong enough to see that the tunnel ended in a brick wall. A small hole little more than knee-high from the floor at the base of the wall showed two sets of feet facing one another within a shaft that appeared at least tall enough to stand in. He sincerely hoped they didn't expect him to follow them through such a tight fit. The four feet visible were crowded so close together, Ford imagined Elle chest to chest with the dimpled and spotty-faced man.

Before he got to the hole, he saw the man's foot stamp and heard rapid, harsh words pass between the two, but in a bizarre language as foreign as anything he had ever heard. The man shinnied down and placed the lantern base on the ground, and the conversation continued, but with the constant stream of words replaced by the sound of skin rubbed together and fingers tapped palms. Something sounding very much like a slap ended the conversation, and Elle crawled back out with the lantern base.

"Did he just slap you?" asked Ford growing incensed.

"It is nothing."

"Nothing? Then I'm going to kill him for nothing!" He lunged for the hole. The man's feet disappeared upwards. Ford got his head and shoulders through the hole when a small cascade of gravel and dirt rained down upon his head.

"Let him go," urged Elle pulling him back by the pants until they slipped loose from his hips.

"Hey," Ford hollered and crawled back out. "You just gonna let him get away with that? Give me a chance at him, and he'll never touch you again!"

The embarrassment of being a victim and having the abuse witnessed by a friend forced Elle's gaze away from Ford's as she scooted around him and crawled back into the hole. What was worse was the fear she had that Ford would scare him away and he would indeed never touch her again.

"I tell you it is nothing. And beside, he is gone, long gone away. Come," she said as her feet disappeared from the hole and the light began to diminish. "We go up."

Ford stuck his head in the hole and looked up the narrow shaft. "Oh, no. No, that is not going to work. I'm too big."

"Hush," called down Elle. "It is safe and fast this way. You must follow." Scuffing, tiny heaving sounds and dust descended the shaft. Ford leaned back out, wiped at his face, and took a few deep breaths to steady himself. After the stint in the confined cell he wasn't sure he was capable of squeezing through such a narrow passage. On the other hand, it wasn't getting any warmer nor more welcoming down here with the dark creeping in all around him. Once through the hole and standing in the shaft, he reached up for the ladder or rope he assumed would be there. No ladder, no rope, only rough stones.

"How do I get up?"

"Shhh! Climb," whispered Elle from above. "Quietly!"

"*Climb*, she says." How, he wondered while running his hands over the wall. Reaching as high as he could, his fingers found grips in crevices he could not see, and he lifted himself a few inches only to fall back down immediately. Eventually, he learned to plant his feet on either side of the shaft to act as braces, yet still his feet slipped, and he fell back down again. "Impossible." He gave it another go and this time also wedged his back, elbows, and knees against the walls. The position held. Shinnying up in small increments seemed to work. In spite of a slight slip now and then, he was able to catch himself and make continual progress, albeit at a snail's pace, up through the tube-like shaft. A trembling in his knees started up at once, and doubt seeped in about whether he could go on climbing much further. The lantern light appeared overhead along with Elle's face.

"Hurry," she whispered.

"What do you think I'm doing?"

"Nothing or sleeping."

"Am I almost there?"

"Yes! Hurry! We can not be here long!"

"I'm going. Hold your horses." He slid up another few inches, barely needing to brace himself now. "It's getting awful tight." A few more thrusts and relief flooded over him as he found himself face to face with Elle, her face framed by a hole that opened out to the liberating freedom of a room beyond.

To help him out of the shaft, she held out a hand, which he reached for but found he could not lift his arms.

"I'm stuck," he grunted. Squeezed tight about the shoulders in the hole with nowhere to go and no seeming way to get through no matter how much he pushed, Ford could do nothing but watch Elle's look of anxiety and her twitchy fingers that showed with their fidgeting how urgently she wished to pry him free. Suddenly, she reached out and began pulling at his head. "Ow, stop that!"

"You shoulders are too fat."

"Wide. Too wide."

"Come, what to do? We are in a bind."

"I'm the one in the bind!"

"No. Understand, we must be gone from here as soon as soon." The exit hole through which she peered back at him from appeared incredibly small, yet larger than the one he couldn't get through. Ford was thinking over what to do when Elle's hand lashed out, smacking the top of his head. "I know," she whispered excitedly as she pushed his head down.

"What are you doing?"

"Back in, then come one arm, then shoulder and then come more."

"I don't know what all you just said, but I'll try." Sliding back down the shaft was easier than expected, especially after he relaxed and let out a long breath. Once far enough down to slip one arm above his head, he reached up and took hold of a stone around the rim of the hole near where he had got stuck and heaved himself up. The stone came loose in his hand, and he fell a few inches until he wedged himself into the shaft with his back, knees, and elbows. The stone he handed up to Elle because there was no room to drop it past his body down the shaft. With a lot of pushing and pulling accompanied by plenty of gasping and mumbled cursing, he finally fought through the hole and fell panting on a wooden floor.

While he rested, Elle busily moved objects about the room, and before he was ready, she was pulling at his sleeve until he got up and followed her to a ladder concealed behind a wall. At the slightest hint that he might speak, she placed a finger over his lips and shook her head. Ford obeyed and followed her further instructions to climb. Each spindly rung threatened to give way under his heavy step, but they held and delivered him to a long but cramped room with a low-rafter, pitched ceiling, a roof if he was not mistaken. The relative warmth and dry air was a comfort compared to the underground cell. Elle's flickering light did not cast far. All that could be made out was a dust-caked fleece blanket lying rumpled nearby upon a flattened layer of straw. Rock-hard rodent droppings crunched under Ford's knees and stuck to the palms of his hands when he rolled into a sitting position. Dust kicked up, and he had to stifle a cough in the crook of his arm.

"Anything to drink?" he whispered close to Elle's ear. She produced a thin vial from a pocket. Her clothing was quite tight, and Ford wondered how the vial had not broken but dared not ask and anyway, he didn't care so much about the how as the what. "Bless you," he said, greedily slurping the liquid down and gagging at the taste. He rubbed his tongue on his sleeve trying to rid himself of the remotely familiar flavor and shot the vial a reproachful glare. "What was that, rotten pumpkin juice?" Elle only grabbed the vial and held it up to the light to make sure none was left. "Ain't you got nothing normal to drink?"

"Now we go."

"Wait. What happened back at the Horseshoe?" Again, Elle signaled Ford to lower his voice. He did, but he would not be put off. "Where were the blue hats that were supposed to get me out of there?" Elle bowed and shook her head. She wished to erase the past day, or at least the parts of it that had not gone as she had promised and as she had been promised they would by those she thought she could rely on. This was a shame she would rather not revisit.

"The purse was not enough."

"What do you mean? From the fight?" Ford looked upon her incredulously as she nodded. "But I thought that was all fixed up."

"Not many bet, and bets was small, few coins." She was sorry for that and wouldn't meet his eye. Wealth and the increase thereof meant everything to her. She assumed others felt exactly the same. In this case, she was not wrong. Ford had risked his future on this gamble.

"How much did we make?"

"Enough for this." Elle raised an open palm to their present cramped confines. "And to pay for the…for the breakings, you did at the Horseshoe."

Ford collapsed upon his back and stared up into the rafters. He had not pulled one over on Barker. He would not have enough to see his plan through. Apparently, he would not even have enough for his next meal. His mind was in such a quandary that he didn't realize he was mumbling. "Now what do I do?"

"Now we go." Elle crawled to the far end of the room and pushed at some boards covering over a window. The whole square section of planks swung open on hinges to a patch of night sky that blew in a hint of crisp air. Elle climbed through the opening and Ford passed the lantern to her, but she shoved it back. "Put it out and come."

"I don't think—" Ford began, but Elle came back to the window to crouch nose to nose with him in order that he might see her seriousness.

"No talk no more. Come."

Ford followed as commanded, but shoving himself through the window was nearly as difficult as escaping the shaft. As he pushed his shoulders through the frame, it bowed out so far on either side that he was sure the planks would snap and the noise would anger his friend. Eventually, he dragged himself through and stepped into the night air onto an adjacent roof. Enough stars were out to outline the rooftops but only outline them. Nothing of depth could be made out. The black sodden wood of the roofs blended perfectly with night's deep drapery. Ford feared to let go of the side of the house and take another step into this unmapped void. A dizzy feeling, the sort he got after his third or fourth drink, came over him as he nestled his back against the house with one hand on the window frame and the other on the roof beneath his feet.

Once an eternity had passed within his mind, the amorphous form of Elle returned and took him by a wrist to lead him along the roof. His head spun, and his feet would not move but for her insistent coaxing to the edge, where he got down on his hands and knees. She left him there and leapt over the side. Ford gasped and gasped again when her head popped back up. There was another roof just a few feet below the top of the one he perched upon, and it was clear by Elle's tugs that she expected him to follow her. He slowly slid his legs over the side and reached with his toes for the lower roof, but his feet swung free and felt nothing. A yank of his pant leg pulled one foot over to the steeply angled roof slick with evening damp. It chirped under his weight as if he were stepping on a nest of birds. His relief at having survived thus far was short-lived.

"Come," Elle whispered in his ear just before slipping away along the roof peak on her toes and heels. She dropped over the side and out of sight as easily as someone walking out their front door. Ford took his time, sliding his feet along the ridge and peering over the edge down into the nothingness below. He shook his head and stepped back, planting his heel on a particular slick patch. Before he knew it, he was on his back sliding off the roof. His whole body went rigid upon hitting the air.

The fall might have lasted a lifetime or the blink of an eye for all he knew, but the resounding *splat* when he landed came quickly and shocked him with its finality, especially because he wasn't dead. He wasn't even hurt, only soaked in cold mud the length of his backside. The sloshing of feet drew attention to rotund shadows looming about. Ford had missed the squeals that burst out at his landing, but now he took notice of the interested snorts moving in his direction. The minder whose duty it was to watch over this pigsty snored away upon his stool where he perched in one corner, but the ruckus caused by Ford raised the house. A light showing through a window from the house into the sty revealed a low pen wall, which Ford made for and dove over as a door creaked open.

"Hold up," Ford called to Elle when they met again down the street and around a corner. Instead of the electric tension that would normally be running through him at a time like this, a peculiar drowsiness was overwhelming him, and he closed his eyes.

"Don't sleep."

"Yeah, think I will, thank you."

"No! Come, more fast than ever!" Elle dragged him by the arm along a back lane and left him propped against a wall while she disappeared through a doorway, emerging immediately in his mind with a tankard of water that he chugged down insatiably. Much of it spilled from his lips and down his neck, but it tasted marvelous. She threw the mug back in the door and dragged him onward. A few yards farther on, his eyes began drooping of their own accord. The shaft and the attic it led to were fading from memory. The next thing he noticed was the thunder of the raging river below him while they stumbled over Ox Bridge. This moment's revival fled from him as soon as they passed it by and trudged up a hill that he thought would drag him down into the earth, where all was sleep and fading dreams and the smell of the color green.

Chapter 8
The Armory of Academia

Not long after noon, Ford awoke flat on his back in lush grass, still groggy from an all-encompassing slumber. The first thing his slowly focusing eyes flittered upon was a pitcher of water. Figuring Elle provided it, he took a cursory sniff, downed it and fell back asleep almost instantly.

The next time he woke up he rubbed his eyes, yawned and saw that the pitcher had been refilled. He drained it again. Sights and sounds came alive for him once he put the pitcher down. Vine-covered walls surrounded him on three sides. The fourth was an archway leading to a quiet lane somewhere off the main streets, or so he guessed by the lack of passersby and noise. This hidden alcove that surrounded him held a verdant serenity seldom seen in the midst of the city. Flowering bushes left quite wild, dandelions popping up where they might, and a shady corner of mushroom caps just poking through the ground were all dominated by a single, towering maple tree full of life, its green canvas above spreading a shady cover over a moss carpet that tickled his palms and fingertips as he lazily brushed the soft ground cover.

Twisting about to see what was behind him, he found himself staring into the bulbous eyes of the two-faced god Dwy Wyneb, or at least the stone embodiment of Dwy Wyneb. This personification of man's good and evil duality as seen in some Haunan idols held one pair of its four hands uplifted to the leaves, the other pair beneath were turned palm down and lowered toward the unseen roots below. The statue, no more than two feet tall, sat facing him from across the courtyard; in fact, Ford realized, it was actually meant to be facing the tree. He just happened to be in the way.

Certain urges forced him to his feet, and he leaned with one hand braced against the maple while he relieved himself on its base. With plenty of time to look about, he admired the holy sanctuary, the impressive height of the tree and noticed for the first time a priest of the Order of the Sud a Waed facing him from where he knelt by a small stone altar in complete repose. He was a grover, one who watched over a sacred grove. This grover's long face, thin lips, and drab robe did nothing to diminish the overall aura of welcome created by kindly eyes and the graciousness implied in his open arms. A ray of sun through the branches caught the wisps of his fair locks and cast a floating ring of gold about his head. Their eyes locked and Ford hurriedly finished.

"Sorry Father, or ah, Goeddyn. Am I pissing on your tree?" asked Ford with a good deal of remorse and genuine embarrassment.

"You are pissing on everyone's tree, brother," said the young priest without scorn, but rather a sincere warmth, as if to say he wished his visitor would continue enjoying the sanctuary as he saw fit.

"Oh. Well, that's all right then," said Ford patting the tree and saying a quick prayer. He moved to go, but the priest's kindly offer of a bowl of boiled potatoes in broth could not be turned down. Lean as he was, the priest did not eat, preferring instead to watch placidly his guest gratefully devour the spuds. Neither spoke, but then the priest came out of his sedate mediation somewhat downcast. Ford feared he had done something else wrong, but couldn't think what it might be and decided to suck down the last drops of soup as fast as possible before being kicked out of the grove.

"I'm to tell you that your relations expect you." The priest's face grew quite long as the corners of his mouth drooped. "I am ashamed to say I nearly forgot."

"Think nothing of it, Goeddyn." Ford took delight in comforting him. "Today's the day I meet up with my cousin, and we go off on a little adventure."

"An adventure?"

"A walk in the woods and nothing more to be honest."

"How delightful!" Though he hadn't actually shouted it with glee, there was an almost passionate enthusiasm that lifted not only the priest's voice but his whole demeanor. For his part, Ford left the pleasant little sanctuary quite looking forward to this journey into the wilds now. Originally he had looked upon it as a means to get away from Barker, which was still of paramount importance, but now a jaunt amongst the trees appealed to him for its own merits.

When the seldom-used side lanes and back alleys weren't available, Ford did his best to blend into the crowds on the busy streets in a continuing effort to elude Barker's men. The idea that someone a head taller than most and dressed in rags would not be noticed walking amongst the freshly scrubbed faces and vibrant attire of Brynseht citizens was ludicrous. Anyone looking for just such a person would spot him quite easily. However, deprivation and the remnants of a haze from the draught Elle had given him skewed his good sense, so much so that he got himself turned around twice and found himself trudging unnecessarily back up Wamb Hill a second time before finally finding the

Malcolmite Brotherhood's Beeswax and Candlestick Emporium and the Armory of Academia just beyond.

"Hello!" and various other shouts drew no response from the vampire bat head above the door to the Academia. Feeling defeated by the bat twice as quickly as the last time and on the verge of giving up, Ford thought he saw the bat wink. Inching closer and standing upon his toes, he spoke into its ear, "Hello, is anyone in there?"

"The word," spoke the bat, rocking Ford back on his heels. The voice was curiously normal, stern, yes, but fairly man-like Ford realized after his initial shock.

Blinking away his confusion, he eventually was able to ask, "What?"

"The word," said the bat.

"The word? What do you mean?" He waited for an answer, but none came. "Hello?"

"The word," repeated the bat.

"What word?" asked Ford with one clenched fist inching closer to his tormentor. "And if you say *the word* one more time I swear I'll knock you clear off there!" The bat remained silent. Ford tried to stare it down, but blinked first and sat down in a huff with his back against the base of the Academia quite careless of the lately ubiquitous puddles dotting the flagstones.

Within the same moment that the damp soaked through the seat of his pants, he jumped back up with an idea. The bat was asking for a password. If it hadn't been for Elle, he wouldn't have guessed. During their time working the streets together, she had introduced a number of such covert concepts to the backwoods country boy. "Um. Open? Open. Open up. Open door. Door open. Open up door!" Every word he could imagine to do with entering through a door he shouted at the bat, but he was no Adeline or Alan and had no endless arsenal of words at his disposal. The hard-headed bat was outwitting him, and he knew it as he slouched against the door and called out at random any new word that came to mind or tried an old word just to be sure the bat had heard him. Eventually he resorted to thumping the door with an elbow, cursing at the bat and challenging it to a fight.

No one idled before the great doors of the Academia. Either they had business within and were welcomed, or they did not and were not. Therefore a ragged loiterer stood out quite conspicuously to those passing by. It made him uncomfortable to be gawked at, so he moved off and found the back of the school in search of another door, a low window, any sort of entry or way of alerting someone inside. Finding none, he strayed away, walking around a block and then another, while trying to think of how to get in or a way to get word to his cousin.

"Does no one come and go from the school?" he asked an idle joiner sitting on his stoop casually flipping a mallet in his hand.

"Go on, you lazy dewbeatin' raggabrash! Get back to your Eastfeld mud hole!"

Ford couldn't know that he had happened upon the joiner on a particularly bad day and that the man was merely spitting back the pent up venom within for his lost trade. It felt like a personal attack and in other circumstances Ford might have struck him down, but he was so surprised by the vehemence of the reply that he only retreated to the Academia's entrance for another try at the door. If nothing came of it he had would have to find somewhere to hold up. Staying in one place, out in the open seemed like a bad idea. Barker would want him dead now, and even though this was well out of his usual neighborhood, the man had ways of finding his prey when he wanted to.

"Maybe the priest won't mind a little more of my company," he muttered as his fist bounced off the door in a monotonous rhythm. The door swung back.

"Ah, there you are," said an aged mage in a worn robe, an utterly old man slump-shouldered by the tyranny of time and dwarfed in the frame of the enormous doorway. Ford recognized him as the mage he had seen with Yonn performing cheap tricks in Brastersceatt Square weeks ago. "We've been waiting for you. Come in. But mind, keep quiet." He glanced over his shoulder back into the Academia, then looked Ford over before saying without much hope, "And try not to be seen."

The long, high-ceilinged, sparsely furnished room immediately beyond the door was lined with benches and clothing pegs along the walls. Crossing as silently as they could to the head of a stairway with the old man leading the way holding a lantern aloft, they were about to descend when a stern cough stopped them in their tracks like a couple of schoolchildren up to no good.

"Instructor Walader, who is that with you?" demanded a tall mage in stately robes from an archway across the room. The deep creases cutting straight down through his sunken cheeks barely moved as he spoke. With a sudden burst, he swept across the room to them with all the noise of a breeze skimming glass.

"A test subject, Overseer Hyldabaern. A *willing* test subject."

"Really?" said Hyldabaern raising a sharp eyebrow which lent a bit of wonder and disbelief to his severe gaze. "I congratulate you on your find."

"Thank you."

"On your way to the potions annex?"

"Yes."

"Well then, don't let me detain you." Hyldabaern gave Ford a final appraising eye before swishing away.

At the bottom of the stairs, Walader prodded Ford into a cramped room lined with shelves filled floor-to-ceiling with bottles and beakers. Scrolls, some rolled with twine, others loose, were all jammed into the cubbyholes of a cabinet. Unlit candles of various lengths stood in holders all around. Tables, benches, and chairs, every available surface but the floor, were covered in books left open. The old mage hung his lantern from a hook at the end of a long chain suspended over a table in the center of the room.

"Shut the door."

Ford gave it a push with his fingertips, but the door hardly budged. He had to shoulder it closed and when it sealed shut the air and sound in the room deadened, blocking up and momentarily deafening his ears.

"Hello?" he called out just to see if he could hear himself.

"Yes, what is it?" replied the old mage.

"What was all that about a test subject?" asked Ford digging a finger into his ear.

"There's no need to shout."

"Well, just so you know, I ain't doing nothing that's going to turn me into nothing weird. Understand?" Ford lowered his voice, but could barely hear himself and was certain the old mage couldn't hear him either. Walader waved him down as if to calm or quiet him, Ford couldn't be sure which.

"Stay still and touch nothing." The old mage rummaged through the cabinet, tossing rolls of paper onto a central table, toppling the lone bottle there. He spun around with a roll in hand and squinted. "Let me see, let me see…Ah, there it is!" Across the room, he shuffled to grab a beaker crowded by dozens of others taller and thinner on a shelf far too high up for him to reach.

"Which?"

"The wide shallow one with the stopper." Ford grabbed it for him, and he took it gratefully, tapping the glass with a long, yellow fingernail. "Drink this," he said, shaking and swirling the cloudy concoction before handing it over.

Ford un-stoppered the beaker and held it to the light. A vaguely unpleasant but mostly muddled memory on the subject of imbibing strange liquids offered in unusual containers kept him up from drinking it down as instructed. But then again, there had been that nice priest who had given him plain, refreshing water.

"Go on," said Walader, his instruction turning into command. He was only doing this as a favor for the pleasant, but shy young student Yonn, who assisted him with the odious task of entertaining the masses with simple illusions for what little coin they were willing to part with. The students weren't allowed visitors to their rooms, but Walader didn't like the overbearing Overseer who set down this rule, so there was that compensation for his time and secrecy as well. "Drink it, then climb into it."

"Eh? Climb into it?" asked Ford looking incredulously from the man to the beaker and back again.

"Don't worry, it will be empty then."

Ford tried the patience of the weary old man by demanding a fuller explanation and then, once satisfied, ventured on a sip. "Ach! It's like moldy dust!"

"Yes, the taste is unpleasant, and unfortunately there is a lot of it, so drink up. It's not a powerful magic. The effect won't last long. A student made it from an old formula using inferior substitutes. Finer ingredients could make a more potent concoction in half, nay, a third the amount without the horrid taste. But now that's where you and your friends come in, isn't it?" The mage waved away Ford's obvious surprise and explained how he was well aware of the planned excursion. An abrupt twist of mood soured his features, and he turned to Ford with a penetrating glare. "Take care of the boy. He is a good boy. A bit timid and not much of a mage, but he has a good heart. I would hate to see harm come to him."

"Agreed." Aside from the magic of which he knew nothing, Ford had formed a similar opinion of Yonn and liked the boy well enough from the little he knew of him. Sagging jowls rose, and satisfaction lifted the mage's wrinkles.

"Very well then, I wish you the best, and very much so considering the school's growing need." Walader looked wistfully about, vaguely waving a hand over the room as if the need was plain to see. At first glance, Ford thought the cluttered room appeared almost too well-stocked, but a closer inspection showed that a good many of the glass containers were empty or near to it.

While Ford finished off the last of the potion, the mage reeled off an exhaustive list of natural spell and potion ingredients that would be most useful. They all sounded as foreign as another language to Ford, whose attention was drawn away to the peculiar wavering he felt in his chest and stomach as if his innards were deflating, his body collapsing from within, and his skin floating down to the floor. He held his hands out before him, but all he saw were a pair of ghostly clouds. His eyes settled at floor level, and everything before him, table legs and feet, all were blurred. "It's like being in a fog. Or no, it's like being the fog itself." The thought escaped through his lips like gas, and the following chortle made no more sound than the puffs of a smoking pipe. All the same, the force was enough to send him drifting slowly and uncontrollably backward across the floor.

"I told you not to move," said the mage, his voice like a distant echo through a haze about a mountain peak, an echo caught up in the haze and slipping down with it into a valley. Ford tried to say he hadn't moved, but the words wheezed out in meaningless whiffs. Suddenly the air sucked into his ears. They popped, and he could hear clearly again. The door had opened and the wind it created pressed on him with the irresistible force of a hurricane, shoving him across the floor and through Walader's legs. *Do not look up*, Ford told himself as he passed under the old man's robe.

Somewhere off in the storm, he heard another voice, lighter, perhaps Yonn's. Ford called out for help as he hurtled toward the wall where he was sure he would smash apart on impact and blow away in a million pieces. But he didn't. He didn't feel a thing; instead he simply gathered together in the corner and slowed. Then there was a soft pressure. He was aware of hands like pillows herding him into the beaker. After some trial and error in which he slipped about the opening, unable to control his amoebic body, he finally poured himself in.

Inside the confined space, he felt more solid. A vague recollection of being squeezed tight in between something or somehow being restricted came to him, but it was nothing like this feeling of containment where he felt more in control of himself. Rolling over in easy somersaults, he brought his eyes up to the glass to peer out into a fuzzy world of dim light, stairs and the passing stones of the floor. A distant wall loomed closer, and a framed picture came into view. A door opened and closed. A far off stern voice, possibly the Overseer, was followed by an immediate darkness that lasted long after the voice died away.

Light again flooded into his beaker. A big white face came startlingly close and broke into his cousin Danny's cackling laughter. Without warning, he was flipped upside down and poured out naked on to an icy floor. At first, the freedom terrified him, but then he settled somewhat, and the unfolding of his frigid limbs felt wonderful. Then the nausea set in. As he lay sweating and trembling, threads of conversation fluttered about his ears as little more than background distraction from the overwhelming exhaustion and the immense weight of being dragged back into a human body. A distant scratching, like that of rodents, finally brought him around with a shudder.

"There he is. Hello, cousin. You are feeling under the weather, no doubt." At a table covered in feather pens, ink, a candle, a few scrolls of parchment, a pelvic bone, and a vial of peach-colored powder, Aedann Goldsmith sat hunched with a pen poised over parchment for the brief moment in which he turned to address Ford where he lay sprawled upon the floor of the dormitory room Danny shared with Yonn.

Ford gurgled a response, cleared his throat, and mumbled, "I..." His spinning head was fending off an abrupt headache stampeding across his forehead from temple to temple.

"Yes," replied Danny in the midst of scribbling a few words. He set aside his work and picked up a book that lay upon his lap. "You took a little nap. That has been known to happen, usually to those slight of weight or mental agility. The effects are wearing off, though, I should say."

"I feel like I just been shat out a cow's arse."

"All is well then."

"You should feel like your, uh, yourself again," said Yonn venturing to lean over Ford. "Soon." The boy sat back, but kept a vigil over Ford and was ready with a cup of water the moment he should want it.

"Though the side effects can be..." Danny trailed off, finding a passage in his book far more interesting than anything going on within the room. He turned to the next page, looked it up and down, and turned to the next, "...unfortunate, they are essential, I assure you. Otherwise, how would we get a mountainous oaf like you through the halls sight unseen during the day? When the Overseer is at rest during the predawn perhaps."

"Visitors aren't a-allowed in the rooms," Yonn explained. As Ford nodded, he found that there was a blanket partially draped over him and pulled it up around his shoulders. He noticed his hands and was glad to see they had returned to hands once more. "Your clothes," said Yonn indicating a bundle at the foot of a bed. Eventually Ford was able to get up and get himself dressed. With a meal provided by Yonn in his belly and feeling like himself again some time later, Ford sat in his obliging host's chair, leaning forward with his elbows on his knees and looking down into a small cup of wine, acutely aware of the young man staring at him from the edge of his bed.

Danny leaned back comfortably in his chair, stumpy legs stretched out, draining his cup with loud slurps. "What do you think of the wine?"

"Prime stuff," said Ford smacking his lips and working his tongue all around his mouth.

"Prime? I would not go so far as to call it prime, but it is drinkable. It is Instructor Runisdotter's attempt to turn water into wine. She has been at it for ages without much luck," Danny said through drawn jowls and a disappointed pout. With a last sip and a grimace, he placed the cup on his table well away from himself. "Best left to the priests, I would say."

Just as Ford was wondering what other odd things the mages were secretly up to within the school's thick walls, his eyes alighted upon a small jar on a shelf. Something inside it made him move closer for a better look. Suspended in a clear gelatinous fluid floated a minuscule creature with a horse's head, the flippers of a duck, and tiny wings folded upon its ridged back. Though it was likely dead and harmless enough, still Ford was glad to see the cork firmly plugged into the hole at the top. He backed away and took his seat once more.

A twinkle of pleasure alleviated the sour remnants drawing down Danny's face. He wiped a sleeve across his lips and clapped his hands together. "Let us get to work! Grab the weapons, would you Yonn?" he said heaving himself out of his chair with a grunt so that a red-cheeked Yonn could slide it out of the way and crawl underneath the boxy frame of the bed. Danny turned pointedly toward Ford with a triumphant smile that added folds to his smooth fleshy face as Yonn fished out a few odd-shaped pieces of wood. "For our journey."

"We're bringing firewood with us?" asked Ford with a raised eyebrow.

"*These* are the weapons," said Danny, each deliberately pronounced word tinged with annoyance.

"Those are sticks."

"Look! Give me the spear!" Danny held out a hand, briefly puffing out his chest, so it came a bit nearer to being flush with his protruding stomach. Yonn handed him a long, relatively straight and substantial, knobby branch. "That's the staff."

"They all look k-kind of the same," murmured Yonn as he shuffled the pieces of wood in his arms and handed over the thinnest piece of all.

"This is a spear, you see by the pointed end here," said Danny, forcing the words through his phlegm-lined throat as he made a two-handed jab with the stick. Ford took it from him, looked at the thin shaft and gave it a slight, yet too strong bend in the middle.

"Oh wonderful!" shouted Danny after it snapped and a shard of wood flew past his ear. "There goes the spear!" Grabbing the two remaining pieces of his broken weapon and glaring at them with pursed white lips, he handed the pieces back to Yonn and took in a gut-bulging breath that he let out in a long, agitated sigh.

"Makes good firewood. Besides, looks like you got another one there," said Ford pointing to a second long piece of wood in Yonn's arms.

"That," said Danny with a catch in his voice, "that is the staff."

"Oh, there's no point," said Ford.

Danny stared hard at him, but seeing that his cousin had no notion of his own wit, he cleared his throat and moved on. "This last one is a war hammer."

He yanked another stick from Yonn's hands. "Or, I suppose, a war club might be a more appropriate name for it. You can see how the heavy, knobby end here would deliver a fine crushing blow, while its shorter size makes it much more handy in tight quarters such as this room." Warming to his topic, he drew back the club for dramatic effect and smacked the wall behind him that divided their room from the next students'.

"No magic in the rooms after hours!" shouted a youthful, but irritated voice from beyond the wall.

Danny and Ford both turned toward the wall, put a fist to their lips, and kissed it, a little known gesture from around their homeland insinuating the target of the insult should suck an egg. Each caught the other doing it, and each felt an inward familial warmth toward the other. Danny muttered something about the club being sturdy enough and handed it back to Yonn. "Here. You can put those sticks away now."

With the day wearing on and an early start for the following day decided upon, they made last-minute preparations and readied to turn in for the night. Although Yonn tried to give up his bed, Ford wouldn't hear of it and made himself as comfortable as he could lying on the floor between the two beds. Danny remained hunched at his table, sorting through a disheveled pile of papers, shuffling the most important ones into a flat lockbox and shoving the rest under the parchment rolls. "This might interest you," he said, tossing a light packet of papers on to Ford's chest.

"What's this?" asked Ford.

"Letters from home. I have received only two thus far. A short note from my father included with a smartly chosen, though poorly made idol of…that goddess, the one of cunning and luck."

"Gwency," replied Yonn and Ford together.

"Yes. The idol was created with the intent of escaping notice as it made the journey from home all the way here. I wish I could have shown it to you. It was quite hideous. No one would want the awful thing." He let slip a wheezing chuckle that sounded more like the suppression of gas rather than a laugh.

"It's right here," said Yonn, retrieving from behind some shelved books a statuette of a hatchet-faced female with sharp elbows and oversized hands and passing it over to Danny.

"What do you know! I had no idea we still had it. Excellent. See here, the head comes off and within is a hollow cavity perfect for hiding…oh, whatever would fit, I suppose. Gold melted down and shaped can be made to fit snuggly with the addition of a bit of wax. Enough to cover tuition for two years, I can tell you that much. It was sent to me as a present around the date of the goddess' holiday. As if I follow that nonsense," Danny said and waved it off as if Ford's faith were a buzzing nuisance. Ford held the totem, caressing its wavering lines and rough surface.

"My father made this," said Ford.

"Did he? I always thought my own had carved it."

"I was there when he made it."

"Oh. Well. Brilliantly done," said Danny taking the statuette back and stretching his lips into what was for him a broad smile, a smile that steadily deflated at the sight of Ford flipping through the pages of the letters. "The second letter was from my brother, letting me know my mother had died."

"Aunt Mally is dead? I'm sorry. I didn't know. How?" The words freely tumbled out of Ford.

"A sickness of some sort, so I am told." Danny shrugged and turned back to the work upon his table. Even if they had a closer relationship, Danny wasn't someone who encouraged consoling, so Ford resigned himself to contemplating his cousin from across the room. Bent-backed and withdrawn, he seemed older than usual, which was saying something. He was ten years Ford's senior and even as a child, he had preferred the mature pursuits of reading and study over song, story, or play. But now, the mention of the loss of his mother made him seem positively ancient.

Ford had nearly blurted out empathetic condolences but caught himself. Certainly he had felt the loss of a mother, but it was not the same. As far as he knew, he was still alive, just merely estranged. Ford's stepmother had died, but that was not at all the same. She had been killed in a terrible accident in which Ford had taken part. A quarrel had erupted, and she had swung a knife at him. He still had a white scar down his chin to show for it, but she had gotten the worst of it. In the end the death had torn apart his family, and he imagined Aunt Mally's death had had a similar effect on the Goldsmiths.

The light in the room wasn't sufficient to read from where Ford lay. Even if he could see the letters well enough, his literacy was limited in the extreme. Besides, they were private and meant for Danny. Ford satisfied his curiosity by asking, "Will you go back?"

"To what purpose?" Danny didn't take his eyes from the papers before him and Ford at first wondered if it wasn't to hide his sorrow. "She will have been interred long since."

"To work the family trade then?"

"My brother is still quite alive and well, and has things in hand. There is no need nor room for me there." Danny's callousness toward his family surprised Ford, but this was soon overshadowed when Danny shoved a piece of paper into his hands.

"What's this?"

"A contract. It lays down the parameters of our little undertaking and makes clear our individual shares, should we make a profit on the venture. Once signed--Yonn, show him where to sign--once signed, our agreement becomes legally binding."

"You want me to sign a binding contract before we go pick some flowers?"

Danny was not one to take much notice of the ever-changing ebb and flow of human emotion, but he sensed Ford's incredulity enough to take notice of the unease in the room. He dealt with it by turning back to the book open before him and answering with an air of nonchalance. "It merely defines the equality of our three-way profit sharing. It is for your good as well as ours."

Ford scribbled his name with the pen Yonn offered him and rolled up in the spare blanket the boy lent him for the night.

Danny slid the signed contract between the pages of his book, put out the light and crawled into bed with a light heart, knowing that he had accomplished all he wished to that day. Ford lay in the dark thinking about the letters and how he had never received one from home. Not that he expected it. Still, it would have been nice to hear how his family was faring. Danny turned once in bed and began snoring almost instantly. The sound was like a signal that sent Ford into a sudden slumber, and the two struck up such a horrendous chorus that Yonn barely slept a wink that night.

Chapter 9
Secrets of Life

Apart from the heaving, shivering sighs and shudders of disheveled homeless bodies tucked in damp corners, fishermen pulling out into the expanding river and the rare cat darting after the city's vermin harassed day and night by man and beast, the city slept even as the first light eased a paler shade upon the pure black night.

In the middle of an Eastfeld street, Weylon Whetstone, the Captain of the Night Watch twisted his neck until it cracked, then narrowed his eyes upon catching sight of something amiss off to his left. Stepping up to the window of a potter's shed, he pressed closed a loose shutter and walked away shaking his head and scratching at the well-kempt beard his wife loved to run her fingers through.

He had warned Wyndal Potter about the shutter before and how it was an invitation to be robbed. "Opportunity provides incentive to even the laziest thief," he had told him. Not that it did a whole lot of good, but sayings of that nature, he felt, were the best way of teaching the folk on his route. He also taught their children how to make fart noises with their hands while they waited their turn to gather fresh water at the well at dawn, and it often gave him no end of joy to hear tiny toots sounding off here and there throughout the neighborhood in the early hours as he headed home at the end of his shift.

Whetstone's lantern swung leisurely back and forth at his side during his stroll through the streets. Nearing the corner where Leoffy's bakery stood, he thought he saw movement in the shadows of the adjacent alleyway. Taking a step forward to investigate, a furtive scurrying of feet behind him down by Issinari Square drew his attention away from the alley, where a somewhat short and slender figure in a dark cloak clutching a thin, sharp knife ducked deeper into the shadows. Whetstone knew from experience that those slinking footsteps crossing the square were the kind that belonged to someone who was likely up to no good. Two, maybe three pair, he surmised. If he went straight for them, they would likely slip away before he caught up. However, if he hurried down Sluice Gate Row and dashed through the vacant shop once owned by Caerwyn, he might catch the scoundrels at the crossroads just on the other side. With no more than a cursory glance back at the alley, where he suspected he had seen nothing more than a cat, he took off for Caerwyn's back door.

The great breaths of cool, damp air he had to suck in as well as the burning of his legs as he ran made him feel every bit his age. Years at this job had reduced a strong, limber youth to a foot-weary middle-aged man, who now realized the passage of time and resented it. Fleet footsteps, almost soundless, raced up behind him as he turned the corner into Sluice Gate Row. He twisted about just in time to catch sight of the tail end of a shadow flying by. His momentum kept him spinning and stumbling forward into the spindly arms of Baldevan Reddy, an emaciated shambling derelict of dubious character currently residing in some hole down in Dwyer's Depression. For all his hanging wispy cobweb-covered rags and even his long gray hair, Whetstone believed Reddy acted much older and decrepit than his actual years. He also suspected Reddy made a living working as a spy for Yuree's Quick Smiths, the dominant thieves' guild of the city. Reddy nodded, smiled, and mumbled something incomprehensible that Whetstone didn't have time for. Whoever had been chasing after him was gone now, so he brushed the old man aside and dashed down Sluice Gate Row to Caerwyn's back door. It was locked. Whetstone chuckled. Then his laughter rang out loud and echoed in the quiet back street. He couldn't believe that of all nights, forgetful Caerwyn had finally remembered to lock his back door.

"Trust old Caerwyn. It really is the way of things, isn't it Reddy?" Whetstone turned his crooked, unbelieving grin up the street, but Reddy was nowhere in sight. That made Whetstone laugh all the more as he headed back to his usual route.

In these waking hours just moments earlier, three figures wrapped in cloaks and robes passed through Issinari Square and the crossroads beyond, moving with caution and keeping mostly quiet. Glancing ahead, behind and down every crossing street or side alley, Ford urged Danny and Yonn to pick up the pace. For their part, the two students were not used to being awake nearly as early as this. Both had known sleepless nights for the sake of study, experiments or to attend to a master's cauldron while some lengthy arcane magic was attempted, but this rising before the sun nonsense just for the sake of getting an early start was beyond reason as far as Danny was concerned.

"Perverse self-flagellation," he grumbled and, when shushed for the third time since they had set out, resigned himself to letting slip small exasperated grunts whenever he might disguise them as strenuous effort to keep up with the other two. To his chagrin, the more noise he made only pushed Ford to drive them faster. Ford had Barker on the mind again, as he did anytime he was out and about on the streets.

Swooping up from behind, two blackbirds with sprawling wings glided through the narrow street just over their heads. Crows or ravens, Ford couldn't tell. Either way, he was sure it was a bad omen, though he kept it to himself. If Danny had been in any mood to discuss birds, he would have said that the pair alighting on an inn sign protruding out over the street were ravens and that their grating, rambling chatter was the giveaway. Ford didn't particularly care what they were; he just wished they weren't so loud. Their squawking, as if maliciously directed at them, was like an intentional alarm to wake and alert the populace. Nothing else could be heard and hearing things was second only to sight in importance to Ford at the moment. He strained to listen between the stuttering cackles of the birds and their own mud-sucking footsteps. He willed his eyes to pierce the morning gloom, but with little success until they latched upon a vaguely defined body standing half-hidden in the shadows that fell between the inn and the last house before the vast city broke up into clusters of farms and long stretches of fields.

Ford feared it might be Grady or Keene. Perhaps Barker had gotten wind of their plans and was waiting in ambush. The rather slight individual appeared to be alone. If Barker planned on jumping him, Ford supposed he would use at least three men coming from various directions, so perhaps this was someone new, and Barker's muscle waited in the wings.

"Watch your back, boys" he muttered glancing this way and that, holding up a hand to warn the other two of the trouble. As if taking the raised hand as a sign, the stranger slipped from the shadows into the street. Two long strides took Ford within one more step of landing the right fist, he held cocked when the figure pulled back its hood, and Elle's face took shape in the dim light.

"Again, you will hit me?" she asked. He hushed her and, without preamble, pulled her along with the group.

Once outside the town, they stepped on to an earthen dam to follow the partially submerged cart road atop it that headed into a countryside washed out by the combination of drought and deluge. Great green clumps of weed spotted the brown fields. To the east the land rose steadily away beyond sight in easy mounds divided by gullies like veined waves. Their path skirted the Down Hills, those soft mounds where Pennaeth Brastersceatt's country house sat alongside a lake of his ancestor's making. When full, as it was now, this reservoir irrigated much of the surrounding fields and poured into the canals of the east side of the city.

"What is going on?" Danny wanted to know as they left behind the tiny village of Tilbury just below the reservoir.

"My friend Elle here," began Ford, "you remember Elle. She's coming with us."

Danny drew Ford aside and lowered his voice to say, "That was not part of the bargain. There is nothing in the contract about this."

"Change the contract." Ford was flippant and quite carefree now that they had escaped the city.

"The contract is back at the school, and as it stands now there is no provision for a fourth share, and I do not speak for Yonn, but I for one am not willing to forego a percentage of my own share."

"Take it out of mine then. She and I'll share a share."

"Very well," said Danny with relief and a touch of surprise. "Your loss."

Ford was happy to have Elle along. He had a guess as to why she too was escaping Port Morton, but couldn't ask in front of Danny and Yonn. Regardless of her need, he figured that with all her resources and connections, there must be a better alternative for her than leaving the comforts of town life for the wilds for which she was not suited. The intensity and seriousness with which she skipped and hopped to avoid the ubiquitous mud puddles and dung piles in order to preserve her self-tailored red ochre leggings and leather boots gave him a good laugh.

However, a more somber mood descended upon them all as they passed farmer after farmer struggling to drain their saturated fields. All the gratefully received rain that had broken the drought had turned into a curse that flooded the land and washed away topsoil. Plowing was near impossible, and seeding was out of the question. These earth merchants, nearly destitute, had resorted to paying priests to chant over their sodden fields and Ford and his companions walked by one poor weeping wretch before they passed on into the wooded lands beyond.

Between his increased panting upon the leaf-covered incline leading up to the trees, Danny began expounding at length on the local irrigation and canal system, the construction of the dam, and crop rotation. There seemed to be no end to his knowledge.

"I'll tell you what, Danny," said Ford for no other reason than to cut off his cousin's flow of words. He had nothing to say in particular, he just didn't want to listen anymore. However, now that he had broken in something was expected of him, and suddenly his mind was a blank. Seeing the lines of sweat running down Danny's reddening face, he plucked the hump-like pack from of his hunched back and tossed it over his own shoulder with the ease of removing a piece of lint. "I love it out here surrounded by trees again. There's something about the air that sends me right back home. Know what I mean?" He took in a deep breath.

The villages ended, and the only sign of civilization was the occasional woodcutter's hamlet. Danny leaned on the knotted branch he called his staff and swatted like a madman plagued by invisible demons at the mosquitoes coming out from the pools and puddles to swarm around him by midmorning.

"How 'bout we stop," Ford suggested. "These packs could use lightening." The fragrance of packed provisions had been driving him mad with hunger. Once settled by a rosemary bush for a brief meal, his eyes went wide with astonishment at the amount of such rich food that had been packed, and all at Yonn's expense, it would seem. As he sprawled out in the grass by the road and let the Osby Blue cheese dissolve in a pleasantly sour, pasty coat over his tongue, Ford gave voice to a mild concern troubling him over the past mile. "We been getting some queer looks. You notice?" All that morning, farmers had leaned on their hoes and plows and given them mean stares as they passed.

"We must look an odd bunch, the four of us together," said Danny with his mouth full.

"Perhaps-s," said Yonn, stopping and starting again. "Maybe they think we're bandits."

"Us," Danny snorted. "This motley band? Not likely."

"No, but I don't think they like us," said Ford remembering the lack of common civility shown by the carters and drovers on the road into Port Morton. Cold shoulders and grunted salutations were the best they had received.

"It is known, the farmer peoples don't like the city peoples," put in Elle, and it *was* known. Ford knew it well enough by the lack of hospitality his friends showed the farmers who came into town to sell at the markets. For reasons he hardly understood, it was unwarranted animosity, and it went both ways. The provinces saw the city as some ravenous leviathan eating the countryside empty, and they resented it.

Such existential ideas flittered in and out of Ford's mind without making much of an impression. It all seemed beyond him, and besides, the loaf of fresh bread he was digging into was so much more tangible and inviting. As he dug out a hunk of bannock and handed the rest to Elle, he began saying, "I forgot how much—" but the words caught in his throat at the glimpse of dye-reddened skin on Elle's wrist peeking out between her glove and sleeve when she reached for the bread. Ford froze but for some reflexive chewing.

"How much what?" asked Danny when the pause grew too long.

"How much…" Ford couldn't remember what he had been thinking of just a moment before and awkwardly fumbled forward. "How much I love it out here."

"So much so it is worth repeating, I see," said Danny shaking his head as he gnawed away at a strip of dried fish. Yonn was the only one who twisted around and around eagerly taking in the object of Ford's affection. Elle was not as oblivious as the other two, and Ford could feel her eyes upon him. He examined the bread far longer than could ever be natural.

Until now her gloves had escaped his notice, but why else would she wear them in the middle of a warm day other than to hide the shame of being caught stealing? The punishment for petty theft was to have a hand-dyed red. By decree of the Iarl the harsher punishments, such as having the hand cut off, had been relaxed, for maimed citizens were not productive citizens, nor could they hold a spear should peasant levies be needed. Even so, a person with a red-dyed hand caught committing a crime was liable to be executed if the offense were bad enough. No doubt this was why Elle had escaped with them, thought Ford, and that led him to wonder what her offense had been. She was quite careful when it came to picking pockets, so it might have been something more severe. But it couldn't have been as bad as stealing the Middlefield journal and maps, could it, he wondered? He turned to Elle to read what he could in her expression, but she had stepped away from the group and faced a line of distant hills visible through the trees.

"Hills are coming," she said with a raised finger to indicate which hills were on their way.

"Yes," replied Danny pulling out a rough map of the area. "But before the hills, there is a river and a crossroads."

"Looks like this forest gets thicker," said Ford as he edged up beside Elle. "Would be a prime place to get robbed." Elle returned and sat back down with the other two.

"Exactly what we brought you for," said Danny flipping Ford a nod as casually as one might flip the contents of a bedpan out of a window. He slapped his cheek and wiped his hand on his robe. "And now that we are all fed and rested let us move on before these pests finish us off."

The afternoon turned overcast, and particularly dark patches rolled into the sailcloth sky above. The rain beat down on them briefly, eased off and gained strength once more, making a trial out of trudging along the rutted road and up and down interminable slopes. Plunging feet into the mud and plucking them out again was tiring work on a dwindling road that didn't receive much upkeep. When a vast, forested valley loomed ahead they were quite exhausted and not pleased to see the other side of the valley rising up like a green barricade.

"A daunting prospect indeed," said Danny pulling his robe tighter around him.

The ruins of a long-abandoned hamlet set back from the road and engulfed by the forest seemed to Ford a likely place for a bandit's hideout. He knew this from his days with the Wayward Boys, an outfit of young thieves, who would have laid an ambush in dense undergrowth such as this. Perhaps they might have lain in wait down by the river where the constant rush of water would drown out noise and make it easy to sneak up on those unwary travelers attempting to pass through Long Wood, a well-named forest of ash and willow that covered the valley and snaked along with Brown River. His gait slowed. He even hesitated between steps and strained to listen. His grip on the so-called club Danny had provided grew tighter where it rested upon his shoulder. So far the stunted log had only come in handy in toting one of the sacks of provisions, but it might actually prove more useful than he imagined. The deeper they advanced into the forest, the deeper he entrenched himself in vigilance.

"Ford, do you, um, s-sense trouble?" asked Yonn trotting up to Ford and peering up at him with almost hopeful eyes. "Let me know if-f I can help." Ford looked down at the wiry young man, all bone, every knobby joint of him, and thought it might be a joke at first, but there was sincerity staring back at him out of those eyes like wobbly marbles rolling about. A quick look over his shoulder showed that Elle had the rear covered, as he knew she would. However, another set of eyes never hurt.

"Yeah sure, stay right beside me there and keep a lookout to your side," he said and watched the young man's demeanor instantly change. The nerves never left entirely, but the pleasure of being thought useful in a potential scrape visibly swelled the boy's whole being. "Keep your eyes open." It seemed an absurd thing to say to someone whose eyes couldn't have been more open, but the boy nodded eagerly and looked all around him.

The hiss of the river morphed into a bubbling rumble, and when a bridge appeared, Ford ushered them over the narrow planks as quickly as he could. All the dark shaded distances, every crooked branch, and each peculiarly shaped stump turned out to be nothing more than what they were, and luck proved to be on their side as they passed out of the forest unscathed.

Awaiting them on the other side of the forest was a modest, but active little village nestled against the impressively steep range that ran alongside the forest and river. Another road crossed their path as it ran parallel to the river and ridge. At the crossroads of this much-used cart road sat clusters of houses in two and threes, with one or two perched above the rest here and there upon tiny plateaus, some natural and others cut by man from the earth like shelves. Though all of the dwellings were surrounded by a winding and occasionally lopsided palisade, the travellers could see almost of all them where they perched upon the slanting hill.

"This would be Uldale," Danny said, pointing at a spot on his map. "They do well with eels. Uldalian eels." Talk of this and the scent of smoke from wood-burning fires hanging low under the ponderous clouds of a heavy sky set off Ford's stomach. These attacks of hunger seemed so much more violent now that he was eating on a semi-regular basis rather than when he went days without a meal.

"Let's see if we can't get some for dinner." With what coin or trade he planned to procure the eels he hadn't considered, such was the command his appetite had over him.

"The rain is abating," said Danny as if it annoyed him. "Only natural, of course. We have shelter before us, and now it chooses to abate, like some embittered grudge-bearer."

The gaze of field workers and sun-darkened women sitting by a pond dressing yard-long eels followed them as they crossed the thin strip of sheep pasture between the river and village's palisade gate. A boy of about thirteen came running to meet them with his jaw dangling. He gaped from one to the next over the gate, and when Ford started to speak he ran back to a weather-beaten barn where he emitted a few tremulous high-pitched shouts that carried easily back to the gate. An old man appeared at the doorway and stared down at them for a breath or two before tugging on a skullcap over wispy white hair and hobbling down to the gate. The gaps between the posts in the palisade began to fill with the curious and grubby faces of children. The old man took ages climbing a ladder to look over the wall, but he took in everything the travelers said with an alert eye and comprehending mind.

"Shelter for the night. Perhaps something to eat is all we ask," Ford announced.

"Doubt we will find much more," murmured Danny leaning in at Ford's shoulder.

The old man's replies came in a country drawl, and his long, drooping nose seemed in constant danger of slipping into his toothless mouth with every other word. Though his welcome was gruff, the gate did swing open for them.

"Name a Ulfred," he said by way of introduction as they followed him in an agonizingly slow crawl back up to the barn. On the way he let them know he was the son of many Ulfreds and the owner of the barn, which had been turned into an inn, "when last cow die in big cattle plague." He also acted as gatekeeper and oversaw the ramshackle mill leaning dangerously over a weedy pond down by the river. By the size of the other Uldalians' noses, Ford and his companions guessed that Ulfred was likely brother, father, grandfather, uncle and cousin to nearly everyone in the village.

Ford was quite willing to sleep under the stars for the night, but when the other two accepted Yonn's gracious offer to pay for a room for everyone, he set aside his objections and crunched across the brittle rushes to a seat in the inn's common room. Yonn worked out the details and price with Ulfred, who insisted on showing him each of the three separate rooms.

"Whichever has the longest beds, right Ford?" Yonn called over his shoulder with a smile as he was led into a room. Danny and Elle sat and stretched out their limbs. The excitement of newcomers having passed, the children who had followed them to the door returned to their play by the pond.

"Boy's coming out of his shell," said Ford. "He's got pluck, but he's a stringy cut of meat. I'd hate to see what'd happen to him in a scuffle. Good thing he's found learning." Having had a taste of education and a feast of fighting, Ford had come to the conclusion that, "It's better to bury your nose in books rather than getting it bloodied." Danny, who would remain a student of learning all his life if possible, heartily concurred.

"That boy, he loves you," said Elle without a hint of humor.

"What?" Ford all but shouted before catching himself. "What are you talking about, *love?*"

"Ah yes, I see it now," said Danny, unable to repress a grin. "He is peculiarly fond of you. I think he wants to be you."

"What? You're both talking nonsense," said Ford refilling a mug he had already drained from a pitcher of chilled, but sadly flat ale that the boy with the dangling jaw had brought to their table.

"Not at all," argued Danny. "Soon after meeting you, I caught him in our room swinging his practice wand around like a sword. Like a sword!"

"But I don't even own a sword," protested Ford.

"Maybe not, but you bring out an adventurous spirit in him."

"Bah."

"I tell you. He was quite eager for this trip."

"Why is—?" Ford broke off for the time it took Ulfred to shunt Yonn into the next room and then went on in a lowered voice. "Why is that? The kid comes from money, so what's he need this for? The risk and reward don't make sense for someone whose purse jingles like his."

"Well, I can tell you he needs nothing material. That his parents provide."

"It is you," interjected Elle with a nod at Ford. "He need you." Danny's cackle could be quite annoying, thought Ford as he went to the door under the pretense of having a look about the village.

"Wherever the misguided youth's thoughts may lie, I hope they are upon supper shortly," Danny said with a distracted look from his ale toward Ulfred's prattle.

"Nothing but friends. Friends at most," muttered Ford to the world beyond the doorway. Ulfred emerged more quickly from the next room and only had Yonn lean into the final room before they returned to the others.

"Where to wash one?" Elle asked, and the old man had his boy take her to the back of the inn to a trough filled with cloudy, gray water. The boy stood watching her with his mouth wide open, not taking the hint that she wanted him gone until she glared with a deadly eye straight into his face. He slunk off, and one of the Uldalian mothers shooed away a few curious children who had crept close, driving them into the squat, weathered hovels.

Once alone, Elle stripped off her gloves off and scrubbed at her reddened hands, even scraping at the skin with a kind of pumice stone, laid there for the purpose, until she couldn't be sure if her hands were red from the dye or blood. As if sapped of life, her hands slowed to a full stop, and her gaze remained upon the murky water. Her head leaned almost imperceptibly to one side, and her face assumed a forced, tight-lipped grin that bordered on a grimace. "Thought you to come and look?" The words fought their way out between her teeth and shot at Ford as he was leaning around the corner of the building.

"Sorry," he said, though he was not exactly sure about what he was sorry, nor completely sure for which reason, being there at that moment or having discovered her secret in the first place. His eyes fell to her red hands.

"Now you know and have no doubt," she said, resuming her scrubbing. Ford turned and walked in lazy circles with his hands held behind his back while staring out of the river valley or up into the hills. A half sigh, half whistle escaped him, followed by random clucking noises as his tongue bounced off the roof of his mouth. The hairs at the back of his neck bristled, and he scratched the spot.

"I—."

"*You!* You want always to *know*," Elle punctuated the final word with a bug-eyed glare straight into his face. "Even when…when you should not. *You* put your nose in all. Everything!" She fought her own anger, but it showed through a twisting smile that bared her teeth.

Ford stepped back, withdrawing not only from her cruel demeanor but from the accusation as well. It seemed wholly unjustified. He wasn't a nosey person by nature, but apparently that was not how she saw things. "*You, you, you,*" she kept muttering. His selfishness astounded her, especially how he had used her to enact this ill-conceived plan of his involving his last fight. It wasn't setting it up and putting it into motion that bothered her, so much as the aftermath and what it meant for her. She doubted he had even given her a second thought while working it all out. And now this. It wasn't even the point of the matter, yet he was essentially questioning her abilities with these intrusive questions. When attacked by such a person in such a manner, she knew only one reaction.

"You want to know all? Fine then, I tell you! Your woman that you love, she is mad!" She nodded vehemently and tapped her temple to back it up. "It is truth! Everybody know this! Everybody!" The main force of her fury spent, the final words fell quite tamely from her lips. "Everybody but you." Hair fell from her sagging head into her face. She blew it away and went back to scrubbing her hands. There was still a taut thread of anger within entwining itself with a sadness that pushed her toward tears, but she was not the crying kind.

The truth was that she loved Ford. Perhaps she only loved him like the boy Yonn did, with a sort of admiration, she couldn't be sure. She had only a vague notion of love, and its many meanings confused her. The little time she had had with her mother and father made the recollection of their love, ever-waning in the intervening years, come to her in fleeting snatches of tenderness, like the few pleasant dreams she could pluck out of the pit of nightmares that still troubled her slumbers to this day. And then there had been little time for affection with the aunt who rescued her and carried her away from the devastation of home and family. Though she esteemed her courageous aunt, the all-consuming cause for which that brave woman fought did not lend itself to tranquil days made for building delicate emotional bonds. They had spent so little time together before Elle had been secretly shepherded from the Forest of a Thousand Names to live with these Aelwyd people.

No, Elle did not understand love, but what she did know was that Ford Barlow was nicer to her than most, at least when he wasn't in a foul mood. They were friends, and she wondered if that were not enough. It seemed not, for he had *loved* other women. Mostly that amounted to spending his money at brothels, which never bothered her. It was meaningless. However, now it appeared he was *loving* this other woman who seemed unworthy of him, entirely unsuitable, and what was worse, she was no prostitute. That bothered Elle, because it meant something else entirely, something she did not comprehend.

Ford's apparent indifference toward her as a woman, as a sexual being, or even simply as a creature to be loved had pushed her into the arms of a mean-spirited thief whom she had met through her guild. This man never showed her affection, but he did show her a form of attention, and then he took her when she did not rebuff his crude overtures. His mere presence made her throat constrict and her stomach churn. She thought this was love. After all, she reasoned, he instilled in her a drive to succeed in order to please him. But then again, there was her fear of him witnessing her failure. Now she was having second thoughts and reexamining the reasons she became stiff and uncomfortable in her own skin when around him. This also happened whenever she met up with Ford, except that a sudden joy sprung up within her, one she feared might make her do something foolish. Her mind would turn somersaults, and her limbs seemed to move of their own accord. When this happened he would laugh. In her opinion he laughed too much, and she particularly hated to be laughed at.

She knew little of the finer points of human nature, so all but his most obviously kind actions lately had been taken as intentional callousness, and her vindictive side wanted to punish him for it. Having charted the path of these thoughts and emotions thoroughly before, they now flew across the map of her mind in the time it took for Ford to bow his head, scuff the ground and look at his friend again, quite clearly confused.

"You mean Addy?" he asked. Elle shook her head in disbelief but then nodded. Embarrassment tinged with irritation welled within Ford. He meant to leave her at the trough, even took a few steps away, but then he turned back around at the corner of the inn with palms upraised. "Look, I don't know why you're saying these things about her, and it don't matter. I don't want to talk about it. But whatever happened"—here he pointed to her reddened hands—"whatever caused that, I'm sorry if I'm to blame." Elle had plenty to say but kept on scrubbing. Ford grew impatient. "Am I to blame?"

"No."

He slid in closer to speak to her, standing side by side, in the conspiratorial way they'd adopted back in the days when their friendship first flourished. "Well then, how'd it happen?" His inquisitiveness showed itself in a tender tone, sagging shoulders, and sad eyes. If he touched her out of kindness right now, she wasn't sure what she would do. She was sure this wasn't curiosity for curiosity's sake. He wasn't looking to mock her, that much she understood. "You didn't get caught, I mean, doing nothing, did you?"

"No."

These were lies, he was sure of it. Elle made a habit of lying when it suited her, sometimes barely seeming to care how transparent the untruth appeared.

"No? How then? That don't make no sense."

As inviting as he made things and as much as she wanted to confide in him, she hesitated. This was guild business and everything to do with the guild was a secret. The pause was nearly enough to finally drive him away, but she caught him just as one of his enormous feet slid back toward the front of the inn.

"I would not do a thing *they* wanted of me to do." She held up her hand. "So they do this for to shame me."

"What was it?" Ford shook his head, knowing he had asked an unanswerable question. He waved it off and went on. "You wouldn't do it?"

"I refuse."

"It must have been bad."

"It was a bad thing."

"I see." He leaned back, found the corner of the inn, and leaned against that, while he breathed deeply and aimed his ire at an organization he knew little more than by reputation.

"Very dangerous," she muttered as she went back to the water and the pumice stone. Something in the way she said *dangerous* triggered Ford's memory.

"It's not about the Iarl's book, is it? Tell me you ain't stealing that thing? Don't even think about it! They got guards all over that place. You got no chance. You'll get caught and end up..."

His misunderstanding she could endure, but not the wound to her professional pride. Elle dried her hands, put on her gloves, and marched back into the inn. Even if his thoughts weren't already in disarray, Ford doubted he could have figured out what was wrong with what he had said.

After a night of sitting by a sputtering, smoky fire being plied with roasted eel skewers in exchange for city gossip by Uldalians eager for word from abroad, the remaining members of the group stretched their feet toward the hearth. Elle had left earlier after drawing too much attention to herself from the sweat-drenched men straight in from the fields. Once the inquisitive villagers discovered she was originally from the Forest of a Thousand Names they were positive she was an elf. The piercing intensity of her eyes, the grace of her slender body, and the hue of her hair like a moonless night set her apart enough to assure them that she could be no mere human. After one foul-breathed farmer leaned in too close and asked, "Wheah a' ya long eahs?" she decided to turn in. After a half night's worth of questions finally exhausted the Uldalians, they hoisted their children on to their hips, hauled up their elderly and shuffled off home.

"It's been a long one," said Ford leaning back against a wall and letting his heavy eyelids close. Yonn sat hunched over beside him, elbows on the table, hands propping up his lulling head. "Too long for some." Ford nudged Yonn with his elbow and nodded to where Danny lay with his face flat against the table, a string of drool dripping from his greasy, parted lips.

"He sleeps...anywhere," said Yonn with envious eyes still on Danny. Ford would have liked to be sleeping on a bed right about now, but Elle had retired to the room they had paid for and, unsure where he stood with her, he decided it was best to give her some space. Sitting like this, he wasn't as comfortable as he had ever been, but he had also been a lot worse off, and like Danny he could sleep pretty much anywhere.

"Me and him got that in common. Must be a family thing," he said with a slight slur as he took the first step toward the land of dreams.

"Do you miss your family?" Ford thought Yonn had shouted the question it sounded so loud, loud enough to shake him awake.

"Family? Uh, yeah. In a way, I suppose I do." Ford was too tired to think straight, but he had never been too tired to forget how little he had been loved by his family. Out of all of them, he only truly missed his brother Leo. Perhaps his youngest sister too, but it was Leo who showed up in his dreams and made his heart hurt for the longing. Leo had been his best friend. No one since had filled that void. "Funny you bring that up, I've been thinking of going back. It was part of this plan I had after my last fight—"

"I saw that fight! You won! You were great!"

"Funny thing is, I was supposed to lose that fight." Ford deflected any more praise by rambling on about his post-fight plan to take the money and run, to flee Port Morton for good. Yonn looked shocked.

"But what about your mother?" If the first question about family had prodded Ford awake again, this one stung him. Yonn realized his misstep with a sinking dread that shook his confidence. "W-what I m-mean...it's just th-that I heard..."

"How'd you...oh." Ford turned a nodding head toward his cousin. "Old tub of brains here must've figured it out, eh?" Yonn admitted as much and began to fidget as he attempted an apology. The boy's face turned so red that Ford feared he might faint or burst. The way he cringed, it looked like he would crawl under the very ashes of the fire and allow them to consume him if given the chance. Ford felt awful for someone going through life so timid. "Don't concern yourself. It's nothing. Yeah, I came out to town to find my kin. She's somewhere in that big ol' place, so the story goes. Well, the real story as I know it was she carried me all the way there and took her best shot at a new life. That shows a mighty fine spirit, don't you think? I guess it didn't work out, because she left and found my father, dropped me off with him and his folk and headed back on her own." He left off when the memories came back too strong to ignore. "I didn't know these people. I remember…" He chuckled to himself, a sour mirth. "I would cry, just about every night at first. I'd look up and see the distant lights of Oren, this tiny village not more than a stone's throw away, but at that age, I took it for the big town, for Port Morton. What did I know? It was a whole lot bigger than Barlow, I'll tell you that much. So I figured that must be it and that must be where she was, so I'd be there crying for the little lights I could see coming from the windows or whatnot, begging my ma to come get me. After a while of that they put me out in the barn. Can't blame them." He threw a sideward smile Yonn's way. "Any road, I grew up and figured maybe I'd try and find her, but no luck. Maybe she ain't even there. I don't know. I looked and looked, but…" He threw up his hands. "So I'm done with the place." Sitting up, he twisted the kinks out of his back. He was ready to call it a night. The floor looked as inviting a spot as any. He even got his feet under him to vault himself up, but Yonn's pleading eyes begged him back into a lounging position.

"So you're leaving Port Morton? F-for good?"

"There's nothing much left for me back there, nothing but trouble. So, as of now, that's the plan."

"But you can't!" Yonn blurted out. The words came from someplace deep, propelled by a force he couldn't control. Revealing the source would have been humiliating to him, and he flushed with the thought that he had just exposed himself, admitting in his mind that he did not want Ford to leave because he didn't have many friends. Danny was the closest thing, but his friendship came with severe limitations, mainly because Danny didn't care much for people in general. Like most of the students at the school, studies came first. That left little time for socializing. They dedicated their all to honing their craft, whereas Yonn had almost no skill at magic. When the others realized how outclassed he was, they ignored him. His parents continued to throw money at the school because they had their own hopes and dreams, but to Yonn it seemed like they only wanted an out of the way place in which to stow him. He had grown lonely and spent many a night crying silently in the dark. So, when Ford came along and showed him a friend's kindness, Yonn became quite attracted to the giant of a man, who seemed to embody courage, strength and an adventurous spirit, attributes Yonn lacked and longed for. He latched on to Ford, unaware of how it might seem to others. Attacked by this sudden desperation, he was hardly master of his emotions. They spoke for him, they fought for his desires. "I mean, you-you haven't found your mother yet."

"Don't think I'm going to, lad. Like I said, I tried. She just ain't there. I thought I was on her trail this once, but no. Funny thing is, I don't even really remember what she looks like anymore."

"That doesn't sound funny to me."

"No, I suppose not. Well anyway, I tried to find her and failed, and now it's time to move on, so I came up with this plan to do this little job we're doing here and grab the money and make my way...somewhere. I don't think family'll really be happy to see me, so maybe somewhere else."

"You don't even know where you're going?"

"Yeah, suppose I didn't think that one through, did I? You're smarter than me, what would you do?"

"I would..." Since he had calmed somewhat, modesty held Yonn's tongue hostage.

Ford elbowed him. "Out with it. I want to know."

"I would try and never stop trying until I found her."

Chapter 10
The Tomb of Grawrall

When Ford and the others finally emerged at dawn from the inn, squinting and yawning, or groaning from various aches and pains, and clutching their cloaks about them as if this mild day was more akin to midnight on some windswept tundra. The sleepy people of Uldale were already weeding their hillside gardens, repairing the rickety mill wheel, and tending their flocks and the long thin fields along the river. For her part, Elle felt fully refreshed, having gone to bed early and enjoyed an uninterrupted night's sleep, while the other three had all slept in various uncomfortable positions in the common room.

The calls of the young Uldalians and the scent of wood fires dwindled and disappeared along with Danny's complaints of foot pain as Ford and Elle left him and Yonn behind upon a switchback trail that climbed the steep hill behind the village. Some called it a mountain for its height as well as for the tumbling slopes and the precipitous drops along its length.

"They're coming. Slowly, but they're coming," said Ford leaning over a ledge close to the peak. The wind tossed his hair about and drowned out his words now and then. "It's going to take us a damn long time to get over the other side of this thing. We'll stop here and let them catch up." He and Elle sat together on a rock, catching their breath. The long trek up the hill had given Ford plenty of time to consider yesterday's events, and he had come to at least one conclusion. "You did the right thing," he said looking out over the land for miles around. "I mean leaving town and coming with us." He was about to lay a hand upon her gloved hand, but thought better of it and patted her shoulder, giving it a quick squeeze before jumping up and stepping across to where the path eroded away at the edge of a scarp that fell for hundreds of feet.

Lingering regret for things she had said the day before welled within Elle and made her wish she was more adept at apologies. "Sorry," she tried to say over the wind, but her voice was not robust like his, and she doubted it carried. But then he turned to her, winked and smiled. She was glad he had heard because she doubted if she could say it again.

She thought of things she had been considering since their argument at the water trough. Eventually, her rational side won over. The simple fact was that Ford had eyes for another, not her. Right now he was simply a good friend to her and nothing more. It was best not to ruin that, she concluded.

"Danny won't be happy to see them," Ford shouted as he pointed toward the east where rolling hills one after another beyond sight awaited them.

A bitter wind cut through their thin clothes, and Ford made for a sheltered nook where two boulders met. He curled up in it, wrapping his cloak around him, and gestured for Elle to sit beside him. She did so, sitting shoulder to shoulder with him, and warming her very soul with thoughts of wrapping up within his cloak with his arms around her. Thinking it would do no good, she knew, but she went on thinking it nonetheless.

"They'll want something to eat and a rest," Ford said and his body sagged in resignation. "This will take forever."

To Ford's surprise and admiration, Danny rested only long enough to get his breath back and would not eat, fearing that once he got comfortable and filled his belly, he might not be able to get up again. He drank some water, took a look around the bald top of the hill, and led the way over the peak and back down the other side. His tentative, waddling steps held them up, but even so, they soon descended below the gusting winds and felt something akin to warmth once more.

Toward the bottom, they picked up speed and just about tumbled into a forest coated in pale blue-green, leafy lichen and covered in climbing vines. Ankle-tangling grass and knee-high clumps of ferns matted the ground. The leaves soon grew into a thick canopy and blotted out the sun, creating a cool, damp cavern-like atmosphere where everything in this primitive forest grew with a creeping inevitability that clogged the very air, stifled sound, and left one with an impression of isolation or even imprisonment.

"There is something about this land. It is as if it could lure you deep within and kill you without even meaning to." Danny said this in his normal voice, but his words met the ears of the others as a muffled utterance, as if they had been spoken from behind a thick drapery. All four of them fell in with the will of the woods and remained mostly silent throughout the day, never raising their voices if they spoke at all. Little more was heard from them than a muffled footfall or an involuntary sniffle.

Their progress that day was reduced to a near crawl, impeded as it was by a fear that they had lost their way. Without the sun or any visible landmarks to go by, they couldn't tell what direction they were headed. In the mid-afternoon, they were drawn down into a valley and allowed it to choose their course. Moss-strewn rocks poked from the sides of leafy knolls here and there, and as they continued the rocks turned to boulders and started thrusting themselves up from the earth like ancient monuments erected by giants. The valley narrowed into a ravine when a twisting brook appeared. They walked against its flow, sometimes stepping upon the slick rocks it slid over when the narrowing ravine left little footing on either side of the water.

"This feels like a good place to get ambushed," said Ford, just before Elle halted and held up a hand.

"Listen," she said, cocking an ear. As still as Ford, Danny and Yonn stood, they heard nothing out of the ordinary. They followed her, moving only when she did, into a curve in the ravine, at which point all of them could hear high, airy echoes. "A siren?" Elle whispered, and the three men blocked their ears. Ford caught her eye and questioned her with a worried look, which she waved away and set to listening with a single-minded intensity.

There were two voices floating vaguely about the air: a rapid, excited talk coming in fragments that were at once joyful and then condescending. A quizzical smirk played upon Elle's lips, and a wrinkle rose upon her brow. She strode forward. The others hesitated and then followed until they came to a high cliff wall from which water dribbled like a glistening serpent's belly that slashed down against a ledge, then rolled over it and slid clinging to a grooved rock until it came peacefully to rest in a small, round pool at the bottom. And there sat a little girl no more than eight and a slightly larger boy facing away from them toward the waterfall with two dogs curled up at their feet in patches of sunlight.

The girl was in deep conversation apparently about her favorite kinds of dogs, alternately patting the ones beside her. Her speech was nearly unrecognizably accented, but it was clear that "brewn poopies" were a cherished favorite. By coincidence, it was the browner of the two dogs that spotted Elle first; however both leapt up together, racing forward a few yards, yapping and growling but coming no closer. When the boy stood and pointed the girl took no more than a wide-eyed glance at them before she dashed off, ascending the steep embankment covered in vines and roots in a few scrambling leaps like a little blond monkey in a frock. In a flash she was gone, but the boy had stayed.

The boy had no plans to leave. He had questions; not impertinent, but intensely curious. After quieting the dogs and overcoming some trouble with understanding one another's accents, he let it be known that they were strangers, the first he had seen in ages although he was already ten and spent most of his time wandering in the woods. From under unwashed straggly hair, his gray-brown eyes stared with fascination at Elle, and he would not be put off until it was explained exactly what she was. It was the sort of question only a child could ask so bluntly without offense.

"I never knew I was so very different," said Elle.

"You must remember, my dear, within the city confines you are one of many. Here you are as rare as finding a fallen star," said Danny.

Though the boy's back-country vernacular was at times indecipherable and his questions endless when they told him where they were headed he explained that the brook would lead them astray and promised to put them on the right path. With him and his dogs taking the lead, they left the ravine and crested a hill overlooking a hollow where the boy's village of a few squat turf hovels lay nestled below. Their grassy roofs blended into the lumpy, green ground.

"These are very old dwellings indeed, surrounded by an equally old wall," said Danny squinting down at the rough-hewn timbers of a palisade dark with age and damp. "One wonders what, if any, contact these barbarians or hill-dwellers or whatever one may call them, what contact these *people* have had with the outside world." Too busy examining the details of the village, Danny was heedless of how his words might be taken by the boy, who was himself oblivious, being too busy examining with extremely close attention the diamond-pattern stitching down the length of Elle's form-fitting leggings.

"Years past, I work for a bitch seamstress," was the extent of her attempt at patient explanation.

From the only structure in the village of any significance, an ancient and crumbling stone hall, the little blond girl immerged pointing and gesturing with a woman in tow and a pack of barking hounds threatening to trip them up. The two dogs with the boy called down to their brothers and sisters with delighted yelps as if saying, "Look! Look! See what we have here! No! No! They are good people!" Spotting the group, the woman ran in a fluster through the palisade gate as far as an unruly patch of beans growing halfway up the hill.

"Brywan! Brywan!" she shouted in a coarse shriek. The boy beside them shouted back that he was fine, he had met one of the "dunaelf!" and she was right here, and did he *have* to come back? All the dogs leapt about yipping, sniffing the strangers, and nipping one another in their excitement. With a fussy reluctance, the boy Brywan finally gave in and started down the hill toward his mother.

"Wait!" bellowed Ford, before he was completely out of earshot. "Where's the…" He turned to Yonn and Danny. "What's the place called? Ask him how we get to the cave, the monk's cave." They did, and in answer Brywan shouted back an excited jumble of words that sounded something like *ahya gonkel bahky,* and that was all. His mother raced up, grabbed him by the hair and dragged him in a stumbling hurry back to the village, hollering the entire way, with the dogs taking up the chorus.

By now it appeared that the entire village had gathered along its walls and were watching them like hawks, hairy and husky hawks in brown fur standing firm and unwelcoming with their hefted pitchforks and hoes. Ford led his group, who all felt keenly defenseless at that moment, back over the ridge and down the other side.

"Regrettable," lamented Danny. "That village would have made a fine base camp from which to work. A roof over our heads at night, possible trades for provisions…"

"And we lost our guide," added Ford.

"Never you mind. The boy served us well. That meager waterway is to our south and as long as we keep it so and stay on this east and somewhat northerly course I am sure soon enough we will find our monk's garden, which should be no more than a day's journey from the monstrous hill that nearly killed poor Yonn." This was the first Yonn had heard of nearly being killed by the hill after Uldale. It had not been an easy climb, but the actual reason he had not been taking it in leaps and bounds, as Ford had, was that he had hung back to look after Danny out of a habit he had developed in caring for the old mage Walader.

Now that they were potentially within sight of their quarry, Danny lagged well behind and of course Yonn with him. They shuffled and tripped more than usual, even though their eyes were constantly scanning the ground. When Ford realized the hunt was on, he joined in along with Elle, but they were both rebuffed and rebuked so often for pointing out worthless impersonators of Larkwine's Rue that they soon lost heart. Ford complained that they were here to help, so Danny suggested they be on the lookout for "fungi or any rare newt that might slither from the muck." While Ford happily kicked at rotting stumps and overturned logs, Elle had no interest in slimy things and did her best to appear productive by poking at the ground with a stick. Whenever it sunk into a squelchy patch, a disgusted shiver ran up her spine.

Ford's calling out every time he came across a new weed or scared up a toad seemed more of a nuisance than his efforts were worth, but for all Danny and Yonn's poking and prodding of grass and bushes, they were doing no better. So far, it had been nothing but common herbs and mundane plants of little value.

The cloud-filled sky and the deeply shaded hollows they walked through allowed night to sneak up on them. A slapdash camp was thrown together on a terraced plot of land near a pear tree.

"Not under it," insisted Ford as he scraped sparks from a flint into a dry bed of twigs. "Don't want to get stepped on by some creature looking for a sweet." It seemed logical to the others, since they could see the trails, beds, and scat of deer littering the wild grass all around, and for all they knew, there might be creatures even larger about.

"Cultivated land, but cultivated some time ago, it would seem," remarked Danny tossing aside branches and pounding out a clump of grass with the butt of his staff.

"Maybe it's part of the lands around an old c-castle?" Yonn proposed while he picked up Danny's discarded branches and placed them by the campfire.

"Could be," said Ford. "I've come across old tombs and such in my wanderings." Ford's support pleased Yonn.

Danny shrugged. "I suppose," he admitted with little conviction. "Stories of the ancient chiefs said they planted groves and gardens and all manner of things about their forts. Perhaps that pear tree is a descendant and all that is left of a once-great orchard."

"There could be more plants or, uh, things around," said Yonn.

"Good lad, Yonn. See, that's what learning gets ya!" said Ford giving the boy a pat on the shoulder, while Yonn smiled and rapped his forehead with a knuckle.

"Yes, yes," said Danny. "But the monk's cave is what will yield us our best chances of success for the herbs we seek. He came out for the solitude, so it would have been long after the old civilization collapsed. Much more recent and thus much more likely that his garden, left untended and gone quite wild after his death to be sure, might still be growing of its own accord. It thrived with the help of his hand. Might it not survive without it? I believe s--Oh, my heart!"

Like a predatory cat, Elle had appeared out of the darkness. Without a word, she slid into her embroidered blanket by the fire.

"Where'd you come from," asked Ford.

"The smoke. For my nose, I need to go away. There is a something like a sweet in the air, more than the pear. Flowers, I think."

"Excellent!" cried Danny, having recovered from his fright. "That is a good sign if ever there was one." He rolled into a blanket and began snoring.

A nominal watch was kept, but the night passed without disturbance. One by one they awoke cold and damp from a night of sporadic drizzle to a moist, foggy morning and the long, sad minor tones of a white-throated sparrow, the random squeaks of a horned lark, and the shrill vibrato of a red-winged blackbird, as well as a score of other random squawking bursts from above. Ford pulled his cloak over his head and let out a lazy, rolling growl.

"Damn winged rats. Sounds like all the birds in the goddamn world up there."

"And yet," Danny began in a slow, drowsy voice, "it is but one. A male, judging by the sheer volume." He cleared his throat, and the forest went momentarily quiet.

"Good, keep doing that."

"Over in the pear tree, if I am not mistaken." Danny tried to peel off the wet woolen blanket wrapped around him. "It is a single mockingbird or perhaps a thrasher. They are one and the same."

"Their voices, they carry so," remarked Elle massaging her forehead.

"There is no mistaking, they are whores for attention and annoyingly unpredictable, as is the case with most birds, or mammals in general to be truthful. Quite unruly beasts." Danny said all this while snorting not unlike an unruly beast himself, as he struggled with his robe which had gotten itself all bunched up around his belly; he thrashed up and down, then back and forth trying to unleash his body from the leviathan-like grasp of the wet robe and blanket. Finally, he flopped free with a half somersault and rolled across the ground naked from the waist down, pasting a smattering of damp leaves over his iridescently pale body.

After breakfasting, Ford left Danny and Yonn to dry themselves by the smoking ashes of the fire and hiked along the terrace and up the hill. There he met Elle kneeling by the remnants of a stone wall.

"What's this? An old house?" asked Ford.

"A house maybe." She pointed across a valley to an adjacent hill. "But there a great house once stood." Along the far ridge among the rock outcroppings, thick bushes disguised jagged tower ruins coated by moss and stone walls disintegrating back into the earth like green teeth in rotting gums. All four were climbing about the time-worn stones when Danny gave a subdued cheer and shouted, "The flowering sun fern!"

"It is a form of valerian," he said while his fingers caressed the plant's long, thin leaves. The others hurried to his side.

"This is the sweet I smelled," said Elle holding one of the white flowers to her nose, "A lovely perfume it would make."

"Ah. Yes, well, it is not overly valuable, and I dare say this moist soil is less than ideal, but it has its uses. For lack of more powerful ingredients, the oils from the root can be used as a substitute in some spells that bring on sleep and other magics that require the target mind to relax." Danny let his lids grow heavy in mock slumber while twiddling his fingers about his temples. "Well, that is something at last, and since we haven't found anything better, we might as well make the most of this. Yonn, grab the sacks."

Danny gestured to the patches of valerian here and there about the hillside, making sure Ford and Elle knew what to look for. They picked and packed the plants in tight bundles for the better part of an hour before Yonn called out. Lower down the hill he showed them where a massive tree had fallen over, and its roots were splayed in the air; a mudslide had stripped away much of the vegetation and topsoil to reveal a length of fitted stones, like the top corner of a box. A crumbling yard-wide hole appeared in the center where some of the stone had broken free. The tree's roots still clutched a few of them.

"Looks like root rot took it down," said Ford.

"That and a combination of the stones giving way," said Danny.

"This is something," said Elle with an eye cocked at the dark hole as she knelt by the exposed wall and ran her fingers over the stone.

"Just some more old ruins," said Ford. He was about to give it up and go back to his flower picking when Danny's words halted him in his tracks.

"I think we have unearthed a tomb or perhaps some secret chamber yet untapped." He clasped onto Elle's shoulder for support and leaned into the hole for a closer look. "This mudslide and the resulting cave-in appear quite fresh."

"There is something of…of the coins and jewels and these things?" Elle was more than asking a question, she was salivating with her entire being when she pressed cheek to cheek with Danny, both pushing their faces further into the hole.

"A treasure horde? Maybe. Nay, quite possibly. We shall have to find out!"

An angry growl from deep in the hole knocked them over backward. Ford tripped and fell up to his waist into a bush and bellowed out in pain. Yonn was up first, helping Danny stagger to his feet. Elle crouched beside a tree with her needle-sharp dagger gripped in one hand, the blade and her wide eyes trained on the dark hole.

"What was th-that?!" Yonn wondered in a high-pitch tremble, darting his eyes from one face to the next as he and Danny backed away from the hole.

"Something's stinging my leg!" yelled Ford. Yonn left Danny's side and ran to help Ford.

"You probably fell in a thorn bush," said Danny limping crab-wise over to investigate. Ford pounded the bush into the ground with his free foot and pulled aside the remaining branches and leaves to reveal a barbed vine wrapped in a spiral up his pant leg with a dozen of its hooked thorns dug in firmly, dark red stains spreading around each.

"The spiny animatus vitis!" The words absolutely leapt out of Danny's mouth. "Have you ever seen such a specimen? Grown to maturity and quite healthy. See how it writhes!" He bent low to get a better look at the vine as it probed, flexed, and squeezed. Its thin, tapered end, bare of thorns aside from some developing soft and pliable hooks, repeatedly curled up and thrashed itself like a harmless one-inch whip against Ford's calf.

"What of the thing in the hole," Elle wondered to an inattentive audience.

"Does it hurt?" asked Yonn examining the half-inch-long spikes toward the base of the stem. Ford stared at him, incredulously.

"I've felt better." His demeanor softened, and he went on in earnest. "It was agony at first, but now it's going all numb."

"Yes, yes!" Danny nearly shouted in his enthusiasm. "It will do that. It injects a mild sort of venom through the thorns, and it is believed that this creates a vacuum which then sucks in the victim's blood!" Ford's eyes popped.

"It's a man-eater?"

"Not solely. Being relatively immobile, one cannot imagine it goes about picking and choosing its meals. Rather it must take what comes along."

"The sound was like a kind of monster, did you not hear?" asked Elle with her eyes still glued to the hole.

"But yes, men, or perhaps children would be more like, have been known to succumb entirely to a full-grown vine, some of which have been recorded as growing as much as ten feet in length! However, anything more than a few feet are rare indeed. Most often, one encounters smaller specimens such as this, and only an arm or leg are lost. Wonderful organisms!"

"An arm or leg?" Ford shouted.

"Will he lose the leg?" asked Yonn while Ford went pale.

"What worrying old hens you are!" Danny let out a chuckle. "There will be a great deal of swelling following this paresthesia, and then the leg will have to come off only as a last resort, should it become infected."

"You're a great comfort, cousin. Elle!" Remaining crouched and without removing her eyes from the hole, Elle glided low to the ground over to his side. "Cut that," Ford directed, and before Danny could protest, she severed the vine at the base. An agonized gasp escaped Ford's lips as he unwound it from knee to ankle, tearing holes in his trousers and releasing trickles of blood. He then flung the vine as far from himself as he could.

"You! Do you know what you've just done?" Danny couldn't believe his eyes. He wrung his hands, stamped his foot, and forgot himself so much as to use contractions. "That was a rare species that would've made a superb case study! I personally know an eminent sage who would have paid a handful of gold to own a living one!" He went on, but they ignored him.

"That noise, was it animal or monster or what?" Elle's intense watch on the hole broke only long enough for a brief glance at each of her companions.

"For all your clever town ways, Elle," said Ford trying to smile through his discomfort, "you sure don't know much about the wilds. It was probably nothing more than a badger." The last word shuddered from him as he dug out a deep thorn. "We could ask him, but…" Ford nodded toward Danny, who had stomped away from the others and was now flinging his hands up in the air and mumbling about stupidity.

"It sounded like a big cat, maybe?" said Yonn.

"Is a shame not to find the treasures, if they be in there." Elle's lingering look of regret toward the hole was blocked by Danny's rotund form.

"A shame? Why do you talk of shame?" He let out a short, barking laugh. "Some scabrous rodent is not about to get in the way of us finding out if there is something of value within! Yonn, run down there to our fire and fetch a charred hunk of wood. It looks to still be smoldering. I am sure you will find something suitable." Yonn came back and handed Danny a stumpy log aglow with embers along one side. "Perfect!" Danny waved it and blew on it until a small flame erupted, then handed it back to Yonn. "Now then, give that a heave down there and stand back." The boy did as ordered. A hiss spat from the hole followed by a burst of growling twice as fierce as before. "Now, everyone ready your weapons." A flash of yellow fur shot from the hole, and they all fell back as a bobcat tore away down the hill and into the forest. "Well, that takes care of that!"

Ford hopped to his feet and toppled over again. "Give me a moment, and I'll lead the way."

"It will only get worse before it gets better. You had best stay here while the rest of us investigate," Danny advised. Seeing as he was having trouble standing, Ford could hardly argue. "Fashion a torch and let us have a better look."

When Danny issued the command, Yonn jumped to without an earthly idea how to make a torch. Ford took him aside and put old knowledge to use. Soon enough they had a bark-wrapped torch ready for Danny to douse with some oil from a small flask he carried.

"Watch yourselves. Be careful," Ford shouted down the hole as Danny, Elle, and Yonn crawled in and inched down a slide of dirt and rock into a stone chamber. "What do you see?"

"Not much," Danny called back. Fresh cobwebs hung in the only two corners of a small, square room that had not been filled by the cave-in. The remaining space was cramped to the point that none of the three could stand. A few small, gnawed bones littered the dirt that had spilled in from the hole where the roof and part of the wall had collapsed. Various insects skittered into cracks along the stone walls and ceiling. Danny swung the torch toward the darkest side. "Oh. There is a door. And a good deal of dirt blocking it."

Half of the door was buried. Elle edged up to it, made a quick examination, and pushed against it. Nothing happened. She was about to call for Ford when Danny made a suggestion. With Elle and Yonn on their backs, they were able to push against the door with their feet and use the full strength of their legs. The door gave way and clumps of dirt toppled inward. Danny handed over the torch and Elle had a look inside.

"The smell is very old."

"What's going on," Ford hollered from above.

"It is safe," Elle said just before crawling through. The other two followed after her and entered another small, stone-walled chamber very similar to how they imagined the first would have been without all the debris.

Ford sat outside the hole, wondering what was going on and thinking about how slow time went by when you were waiting on someone else. He tried another shout and again got no reply. A moment later Yonn's head popped out.

"What's the word?" asked Ford as he hauled the boy up.

"Not much," replied Yonn, but the light in his eyes betrayed his excitement. He went on to give Ford a detailed account of the two chambers. The second differed from the first in that without the layer of dirt a flagstone floor was visible, and the walls were painted in fading landscapes of forest and hill. All around the room low relief carvings in the stone of wolves, foxes and a few other kinds of canine stared back with open mouths and tongues wagging. Some sat on all fours, while others stood erect and held tools or weapons. "They're checking each mouth," Yonn went on and in his exhilaration he never once stuttered. "It's like the dogs are sticking out their tongues at us, taunting like. Nothing so far, but Danny isn't giving up. It may take a while yet. I'm to bring water. And another torch. Oh and Danny said to say, *kick up that fire and fashion more torches.*"

"It'll be as long as that?"

"It may be," Yonn agreed distractedly while filling his arms with everyone's water-skins. He would have to come back for the torch, he thought to himself, hardly listening as Ford went on.

"I suppose, there may be more than meets the eye," said Ford recalling the time he had encountered strange little men in a ravine while lost in the wilderness. The naked and pale creatures, almost human but for their oversize skulls and olive-like eyes, had a secreted treasure trove in a cave that lit up from the glittering jewels and precious metals. Only, they possessed a magic Ford did not understand –he understood very little of any sort of magic for that matter– with which they had subdued him, knocking him unconscious momentarily, and when he awoke almost all of the treasure was gone. "There might be something hidden away down there. Danny'll overlook it if he ain't careful. I'd better…"

In his impatience and eagerness to be a part of the most interesting thing to have happened since they set off, Ford tried his gimpy leg again and found it to be worse than ever. "I could crawl through the hole all right and if I just had something to hold me up, like Danny's stick…" Looking about for something he could use for support and finding nothing at hand, he turned just in time to see Yonn disappearing back down the hole. A deflating sense of uselessness washed over him.

"Any luck?" Yonn asked as soon as he entered the second chamber. He received no reply. After scouring all the walls, sticking their fingers into every mouth and even pulling each dog's tongue, they felt they had exhausted all possibilities. Again he asked upon returning from his next trip with a fresh torch.

"Damn it, no!" Danny shouted and slammed down his staff. The butt made a hollow cracking sound upon the flagstone. They were all drawn to the spot. He tapped it again and then tried others around it, all of which sounded more solid.

"I should know this," said Elle from her knees as she worked double-time with the tip of her blade to pry the flagstone free. Once a gap was made, they used Danny's staff as leverage, lifted the flat stone and moved it aside. The black square hole left behind in the floor seemed as inviting as an unknown afterlife. All three leaned away from the musty smell of old earth wafting up from the hole. They listened and imagined in the absence of sound countless horrible possibilities silently awaiting them below.

"Anything may be down there," said Yonn with more than a little apprehension tugging at his voice.

"Might be nothing, but we will be none the wiser if we only hang about up here," said Danny grabbing the new torch from Yonn and dropping it in the hole. It clattered a second later against a stone floor below. Danny grunted his way to his hands and knees and poked his head through the hole. "All clear.

And as luck would have it, there is a way down." He disappeared over the side, and used hand and footholds cut into the rock against one wall to descend into the lower chamber. When the other two joined him, Danny was holding the torch aloft, and they all stared about them in perplexity and revulsion.

"It's awful," said Yonn.

"Most sinister," commented Danny.

"Hello?" came Ford's muffled and echoing voice from a distance. Whether they heard him or not, none of the three made a reply or took much notice.

"It is a veritable grotesquery," said Danny stepping forward to examine the murals that covered the walls here as they did the chamber above. However, these fading paintings depicted a story of base violence between human and canine, of a slaughter and torture so graphic as to inflict horror upon the viewer: flayed skin and torn fur; gutted individuals with organs askew to the delight of madmen; decapitation. Hardly could it be determined who was the aggressor and who was the victor.

They soon turned away from these to inspect the few articles contained in the room. At one end sat a few low tables against the wall and on the floor before them were scattered fragments of overturned vases and jars decorated in faded symbols and images difficult to make out. They took little notice of these, guessing that whatever had been inside, likely food or drink Danny guessed, had been scoffed up long ago by some form of critter as evidenced by the numerous tiny holes all about the room, as well as the droppings that crunched underfoot.

What interested them most was the mammoth sarcophagus against the wall opposite the tables. Certainly, the murals distracted them due to their arresting hideousness, but since there seemed to be nothing else of value in the room it was this that most intrigued them. The box itself was simple, rectangular and made of stone. Wide paws and thick claws made up the base. Countless v-shaped gauges covered much of the rest, but for a broad band about the middle where a scrolling group of tiny figures in a variety of positions enacted a scene none of them could make out.

Crowning everything, in one literal sense, was the most mesmerizing exhibit of all: a giant skull perched atop the sarcophagus. The first thing one noticed was its enormous size, like that of an Aelwydian drum. The cranium was relatively small, though, so that the jaw and snout jutting out beyond the sarcophagus' lid made the whole thing more angular in appearance than a human skull.

"It is not real or yes?" wondered Elle.

"Perhaps of porcelain-make," suggested Danny after squinting at the skull that had been yellowed with age and grayed by dust. Dust had settled thickly on most surfaces and dulled nearly everything to the extent that until just now no one had noticed the stone held between the jaws of the skull. "Yonn, slide over one of those tables." Once it was in place before the sarcophagus, Danny adjusted it to his liking and heaved himself up upon it, but could not reach the stone, which would have been out of reach for even Yonn, the tallest of the three. Danny tapped at it with his staff. "It is wedged in there tight. Yonn, the light, hold it closer." He scrapped away some of the dust. "Yes."

"What? What do you see?" Elle demanded as she slid over two more tables. Stacking one on the other, she climbed atop them both, but only got close enough to touch the boney, white chin with the tips of her fingers while standing on tiptoe. More scraping with the end of the staff and her eyes lit up at the sight of the twinkling light reflecting off what appeared to be a very large and potentially valuable gemstone. Wedged deep, there was little room between the stone and the corners of the mouth, just enough that Elle could slip the point of her knife in to try prying it out. The blade bent right up to the point of breaking before she gave up.

They traded places and, although Danny's weight and lack of coordination made even the most novice of acrobats look solidly in control of their craft, his sheer determination kept him upright enough to wedge the butt of his staff into the front of the skull's mouth in order to use it as a lever. The incisors and impressive canines snapped and crumbled, but the lower jaw held firmly again the top of the sarcophagus. Danny hung a touch more of his own weight on his end of the staff.

"It shifted!" cheered Yonn.

Danny pulled at the staff and Elle pried with her knife. There was a scraping. Danny made a leaping grab and out of the mouth popped the stone, and with it shot a snake. Its wide, fanged mouth clamped around the stone and the tips of Danny's fingers. Elle slashed with her knife, and the snake's severed head toppled with them to the hard floor where they crashed amongst splintered tables, and the many tiny fragments of the shattered the stone. The jaws of the skull snapped shut the instant the stone – nothing more than a worthless bauble – was removed, thus releasing the skull from where it was wedged between the top of the sarcophagus and the ceiling. The door to the sarcophagus swung open and out tottered a massive skeleton clinging to the barest of ligaments, headless but still taller than them all and with a ribcage as rotund as an ancient oak. It lurched forward upon its rickety limbs and, whether from momentum or of its own volition, one of its arms raised up as if reaching out for Danny and Elle where they lay sprawled upon the floor before it. Suddenly Yonn flew sideways across the room, and the skeleton whipped around with Ford gripping it by the wrist and hurling it straight into a wall. Bones burst in the air and fell clattering like sticks upon the floor. Everyone and everything but the writhing snake's body went still. If there had been any life in the skeleton these past hundreds of years, the scattered bones were devoid of it now.

"Are you hurt, any of you?" Ford shouted, hopping and limping about, trying to help up the others. Danny held up his hand and twisted it this way and that in the light.

"The snake's fangs bit down upon the stone and seem to have missed my fingers entirely."

"Luck is with you, cousin. Elle? Yonn?"

"I'm all right. I'm all right," said Yonn in a twitter while getting to his feet and retrieving the torch before brushing the dust and droppings from his robe.

"What have you there?" Danny asked of Elle, who held dangling by a chain an amulet she had found amongst the bones.

"It was over the monster's neck. I saw it!" Yonn all but shouted in his high spirits. Ford took the torch from him, and they all gathered around Elle to examine the amulet. A red decagonal gemstone set in tarnished metal gleamed back at their eager faces. Engraved upon the back they found runes writ in a language that befuddled even Danny.

"If my father were here, he could identify this metal at least, of that I am sure. For all I know it may be worthless." Danny flipped the amulet about to peer lovingly at the stone. "The gem, however, this must be worth a good deal. A ruby, perhaps." The others mouthed and murmured *ruby*. "My honorable companions, I believe we have found ourselves a small fortune!"

CHAPTER 11
IN THE RECLUSE'S DEN

"Do not move," muttered Danny mere inches from Ford's ear. Though all of Ford's muscles jerked to attention, he remained otherwise still.

"What is it," he asked through barely parted lips, fighting back the urge look about. Having sat on the ground for a good long while now, his mind could easily conjure up any number of horrible dangers creeping up on him from out of the undergrowth. Venomous spiders and poisonous snakes were at the forefront.

Danny nodded down to where a trail of determined ants trekked back and forth over the sleeve of the arm Ford had laid over the log he reclined against. "Look, see, they carry aphids. Very tiny aphids, ever so gently." He lifted Ford's arm, slid it a few inches to one side, and settled down to some intense observation, hoping to study the ants' reactions. Initial confusion and apparent panic was followed by investigation and then innovation that culminated in a calm and progressive trail leading over Ford's unmoving wrist, just a few inches from Danny's broad satisfied smile.

"How poisonous are they?" inquired Ford barely above a whisper.

"Poisonous?" Danny gave a snort. "There is not a spittle's worth of poison in them." When he turned to retrieve a pen and paper from his bag so he might scratch out some notes, Ford shook his arm free of ants and found a new place to sit. Only mildly perturbed, Danny went on studying the ants with no end to his curiosity.

On the day following their descent into the tomb, Ford could do little more than rest with his leg propped up. While the others wandered about in search of rue, that increasingly elusive flower, he thought over what had happened and discussed it with whoever came within earshot. They could come to no conclusion as to whether the thing that had emerged from the sarcophagus was alive or not. Danny repeatedly returned to the possibility of yet another secret passage leading to perhaps an even richer tomb that had been overlooked. Ford doubted it for the sake of Elle, who felt affronted every time Danny unwittingly questioned the thoroughness of their search.

A surge in the throbbing pain of his swollen leg cut short Ford's current train of thought and once again he regretted his foolish insistence to keep moving after being warned not to. The calf was beet red, the wounds angry, but at least they weren't festering. Pus had formed. They all remarked at what a quick healer he was. Twenty-four hours later, the swelling, if not actually receding yet, had at least leveled off.

He lay back against an oak tree looking up through the tiny gaps in the leaves above and trying to release the irritation building within him. He hated feeling weak and dependent on others and wondered how the young and elderly could bear it. Even as a boy he had always been big for his age, which meant hardly ever having to endure the cruelty of older children.

"Is that all you're going to do all day?" he asked through a grimace while rubbing down his sore leg. "What's so interesting about ants?"

"Their anatomy for one," began Danny. "Not to mention their diet, efficiency, organization, predictability—"

"Fascinating."

"Quite. Humans could learn a lot from ants, perhaps even you."

"Doubt it."

"You are probably right," said Danny starting in on his second attempt at drawing the spiny animatus vitis. "I am also taking notes on our journey thus far, certain aspects of which may be of interest to instructors at the school as well as to fellow students. Perhaps one day they may even lead to an invitation into the Academia's Society of Colleagues, I should think. Would you not agree, Yonn?" When there was no reply, he looked up and was surprised to find that Yonn was nowhere to be seen. Ford explained that he and Elle had wandered off together some time ago to scout the area and see what they could find. "And much luck to them. The school could use more variety than this lot." He pointed an elbow at a sack filled to bursting with a white and pink flowered plant called yalcadal, a fairly powerful valerian, but common enough to render the find barely worth carrying all the way back to the city.

Danny was back at his notes, and Ford had fallen asleep when Yonn came tumbling down a slope through the brush shouting "A cave!" He skidded to a stop in the middle of camp, sweaty and filthy, but triumphant. "Elle spotted it from afar! It must be Larkwine's!"

Climbing a zigzag path into the valley and up again to the next hill, they could see across the way the cave entrance from various angles and had plenty of time to admire it if they wished while waiting for Ford who came hobbling after them with Danny's staff as a crutch. At first, it appeared to be nothing more than a natural a gash in a rock-capped hilltop when Yonn first pointed it out through light tree cover from the far peak. But as they progressed, the human touch revealed itself in the jagged chiseling done to widen the opening, in a stairway leading from the mouth down the slope toward them, and the boulders like bulging sacks of wheat placed on either side of the entryway. Leaving the cave at a right angle, the stairway descended some fifty feet and ended where it met with a circular landing. This was mostly covered in weeds that reached as high as their waists at times; it was surrounded by gold mop, an evergreen shrub that had grown unruly invaded the landing and engulfed most of a rotted wooden bench made from halved logs. Sitting at one end of this bench, Elle tried to appear relaxed and ambivalent while waiting for them, but her posture was so unnaturally upright that it belied the pride and eagerness bubbling within.

"An open-air antechamber for those seeking an audience with the monk?" Danny wondered aloud. "Or perhaps an auditorium from which the man spoke to the people?" Ford's grunts and stifled groans came from the trees and gradually grew closer.

"It must take the monk much time to make this all," said Elle, mostly indicating the stone stairway.

"He got help, so the story goes."

"Story? What story? What've I missed?" asked a red-faced Ford upon finally joining them. "Hey there, look at that! The monk built all that by himself?"

"He got help," Elle promptly answered.

"Yes," said Danny shooting her a dirty eye. "His devotion…no, let me see. I believe the passage goes, 'His self-inflicted solitude touched the hearts of the people.' That is from Ceddale's *History of Devotional Worship Specific to the Adherents of the Hau Religion within the Central and Eastern Regions of the Domain Known as Aelwyd*. His followers made pilgrimages to see him, and I suppose they must have assisted with building this and that."

"Ha! So the old man came out here to get away from the people, and the people came all the way out here to be near him?" Ford's uproarious laughter let everyone in the area know just how funny he found it.

"Yes, the bitter irony is ever so humorous," said Danny in a distracted undertone. "But getting back to the matter at hand, we came for rare plants and a look around; however, there is nothing here but weeds." With his open palms up, he gestured to the sea of wild greenery they appeared to be floating in, spreading his arms and inadvertently brushing through the insubstantial pale bushes about him. Instantly hundreds of tiny buds leapt into the air and fell in a deluge of verdant, curly seeds down upon his head and shoulders. "What in the name..." He waved a hand through the bushes again, and a few dozen seedlings jumped up two or three feet into the air. On the third swipe only a half dozen. He moved ahead a few feet, swiped, again and again, an emerald cloud flew straight up and right back down again. "Amazing! Have you ever seen such a thing?" Ford had. His time living in the wilderness had shown him many things like this, but he kept his mouth shut and just smiled at the sight of the little round man dashing about with puffs of green dots exploding around him. Quite quickly Danny's childlike joy turned to an equally childlike frustration when he discovered he was unable to obtain a specimen without all of the buds leaping off the bush the instant it was touched. However delicately he handled them, the conclusion was always the same. Thousands of curlicues bounced off his face before he gave up.

Ford limped up the stairs toward the cave, last in line and keeping up as best he could, but cursing every time he stumbled to his hands and knees. As the strongest among them, he felt he should be leading the way whenever they moved ahead into the unknown. A misstep sent him down once more, and when he cracked his knee upon the step he threw aside the staff, dropped the sack slung over his shoulder and smacked the club down on the stone. He was sick of being hurt and being a liability.

"Don't go sticking your noses in that cave 'til I get there!" he shouted up to them as he sat back, massaging his knee and had a look around. Being one of the higher points in the area and rocky, the hilltop was a touch drier all around, especially the stunted shrub-like trees sprouting from between granite boulders. Tiny terraced earthen plots between or overlaying the rock were overgrown with clumps of new grass poking up through last year's crisp, yellow brome.

"Aha! Victory at last!" cried Danny.

"Is that it?" asked Yonn.

"That is it, my friend. Larkwine's Rue of Hope!" Like many varieties of common rue, this cluster sitting at the mouth of the cave had flowers consisting of five yellow petals, but the orange that trimmed each petal distinguished Larkwine's Rue from others. Ford limped up to them as quickly as he could in order to admire the flowers with the rest, each running their hands over them, caressing the petals and drab blue teardrop leaves as if the plants were newborn babies.

"Well then, shall we begin?" Danny said with a big grin while searching through the sack of provisions for the pouch he had packed for this particular purpose. They each began plucking off the flowers with feverish fingers. Danny honed their technique, suggesting a method of removal that would preserve the plants for the future. He also dug up a plant, a small specimen but a rue plant in its entirety, and tenderly placed the clump of dirt encasing the root ball into a small sack. "Did you ever consider the irony of Larkwine's flower?" he asked while tying it off. "I mean to say, the *rue* of hope? The flower bestows hope and a sort of false sense of courage from it, yet the name belies its attributes, in a way." Only Yonn had any notion of what Danny was getting at. Neither Ford nor Elle knew the meaning of the word *rue*, so Ford only nodded blankly, while Elle would not reply for fear she was being made game of. "Ah well, I found it humorous," Danny concluded with a benign smile.

For his part, Ford didn't know or particularly care what Danny was going on about. All he knew for sure was that he was holding a flower that granted hope and courage, something he could use a good deal of. Even the thought of it bolstered his confidence. No doubt it went contrary to the code of conduct laid out in the contract he had signed with Danny, but Ford took a sprig of the rue for himself anyway and secreted it away.

"Too dark," said Danny after the rue harvesting was through and they were poking their noses into the cave entrance. He stepped back and folded his arms, "Too dark to see much of anything."

"It's probably filled with bats," muttered Ford with a spite born from unpleasant childhood experiences of spending nights in the loft of a barn. "Nasty, filthy bats."

Elle came forward to investigate for herself. She had kept her eyes closed for a few moments and only opened them fully when she stood directly in front of the mouth of the cave. "Oh! There is a stink!" she exclaimed, jerking her head back. With nose pinched shut, she leaned in again. "The room is not large, and maybe there is more back, away back."

"Room?" wondered Ford.

"Yes. It is very like a room for living."

"If there is a continuation, descending into dark corners with accumulated moisture, there may be fungi and such. Something of worth or edible in the least." Though Danny said this in jest, the truth was they had already gone through most of the food they had packed and were left with only half of a small bag of dried peas, enough for about a day, maybe two if they rationed them. "I must admit a curiosity to see how the monk lived."

A torch was fashioned out of the driest bark Yonn could find, a white strip of birch they shoved into the split end of a stick. Once lit, it wouldn't last long, less than half an hour.

"Hope it don't go out and leave us in the dark," said Ford taking the torch from Danny. "If I ever do this sort of thing again, I'm coming more prepared."

Ducking his head under the low ceiling, he sniffed and balked at the smell. "Dear gods, you're right. Smells like something died in here a while back." He inched Danny's staff forward and tapped the side of the wall with his club. "Hello?"

"My dear cousin, since the monk is dead, there is very little chance he is still in residence."

"That's no call for being rude."

"Just hold the torch still. You are throwing shadows everywhere." Danny squeezed and shoved past the others into the cave. Ford came in next and stood beside him. The other two crept in behind.

"There." Elle pointed between them into the darkness ahead. "It goes on." At the back of the shallow cave, away to the right, a darker void was evident. There the rock glistened ever so slightly in the light that remained. Everywhere the rock shone a murky blue-grey granite, but underneath the damp, toward the back, the rock appeared black.

"Look, there's a bowl on that rock," said Yonn.

"That is more than a rock. See, a basin has been dug into it," said Danny snatching the torch back and stepping heel-to-toe over to a thigh-high block of granite sitting near the center. As he moved, the flame of the torch danced along a pattern of designs etched into the sanded rock of the ceiling. "Odd, there is still water—." The torch spun from Danny's hand as a spear ripped through his robe, tearing it half off his back before smashing into splinters against the basin block. A snarl and a growl echoed in the dark. The torch, almost extinguished, came back to life and cast a flickering light from the floor that barely caught the back of the cave where there crouched a half-starved man-beast with a wolf-like head and a scabrous body matted by patchy gray hairs. A ragged animal-skin wrap draped over one shoulder was not cover enough to hide the wiry muscles of its arms and the clawed hands twitching and flexing as it clenched two more spears. Its almost human jaw-line widened its lengthy snout. Its purplish lips curled back into a sneer as the beast glared at them with eyes that glowed red in the light.

"A warghadoc..." From the darkened alcove beyond the basin came Danny's astonished utterance at seeing a living version of something he had only seen as a sketch in a book on legendary beasts.

"Nobody do nothing," said Ford in as low and steady a tone as he could manage. The beast hadn't moved, and if everyone remained calm and didn't alarm it by sudden movement they all might back out of the cave and escape unharmed. His voice drew the warghadoc's attention. It crouched still lower and its fangs caught the light. "Look out, it's going to strike." There was no retreating, not for the hobbled Ford, who limped before the others, presenting himself as a target, but keeping his club hidden behind his leg. The warghadoc growled again, then let out a long howl that reverberated throughout the cave so that nothing else could be heard, not even the sound of Danny shouting as he raised a handful of a sulfuric mixture high in one hand. The warghadoc feigned an attack with a thrusting half-step forward, and then it barked sharp, threatening yaps and yips. Another thrusting half-step. When they did not back down, the barking quieted and became rambling guttural croaks sputtering through gnashed teeth. Then it stopped altogether, and the creature's sharp chipped incisors disappeared behind relaxed lips. Unbending its knobby spine, it stood erect nearly to Ford's height and seemed to listen to Danny's chanting.

"It spoke," said Yonn amazed and curious, sliding out from behind Ford for a better look. The beast's eyes darted to the young man, and it howled as it went back into a crouch. Danny's incantations grew in volume.

"No!" shouted Ford as a blazing red flash shot from the alcove across the room, scorching the beast's flank before spending itself in an eye-blinding blast against the far cavern wall. The stench of sulfur filled the air. The warghadoc flung sideways, shrieked. The torch died away to nothing and the pale day threw the only light in the cave faintly in at their feet. All else was shadow, and random sounds: scraping nails, padded footsteps, a wooden shaft dragged over stone, and an escaped whimper from one of the companions.

A blunted stone-tipped spear slid out of the darkness with the chance imagery of a dream and the whetted terror of a razor-sharp nightmare. Behind it, the beast's gray snarling muzzle dripped saliva as it pushed the weapon into Ford's gut. Gasping for air, he spun away bent double and stumbled into Yonn, who stuttered an incantation while kneeling on the floor where he scrabbled to scrape up purple dust fallen into the dirt. Plucked back, the spear immediately jabbed at Ford again. He swatted at it with one hand and brought the club straight up with the other, catching the beast's chin and sending it reeling back into the darkness. Ford brought the club back for another swing, and it smashed against the granite block splitting into two useless splinters. He cast it aside and took up the staff, readying for another attack as he kneeled over Yonn, who stretched out his fingers, covered in purple dust and brown dirt, and repeatedly stammered a chant with his eyes closed. He finished and gave an expectant wince, but nothing happened. Springing from the darkness, the beast leapt upon the granite block and lashed a yellowed claw down at Ford, who jerked back and slammed his head against the wall. His inert body slumped over and dropped to the ground.

Indistinct growls and muffled shrieks rolled about Ford's ears like distant thunder. The black shade before his eyes blinked into a fuzzy gray. He tried to shout, "My legs! I can't stand!" but the words merely floated in his mind, refusing to come off his tongue. His head felt much as it had when the old mage had turned him into vapor. A whining and a husky bark emerged from the stirring shadows about him. He swung a fist or thought he had. His arms and legs hardly seemed to belong to him.

"Get up!" he heard himself shout when a brilliant light lit up the cave. Rising upon one hand, he blinked as the blurred images came together into shapes that could have been Yonn holding up a torch and the warghadoc crouching in the middle of the room. Details slowly filled in the outlines. Elle's face, so small and pained where she leaned against the back wall, her bare hand still painted red, no, bloodied.

Ford shook his head, knelt to get up and found the staff trapped beneath his leg. He rolled over and brought it up in both hands just as a crack echoed off the walls followed by a fierce, exhilarated nasal whinny and Yonn flopping flat upon the floor with a tear across his cheek and a magical ball of glowing light in one hand such as Ford had seen the old mage Walader cast. He spun around to see the beast jump from the basin block, jerk down a rock held high above its head and dash it against Yonn's skull. Ford cried out and jammed one end of the staff into the beast's ribs, rocking it on its heels so that it stumbled backward into Elle's blade. She stabbed twice before the howling warghadoc jerked away from her. Ford met it in the middle of the room and caught it under the chin with the staff, driving it into the basin block and pressing the shaft against its throat. The beast kicked and scratched, but Ford's weight held it down while he endured its frantic claws tearing at his clothing and skin. He stared straight into its red rolling eyes that passed back and forth between fury and fear as the realization that it could not escape set in; it began slithering and squirming, scrabbling with its claws to gain purchase upon the staff. Gusts of its foul breath blowing into Ford's face turned to gasps, slowed and then stopped.

Crouched against the back wall with her blade gripped in her trembling, white-knuckled hand, Elle kept an unblinking vigil upon the darkness of the narrow passage leading further back into the cave. Danny came from the shadows and stood over Ford where he collapsed in the blood spreading from Yonn's head. Ford rolled his lifeless body over and peered into his motionless eyes. The flow of blood finally ceased and along with it any lingering hope they had for the boy.

No one moved. No one spoke. They stared at the ground or at their hands, perhaps outside, anywhere but at each other. Their breathing collectively slowed, and eventually Ford got up and sat on the steps out front. A trail of Yonn's blood ran out of the cave and dripped into an expanding pool upon the stairs beside Ford.

There followed a hazy, lethargic time of examing themselves and each other for wounds. Elle's slashed arm was wrapped; Ford's head throbbed, and a sizable lump had formed; there was no stomach puncture, only an angry red bruise; and Danny felt shaken and worn down, the sapping cost of magic coursing through the human body. Afterward they cleaned Yonn as best they could, gathered up his body and carried him from the cave.

"Let me," said Ford halfway down the stairs. Danny had done his best, but Ford grew frustrated by his cousin's fumbling about upon the stairs. Hoisting Yonn's body over his shoulder, he limped the rest of the way one step at a time, adrenaline and distraction blocking most of the pain in his leg.

Not a cloud blotted the late afternoon sky. The seasonal weather change flexed its muscle and dragged out the heat of the day. A stream of sweat trickled down Ford's back and soaked the matted layers of cloth between him and the dead boy before he made the bottom landing. After a short rest, Danny cleared his throat.

"The funny thing is—"

"There is nothing funny," said Ford with a finger raised to him. "Nothing." Danny held up a hand in a sign of surrender.

"Please. Let me rephrase. The amazing thing is, Yonn never cast a spell before."

"What?"

"Yonn. To my knowledge, he never managed to cast a successful spell before now and yet, there he was with components in hand still trying. Seems like a damn fool time to practice."

"He was no fool," Ford said reflexively as he meditated upon what Danny had just said, and it dawned on him what had just happened. What the boy just done struck Ford as hard as any blow he had ever received. "He tried. He kept on trying."

"Yes," said Danny. "I believe he was braver than I gave him credit for."

"His folks would be proud."

"Now what?" asked Elle, still shaken and struggling to find the right words. "I mean, with him? Now with him, what do we do?"

"I suppose we bury him here," answered Danny.

"No," said Ford. "No, we take him back to his folks." Danny wanted to point out how far they had to travel with such a cumbersome load. That didn't even take into account the numerous sacks, never mind getting it all up and over that precipitous hill before Uldale. However, he could see the danger in crossing Ford at this moment and held back for the time being.

On the following day, they were trudging through in the depths of a high-banked trough created by a river that now only existed as a faint trickling over rocks and apologetic sliding through the sodden ground. Ford laid down his burden and reached for the only salvageable piece of warghadoc weaponry, a two-foot-long stub of a spearhead he had tucked into his belt. Danny and Elle, plodding along behind him so wearied from the burden of the stuffed sacks that their heads drooped, pulled up just shy of bumping into him.

"What is it?" asked Danny, gladly dumping his load on the ground and plopping down with it. Ford pointed to the top of the bank some distance ahead. Squatting by a tree sat a brown lump of hair and rags, one bulbous white eye targeting them down the length of an arrow upon a drawn bow. It watched them without moving, and when they too remained still it rose almost imperceptibly on stumpy legs, eased back the bowstring and waddled away at a surprising speed.

"A human?" asked Elle from behind the nearest tree.

"Don't know," replied Ford looking after it in wonder until the shaggy apparition disappeared.

"Whatever it was, we are at a distinct disadvantage here," said Danny. "Now is a good time to get out of this gully or whatever you might call it."

Even after finding the most gradual of inclines, it still took a great deal of sweat and the better part of an hour to haul up Yonn's body. And no sooner had they dropped upon their backsides for a rest than a pack of hounds came crashing through the woods from behind, howling out a shattering din.

"It's the boy," said Ford and their spent bodies relaxed in a flood of relief at the sight Brywan tearing through the trees after the dogs.

"Hahaa!" shouted the shaggy-headed boy as he leapt in the air, not believing his luck and beside himself with joy at finding them again. He stayed as long as he dared, listening to the scant details they were willing to provide of their adventures since he had last seen them, but he had to be home soon, or it meant his hide.

"Before you go," said Ford opening the sack Danny had been carrying and pulling out a bundle wrapped in the warghadoc's ragged animal skin, now encrusted with dried blood. He let the skin unravel and out rolled the severed beast's head. Everyone but Ford jumped back.

"You put that thing in *my bag*?" shouted Danny. "I wondered why you went back to the cave."

The whites of Brywan's eyes flashed, and he trod backward on to a dog's foot, yet the yelp didn't phase him in the least. Amazed, he murmured, "Bahky."

"Barky. Ah," said Ford with a tired nod. "I thought you might know him."

That was the end of their mortal lives in the eyes of this child, for they had killed the howling, midnight terror of these hills, and now they were gods to him. He begged them to come back to his village. They *must*, he insisted, otherwise the others would never believe him.

"Dey nare dah," he complained, kicking the crumbling wood out of a rotting stump.

"They didn't look too happy to see us last time," said Ford when the three of them gathered together to discuss the matter.

"Things have changed since then," Danny countered. "And besides, there is no way we will climb over that hill and arrive in Uldale before well after dark. Not at this rate." When their lack of provisions was pointed out, and the possibility of purchasing something from Brywan's people was put forward, they all agreed to at least test the waters at the boy's village. So, away over the hills the boy and his dogs led them in high spirits and endless chatter.

At the gate of Brywan's village facing steely glares and brandished weapons, they were surprised at just how quickly the villagers' cold reserve and defensive posturing melted away at the sight of *Bahky's* head. When everyone was huddled shoulder to shoulder about the central fire pit within the stone hall, the beast's severed head was passed around, admired and made even more gruesome when the villagers placed it on a short spike in front of the wavering firelight of the central hearth. The sallow gray face with its jaw hanging loose and those almost human eyes looked even more human than ever with the whole thing having adopted the universal death-mask.

Over the rim of a wooden mug of gloppy bread-yeasted ale and through the flames across from him, Ford recognized the brown lump of hair and rags they had spotted in the forest pointing a drawn bow at them. Under that great bush of hair, welcoming eyes wrinkled and the wide bird's nest of a beard parted in a near-toothless smile, like a bowl with a few kernels of corn stuck around the sides. His name was Mab Dermot, and he was the son of the long white-bearded village chief Gab Dermot. The two of them made up half the village's grown male population.

Mab knew they had come from the direction of Larkwine's cave. What had happened there none knew, but all desired to know, so Ford and his companions told and retold the story until Dermot's people knew it well enough to recite it on their own. To them, it was a tale worth a hundred legends from foreign lands because it was so intimate and contained a satisfying conclusion, which would immediately impact their day-to-day lives.

Bahky, the recent scourge of the hills and bane of their nights, had been defeated and the yoke of fear lifted. Though there was heartfelt sorrow all around for Yonn's death and a reverence for his body, this was cause for celebration. They ate and drank, sang and danced, and traded stories for hours on end.

Ford could not match their enthusiasm and exerted only enough energy to appear jovial. He ate everything put before him, drank when plied and stood up the countless times they begged him to, obligingly pretending to bump his sore head on the ceiling just as he had done in earnest the first time so that they all might laugh hysterically each and every time. They never did tire of admiring his extraordinary height, even handing over the babies of the village to be kissed by the giant.

After passing back the last of the sour-smelling bundles to its proud mother, Ford noticed the little blond girl that had just a few days prior climbed the ravine wall with the dexterity of a monkey, turn away from him as if afraid he might try to kiss her, too. During the evening, his eye had occasioned to fall upon this tiny pale sun sitting amidst ragged brown clouds. Even a sliver of such light cast warming rays like gold through gloom, light that twinkled in the rain so that even one drenched to the bone might welcome such a prismatic soaking. But now the little sun hid away in her foster mother's gray tunic, refusing to have anything to do with him. Though it was merely a child's irrational fear and stubborn reluctance to accept him as anything but a source of dread stemming from the fright they had given her back at the ravine, all the same, it had a souring effect on him. "By the gods, I beg my own sons and daughters never look at me in that way," he thought later as he lay back and tried to get some sleep.

Danny's artful conniving, the enthusiasm of the villagers, and his own wearied body and mind finally won Ford over, so that by the next morning he accepted the idea of having Yonn's remains interred in the Dermots' village. As soon as he had agreed to this, he asked for the most suitable blade the Dermots could provide and spent the morning carving a foot-tall wooden totem to use for the burial ceremony. He worked hard to make the face as similar to Yonn's as he could, but in his desire to be kind and to give him more pleasing features, and because of his need to occupy his own mind, he overworked the wood and was not at all satisfied with the result.

His dissatisfaction with the result went deeper than the piece of wood he now stared straight through. "If only, if only, if only," ran the relentless inward refrain as he wished he had done something different, anything that might have changed the outcome. They were self-defeating regrets that did nothing but mire him deeper in ill humor, but still, his mind ran repeatedly through yesterday's tragedy until he thought he might take the carving knife to his own throat. A hand pressed upon his shoulder and woke him from his despair.

"Goot," Mab assured him, leaning over his shoulder for a better look at his work. "Bary goot!"

"That will do," agreed Danny and gave Ford a nod, a visual nudge to let him know it was time to move things along.

Carrying Yonn's corpse the entire way back to Port Morton could have taken all the time in the world as far as Ford was concerned, but as Danny pointed out, there was decomposition to consider. The Dermots' cold, hillside tomb would preserve the body, while a speedy interment would preserve the soul. Should Yonn's remains need to be retrieved in the future, they could be. So they laid the body to rest within a manmade cavern excavated for housing generation after generation. Although Ford and his companions were outsiders, they were honored guests of the Dermots and thus permitted to carry the body through the great stone doorway with its fading scrollwork carved by some ancient relative and into the underground catacombs whose niches were filled with the exposed bones of Dermot elders and innumerable children.

Ford wanted more than anything to carry the boy back to his parents, but amongst his own kin, Yonn would have been mourned as "that shy unfortunate boy," his memory fading in the minds of all but his immediate family. Here though, the final resting place of the body would be cared for and revered by Dermot's people, for Yonn was a hero to them and would become a part of their lore.

Chapter 12
Law and Ardor

Two uncommonly vigilant guards dressed in chainmail shirts stood by the bar and guardhouse entering Port Morton quite impervious to the rain and watched with keen eyes as Ford, Danny and Elle approached the city. It was not unusual to find gatehouse guards asleep at their posts, but that was not the case this day. The meatier of the two stood back so that he might take them all in at once and kept a hand on the hilt of his short sword for the entire time they were given a relatively thorough search by his comrade, a jerky and clearly nervous man possessing more brain than brawn. During a somewhat intense questioning that Danny handled, Ford's attention wandered; he gave a small start of surprise upon finding himself staring into the inimical eye of yet a third guard watching them from the window of the guardhouse nestled against the Two Oaks Inn. The deadly accurate crossbow was normally equipped only by the likes of castle guards, yet here on the outskirts of the poor east side of town, Ford found this third guard pointing a loaded crossbow straight at him.

"Why all the muscle?" he asked and might have added, *speed*, having noticed the hindquarters of a horse sticking out from around the side of the guardhouse.

"You haven't heard?" replied the nervous, brainy guard in plain astonishment. "The poor Iarl's been assassinated."

"Poor my ass," scoffed the meaty one.

"I don't mean in the way of coin, you thick-headed mule."

"She got plenty of them, too, I'll wager." The two guards began anew an old argument over the Iarl's supposed wealth and greed with the nervous brainy one doing his best to defend her while the strong one summed up his side by saying a man like the Pennaeth ought to be in charge of the city, "not no woman."

Eventually, they explained that the increased manpower at the guardhouses was due to the murder of the Iarl as well as other recent assassinations. It seemed security had also increased a good deal on the city streets in general.

From a posting nailed to the guardhouse door Danny read aloud of the hiring of new watchmen and Ford's ears perked up at the mention of jobs to be had.

***

The very next morning Ford found himself in a long line outside of Lygade Hall, a bulky two-story stone building where the city watch was headquartered. A procession of the poor and positionless waited in hopes of being handed the heavy oak club designed especially for cracking skulls as well as the watchman's special jerkin that would signify their newly gained profession. The interviewers were taking their time with some hopefuls and dismissing others almost out of hand so that the line lurched ahead in fits and starts like a hesitant tortoise. Even though most had gotten up before dawn, none seemed to mind spending hours in a drenching downpour.

At the door, Ford saw over the heads of those before him into the hall where the Master of the Watch was asking all the questions, while his two silent subordinates, the one-eyed day watch captain and the grim-faced night watch captain, sat looking glum and unimpressed.

Ford had never taken part in anything like this before, and the idea of standing before a group and answering questions unnerved him. He wished he had the confidence of the two applicants in front of him, a father and son ready to give up their floundering farm if chosen.

"What if they pick only one and not the other?" questioned Ford.

"If they pick one, stands to reason they'll pick both," said the father incredulously, looking Ford over for signs of drunkenness. Turning fully around to face Ford and speaking slowly as if to a mentally challenged child, he went on, "You see, they's picking 'em by size and strength. There's not sixteen years between me and my boy, and we're same-ish in the physical way of things, as you see." Ford did not see but held his tongue. "I can still whip ya though, boy! Eh, eh?" The father, half a head shorter than his son, jostled the boy, a lad of five and a half feet still in the grips of puberty, who wilted and giggled as he shied away from his father's playful digs to his ribs.

Ford could only wish to be as much at ease as these two, so sure of their coming good fortune, but after enduring the failure that sent him to Dwyer's Depression he didn't hold out much hope. If he was one of the decision-makers sitting up there at the heavy oak table in front of the glowing hearth, looking sharp in warm furs and high boots, he wouldn't hire himself, not by the sight of him, he reflected as he looked down at his torn and bloodstained pants with the lone pocket that was hanging on by threads, and hanging open so that he caught a glimpse of his sprig of rue. His fingers dove in and wrapped around it ever so tenderly, and an immediate sense of hope surged within him. He became alert, and an urgency to grab his chance enveloped him. Standing at the doorway, he leaned forward to hear the questions being asked, and he would've heard each and every word plain if the damn lip-smackers behind him had shut their godforsaken pie-holes.

Next up, just ahead of the father and son, was a stout young man Ford thought was perhaps a sailor he had seen while offloading a merchant ship back in his porter days. The look of the man made Ford worry about the number of watchman vacancies available, for he was sure this man fit the mold. Though not overly tall, he was obviously strong, could probably handle any rough work and didn't look like he would take any nonsense from anyone.

At first sight of him, the heads of the watch-master and captains nodded, but when they got beyond his name and former profession to ask, "What would your actions be should you happen upon a body lying unconscious in the street?" All they received in reply were grunting, confounded huffs, blinking eyes and an increasingly frightened stare as the man fought in vain to come to grips with such abstract hypotheticals. He might have been a dab hand at hauling upon a rope, but they had seen this before, and he was soon mercifully dismissed.

Next, the father and son strode up to the table and before either were even questioned, the Master of the Watch simply pronounced, "Too small! Next!" and "Too young! Next!" It happened in a flash and the suddenness with which Ford now found himself standing in the middle of the room in front of these officials and the nerves that overcame him almost made him forget his own name.

"What would your actions be should you come upon a blaze?" said Ford later that day in Elle's room with his chin doubled up while speaking in the officious tones and blubbery lisp of the Master of the Watch. Elle stifled a snicker as she leaned back against the wall and stretched her legs up on her bed. The small crate under Ford creaked with his own bouncing merriment.

"You answer what?" she asked.

"I almost told old buttertub if it were going good you might as well sit back and enjoy the show, but then I remembered about calling out 'fire!' and getting buckets. Then he asks me what I'd do if I caught someone stealing and I said I'd wring his neck and give back the goods. Not in them words exact, mind you, but nice like. Tell them what they want to hear, right? I mean, I'm no priest, but I'll pretend to be if it pays." Ford had once pretended to be a priest in order to rob, and as the memory came back he earnestly wondered if he could do that again, logistically as well as morally.

"So now you will arrest me?" asked Elle. Surrounding them was a plethora of goods she had stolen. It was too much for such a small room, but the space was not cluttered, so much as crowded. The random collection had been organized to the best of her ability, utilizing shelves and boxes. Some of the goods she used, some she sold and some she traded for things she could not steal. Giving something away seldom entered her mind.

"What?" said Ford, whose initial confusion faded as he looked about him. "Oh, no, forget about that. I'm just doing this to make some coin. Nothing more."

"So, you give the answers and what they say?"

"Oh well, they all just sort of nodded and it looked like I was in, but then this one fella, the night-watch captain, an irritable looking son of a bitch, he says he recognizes me, and I figure it must be from what I done in the past and I'm thinking it's all over, but next thing I know they're handing me this thing!" Ford held up a two-foot-long, smooth oak club with a leather-wrapped handle and an iron band fashioned around the fat end. "Woulda come in handy back at that cave..." His voice trailed away as thoughts of their journey into the wilderness came back. "They didn't have one of them jerkins of theirs in my size, but they said one'll be ready for my first day." Shouting between the Dadha man and woman in the adjacent room nearly drowned him out.

"Bastard," Elle muttered at the wall.

"And they said I needed new trousers." Again, he doubled up his chin and adopted his new boss's manner of speech. "So as to reject well upon the offals of the watch!" Regardless of Ford fudging some of the words that escaped him, the return of the character got Elle laughing. It was subdued. Ford had been downcast since Yonn's tragedy, and Elle had caught his mood. But hearing her minute twittering brought out the joy in Ford. "Or some such nonsense. I don't remember what he said." After having his fun, he ran a hand over the threadbare and filthy material covering one thigh and sighed. "I guess they have seen better days."

"I will make the trousers for you."

"Will you? I didn't want to ask, but you do such good work."

Amongst the rolled-up cloaks and tunics, stacked hoods and hats, hanging hose and frocks, folded handkerchiefs, and jars and pots filled with hairpins, combs, decorative clasps, broaches, rings, bracelets, earrings and more, Elle located a neat pile of colorful fabrics in the corner of the room where the pitched roof brought the ceiling slanting down low. Needle and thread rested on top of the pile. Taking it all to the room's only window, she flipped through the folds in the light looking for one she liked.

Ford occupied himself by running his nose over a shelf of vialed scents. Unstoppering one with a yellow liquid, he drew in a deep breath and coughed. "What you hanging on to your piss for?"

"It's—"

"I know," he said, taking up another. "You think I'd open it if I didn't know?" He held the new one under his nose and sniffed a subtle, odor-neutralizing scent. "So that's how you're always smelling good."

"Put them down. You will break them."

"Which one of these you use for drink?" Ford asked peering into the three clay pitchers sitting next to her empty water basin.

"Any. All."

Ford grabbed up all three and headed out the door. Fetching water was the least he could do, considering she was putting him up for the night and perhaps for several nights until he got back on his feet. "Would you just...?" The door had a latch, a bolt, and a lock, rather intricate for the time, which Ford would have had trouble with even if his hands weren't full. The clicks and clacks might have been relatively silent, but the squeaky floorboard just outside the room sounded off like a cat whose tail had been trod upon. Just as Ford reached the top of the stairs, the door opposite Elle's shot open and out popped a slender man nearly as tall as Ford.

"Hello, Elle!" leapt from his long face, where thin lips and sleepy eyes could not hide his pleasure. Ford recognized the priest from the Sud a Waed grove where he'd woken up lying flat on his back. The young man's exuberance dissolved at the sight of Ford instead of the expected Elle, but the recollection instantly dawned on him as well, and his pleasant demeanor revived into a somewhat welcoming gaze as they greeted each other.

"Fine day! Good to see you again," Ford bellowed with an accompanying nod in lieu of a wave. In return, the priest raised a hand in which he held a jug, which he would have preferred to hide so that he might slip back into his room. However, it would have been absurd to pretend it hadn't been seen, so he joined Ford in gathering water downstairs in the lodging's kitchen.

"Met your skinny friend across the way," said Ford after getting back to the room.

"Willem he is called," Elle said. "Put those down and stand still."

"He was that priest there at that grove, wasn't he," said Ford conversationally while Elle took his measurements with a length of string. He reached over her, grabbed a jar of ointment, and poked his nose into it. "That's how you came to drop me off there."

"Do not touch my things. You will break them." She took the jar from him, affixed its lid and replaced it. "And do not sleep in my bed. You will break it." Ford thanked her again and reassured her he wouldn't stay long, just long enough to afford his own room. "Stay long if you need. I am not here all the day. I come, I go."

"I take that kindly. Hey, this is nice," said Ford reaching for and drawing his hand back from a thin ribbon with tiny green and gold oak leaves on a black background. It hung from a peg with other, plainer ribbons. "Reminds me of my clan colors almost."

"It's the only thing I have to remember my...what do you call...mother's sister."

"Aunt."

"Yes. Last I see her, she give it me."

Clearly this was more than a mere ribbon, and the significance it seemed to have for Elle did not escape Ford, but just then something else caught his eye. "Hullo, what do we have here?" A playful joy lifted each word at the sight of a bottle of liquor stashed behind the water basin on top of the table by the window. The vessel had been molded into a hare and horse hybrid creature, a pooka of legend made with impressive craftsmanship.

"How'd I miss this? Can I? Just a sip?"

Elle shrugged. "It is strong. For cuts and such things as this."

"All the better." Ford sat on the floor with his back against the bed frame, one of the finest bedframes he had ever seen, which wasn't saying much since he hadn't seen more than a handful that he could recall. A few sips from the pooka bottle later and he was by the door absentmindedly gazing up at a portrait of a woman with impossibly white skin, a mass of red hair atop her head, and the bearing of the immensely proud. She could have been more beautiful–a strong chin dwarfed her flat nose considerably–but if Ford had his way he would have been happy to go on drinking and gazing upon the picture for the rest of his life. Though seeing a person hold that unending pose, frozen in time forever, seemed spooky, all the same, he promised himself that he would have a picture made of his own loved one made one day, perhaps even himself. While the woman on the canvas was enticing in her way, it was the novelty of the object itself that enthralled Ford. Few people had portraits, and as small as it was, it still could have belonged only to someone quite wealthy. "Whoever you got this from must've been able to rub more than few coins together."

"They have much. Never they see it gone, I think."

That seemed logical enough to Ford, at least at first. Then he looked around him at all the things Elle had accumulated, and even though her loot was considerable, he knew she would notice if something went missing. He wasn't noticing much himself at the moment, other than that whatever had been in the bottle now seemed to be swimming about his head.

Elle glanced at him over her shoulder while cutting fabric in the window's light. "You come back. Why?" At first, she had been perturbed at having gone through all the trouble and expensive on his behalf only for him to suddenly and inexplicably change his mind, but she couldn't deny that she was glad he had come back. Still, it was a question she was too curious not to have answered and now that they were alone and at leisure, she decided to broach the subject.

"Eh? Oh, why the change in plans? I don't know. I mean, that is, I do, but..." he shrugged. "I don't know. I suppose it was something to do with that boy. Yonn. He said something to me. Made a lot of sense." Even if he hadn't been stewing in alcohol after a long day, his concentration would still have been distracted by the recent events. His hesitation grew general, pauses frequently. Sad little groans and sighs slid from him without him realizing it. "Smart kid. And brave. You wouldn't know by looking at some people, but they can surprise you." He took a long pull on the bottle, breathed deeply, let it out slow and steady, and then smiled at Elle. "And you, too. I couldn't leave you behind. Who'd look after you?"

She would look after herself. There was no need for anyone, just a desire for someone. She had done fine on her own for years now, and yet she was glad he wasn't going anywhere. None of this did Elle speak. A diligent focus upon her task was her only answer.

She made her first stitch at sundown and was crouching by a candle just before midnight when she ran out of thread. Off into the night, she slipped with Ford asleep on the floor and none the wiser about her comings and goings. With the sun just on the rise, she had completed numerous errands and had returned, but still without thread. In a flash of ingenuity, she realized she could use her stash of ribbon to complete the trouser seams, and with the final stretch of leg still remaining, she made the hesitating decision to use up every last bit of the ribbon, as much as it pained her to do so.

As Ford marched doggedly through the busier streets that afternoon with his chin up, he thought the laughter erupting around him seemed a little much, while those pointing at him were practically begging to have their teeth knocked out. The jibes that ranged from "Is your mum a canary?" to "Did you soil your trousers?" he took without retaliating.

The red shirt was one thing, but yellow would not have been his first choice if he'd had his pick of colors for new trousers. All the same, Elle had spent hours working on them and used her own prized fabric at no cost, so he could hardly complain. She had even sewed in a useful little pocket on one side. Still, in the poorer part of town where no one had new clothes and no one would have worn such a very bright yellow even if they could have afforded it, he stood out like a foreigner without the excuse of being one. But at least his clothes were clean and presentable for his first day on the job.

"A little tight though," he said, pulling at the material wrapped too snugly about his groin.

A wizened, slack-jawed laborer Ford had seen during the interview was scraping away with a frayed broom at the spotless floor when he arrived at the otherwise empty watchmen's guildhall. Even the furniture had been stacked away so that the large, red timbered main chamber echoed with Ford's footsteps and voice when he entered and asked for assistance. The wrinkled and sluggish man, the hall's keeper, either didn't hear him or kept on sweeping by way of ignoring him.

"Name's Ford. I'm one of the new watchmen. I start today. I was told to come for my jerkin? Where is everybody?" Mesmerized by Ford's appearance and befuddled by the questions, the keeper was of little help. He knew almost nothing, nor would he venture to explain Ford's duties to him, but he did have the presence of mind to give him his special watchmen's jerkin. Ford asked where he might find the Master of the Watch or the night captain. The keeper remained stunned by the brilliance of Ford's clothes and his mouth merely drooped for a time before the words "Derry Child" came out.

On his way out the door, while doing up the wooden buttons of his jerkin, Ford felt a sharp pain in his abdomen and found a pint-sized man had bounced off his midsection and fallen over backward down the front steps. "I'm real sorry about that!" he cried leaping down the steps and hoisting the thin, ghostly young man with a hangdog face back to his feet. "Are you all right?"

"Oh sure, I'm fine," said the man reaching for his backside, which had softened his landing.

"You don't look so good." Everything in the man's otherwise open and uplifted face was pale and harried.

"Am I too late, sir?" he asked, staring nervously through perpetually doleful eyes at the guildhall door while vainly struggling to escape Ford's vice-like grip upon his shoulders.

"Late for what?"

"I was hired as one of the watch only yesterday." He retrieved his watchman's jerkin from where he had dropped it and hurriedly put it on. "All the family's sick and I'm afraid I hadn't time to put it on. I'm afraid I'm late. I can't lose this posting, sir, please." Ford didn't doubt that the fading skeletal frame in his grasp could afford anything that would keep one more meal from his table. The man looked to be worse off than himself. The sight of him in his terrible agitation put Ford's worries into perspective and conjured a confidence that came out as a reassuring smile.

"Name's Ford."

"I'm Dillon, Dillon Baw."

"We're in the same boat, Dillon," Ford said while swatting the dirt from his new friend's backside and shaking the jerkin straight upon his shoulders. Dillon gave up the struggle against Ford's kindliness but didn't look much more reassured. "You got all your gear?"

"I think so, Master Ford."

"Do you know the Derry Child? I know it by name, but its whereabouts...I...." Ford looked around them as if he hoped the place might suddenly pop up. The only thing he saw was that the sun was going down.

"I know it. It's not far."

"Come on then! Hurry, and we might still be employed when we get there!" They rushed off, and Dillon led him around the block to where the unique sign of the Derry Child, a saucer-faced redheaded boy with freckles, that Ford immediately recognized. Being the closest tavern at hand to the guild, over time it had become the default meeting place of watchmen. Ford's porter duties had taken him by the place several times, but he had taken little notice of it since it was a quiet establishment on one of the more genteel streets in the neighborhood. However, it now rumbled with wide-ranging chatter mingled with disgruntled complaints and occasional wry laughter under a cloud of smoke that battled for supremacy with the sour smell of spilt beer. Though fairly clean and tidy, it was a snug hole of a barroom, and its few seats were taken up by watchmen and even higher city officials.

"There he is," Ford said to Dillon in an undertone by the door, "that sour-grapes captain of the night watch." The talk died to a whisper so that his last few words carried into the room, and the entire room turned its raised eyebrows and smirks full upon Ford to take in his attire.

"You're late," called the night captain across the room, beckoning them over. "My name is Weylon Whetstone. You check in with me every night before..." The bell at the nearby Temple of Awyr rang out. "Before that bell sounds." He turned to the room and called out, "The bell, gentlemen! Drink up," and casually gathering his possessions, he tightened his belt. "Old-timers partner up with the new lads. And lass," he said with a nod to Moll Turner, the one woman who had been hired for the night watch, a beefy-shouldered former drover. Looking around for someone to partner with, Ford stepped toward a salt-and-pepper bearded old-timer in a faded jerkin. Whetstone grabbed his arm. "You're with me."

The tavern cleared out in a hurry, leaving Ford rocking from foot to foot by Whetstone's table and wondering what they were waiting for when in walked a short-necked, wide-bodied woman with a patch over one eye. Ford recognized her from the interview as the day-watch captain. She dropped down on to a bench across from Whetstone, threw her hat on the table and scratched at her tangle of blond hair.

"Tough day?" Whetstone asked.

"A hog's hide of a day, but nothing unusual," she replied, pulling off her boots and stretching out her legs. Her drooping head and eyelids perked up slightly when the proprietor placed an ale in front of her. A brief, efficient exchange of noteworthy news passed between the captains, and then Whetstone was off with Ford in tow.

"Where's your torch?" Whetstone asked Ford out in the street.

"Torch?"

"Your lantern, boy! Didn't Alden give you one?"

"Who?"

"Alden the hall-keeper. The old duffer back at Lygade."

"Oh, no, he didn't give me nothing but this." Ford patted his jerkin.

"He's a good ol' fool, but either he's losing it or could be we're plain out of them. I wouldn't be surprised. That's what comes of hiring fast like that. You end up with no tools to do the job." Whetstone shook his head and seemed to be talking to himself before returning to Ford. "Worry not, we'll dig one up sooner or later. What's just as important as the tools is the knowledge to do the job right."

Night blotted out the day as they settled into a leisurely stroll, lighting every other corner lamp, filling those that needed it from an oil flask hanging from Whetstone's belt. Following a route the captain could walk in his sleep, he cordially introduced Ford to the few people they ran into along the way, while also giving Ford a rundown of a night watchman's duties and providing tips on how to do them well. "Mostly it's easy, just making sure nobody's up to no good. Should be easier now with all these extra hands."

"Is the rumor true?" Ford ventured to ask. "I mean, why they hired us all?"

"Clarify yourself, son."

"That the Iarl is dead?"

"Oh that. No, she's still alive as far as I know. Her cousin's wife is doing poorly though. She and the Iarl were out walking, just them and a house servant, so I hear, when all of a sudden they got mobbed. Someone threw a stone meant for the Iarl that caught the poor woman upside the head, the cousin I mean. But I suppose that's got something to do with why you all got hired, the trouble in the streets, I mean."

A shopkeeper called out to them and waved, upon which Whetstone explained that "Master Aelfgar likes to work late." Ford wondered aloud why someone would want to do the Iarl harm. Whetstone shook his head. "I don't know. Some say since her husband died she's fallen apart and so has the whole town, but I just don't know. Seems no one's to blame but the weather. Too much sun and now too much rain, it's killing the crops, and that's no good." The mist coming in from the sea rolled through the streets as it did most evenings, causing the lamplights under their charge to flicker. "The Pennaeth could do better, some say, and maybe they're right. What do I know? I'll tell you what I do know. If Brastersceatt took over, the Weaverites would move in and make big changes. They'd shut down all the brothels for a start. Some might say that's a good thing and perhaps it'd make our jobs all the easier, what with there being fewer bodies on the street at night. But I tell you what, you close down those houses and where do the patrons go? They go out and find what they're looking for in other ways and places, and that just might make a whole lot more problems, much worse problems that the likes of you and me got to deal with. No, thank you! Keep things as they are, I say. The Iarl's a good woman, and I'll always stand by her."

For a block's length, Ford absorbed Whetstone's words like a sponge. He liked the way the man spoke with conviction and filed away his confident manner as a trait worth emulating. However, what made a truly strong impression upon him was that Whetstone's convictions meshed so well with his own. Shutting down the brothels would be a terrible idea. He had sometimes doubted that this was a conviction rather than just a desire to see the trade continue. There was the fear, a minuscule one yet persistently floating about the rearguard of his thoughts, that perhaps his mother had turned prostitute for lack of more suitable work. After all, jobs were hard to come by, and for all he knew, she was an unskilled laborer like himself. Caught up in his own contemplations, Ford forgot he was walking beside Whetstone until the man broke into his ruminations.

"Now, as for why I hired you in particular," said the captain with a sidelong glance at Ford. "I wanted to see what you're made of, what kind of man you are."

"Me?"

"You. I've seen you around. I know about your past." Deny it, flee, or knock him over the head with the club, all three alternatives immediately sprang to

Ford's mind before Whetstone went on. "Calm yourself. You put in your work, keep your palms clean and you and me, we'll have no problems. You were hired, well, because look at the size of you. And besides, it's better to be on this side of the law than the other. Am I right?" Too busy recovering from the shock to hear the question, Ford dithered. "I said, am I right?" Ford nodded, and Whetstone decided he would have to keep an eye on the new recruit.

Some of the strain between them eased when they were greeted most merrily by a tipsy tavern owner closing for the night. However, happening upon the back half of a man stuck in an open window really wiped away the tension. Wearing the kind of knowing grin that said he had seen this before, Whetstone nudged Ford and pointed out the miscreant. Without saying a word, Ford grabbed the man's dangling legs and was surprised that he didn't seem alarmed in the least. After dragging him out of the window, he figured out why. The man was exceedingly drunk. He didn't appear to be the least concerned about being caught trying to rob a tobacco shop, and Ford wasn't concerned that he had been successful. The shop had closed up the year before, and he knew the stock was gone because he too had sneaked in to see if there was anything left of the dried leaves that brought such sweet comfort.

"What you got to smoke?" demanded the swaying drunkard after being safely set down on solid earth once more.

"Nothing," said Ford. The man fingered Ford's new jerkin and bright red shirt.

"Then go get some from your fancy friends." A mean little smile distorted his face, which suddenly planted itself squarely on Ford's chest. Ford scooped him up before he slid headfirst to the ground and they stumbled along with Whetstone arm in arm back to the drunkard's ramshackle house.

"Get 'em off the streets," said Whetstone over the screeches of the drunkard's equally decrepit wife as they left them behind. "Sometimes that's the best you can do."

"Let me in, woman!" shouted the drunkard a block behind them.

"You no good, lousy, feckless, dimwitted…" The wife went on and on until eventually fading away with the distance.

***

By the time dawn ushered in the new day, Whetstone hadn't uttered another word about Ford's past transgressions, and Ford relaxed enough to feel the aches from putting in a long night's work when normally he would have been asleep.

"This'll take some getting used to," he said to a fellow new recruit upon collapsing at a table at the Derry Child, where he lay his head down and promptly fell asleep. The next thing he knew, he was trying to blink his eyes clear and make out the face that belonged to the man poking his shoulder and saying his name.

"I beg your pardon friend. Should I come back later?" whispered Alan with a cautious glance around at the few other lounging watchmen, who like Ford had not made it home and had slept at the tables after their first night as watchmen. "I'm sorry to wake you." Ford sat up coughing and clearing his throat. The skinny writer leaned away.

"That'll happen when you prod someone like cattle." Alan apologized profusely laying a hand over his heart and stepping toward the door. "Stay! Stay. I'm awake now," said Ford rubbing at his eyes and massaging his forehead. "I'm sorry. Have a seat. It's good to see you, but how'd you find me?"

"Your friend Elle found me and told me how to find you."

"She gets around."

"She does."

"Wait. Why'd she go see you?"

"She wanted to talk to me about the Iarl's journal. She's quite keen to see it, which is unusual in someone who—correct me if I'm mistaken—can't read. Please, forgive me. I mean no slight in the least, but I admit, I thought it a bit odd." Ford didn't think it odd at all. He had a very good idea why Elle wanted to question Alan about a valuable object. Alan had plenty to say about their visit, being pleased as he was to find someone so interested in his work. However, with a headache coming on, Ford was glad when he eventually moved on to his true purpose, and the end of the conversation was in sight. "What I really came here for was to ask you for a firsthand account of your recent adventures."

"Adventures?" said Ford noticing for the first time that Alan held a quill and scroll. "Oh, our little walk in the woods?"

"Nonsense," said Alan. "It's more than that. Elle evoked entrancing images and scenes of daring that might a play be made of!"

"Perhaps," said Ford doubting very much that Elle had done any such thing, for she was not a woman prone to poetic flourishes. "Thing is…she tell you about the boy?" Ford kept his eyes on the table where his fingernail dug into the soft wood and pulled up a spongy splinter. More splinters came up as he explained what had happened to Yonn.

Alan expressed his heartfelt condolences and after a decent time, asked Ford to continue on with the whole story of their journey into the eastern hills.

"I'm not flush with coin these days, but I could stand you a drink and perhaps a lamb shank for the tale." That was a drink and a shank more than Ford had expected that day, and so he forced himself to relive the events once more. No sooner had the proprietor placed the lamb and ale on the table than Ford devoured his portion. While winding down his story, he was still licking his lips and so were a handful of the Derry Child's patrons, but for a different reason. They had gathered around the storyteller, and the scribe enraptured by the emotionally taxing conclusion of Yonn's horrible finish and had questions aplenty of their own when Ford casually mentioned handing over the monster's severed head to Dermot's people. He had to backtrack and explain how, having once witnessed the beheading of a vanquished foe during a border skirmish, he was merely mirroring the old warrior's code and exacting revenge for the dog-man's brutal slaying of his friend.

"Adeline asked for you," Alan said when the story finished, and the gathering broke up. He tried to say it with the nonchalance of an aside, busying himself with rolling up his papers and cleaning his quill, but he was a lousy actor and could not disguise that it had been his main reason for coming to see Ford. "It would seem she got it into her head that you are avoiding her."

Ford sank within himself and set aside the bone he had been gnawing. "Is that so?"

"Yes, though I reminded her that you had this, this thing you were doing." Alan shook the roll of papers. "But that didn't seem to pacify her. I tell you, she was nearly going out of her...she was quite worried about you. She stopped going to the Three Sheets entirely. The thing is, she's a bit on the delicate side. I'm not one to spread family secrets, but she has had some trouble in the past. Abandoned by loved ones, that sort of thing."

"Ah." Ford didn't know what else to say and wished Alan would stop. He wasn't at his best, and even if he were, all this talk still would have befuddled him, it being beyond the realm of his experience.

"She's easily hurt and"—here Alan lowered his voice—"this goes no further." Ford nodded. "She's easily upset if you know what I mean." Alan made the briefest of gestures toward his head and thought better of it. A flush of embarrassment spread over his cheeks, and he hurried from the tavern in a rush of words. "I'm off! Good to see you! Truly!"

Ford felt terrible. He hadn't given Adeline much thought recently, and now he wondered if he actually did love her. Alan had once talked about a thing called infatuation, and perhaps this was it. Certainly he had a tendency to fix upon women that were in front of him and forget about those who were not—even he had to admit that much. But no sooner had the thought formed than it was brushed aside by another. Now that he had work he would soon be in coin again, and he might see her once more on his own terms, feeling like someone of worth.

The original plan was to stay at the Derry Child until it was time for work. The tavern provided at least a feeling of safety. Better to spend as little time as possible traversing the streets where he might be picked up by Barker. On the other hand, there was the share he was owed from his cousin. If he could just make it to the Armory of Academia he would have more than enough to pay back Barker, maybe even throw in a bit extra as a sort of goodwill tax to smooth things over. And while there he could pop in and say hello to Adeline. Smooth things over with her as well. He liked the sound of this alternative plan. "If I can only make it there alive," he muttered as he stood in the doorway, that entryway to the many and long streets, he would have to walk alone.

Even if the tavern's proprietor were run off his feet, it would have been hard to miss six and a half feet of man in his doorway, his shoulders nearly touching either side of the frame. But it was the slow time of day, and he was at leisure to lean against his bar and observe the giant poking his head out the door as if looking for something up and down the street, leaning forward and retreating back, and then taking from the pocket of his ludicrously yellow pants a flattened flower that he seemed to caress just before dashing out the door with the sort of ridiculous grin only a loon would flash about in public. "Odd ducks come in all sizes," he said shaking his head and going back to work.

Ford was the embodiment of urgency and stealth on his way to the west side of town until he found himself mesmerized by the spectacle in Brastersceatt Square. The place was alive with a magnetic activity that drew a larger crowd than usually came to purchase the ruby red tomatoes and emerald green gourds. People mobbed the street performers found there: a girl conversing with her pet bird, a cat master, a man running circles about the square with silver-striped foxes trotting at his heels and weaving artfully between his legs, and the bear baiter rehashing his increasingly popular performance from the Horseshoe Inn. Some of them were natives of the Forest of a Thousand Names who had traveled all the way to Port Morton to take part in the festivities in celebration of the peace and harmony that flourished between the peoples of Aelwyd and the Forest. After dallying by a large, potted cucumber-shaped plant with the glistening, supple skin of a slug that was supposed to sing but was not at the moment, Ford realized he was allowing himself to be entranced at his own peril and finally dragged himself away from the entertainment and headed for the Armory.

That turned out to be just as much of a waste of time. He never did get in to see Danny, but rather had a frustrating and fruitless conversation with the door bat. Even if he had made it past the bat, Danny would not have had his share for him. The school wasn't ready to buy the stock of rue and valerian he had brought to them, and nothing had been discovered yet about the worth of the strange amulet.

Danny valued wealth for what it could do for him, but his true passion lay in learning and perfecting the craft of magic, so while Ford banged on the front door to no avail, Danny remained oblivious within as he was at most times, sitting at his table in his room absorbed in reading. "Yonn, hand me that…" he began; turning about and seeing the vacant bed and table swept clean of his lost friend's possessions, he realized anew that one of his very few friends in this world was gone. Turning back to his book, he sighed, and a tremor shudder broke it midway through.

In the clean, well-drained streets lined with inviting shops between the Armory and where Adeline roomed on an upper floor of a building owned by a mercer, Ford heard a wine crier calling out his review of a local winery's latest batch. The call died away behind him and was replaced by the shrieks of someone torturing a cat, or so it sounded to Ford. Loitering by the window from which the offending noise erupted, he caught a glimpse of a short-haired, clean-shaven man attacking with a stick a fiddle tucked under his chin, which produced the horrendous scratching racket.

Dismayed and glad to get his ears clear of the clamor, Ford hurried away with a pace doubled by the guilty realization that he had been dragging his feet once more. The reason why vaguely played about in the back of his mind and his bustle quelled the telltale nerves within him, but he knew he had neglected her and no one liked that, especially not those who held affection for you. Also, he was meeting her on her own ground, this affluent part of town that always made him feel inferior whenever he visited it.

Though he had never been further than the front door, the Mercer family knew of Ford and guessed the manner of his relationship with Adeline. When he walked into the shop the wife was holding up a broad piece of silk to the light, two daughters were folding linen, and the mercer himself had his tally slate in one hand while leaning nearly bent double over his accounts book. They all froze in the midst of their duties as their eyes shot to Ford and remained glued upon him as he spoke. The mercer blinked, sputtered and managed to spit out, "You're asking for Mistress Linkman?"

"That's right, I wanna talk…I would like to speak with her, if I may, please."

The girls tittered and the mother cast scorn at random. None of this was proper, in her opinion. The mercer, tenderly laying aside his slate, walked over to the foot of the stairs with a bent back and the hobble of one accustomed to sitting, and admitted, "She's up there…in her room." It was a statement, not an invitation. Guessing that one would not be forthcoming, Ford thanked him and dashed up. The family burst out in a bustle of confused babble.

"Wait! Wait!" shouted the mercer's wife up the stairs as she followed after him. "Wait!" He was sure she would try to stop him, and he didn't know what to do if she did, so he took the steps two at a time and pretended not to hear. "It's the top floor! The door straight away on the top floor! Not the second floor! Keep going!" Seeing she wasn't going to throw him out, after all, he let the red-faced woman catch up. "Not that door! All the way back!" She came to a clattering halt two steps down from the landing and leaned against the wall, her mouth agape and her chest leaping.

"This door?" asked an innocently smiling Ford, pointing to the first door on the second floor.

"No!" she gasped, and unable to say anything more, she flicked a finger up the stairs to the third floor.

As he began knocking on Adeline's door at the top of the stairs, the mercer's wife made sure the door by the landing below was still locked. It was, but she remained there leaning on it for support, nonetheless while watching him. As he continued knocking, Ford turned toward the woman and smiled down at her again, a little less assuredly. There was no return smile. Her arms were folded now and her face, a lighter shade of red, remained rigid.

"Addy?" No answer. He banged on the door, called out her name and banged some more. The door swung open a crack. With the tips of his fingers, he pushed it back enough to lean through and peer in. "Hello?" The shutters were closed, and he couldn't make anything out. Behind him he heard the mercer's wife's give a haughty huff as she finally descended the stairs.

"Adeline?" He pushed the door in another foot and took a half step forward. In the dark, he could barely pick out pieces of furniture: a bed, a chair, a table with something he assumed was her harp standing on it. There was movement by the chair, and a gaunt figure came into focus. "Hello." Having come all this way with all this time to come up with something, that was all he could think of to say, and so he repeated it. As his eyes adjusted to the dark, he was able to take in her rigid form, the one hand resting on the back of the chair, the other on her stomach and her features, though mostly indistinguishable, appeared drawn and pale with pinched lips and narrowed eyes, as if disapproving of his very existence. Her moody silence filled the darkness and oppressed the stifling atmosphere of a room perfumed to cover the underlying stench of sickness. The wheels of his mind turned faster and faster to come up with the right thing to say and suddenly ground to a clanking halt. Even if he had come up with something he wasn't sure he could trust his tongue. Turning on his heel and leaving without a word seemed a better alternative to saying whatever came out of his mouth.

"So, you're alive," she said as if speaking of the weather.

"Uh, yeah. Yes."

"That's very good for you." She was being deliberately aloof, which was not uncommon for her, but this was as cold as he had ever seen her.

"Yes," he replied and hearing it he thought his tone sounded too light and self-congratulatory, but any amount of hubris would have seemed smug in the circumstances. She receded back into the shadows. A long, nervous pause ensued before he finally found his voice again. "I went away—"

"You certainly did!" her disembodied voice stabbed out from the darkness.

"I mean, I was away from town."

"I know." It was the first thing she said that wasn't coated in ice. Grasping at the hint of warmth, Ford's tongue loosened and he launched into an explanation that evolved into a retelling of his journey. Overall it was short and to the point, although when he got to Yonn's death, he caught her sharp intake of breath and her nails digging into the back of the chair, so he lingered on the scene to his immediate gratification and shame.

She took a hesitant step forward wanting to read his face, then darted for the window and flung open the shutters. The light streaking across the room struck him head to toe, and he threw up a hand to deflect the glare. The bottom of the diamond-patterned robe wrapped about her under a matted fur cape swished along the floor up to him. Taking his tightly-curled, sweating hand into hers and peeling away the white-knuckled fingers of the other from around the door, she led him into the room like a mother cajoling her shy child in to see the doctor, studying him all the while with penetrating eyes as she placed him in the chair by the table, knelt down beside him and laid her hand on his knee.

"Go on," she said, and the sour smell on her breath made Ford turn away to hide his grimace. She began caressing his knee and her face contorted in an anguish she had made all her own as she looked up into his eyes with pity. He devoured it and began embellishing the tragedy, drawing both of them into the sad story for his own selfish purpose until a nauseating guilt sprouted within him and he had to stop. Feigning to look out the window, he massaged the aching muscles of his tight forehead. Adeline all but swooned at what she took for a deep sorrow and pressed her lips to the back of his hand. At first his whole arm seized up, but it began relaxing as the realization came over him that perhaps no words were needed, only action, and this he could do. He stood and lifted her to her feet. Her shoulders drooped, her cape slid off, and she gripped his arms with her cool, bony fingertips.

Arm in arm, they shuffled across the room, but when the bed brushed against the back of her legs, she swung away from him, her long face registering mistrust. Mute and confused, he watched her slide across the room to her harp. Wrapping it in her arms, she sat and played a slow song so piercingly sad as to accentuate her strange aloofness and utter detachment and stun him into an immediate depression.

"I didn't know if you were alive," she said after into a repetitive succession of descending notes that sucked the desire to live right out of him. Right then he caught a glint of steel from a short, thin-bladed knife next to her elbow on the table. "Or if you just stopped loving me," she said with a cracking voice and hands that trembled. The whole conversation might as well have been spoken backward for all Ford was able to cope with it. He could think of nothing else to do, but walk up behind her, slide the knife behind a bowl, slip the harp from her hands and lift her by the arms to guide her back to the bed. She spun around, pulling him down next to her, lust morphing her face yet again, like an actor donning masks in a bizarre play. "Don't leave me like that again," she pleaded and pecked at his cheeks and chin with her cold and chapped lips.

"I won't," he replied as he lifted her chin and kissed down the front of her neck like he did with the prostitute who would perfume her plunging neckline with a sweet scent. She closed her eyes and exhaled an absurdly drawn-out sigh. He laid her back against the bed, hovered over her and drew back the robe stuck to her from the cold sweat covering her pale body.

"Tell me—," she began, but he sealed her lips with his own. When she subsided, he buried his face in her hair, kissing behind her ear where the sick, unwashed smell was strong. "Never..." she said, her voice quivering. "Never leave me wondering." He leaned back. Her eyes were glassy and darting with an ungovernable energy from his left to right eye.

"What?"

"If you love me."

"No," he replied and went back to the front of her neck.

"I love you," she said, twisting around, climbing on top of him and staring down into his eyes for an answer. He craned up for a kiss, and she leaned back. He pulled her down and jammed their lips together. She pulled away, inhaling deeply and flashing a grin full of pleasure that just as quickly fell away. "I love you," she repeated with deliberate emphasis on each word. He flipped her over on to the bed. She let out a tiny involuntary screech, covered her mouth and giggled like a girl half her age as he rolled on top of her. "Tell me you love me." The fingers he was using to brush away the hair and caress her face ran over her lips. She took them into her mouth and sucked on the tips, while he grabbed one of her arms and nibbled his way down along the tender flesh. She squirmed up the bed and whispered, "Don't stop." Back up the arm went his lips and then his tongue slid down her collarbone. He blessed the education he had received at the city's brothels as the tip of his tongue licked along her shoulder and down her chest to the inside of her breast.

Carrying all the way from the shop below, the distant voice of the mercer's wife snapped Adeline out of the moment. She forced up his head up and met his eye. "You didn't say it. Why won't you say it?" Her eyes wrinkled at the corners, making her look every bit her age and more. They went glassy, then filled with tears, making Ford's heart sink. She read the despair in his face and perked up. "Oh, did you already say it and I forgot? I've forgotten, haven't I? I am a scatterbrain sometimes. It's fine, you don't have to say you love me again. I know you do." He grunted a vague affirmation and buried his face between her breasts. Her voice, serious again, burrowed into his ears, "But don't ever leave me. I couldn't bear it. Do you promise me? Do you? Don't make me beg." Cracking an uneven smile, she tried to giggle again, but it came out false, a laugh forcing its way through a crying spell. When Ford didn't respond, she jerked his head up by the hair with shaking hands. "Do you?" He avoided her wet, jittery eyes, but even turning away, he couldn't help notice the tears running down her red cheeks. "Please—."

"I do. I do."

Her whole body relaxed beneath him in a sigh of contentment. She pulled up his tunic, and her hands moved up and down his chest and over his black and blue abdomen, still painful to the touch from the wound he received at Larkwine's Cave. Wincing, he grabbed her wrists, entwined his fingers in hers and held her hands down on the bed.

"Yes. Bed me like a whore." Once inside her, he tried to take it slow, but she bucked against him with rapid, erratic thrusts that threw off his rhythm. "Call me mommy." The murmur in his ear sapped what little passion he had mustered to that point.

"What?" he asked, and now he was the one delving into her eyes for answers.

"Call me Mommy, if you'd like. I don't mind." His stomach lurched at the sight of her knowing smirk.

When he bolted from the mercer's front door without saying a word to the astonished family and hurried down the street hunched over and withdrawn, the sun was going down at an alarming rate. Cutting into the first cross-street he came to and slowing down, he threw a nervous glance over his shoulder before stopping to take hold of a cart for support while he caught his breath and wiped the sweat from his brow. Oblivious to the world around him, his mind whirled about with images and sounds, the freshest of memories he knew he would not soon forget. They echoed and bounced off his present thoughts: the cajoling, the crying, the begging; the insinuations of self-mutilation, and the threats of worse. It was like nothing he had ever witnessed. "Why did I go? And why did I stay?" He shook his head at the thought of lying in her bed, holding her in his arms while she rested fitfully, shivering one moment while breaking out in a muck sweat the next. "Worse, the promises." He had promised to see her the next day and said many things just to getaway. How much of it would come back to haunt him, he dared not think.

When finally able to face the present again, he released his iron grip on the edge of the cart and leaned his back against it, wiping his forehead again. "I need a smoke or a drink...what's this?" A woman's lacy handkerchief dangled from his fingertips. Stifled chuckles grabbed his attention. Not ten feet away, the Butcher of Flank Street, the infamous barber-turned-mender, had quit his conversation with an alchemist outside of his shop and both men were gawking at him, bemused. With his wits and heart rate more manageable, Ford took in a deep, steadying breath, tossed away the handkerchief, stood tall, and marched back down the hill.

"Mad! Mad!" he shouted as he trod across the timbers of Weald Bridge. Two men walking in the opposite direction shied away from the wild-looking young man coming at them like a craze-blinded bull. When he picked up his pace, the men were prepared to leap into the river to escape as he trotted by them. His trot turned to a run through Brastersceatt's Square and the streets beyond until he barreled through the door of the Derry Child just as the chiming temple bell died away.

CHAPTER 13
PROBLEMS AND SOLUTIONS

People. Plenty of people. That was what he wanted around him, thought Ford as he left the safety of the tavern and the night watch dispersed into the streets, leaving just him and his new partner, a man whom Whetstone had described the night before as "something you want to scrap off the bottom of your boot soon as you can." The warning came with an apology. "Fact is, I been looking to pair him with someone like yourself, a big guy. He needs keeping in line. The belt around his brain's a little loose," Whetstone had laughed, "but he does his job thorough. Some would say too thorough for his own good. You'll see."

"Grant?" Ford had asked with a thrust out hand when they first met.

"Gerrant," replied his new partner with insistent emphasis. Ford stared at him. He was sure that's what he had just said. Whether it was a joke or a word game, he could only wonder while they grasped each other's wrists in the usual greeting. Gerrant jerked his arm back and forth, trying his hardest to rip Ford's from the socket. Ford hardly noticed anything aside from Gerrant's slicked-back, stringy head of hair.

Determining his age was nearly impossible from his lined and lumpy contorting face. Squinting and twitching were to him as breathing was to everyone else and he would have bouts wherein he puckered his lips, wrinkled his nose and snuffled repeatedly as if working at an inward itch. His whole body seemed to itch at some point. Often, even within their first hour together, Ford witnessed him scratching at his backside. Before half the night was through Ford could no longer look at the man. His jerky movements were too disconcerting.

Whetstone had found an extra lantern, which Ford now held aloft as they canvased the streets lighting the lamps in their section of town, a strip of streets that ran through a respectable if not well-to-do neighborhood down to the river and part of the dockyards.

"Hold up, pup," said Gerrant pressing a hand against Ford's chest in an attempt at holding him back. The presumption that he could lay hands on him in a blatantly disrespectful manner might have angered Ford if he had been arrogant himself, but as it was, he barely noticed, aside from a slight annoyance. With his perpetually puffed out chest and the platform shoes that gave him two more inches of earnestly desired height, everything about Gerrant, including this straining attempt at manhandling Ford, seemed more comical than anything. And in the end, the reason for it proved to be nothing of consequence. While Ford waited, Gerrant made him hold his lantern as he took out a comb, dipped it in the lantern oil, flicked the excess off, and ran the comb through his hair. Ford had never seen such a thing. Then again, he couldn't remember ever seeing a man use a comb before either.

"I don't like working with a partner. I never got used it, and I don't like it." Gerrant made the declaration and pouted like a grumpy child while staring Ford up and down before finishing his combing.

"Is that so?"

"It is," Gerrant affirmed, but it was an affirmation weakened by distraction. "Come on!" The brilliance of recognition in his eye and urgency with which he spoke said to Ford that Gerrant must have spotted someone up to no good, so he raced after him up the street to the steps of a temple.

"Hey! Hey, you there! What are you up to?" cried Gerrant, and by the end of the night Ford would be sick of hearing those words. *In the early evening, give them a chance to get to where they're going.* These were Whetstone's words, his code of conduct. Either he hadn't told Gerrant, or Gerrant was making up his own code. This time he was shouting it at a young acolyte, who was unlatching the hooks that held the temple's shutters open.

"The—" started the determined temple assistant with an exasperated wave, but Gerrant cut him short and questioned his right to be at the temple. The acolyte said it was his job, Gerrant doubted him, and the two argued the inconsequential matter longer than necessary.

Thus began a tedious night of aggravating citizens, the likely cause of Gerrant's two black eyes Ford guessed, and he was right. The fading purple crescent bags under his partner's eyes were the result of getting his nose punched recently by someone who thought he had taken his nosiness too far.

"Goddamn, Gloinites. Miscreants one and all," grumbled Gerrant when Ford was finally able to cajole him away. Until they ran into the next unfortunate passerby, Gerrant spent the time extolling his religion, Weaverism, and damning all others. Anyone who worshipped outside of his chosen faith was a miscreant. "They're all out to steal and rob, all of them. We ought to send them along with the thieves to Polecat Island."

"Eh?"

"Polecat Island! Don't tell me you never heard of Polecat Island?" Gerrant's gremlin smile contorted with his writhing shoulders in the giddy excitement of holding knowledge over the head of another. "I can't believe you never heard of Polecat Island!"

"You gonna tell me about it or no?" The name did sound vaguely familiar, but Ford was too tired and was already too exasperated with his partner to think beyond the here and now. Eventually, he pulled out of Gerrant that it was an island somewhere out in the sea where some petty criminals such as common thieves were sent if their crime was deemed less serious than punishable by death.

"It's a prison island. Have you ever heard of such a thing? That pussy willow of an Iarl is just afraid to cut off some hands and hang a few people is all. It's a mistake. They should all be executed. A criminal's a criminal. None of them are no good. They get off light. The place shouldn't be. Shouldn't be a place for folks like that. The rope's the only thing for the likes of them! You've really never heard of Polecat Island?" Ford shrugged. "I can't believe you've never heard of it!"

Ford couldn't believe that this was his life now, stuck out here night after night with this irritating fool. He endured another hour of it before he needed a break and suggested they split up for a while.

"Can't," Gerrant blurted out adamantly while his nose went into a spasm of twitching. It was true that the watchmen had been warned to stick together until further notice.

"Just for a street or two, to cover more ground quicker." It was something Whetstone had done with him the night before in order to be more effective. If Whetstone was willing to bend the rules, Ford was all for it.

"We can't!" barked Gerrant. For someone who professed not to like partners, it didn't seem like he wanted to be parted from his.

"It'll be fine. I'll just slip down this road here and meet you on the other side." They were at an intersection of numerous small roads, lanes, and alleys. Ford knew he was pushing it, but he thought if he started small, he could lengthen the time spent away from Gerrant in the future; he'd do anything to get away from him for even a short while. Finally he hit on the right note for his audience. "We stand a better chance of catching them damn miscreants."

Soon after, Gerrant was headed alone down the main road that cut through their section of town, while Ford stepped into a road that forked away. At the next cross street, he would cut back across to the main road. That was the plan, but Ford thought he might stretch it out a little, perhaps tell Gerrant later that he had seen something suspicious in another lane that branched off. He could turn the detour into a nice quarter-hour reprieve.

When he came to that next cross street, he saw a block ahead of him three hefty men in long-coats cross on their way toward the docks. One of them halted and stared back. Ford froze. All three men stopped and watched him. Ford took to his heels and nearly ran headlong into Gerrant.

"That was quick. Did you see anything?"

"No, nothing." But as he said it, Ford kept throwing worried glances over his shoulder.

"See," said Gerrant while hitching up his trousers and puffing out his chest. "I told you. There's no sense in it. We stay together from now on." Ford nodded vigorously. "What are you looking at?"

"Nothing. Nothing." Ford tried to regain his composure, but even once he had relaxed a little, the feeling of shame and embarrassment of having run back to Gerrant remained. Just moments before, he wouldn't have imagined welcoming Gerrant's company, and yet here he was doing just that. "Let's move on to the next street over. I thought I heard something." As he led his partner away, it was behind them that he listened for approaching danger.

The sun was still working its way over the horizon that morning when Ford slammed shut the door to Elle's room and threw home the bolt. She wasn't in, so he collapsed on her bed and tried to fall asleep. It was useless. His nerves were still too rattled, and thoughts of when and how he would get his share from his cousin spun in circles in his agitated mind. Then there was the promised return visit to the madwoman Adeline. To cap it all off, the neighbors were yelling at one another as they were oft-heard to do. Mostly it was the man shouting long and loud enough to distract Ford's thoughts. Yet when one of them eventually left for work, his mind went blank in the relative silence and he fell asleep.

In what seemed no more than the blink of an eye he was awakened once more to what sounded like the neighbors again, but now it seemed as if they were carrying on their squabbles in Elle's room.

"Damn you!" came a woman's cry. He pried his eyes open and jumped to see Elle hovering over him with the look of someone absolutely prepared to end another's life. "Get out!" she shouted. He flopped out of her bed, and either that or his painful thump upon the floor, perhaps both, appeared to mollify her a great deal.

"My clean sheets and blankets and pillow," she bemoaned under her breath. Through the groggy haze of his waking senses, Ford noticed that even after she had gotten over his abuse of her hospitality, she still seemed out of sorts as if disturbed by some other underlying agitation.

"You upset?"

"No," she said.

"You seem upset."

"No!" she snapped back.

"Of course not, but what's wrong?"

She sat heavily upon the edge of the bed and blew out a long breath to keep her temper at bay. For a friend, Ford could be quite trying at times with his prying, she felt. Then again, the necessary secrecy of her trade could be tiring, and the idea of unburdening herself at this moment seemed sublime. "It is the…I am to do a thing, *the* thing I said of before. I must. They say 'you must!' so I must." She shrugged.

A little slow on the uptake as he was at this early hour without having had all that much sleep, her main point had not thrust home. He picked himself off the floor, plopped down onto a crate and rubbed his eyes with his palms. When it came to him, the realization felt like a slap. "Don't steal that book. Do *not* steal that book!" Thinking of nothing else to say, he said it again, each repetition rising farther from request to demand. He stood. He stood over her. He pointed down into her face. This was going too far, and he knew it, but he couldn't stop himself. There was too much at stake. "If you do this and get caught…what happens? They'll come and take you and hang you!" He waved around the room. "They'll take all of this and then where will I be?"

"You?" she cried. The implication that she would be caught irritated her, but because of the underlying concern for her wellbeing, she endured his loud tirade up to that point. Now she grew angry. "Always you think only *you*!"

"I do not!"

She dodged around him and fled the room before he could say another word. By the time he pulled open the door again, she had already disappeared down the stairs. "Fine! Hang for it!" he shouted down the stairwell.

Back in the cramped room, he stalked back and forth like a bear in a cage. After treading on the framed picture that had fallen after the slamming of the door, he hung it back up just so and then nudged it crooked to one side. Dropping on to her bed onto his back, he thought about what had just taken place, trying to work it all out in his mind. Then he flapped his arms about to mess up the blankets.

After giving the whole scene more consideration, he thought that if he had had a little more sleep, he could have handled it better. But sleep would not come now, even though that was all he wanted. The hours passed, and he went on thinking. Occasionally new problems arose from the dispute, such as getting their share from Danny. He was going to ask her to go see him. She had means, more than he, to get such things done. The chances of that happening seemed slim now.

"If only she'd stayed," he said, getting up to stare into the eyes of the portrait, "we could've threshed it out. Stubborn fool." Not an hour later his image of her went from stubborn fool to someone who would likely see sense soon enough. "After she gives it a good-think she'll see I'm right and come around." Such a comforting thought nearly sent him drifting off to sleep, but as his eyelids flickered, the notion that she might do the job that very night stirred him once more. The idea festered into a palpable fear that only slightly relented to the worry of not getting to work before the temple bell. Already a dislike was mounting for that bell. From the window he got a better gauge on the sun. There was still time, but he couldn't risk cutting it as close as he had the night before. Whetstone had not been pleased.

Whetstone.

Ford's face lit up. An instant later, elation propelled him from the room and down to the Derry Child where he found Whetstone drinking ale and staring out a window while toying with a small wooden figurine he had bought for his daughter.

"I want to turn in a thief," he said clear and loud to his captain.

CHAPTER 14
BETRAYAL AND THE BREAD OF LIFE

"Hey! Hey, you there! What are you up to?" Gerrant was at it again. For all the pride he took in his work and the strategies he came up with to entrap victims, such as opening unlocked doors and leaving them ajar to tempt people, he could be incredibly unaware at times. The moon was pressing on that night when he and Ford came upon a lone man shouldering a heavy sack through an unlit back street straight from the docks.

"I'm sorry for being about late, sir, but it's the family's washing, sir," said the haggard man sounding worn from the labor of his bulging load. Gerrant stepped into his path.

"Is that so?" he said, poking the sack with his club so that it unbalanced, toppled off the man's back and thudded upon the ground.

"Whatchu go and do that for?" shouted the man.

"Awful heavy for washing," said Gerrant.

"It's still wet and packed in there tight." The man staggered as he hefted the load back on to his shoulder.

"All right then," said Gerrant, suspicion draining off him like water from a duck's back. "Off you go and be quick about it!"

The man fought down a grin as he politely bowed to Gerrant and stepped around him to disappear into the night. If that wasn't a pilfered sack of flour, then Ford had never seen such a smooth and heavy bag of clothes. He might have said or done something, but since the man had come up from the docks, there was a distinct possibility one or more of Ford's dockyard friends like Stocky might be in on the theft for a kickback. Besides, Ford had far too much on his mind to be bothered with Gerrant's trifling. There was Adeline to consider, he hadn't even resumed the search for his mother yet, and now all this mess about Elle.

At the rotting corner of a sailor's tavern on the far western edge of their route where the streets opened up somewhat to the docks and where they were most likely to happen upon the watchmen running the routes on either side of them, they did indeed bump into the pair that canvassed the area to the north. Of the two, the one with the more agile wit and tongue spoke of theft from a merchant ship moored at the docks.

"Looks like the ship's watch was paid off and they got away with a few sacks of flour," he said. Ford shook his head.

"We'll do more than shake our heads! We'll find them and have them thrown in the Hold," said Gerrant, shaking a raised fist. He referred to the gray stone monolith-like Stanrocc Hold, the keep-turned-prison that towered above all the other buildings along the waterfront.

With some true miscreants to track down, for most of the remaining night, Gerrant was in an upbeat mood. Not only that, but he was also looking forward to the following day. "There's going to be a hanging tomorrow!"

"What?"

"Are you deaf? A hanging! At dawn! Don't tell me this is the first you heard of it!" The festival in honor of the Forest folk still carried on in the streets, and he was missing most of it. His friends he hadn't seen in days and in some cases weeks. Working all night and sleeping most of the day, while spending the rest of the time cooped up in Elle's room, Ford knew almost nothing of the town's news and was forced to rely on an odious source like Gerrant for information.

When he wasn't kicking the homeless or worrying a curious old woman back into her home, Gerrant talked excitedly about the coming day. He reminisced about past hangings he had enjoyed, the erection of the gallows earlier in the day, how Roolf Atwater the hangman had taken the job in order to get out of being hanged himself, and endless things more.

Ford did his best to block out his partner's incessant nattering and in a surprising way, found it only made matters worse. Ignoring Gerrant left quiet, fertile spaces for his thoughts to develop and expand, and fairly soon he was doubting that he had done right by turning in Elle. His plan appeared asinine upon reflection. At the very least, he knew he hadn't thought it through carefully enough.

If they broke into her room, the preponderance of accumulated loot suddenly seemed well above what could be described as petty theft. The portrait alone was worth more than anything he had ever possessed and could be a hanging offense, he worried. "Some friend you are!" Whetstone had laughed when Ford gave her up to him as a thief, and he was right. Ford knew he had been a terrible friend, and it tore at him because he valued few of his friends more than Elle. And now to discover a hanging was scheduled for the very next morning nearly sent him running off into the night in search of her or Whetstone.

"Yes," he blurted out and ignored Gerrant's questions. If he could find Whetstone, he could call it off, say it had all been a mistake. He almost bolted, but the realization that it was too late for that set in quite quickly. Whetstone would not simply forget information about a career criminal because Ford asked him to. Finding Elle was not likely to happen either. Since joining her guild, she was seldom home at night. There was nothing to do but wait. Dawn would come soon. It could not come soon enough.

Risking being fired for not checking in at the Derry Child, Ford ran with the kind of unbridled impetus he had not felt since he was a boy. Sweating and his pulse pounding, he stumbled up the stairs to Elle's room. When he didn't find her there, he tumbled back down to the streets and along to the one place his troubled imagination said she could possibly be.

Seldom had Brastersceatt Square ever been as packed as it was that morning. Ford wished he had his club on him to clear a path through the crowd, but it was back in Elle's room. His watchman's jerkin, which he still wore, impressed none in the excited mob. He could stand at the back like the rest of the late arrivals for all they cared. Only his bulk got him partially through some of the crowd before the mass would move no more. Wanting sleep and footweary, he gladly leaned on shoulders and let himself be held up by the press of bodies, their babbling voices gathering to a deafening waterfall of thousands that crashed in echo off the high surrounding walls of the tall houses from which sheets and handkerchiefs waved in the hands of gleeful onlookers dangling from the windows.

Off to the right of the gallows platform, in front of the House of Brastersceatt stood a hastily erected grandstand that provided exorbitantly priced seating for the wealthy. This moneymaking venture was overseen by a decrepit though impressively industrious aunt of the Pennaeth's, along with her grandson and a burly nephew to provide muscle. The raised seating obstructed the view of some, but she had a right to her grandstand just as the Pennaeth had a right to hang criminals. Rights or no, some questioned why he would choose this day, in the middle of the Iarl's planned festivities, for a mass hanging.

Though standing far from the gallows, Ford had a head of height above most of the throng, affording him a decent view. Even so, he still could not see Elle or tell if any of the prisoners had even arrived yet. An assemblage of officials waited on the gallows platform, and Ford was surprised to see among them the broad-rimmed wicker hat and diminutive figure of Tintot Song. He seemed to be speaking to the crowd, but little could be heard at this distance.

And at any rate, a rising blare and beat of horns and drums now drew everyone's attention to the river.

Cries and pointed fingers shot toward a jubilant mass packed around a wagon rolling over Weald Bridge into the square. On the wagon, a man with feet bound sat upright on top of a coffin in the center of a small forest of upraised pikes and spears. A crowd was already following the wagon, and some from the square rushed on to the bridge to join the procession.

"There's so many they'll collapse the thing," laughed someone nearby.

"What is it?" a few wondered and smug folks were thrilled to give the knowing answer that it was Lem "Long Knife" Sorley, the infamous robber known for galloping about the countryside on a ferocious black steed terrorizing the roads leading to Port Morton, sometimes with his cutthroat gang, but often alone. Taking advantage of her due privilege to ride the wagon was his captor standing like a grand statue behind him. Myranna Holyoak, a woman with a mountain range for shoulders set either side of a jaw so strong and sharp it looked as if it could cut rock, had brought Sorley in alive and on her own.

"They been driving that cart all round Brynseht since first light," called out a fisherman, who usually woke earlier than most, but who had eschewed work that morning upon catching sight of the wagon being loaded with the prisoner. "All through the hills over yonder like a regular parade!"

The crowd in the square surged like a sluggish mudslide toward Sorley to get a closer look, and from the crush of bodies a cry occasionally rose above the din. The congestion at the back eased enough to let Ford and his neighbors push closer to the gallows.

All were not jubilant. Fragments of heckles, clipped insults and the occasional boo and hiss mingled with the cheering and the general festive atmosphere creating a chaos of sound that intensified as the wagon pulled closer to the stage. Some called out the prisoner's name and wished him luck in the afterlife. Some called out his name and cursed it, while longing for some soft fruit or rotten vegetable to hurl for good measure.

Sorley stood out clearer now, dressed in a clean, bright blue cloak with wildflowers overflowing his new hat, tucked into his waist and strewn all about the wagon. A sleek black horse on a short lead tied to the back of the wagon clopped along behind flanked by a small group of men and women dressed in black, openly weeping and occasionally crying out in studied anguish. Sorley ignored the mourners and stood to bow to the howling horde a few times, then smiled as he waved to them with his one good hand. As an afterthought, he waved his stump and broke out in a wide impish grin as the audience laughed at his jest. His antics were repeated twice more to his audience's growing delight before the wagon, slowly passing through the parting crowd, jerked to a halt beside the gallows.

When Sorley was let down from the wagon by the guards and disappeared from view, there was a great push forward as the people jockeyed for a better view. Arguments, shoving, and isolated fights broke out, for many of the onlookers had grown surly with waiting and killing the time with drink sold by enterprising tavern owners with the capacity to wheel kegs to the outskirts of the square.

The guards shielded their prisoner and led him safely through the riotous folk surrounding them. Fists, stones, and slurs were flung at them, and it was hard to tell who was the intended target. Approaching the rickety set of slapdash steps, Sorley motioned to his bound feet and asked of the guards, "Would you help me up? I would hate to fall and break my neck and deprive the hangman of his fee." Upon reaching the raised platform, however, all of his remaining frivolity left him and his smile faded. Though paling fast, he held his head up and placed his stump upon his chest in a solemn prayer, unintentionally eliciting quite a few guffaws.

The sight of the Warden of Justice and Forfeiture standing before the prisoner, unrolling a scroll and reading from it quieted the crowd to a murmur, allowing a few of his words to carry to the farthest points of the square. "The waylaying of…carrying away…assault on a…pilfering the small clothes of the ladies of…lock breaking and entering…many a count of horse thievery…murder."

The hangman then led Sorley to a short flight of movable stairs placed at the front of the platform just below a dangling noose. Sorley stopped the hangman, speaking a few private words with him before ascending the short steps with little help and placing the noose around his own neck. When it could not be tightened sufficiently with the use of only one hand, the hangman offered his deferential assistance. With surprising suddenness and violence, Sorley threw himself off the steps in an attempt to snap his own neck. The framework of the gallows shook, and though both it and the rope held, the plan failed, and the prisoner swung in a wide arc over the front of the crowd, kicking his legs so that the backs of his heels came back and struck the steps, toppling them over backward. The shocked hangman and guards rushed forward, righted the steps and drew them back. A collective gasp seemed to strip the square of air and sound, the eerie quiet broken by individual shouted insults or sobs, while the audience watched Sorley's thrashing body twist and twitch. At one point, Ford stepped aside as an agitated mother carried her swooning child out of the crowd. One final paroxysm and the body went limp, swaying gently at the front of the stage.

Even before the last of Sorley's convulsions, the other convicted criminals were led up to the gallows to have their crimes read out: grand-scale theft of various kinds, usually of livestock and other sorts of property; a very controversial case of illegal sacrifice; an assault and rape leading to the death of the victim; and a grain speculator profiting off the misfortunes caused by the drought, a crime which had once warranted a steep fine, but now carried a death sentence. Each criminal was tied to a new rope along the gallows and hanged one after another.

Though he had hated hangings ever since the first he had witnessed, this was what Ford had come for. So far all was well, but at the sight of the fifth prisoner, Ford's heart leapt into his throat. He couldn't breathe. He could only stare. Walking up the steps, before his unbelieving eyes, he swore he saw Neb Towns, an outlaw, and murderer, with whom Ford had once been forced to band together for a short while. The last time he had seen him they had wanted to kill one another. But that had been years ago, and this man had let his hair grow out. A wiry beard covered his mouth and hair disguised his eyes so that Ford could not make out Neb's scarred lip or heavy brow. Still, Ford would not soon forget the man and the evil he had wrought upon his friends. He hoped not only that it was him, but also that he suffered long at the end of that rope.

Each subsequent convict led up to the platform, tightened his chest and squeezed at his throat until his breath came in short gasps with the anticipation that this one might be Elle. Most of them were men, but at this distance it was sometimes hard to tell. Eyes will play tricks on you, Ford thought as he squinted all the harder. Not only was he having difficulty identifying them at this distance, but when their names were called out, Ford sometimes misheard or missed them altogether. When the name of the man he thought might be Neb was read out, Ford strained to listen, but someone between him and the scaffold shouted something, and he didn't catch it. Even if he had heard, it was possible a different name would have been read out, since Neb Towns was the outlaw's pseudonym.

After six had been hanged, the gallows was full, and a delay had to be endured until they were confirmed fully dead. "Get cracking!" or "Whip it along!" some called over the wailing of family members watching the end of their loved ones. Such shouted complaints piled one on top of the other and unnerved the officials on the platform. Though some did grow genuinely impatient, to their credit most were not blatantly callous. This was gallows humor, that dark mirth birthed in the face of inhuman despair. Much of it came from those close to the front who had just started their day by witnessing horrendous death in a particularly personal way, as personal as could be without being victims themselves. A random lull in the rambling cacophony quieted the square for a fleeting moment in which could be heard words of comfort and snippets of prayer spoken to the remaining convicts. "Dear" and "Honey" floated back to Ford, jerking him to attention.

"Is there a woman up there? Is there?" he begged of the people around him, ignoring their irritation and elbows while he leapt upon their backs to see what he might over the heads.

"That's the word," someone finally answered. "Next up's a tiny little thing." A shudder shot through Ford, and he slumped off the grumbling people before him. More word of mouth spread from the front and filtered back. "They say she beat her husband to death."

"He musta been a dwarf then!" shouted a man nearby which kicked up a good deal of laughter.

"Half a one!" said another joker.

"Missin' both arms!" said yet another. All around Ford were hoots, and the slapping of backs as the jokes were repeated.

"This day will do me in yet," he murmured. Their flippancy annoyed him. Not only were lives being taken, but a life was still in the balance, and he was to blame. He had only meant for Elle to be caught as a common street thief and sent off to Polecat Island, but if she tried for the Iarl's journal and maps and were caught she would definitely be hanged.

A commotion from the direction of the river gradually drew the attention of even the remotest of the onlookers to a small caravan of wagons guarded by pikemen trying to push its way into the square through the people clogging the bridge.

"It's happening all over again?" said Ford thinking, as many did that this was another shipment of prisoners to be hanged. There was indeed a mob as before, but gone was the parade-like celebratory atmosphere. Fierce and demanding people pulled at the drivers, jumped on the wagons themselves and had to be yanked off or shoved back by the guards.

Like leaves blown ahead of a hurricane, word spread that the wagons were full to bursting with bread, bread that was to be distributed freely. The brute force with which the people now rushed the wagons could not be controlled. Any lingering goodwill and camaraderie were dashed by a ravenous panic pervading the unremitting flow of bodies that wanted to get their share before it was gone. No one could be deterred, even if it came to blows, and it did. A smiling boy, leaping repeatedly well above the heads of everyone to get a better look, caught a vicious elbow under the chin from the man next to him who had had enough. A nervous-eyed girl with a clump of hair missing fought against the manic flow to drag herself to safety. An old man bleeding from the forehead fell and was trampled as he cried out, "My brothers! My brothers!" Though high and panicky, the words were lost in the din. Not even the bellowing of the oxen pulling the wagons could compete with the clamor of the crowd.

Few noticed or paid attention to the catastrophe behind them. Regardless of the strenuous efforts to deflect them, the extra weight of the people climbing on to the grandstand for a better view as well as the bodies surging around it, pressing on the scaffolding supports was enough to collapse one corner, bringing the whole grandstand down and crushing numerous unfortunate men and women.

On the gallows platform, Song mounted the movable steps to reach a maximum height. From between two convulsing bodies, he implored the people to calm themselves, to restore order and civility, and to come back so they could finish the hangings. Though a persuasive man, he held no sway over hungry bellies. Nor could he compete with the team of bread distributors bellowing, "Free bread! Compliments of the Iarl! Free bread for the people!" A war had begun, and this was the Iarl's counterattack to the Pennaeth's grotesque show, his bloody-minded attempt to dampen her trade-strengthening, peace-promoting celebrations.

Such grand-scale chaos overawed Ford for a time, and he allowed himself to be carried along with the mob toward the river. After the initial confusion, he picked a path through the current of bodies making for the gallows, where he found the hangman yanking the dangling legs of those who would not die while cursing the air and shouting about the need for ankle weights. Guards in helmets and ring-mail tunics set up a crescent defensive formation with spears and pikes around the hangman to fend off the relatives of those being executed. The guards threatened and thrust people back. A woman took a gushing gut-wound and fell into the arms of the incensed group.

With all the people swarming about, Ford wasn't absolutely clear who was who, but he saw only three remaining people at the foot of the steps leading up to the gallows platform who appeared to be bound, and none of them was Elle. Again and again, he scanned the people throughout the hectic scene. Beyond any doubt, Elle was nowhere to be seen about the gallows. He breathed easy once more.

Unable to attain their goal to using the gallows platform as a point of distribution, the admirable determination of those in charge of the bread wagons evaporated, and they now dispersed the bread right where their wheels had ground to a halt, with the last wagon still stuck on the bridge. Relieved of an oppressive worry for the moment, Ford felt his appetite come roaring back. He waded into the mass with a few parting lunges that drew oaths and elbows from the people thrust aside, and those Ford left trailing in his wake. The mob attacked like rats, scratching and even biting as they crawled over one another. One man near the bridge jumped up onto the river's retaining wall to dodge a guard and received the blunt end of a pike in the gut for his troubles, which toppled him over. The river, swollen by the rains and rising up to the top of the wall, whisked him away in a flash. A few cried out, some gawked, but no one ran to help him. Ford never did see if he made it out alive. He, like everyone else, kept on pushing forward to get a share of the bread.

"Free bread! Bread from the Iarl for the people!" called out one of the wagon drivers over the sea of greedy, grasping hands. The smart fellow had taken to hurling loaves as far away as he could. Like dogs running to fetch sticks, many of the mob took off for them. He had even been clever enough to hurl them into the few open spaces of the square, thus relieving the pressure of the packed crowd somewhat. Loaves dropped on to the damp flagstones and flooded spaces where the raging river had topped the retaining wall. Soon the empty spaces filled with enough people so that no matter where loaves were thrown, they were caught before they hit the ground. With his height advantage, Ford caught the first loaf thrown his way and made off with it.

When he reached the back of the crowd where the press of bodies finally let up, he took the loaf from where he had tucked it under his arm and found that both ends had been torn away, leaving him with the clump in the middle. It was a clump's worth of bread more than he had had moments before and he swallowed it gratefully with greedy speed and mean glares at all who eyed his prize.

As the dry lumps struggled down into a stomach long-tightened by hunger and his mind was relieved of that concern, self-preservation came hurtling back at him like a trap sprung. Barker. Here he was out in the open, standing taller than most, occasionally hearing his name called out and being recognized for his fighting, and he hadn't even given Barker a thought up to this point. Suddenly he felt more exposed than if he were naked. Turning rapidly this way and that, he fully expected Grady or Keene to come flying at him. He backed from the square and hurried down the nearest lane, throwing glances over his shoulders and checking around each corner. His timid trek from the square to Elle's room stretched his nerves to the breaking point right up until he threw home the bolt on her door.

She wasn't there, but the place seemed neater than he last remembered it. His club was propped against a box, and that wasn't like him. He threw himself down on the smoothed out bed and tried to sort through all that had happened since the previous night, but his racing mind was slowing considerably, and soon he was overcome by a fitful slumber full of nightmare.

"Too soon…too soon," he heard himself mumbling some hours later as he came to. It was too soon for Elle to have been apprehended and sent to the gallows. The wheels of the law did not turn so quickly in this town, he assured himself while swiping a palm across his eyes and down his cheeks. There was still time. He swung the shutter open. Yes, there was still time. After filling the water pitchers downstairs, he drained one back in the room and then drank in a more leisurely manner from the next while absentmindedly running a hand and eye over all the interesting items Elle had accumulated. One of her dark cloaks was missing from the line of pegs where others of various deep hues hung. If it had been there this morning, he couldn't recall it. He had no idea where to find her, but he would try. And he would to talk to Whetstone, even if nothing came of it and he did not know what he would say. "It'll work itself out when I get there."

The idea of passing through the streets set him on edge once more. Before, when his blood was up, marching through the streets had been nothing. He would have bullied his way to the gallows and cut Elle down if need be. If any of them had tried to stop him, he would have fought them all off to get her out of there. Now he didn't want to leave the room. In a movement nearing instinct, his hand dove into his pocket and pulled out his crumpled sprig of rue. One loving caress later and he was ready for another furtive journey into the city.

The narrow street in front of Elle's building was often cast in shadow, but today of all days it seemed unusually lit up. Ford craned his neck out the door and looked about warily at the few downcast faces passing the closed shops and abandoned dwellings under an overcast sky. Though the sun was hidden, it shined bright through the clouds, making it apparent that the day was further along than he first realized, so much further that he made up his mind to go to the Derry Child at once. When he arrived, he found the tavern full of night watchmen having a bite and a last drink before their shift. Sitting quietly waiting for his partner to finish his food and drink, Dillon Baw spotted Ford and came over to him.

"Master Ford, how are you?"

"I'm not sure. Seems I went and slept the day away." Ford scanned the tavern. "Where's the captain?"

"Off up the castle," said Dillon, referring to Bowen Dome, the Iarl's seat of power, though she did not reside there due to its sparse accommodations. Instead, a castellan oversaw its daily running, a monotonous task over the previous years of peace. "Something's gone wrong up there." He couldn't elaborate on what exactly was amiss, because like everyone else in the tavern, he didn't know. Information hadn't trickled back yet on what had drawn the captain away. When the bell rang for work, the day watch captain didn't show up at the tavern either. So, Ford was dragged off by Gerrant to do a night's worth of their route once again without finding Elle or Whetstone.

Across the river at Bowen Dome not long after midnight, a team of bakers employed by the Iarl showed up at the gates as they had done the night before to begin the process of baking a massive amount of bread to be distributed free to the people once again. This time, however, they were turned away by order of the new castellan of the castle, Cynrig Colwyn-Delwyn, a pliable man, indebted to his cousin the Pennaeth Brastersceatt. Colwyn-Delwyn had been overjoyed to find the stewardship newly vacated and offered to him upon the sudden demise of the old steward, who met a gruesome end not a week prior when the very spitting image of his favorite scullery maid, a flirtatious and round-bottomed girl, delivered his usual steaming pot of honeyed porridge, dumped it on his head, and stabbed him in the heart. The killer had slipped back out the way she came, even stepping over the real scullery maid's body down in the kitchen in order to sneak out a back door. One day later Colwyn-Delwyn was hurriedly named castellan to placate the increasingly truculent Pennaeth Brastersceatt and as an expedient to maintain the peace.

While the confused bakers shuffled home and across the way on Wamb Hill the Iarl slept soundly in the House of Middlefield, her fortified manor house, two figures crept up to the wall surrounding the house as silently as the still night veiling them in darkness. The larger of the two knelt to provide a broad shoulder for the shorter, the slighter one to place a soft shoe upon and vault to the top of the wall. Within moments both were over and stealthily sliding down the other side when Stripes, the Iarl's mouser who just as happily spent his nights outside as in, yowled and hissed at the mysterious invaders alighting beside him. One of their boots came down upon the cat's neck, and silence returned.

The intruders padded across the flagstone yard to the house and the larger of the two lifted the other up to the lowest window. A thin blade slid between the shutters and flipped the latch on the inside with a flick of the wrist. The shutters were eased back ever so slowly to avoid as much squeaking as possible. Once through the window, the two slipped into a room of pristinely whitewashed walls furnished with intricate yet sturdy tables and chairs. Flags, tapestries, and paintings hung between the sconces with their doused candles and soot-darkened walls. Chests, cupboards and a couch took up so much space at one end that they encroached upon the center of the room. Various vases, a top-heavy alabaster statuette of Aaharuhya the Mother of Milk on a wobbly table, the massive antlers of the high-bladed elk, and a stand of flared spears created a perilous maze that needed traversing if they were to obtain their objective. Each object was skirted with painstaking care. They were halfway across the room when a small nugget of charcoal on the marble tiles that spread before the room's vast hearth crunched under the larger one's heel. The unexpected noise shattered the tranquility of the night and caught them up, but only momentarily, for this assignment demanded swift and decisive action. *In and out. Get it done quickly and quietly*, so they had been ordered.

As they turned into the hallway leading to the bedchamber, a startled and affronted bellow erupted. Blades flashed. The sonorous-throated bellower cried out, "Guards! Guards! To me!" as he fell back to defend himself against the knives that lashed out toward him. Stamping boots on stairs somewhere within the great house added to the cacophonous and confused scene as the man went on shouting, "Assassins! We are under attack!" Soft-soled shoes scurried back across the room. Crashing vases and toppled chairs left disorienting obstacles for the pursuers so that the intruders might leap through the window, climb over the wall and escape into the night.

CHAPTER 15
THE JUNIPER

Ford marched back and forth along the lanes like a garrison patrol on wall duty willing the night to pass as quickly as possible. As often happens, because he wished it to pass, time dragged on with an endless sluggishness. Block after block of annoyingly quiet streets stretched before him, with the only distractions being the occasional citizen dashing away, vagrant masses lying still in their dead-end corners, and the rain. At times it poured with screaming fury, and that was at least something to talk about with the small congregation of watchmen with whom he sheltered under the overhang of an abandoned shop. Dillon was there among them. No one had much news to relate but seemed content to while away the time undercover. When it came down hard enough, even Gerrant was willing to suspend his duties for a short time. Ford couldn't help fidgeting, briskly tapping his foot and walking in tight circles. At the slightest sign of a let-up in the rain he bolted.

"Yer gonna get soaked, ya halfwit!" Gerrant shouted after him into a whipping wind that tossed droplets like daggers. He had never been so pleased with his new partner. "He ain't smart, but at least he's keen for the job!"

Gerrant had not followed him immediately, and Ford was able to put some distance between them. Turning a corner or two, he felt sure he had lost him. Maybe it looked as if he were being an overzealous watchman, but the job be-damned, he was thinking. Right now it only served to keep him from more urgent business. What he yearned for was an excuse to leave work. Barring that, something to break up the monotony and help get this night over with would do. Nestled in an alleyway, he watched his partner hasten by, then resumed his burrowing into the depths of the nook he had found, squeezing between the two sagging walls on either side of the alley and away to the other much darker side. This was the most artful disappearing act a giant of a man like himself could manage.

The storm eventually abated, leaving behind an innocent pitter-patter that tapped like fingernails upon the thin metal plate shielding the extinguished lamp by the door of the One-Eyed Whale tavern. The tapping turned into a mere tinkle that dissolved into more musical tones. No, Ford realized, it was actual music. At the end of the alley, he poked his head around the corner, and there was the player, across the street tucked away in the cellar stairwell of the tavern. In the dim light – he had left his lantern behind with the other watchmen – it was difficult to make out much, but Ford believed he saw cradled in the musician's arms a gittern, a teardrop-shaped stringed instrument popular with the people from the Forest of a Thousand Names, which he had seen played at the Three Sheets and in Brastersceatt Square. Above the player, a creamy white hand and part of an arm rested on the sill of an open window. Ford had once lingered beneath this window on a night when lantern light in the room clearly illuminated those within, so he knew the window looked in on the bedroom of the tavern owner's daughter, a vivacious young woman with plenty of memorable assets.

"Lucky man," he thought. The musician 'had her hand,' as the saying went. This was love, this simple and tender song that broke the noise ordinance with its slow but persistent tones so sensitive in their solitude, yet passionate with their insistence, like a steadily rising heartbeat in one who is gradually realizing the true meaning of that difficult to define word: love. Perhaps this musician understood it, but for his part, Ford had stumbled over the concept, making a mess of his attempts with Genevieve, Adeline, and yes, even Elle in a different way. Perhaps his thoughts would have taken this moody turn of their own accord; however, the musician's choice to switch to a song in a minor key certainly encouraged somber contemplation. How it could possibly perpetuate love, Ford was at a loss to know. "Well, he's lost her now," he thought as the song wound to a sad close, and he felt his heart hanging heavy within him. A tear-laden bar towel hovered in the window frame a moment before dropping down into the musician's waiting hand.

"Aha, found you!" shouted Gerrant from directly behind Ford. A twang of strings rang out in the street. "Thought you could hide from me, eh? Come on, we don't get paid to stand around doing nothing." Chastisement from someone like Gerrant was one thing; Ford could ignore it mostly. But coupled with a shove in the back at a time when his emotions were so raw was too much to bear. He spun around and slapped away Gerrant's arms as they stretched out for another shove.

Ford drove a finger into Gerrant's chest and shouted, "You do that again, and I will drop you right here in the street!" Stalking off, he left Gerrant astounded and sputtering gibberish. The confrontation put the edge back on his nerves. Finding solitude was now of paramount importance. Finding something to smoke came in a close second. Without either, his emotions seemed ungovernable. Footsteps approached. He turned this way and that, and spotted a boatwright's long warehouse jutting out two feet further than the houses around it. Pressing into the corner it created, he flexed his fingers about his club as he waited and hoped this nook was enough to conceal him and let who he assumed was his partner pass him by unnoticed.

The person that passed looked similar to the flour thief he and Gerrant had encountered recently. Whether it had been the night before, two nights or more, Ford couldn't recall. Still not accustomed to working all night, he was having trouble just keeping his eyes open, never mind remembering when he had last seen some common thief he couldn't care less about. For all Ford knew, the flour had ended up in hands as worthy as those it was originally intended for.

But if this was the same man, he was carrying a much smaller load this time, and his manner was far more furtive. His side-to-side glances flashed the whites of his wide eyes. That the man carried his bundle toward the docks and not away drew Ford from the shadows and made him follow at a discreet distance. Quite casually he pretended to check that the occasional door was locked and shutter tight. One of the doors squeaked open, and the man jumped, spotted Ford and fled. Propelled by curiosity and the instinct to chase the fleeing, Ford took off after him in the direction of the river.

"Stop!" The thunderous command surprised even himself and sent the man racing on even faster. Ford broke into a sprint hampered by the mud-strewn streets. Though not a swift or nimble runner, once his long, powerful legs were in motion, he could make up ground quickly. The fleeing man threw more and more fearful glances over his shoulder as Ford gained and the docks neared. "You there, stop!" roared out Ford with a terrible god-like ferocity that provoked his quarry to fling his bundle toward the river. It flopped on to the wharf, rolled over once and came to rest at the edge of the rotting planks. Ford couldn't slow down quickly enough to keep from crashing into the man, but just before he did, the man collapsed to his knees, and Ford sailed over him, tripping and falling flat upon the wharf. He scrambled to his feet and grabbed the man by his fraying collar, shoving his head back and finding an anguished face awash in tears, but not the flour thief.

"We couldn't afford it!" wailed the man. Despite the grief wrinkling his eyes and warping his mouth, it was apparent that he was rather young. The heat of the chase died away, leaving Ford with a tepid and confused kind of sympathy. Nothing of the limp man within his powerful gasp threatened fight or flight, so Ford let go and went to retrieve the bundle. As he knelt to pick it up the young man dissolved into a miserable pool of tears and saliva through which he choked out, "It's not my fault!" The cat-sized bundle was wrapped in a thin, dirty linen and as Ford peeled it away, a tiny bare arm fell limply from the cloth. Then the rest was revealed. The young man stood on trembling legs, peered over Ford's shoulder and let flow a garbled stream of grief. Ford paid him no mind, so focused was he on the little scrunched up face, its eyes mercifully shut, unnaturally red and purple, no doubt from the rigors of a recent stillborn birth, he thought. A queasiness crept up on him. He looked away and held a hand to his mouth and felt immediate shame. A muttered plea for forgiveness from the child's soul forced its way up from his constricting throat.

Ford knew little of babies and even less about birth but had lived in the city during a time when poverty and starvation gripped the lowest rung of society. Infant mortality had risen so high that it was nearly impossible not to have seen it displayed in all its monstrosity. The first time he had happened upon a dead child, he was leaving a tavern after closing time and had just stepped into a stairwell to relieve himself. At the bottom of the stairs a little boy lay naked, no more than few weeks old. Coming out of his shock, he wanted to do something, but a friend told him, "Best just leave it," and Ford had heeded this advice. Over time, death in the slums became so commonplace one hardly noticed it, but this was something different. This he held in his hands.

Pity drew his eyes back to the straining face. The child's weight shifted in his hands, and its head rolled back, revealing red markings around its neck the size and shape of clenching fingers. Ford's core wilted like the malleable little creature in his hands. This was more than a dead baby; it was what was known as a juniper or gin-baby: a child born to an unwilling mother, often a prostitute, who drank large quantities of gin in the belief that the fiery liquid prevented pregnancy and when it didn't work the resulting child was often abandoned, drowned, smothered or strangled to death.

All pity evaporated as Ford jumped to his feet, ready to unleash a deep-seated and all-encompassing rage upon the young man. But the man was nowhere to be seen, even after Ford cleared his eyes. "Shit!" He took a few abortive steps along the wharf one way, then the other. There was no sign of the vile man, so Ford ran back up the street from which they had just come with the child tucked under his arm. The finite incandescence of the street lamps cast such irritatingly small spheres of light, thought Ford; they revealed no one as he ran from street to street, stopping every few yards to listen, straining to hear over the thumping in his ears, but there was nothing. Down every lane, row, and alley there was no one, but for a single homeless man and a local insomniac, who regretted stepping outside his door to walk himself to sleep. "I ain't seen nobody! Nobody!" he screeched at the mad-eyed watchman running wild through the night, shouting for a man to come and face what he had coming. Never before had Ford felt the tall buildings looming above to be so confining, to work with the night sky to create a constricting tunnel that seemed to squeeze the air from his lungs, from which he summoned one final bellow.

"May demons hound your every step!"

Dropping on a stoop, he slouched against someone's door. The wrap had come off most of the child, a girl. He bundled her snugly and was about to place her next to him, but couldn't, not on the wet ground. Somehow it didn't seem right. Instead, he cradled her in one arm that he rested upon his leg, then leaned back to close his eyes, if only for a moment. Images and ideas shot across his mind like lightning blasts and made closing his eyes physically unbearable. The new hurts – Elle, Adeline, Yonn and the rest – were all there, but it was the old pains that stung the most. They appeared before him like brash paintings of his past: his mother abandoning him to a father he did not know and who did not seem to love him; being left crying as he stood alone in the dark seeking his mother in the faint and wavering lights coming from a village in the distance; even the dim stars in the cobalt sky above twinkled with an unnatural brilliance through the prism of his pooling tears as he wondered if she too gazed upon these same stars.

He wiped at his eyes, and they fell once more upon the bundle. Covered or not, he could not now and likely would not ever forget her face, the face of an unwanted child killed soon after birth. Someone held this innocent, defenseless life in their hands and ended it. An unwanted child himself, he couldn't help but think that he too might have ended this way. His mother could easily have solved all her problems by ending his life, but she hadn't. She had kept him, in an unselfish act that he had repaid by becoming a selfish, purposeless wanderer neglecting the very reason for coming to Port Morton in the first place, to find her, to be with her again and possibly be there for her if she needed him. "I will find her," he swore aloud and dropped his head into his free hand with his elbow propped on one knee.

To the soul of the child, he swore, "I will do better to protect little ones like you." *Watch over those who need protecting.* They weren't exactly his father's words, but close enough to one of the few pieces of paternal wisdom he had ever received and wished to abide by, but hadn't. The gods had granted him size and strength, his father had instilled the necessity of using these traits for an honorable purpose, and now it dawned on him how much he had recently neglected his duty. The neglect had spread to his friends and loved ones. "A failure all around. A tired, miserable failure," he murmured between heaving sighs, sighs he hoped might release some of the misery building within him.

A timid hand with an oil lamp stretched out from a window not far above his head. With his head bowed he didn't notice it, but in the new light coming down from above he did notice the thin ribbon with tiny green and gold oak leaves on a black background woven into the inner seam of his trouser leg: Elle's ribbon, the only thing she had to remember her aunt by. She had run out of thread and sacrificed one of her most precious possessions to finish off his trousers. The tears came then, and he could do nothing to stop them.

After letting that settle in on top of everything else and beating himself up for it, out of a sense of self-perseveration, his mind went blank for a time. Eventually, footsteps approached in the muddy street. "Master Ford? That you?" Dillon Baw took a tentative step closer. His watchman partner stood a few feet back holding a drunkard they had been walking home. "We heard something and…"

"What you got there?" asked the partner. Ford hardly looked up, he just handed over the bundle and heard a gasp a moment later.

"Aw, by gods," slurred the drunkard. "The poor thing."

"Where'd it come from?"

"Docks," Ford replied, massaging his forehead. Something was shoved under his nose, and his head jerked back at the powerful smell of a potent corn whiskey coming from a proffered bottle.

"Here, you drink you some o' this," said the drunkard. Ford staggered to his feet, took the bottle and walked off, ignoring the questions and complaints that erupted behind him.

Forcing down large gulps of the harsh stuff, he finished off the bottle before reaching Elle's room. It worked fast, and a grateful Ford felt its numbing effects rush over him in a warm wave. Still, there had been plenty of time to think during the walk home, plenty of time to realize and regret that he would probably lose his job over this. On the bright side, now he could spend his free time trying to find Elle.

"Fuct tick, I'll find work somewheres else," he said as he swerved about and stamped his unreliable feet down on the steps that kept appearing and disappearing on him. "I might be a little bit drunk. Too much to eat, not enough to drink," he said to a wavering figure peering through a door cracked open just enough to see what the problem was. "Or wait…." Someone helped him up the last flight of stairs and left him swaying in the hallway. There were only four doors, but he couldn't remember which was Elle's. He tried one at random, and it opened to a dark room. Willem, the priest, shot up in bed shouting.

"Who's there?"

Ford grumbled an annoyed apology and slammed the door. After some loud deliberation, he found Elle's door and plodded in. By the light of a candle stub left faintly flickering on the table by the window, he could see that the order and cleanliness of Elle's room had been reduced to chaos. Some of her jars had been tipped over or knocked off the shelves. The neat pile of fabric had been toppled. The mattress was folded over revealing the objects stored underneath the bed frame's rope suspension. Whether a robbery or a fight had taken place here, it was too hard to decipher without more light, and even then it seemed too impossible to tell. Elle wouldn't have done this and left the place in this state of her own accord, but if this was Whetstone's work, he had made a real mess of the place. "Barker," Ford growled, figuring he must have tracked them down and taken some of her property to offset what Ford owed him. But if something was missing, he couldn't tell.

In the end, he realized it didn't matter which it was, Whetstone or Barker. Ford had made mistakes, and Elle had paid for them. Another survey of the room didn't answer whether she had escaped, been caught or killed, or if she had even been here at all. "My fault," he moaned as he dragged the mattress into place and collapsed on the bed, beyond tired and as angry and irritable as ever. His head hurt, and it wasn't helped by the shouts coming from the foreigners next door. He couldn't even shut his eyes for fear of the reeling images ready to inflict their pain upon him. His headache swelled with each beat of his heart. A hand clasped over one ear did nothing to block out the shouts of the couple coming through the wall. His skin twitched and pricked him from the inside as if his own body were attacking him. Back and forth went the husband and wife. He tried to concentrate on his own problems, but it was too much to ignore. Now the fight took a decided turn in favor of the man, who shouted down the woman, doing his best to drown her defense. She went quiet. He went on. It was almost as if her silence had somehow escalated the tension between them. Suddenly there was the crack of a slap, and the woman cried out. Then came another slap.

Ford couldn't tell how he got there. He had been lying on Elle's bed one instant, and in the next he was crouched over the foreign man from next door. His body heaved and his fists clenched. If the man got up, he would strike him down again. The stringy, gap-toothed and flat-nosed Dadha man did not stir.

Blood streaming from his forehead pooled on the floor about the chest his head had struck after crumpling under Ford's savage blow. Red-faced and dripping sweat, Ford trembled from a rage half spent. He was ready to throttle the woman cowering on the bed in the corner for her incessant screaming and was only vaguely aware of voices and movement behind him. The priest Willem peered in through the splintered door horror-struck.

CHAPTER 16
STANROCC HOLD

A square of checkered morning light from an iron-barred window crept up his face, spreading over his eyes, rousing him from a near bottomless slumber. A slow, painful recollection of the night before unfurled in his aching head, an aching surpassed for the present by the agony of his back from hours spent lying on a stone floor. The window drooled a steady stream of brown water. Down the wall, it dribbled, through the middle of the narrow room where he was lying to disappear under a wooden door.

Ford dragged himself up and looked out the window. What would have been the street on drier days was instead a wash of slowly churning, russet water at eye level. He strained his head against the bars to see what he might in both directions. It was as he suspected. The river had flooded over, and last night he had been locked away in the bowels of Stanrocc Hold, once an ancient chief's bastion known for keeping bloody murderers out, now fortified as a prison infamous for keeping bloody murderers in. It also housed inmates whose only crime was to express a deviant thought or to commit a thoughtless act of deviance, but increasingly these days it was being used as a transitional facility to hold criminals until their fate could be decided and fines paid. They were holding him and deciding his fate. He wondered if that Dadha man was dead. He had certainly looked dead last night. If that were the case, it would be a quick end for him. The realization that he was probably fired from the watch seemed a laughable concern now.

An intentional cough drew his attention to a window in his cell door. It too was barred, and between two of the bars a slender, drawn face frowned back. From between thin lips a reedy, mechanical voice conveyed a string of words made banal by repetition, which explained to Ford where he was and why a person would end up here, all things he already knew until finally coming to something he didn't know.

"I am the Jailor of Stanrocc Hold." The Jailor rustled through sheets of paper, his attention split between them and the water coming in at the window.

"Let us see…number five. You have been convicted by the testimony of two or more witnesses of committing the crime of a violent assault upon the body of a fellow citizen of the City of Port Morton. Your fine has been determined at fifteen pieces of copper. An additional silver piece has been added for one night stayed at the Hold, for a total of one and three-fourths pieces of silver. Are you able to recompense the aforementioned dues?"

"What?" asked Ford, his whole person enveloped in an uncomprehending stupor. The Jailor repeated his speech precisely, which helped some, but did not completely erase Ford's surprise. "You're letting me go? So, he's not dead?"

"If you are referring to the victim of the assault, yes, I am told he survived his wounds with some assistance." Ford, bursting with renewed life, would have hugged the impressively indifferent man if he could, but resigned himself to a big grin and pounding his fist into his palm. "Have you a bondsman?" Ford could only think of one person who would help him out of his predicament, only one person he could rely on and felt comfortable asking to stand in and take legal responsibility for him, not to mention fronting him the money for the fine. The Jailor summoned a boy and no sooner had the commission to find the bondsman been given when the hasty slaps of the boy's soft shoes could be heard trailing off down the stone corridor.

"Should the boy locate your bondsman, he will expect remuneration for his task completed. I believe a copper is the norm. I would not suggest more. A spoiled child is soon a useless child," said the Jailor as if it were a matter of fact. "He won't be long, but I must attend to the needs of the Hold." After a final, worried glance at the water coming into Ford's cell, he vanished from the door's window, and Ford listened as he went on to the next cell, reciting his spiel with only minor variations as fit the case of the inmate and marching through it with straightforward efficiency.

One repetition was tedious enough for Ford, so he turned back to his window to contemplate the water coming in and wondered where it was going after it slipped under his door. A woman's shout, half scream and half growl, shrill and manic, ricocheted down the hallway from some distant cell. There were words in the outburst, but Ford missed them in the unexpected jolt of sound, and after that she descended into an indecipherable garble in which all was lost in a hushed rambling, though it was clear she was troubled and quite likely insane.

Eventually, the disturbance drowned in the general simmer of Hold noise – random shouts, moaning, jingling keys and occasionally coins – which Ford was already becoming accustomed to. He went back to his window, and over the course of the next hour and more, a whiff of smoke occasionally drifted into his cell to stir his appetite. A murmuring cripple from the Hold's kitchen came by ladling out water. He answered Ford's query about food with only a quiet, embarrassed jumble of words to explain that Stanrocc Hold served food only to long-term prisoners. Ford resigned himself to curling up on the rapidly disappearing sunny patch of floor until he was released.

"Get out! Get out! The Hold is flooding!" shouted the breathless Jailor throwing Ford's cell door open and flying away in a frenzy of shouts and flailing arms. Ford's first thought was that he must have fallen asleep, the second being that his back was soaked. The floor was awash in the water now pouring freely in from the window. He stepped from his cell down into ankle-deep water in the corridor. The Jailor, frantically fumbling with cell door keys, shoved the entire ring of them into the hands of the man from the kitchen, leaving the hapless cripple to free the remaining prisoners, whose arms and hands stretched out from their cells while their cries rang deafeningly off the stone walls.

"Transfer the prisoners to the upper levels! I must look to the stores!" the Jailor shouted over his shoulder as he disappeared up a flight of stairs at the end of the hall. The kitchen man was a perfect picture of one dumbfounded. He stood blinking at the key ring longer than the prisoners could stand before he finally began choosing a key and poking and jamming it again and again into the closest lock until absolutely confounded by repeated failures and picking another with a great deal of deliberation. The curses and pleas of the prisoners only exasperated him as their howling fear of being left to drown turned the place into a madhouse.

Having been led into Stanrocc Hold in the middle of the night while only half aware of his surroundings, Ford could not recall the way out. He sloshed by other cell doors, some open and many still closed, heading toward the bawling of the Jailor coming from some distant chamber. "The bread must be kept dry! Who will help me?"

In one of the open cells, a prisoner had actually remained behind. Ford hesitated by the door and was about to urge the inmate on, but held his tongue after taking one look at the woman curled up in corner, her face covered in a mat of ragged hair that stuck to a diamond-patterned robe soaked in the dirty water swirling around her. This was no doubt the madwoman he had heard earlier, he reasoned. Her robe somehow looked familiar. Perhaps she was someone he had seen in the streets or delivered something to during his porter days, he figured, but still, he wondered what she was doing here. A prisoner scurrying for the exit knocked into him and pushed by. The murmuring cripple from the kitchen lumbered up the corridor from behind and implored him to move on.

"Ford! Come on, son!" Stocky cried from down the hall. Even in this chaos, his friend smiled. "The sooner we get out of here, the sooner we get back home." The whole scene seemed too surreal for belief. Hardly aware of himself or his surroundings, Ford staggered toward Stocky. Nothing seemed certain, not his friend's affectionate embrace about his shoulders, not the fading prisoners' shouts, nor the doorway opening and the light of day upon his face.

Led by the arm on to Weald Bridge and hardly aware of himself in all this tumult, Ford took notice that his friend's once pink and chunky cheeks were now sallow and hung like deflated bladders. Concern formed into questions, but these never left his mouth as his attention was snagged by what hundreds of others couldn't help but watch: the turbulent brown deluge thrashing about beneath him, more like a mudslide than a river.

"Hold up," said Stocky pulling him off to one side. "Captain's in a blazing hurry." The bridge trembled, and its boards rattled as the Captain of the Iarl's House Guards on horseback, and a straggling band of no more than a dozen lightly armored guardsmen and women all thundered by and through the bridge gate leading into Brynseht. They were not regular house guards, but a contingent of mercenaries the captain had had to rally.

"I wonder what—" Ford broke off when cries drew the attention of everyone crossing Weald Bridge to the high embankment, where people there were shouting and pointing at a great beam under Ox Bridge upstream that had just snapped. Another let go, and then the whole bridge disappeared into the river along with nearly two dozen people and cattle.

"Gods save us!"

A head or an arm broke the surface here and there. The people along the embankment tried to throw wooden objects or anything that might float into the river. Someone tossed a rope, but the end fell miserably short of anyone's reach. Massive pieces of the ruined bridge's support structure bobbed about, and someone tried to grab hold of a section of trestle coming toward him or her but was knocked under by it. Some of those gathered about Ford set to praying. Others shouted "there!" and many were pointing. They all cheered when a cow raised its head above the surface and bellowed. It went under once more and wasn't seen again. From the embankment, someone jumped into the river and made for a very small form flipping about upon the breaking water. Both went down and were lost below before their bodies reached Weald Bridge. That was the last anyone saw of man or beast, and just like that, most of Ox Bridge and all the unfortunates upon it were swept away as if they had never existed. The river flowed on, bucking and crashing into the embankments on either side.

Something under the surface slammed into Weald Bridge. Ford, Stocky and all the people around them hurried off.

"It was nothing but a shithole before, but now the old town's really and truly falling apart," commented Stocky in wonder when he and Ford waded into the flooded Brastersceatt Square. Everywhere there were shocking signs of a city in turmoil. Some of the streets had been replaced by roiling waterways. Smoke from at least two separate fires hung over rooftops. Civilians acted anything but civil: looting here, fighting there, and spreading fear everywhere with their unruly behavior. Port Morton was indeed falling apart.

Stocky kept up a rambling monologue about the happenings around them and the news he'd heard. He knew little more than what could be seen by them both and Ford only half-listened, being caught up in his own concerns as to where he needed to go and what he needed to do next. Eventually Stocky dragged from him an explanation as to how he had ended up in the Hold, but it came out in fragments. When the words stopped coming completely, Stocky saw that Ford's attention had been arrested by a slight figure some fifty yards ahead of them in a hooded cloak of a red so deep as to be almost brown. From the side view of the figure crossing their path at the first intersection beyond the square, it appeared to be a woman of a rather diminutive stature. "It can't be," Ford said, staggering forward. However, he had glimpsed enough of her face to believe what he thought he had seen and broke into a run, whistling and clapping and calling out, "Mother!"

The woman turned and pulled her hood across her face. Seeing a hulking beast of a man barreling toward her, she fled down the street in a flutter of cloak and slender churning legs. Ford rounded the corner, and a sudden dizzy sensation overcame him. He leaned against the nearest wall to prevent himself from falling, and his other hand instinctively went to his swimming head. When he looked up again, he saw what he felt in every fiber of his being to be his mother slipping into the back door of the Pennaeth's great house.

"Ford! Ford! Hold up!" Stocky hollered from behind. Just when he reached Ford, Ford took off for the house.

"Hello? Hello!" He shouted as he pounded on the Pennaeth's back door. He tried the handle. It was locked, and no one came to answer. "Hello?"

Stocky caught up and asked, "What in the name is going on?"

"So strange. I don't understand. Why'd she run? Why won't she open the door? It's my mother, Stocky! She's in there! I saw her!"

"You saw your mother go in there? Into the lord's house?"

"Yes! Didn't you see her?"

"I saw a short, wisp of a creature."

"That was her!" Ford looked over the door, taking its measure as if considering the best method of dismantling it. As he knocked again and pushed on it, he didn't notice Stocky shaking his head.

"I don't think you saw your mother, son. Least of all going into Pennaeth Brastersceatt's house."

"Why not? Could be she's a maid or something." At this moment, Ford would hear nothing from any naysayer, even from a good friend. Without giving consequences a second thought, he stepped back and threw his shoulder into the door like a battering ram. The wood around the lock cracked and splintered on his second attempt.

"Ford! You can't just barge into a lord's house," reasoned Stocky.

"I'm going in! You don't have to. Wait here if you want." Once inside with the door left open a crack to let in some light, Ford went quite rigid with the shock of what he had just done. "Hello?" His whisper was so quiet he could barely hear it himself. This back hallway, he found himself in, with its high ceiling and immensely wide overlapping boards of dark wood, was impressive enough, and this was a mere servants' entrance. Any noise above the faintest sounded sharp and magnified, discouraging in him any desire to stir. Instead, he held himself as still as he could in the moment and pricked his ears. However, it was his nose that first alerted him to something peculiar. An unnatural, sour scent clung vague and fleeting to the air that brought to mind the time when, as a boy wrestling with his dog, the animal had gotten excited. When it sat on its haunches to lick itself it gave off a musky odor not unlike what he smelled now.

There were doors to the left and right a few feet away, and, after a rub of the rue sprig in his pocket – so reliant had Ford become on Larkwine's Rue, so assured was he of its power that he had come to imbue it with more attributes than he was originally told it possessed – he summoned the courage to finally creep forward. Unwilling to commit his full weight to each step, he moved with a heel-to-toe tread that eventually carried him to the door on the right. It was shut, but even so, the smell grew stronger here. He tried the handle, but the door appeared to be barred from the other side. A gentle push on the other door and it gave way easily, though with an annoying creak. "Hello?" he whispered again.

Peering in and waiting a moment for his eyes to adjust further to the darkness, he saw that the room was a large kitchen devoid of all but a few cooking utensils and the barest crockery. He tiptoed over the stone tiles past the wide hearth and on through another door to a long main hall with a lengthy table and another, though smaller hearth of its own. By now, he was beginning to believe he was alone in the house. Though he knew that wasn't entirely true, he was sure that the house was not occupied by its owner. If the lord was in residence, he reasoned there would be fires lit and activity in the kitchen, as well as noises about the house. Feeling more confident, he undid the latch on the interior shutters to one of the windows and pulled it in a few inches to let the light in through the wavy glass panels. That someone would have shutters inside their house instead of out seemed strange to him, but then again, if he owned glass windows he would want to show them off, too.

Letting in the light displayed the room's opulence: high-backed and cushioned chairs; side tables with spindly legs; two decorative swords displayed atop a cherry wood chest with impressively intricate carvings; a massive, browning portrait above the hearth that Ford took for Pennaeth Brastersceatt though he had never seen him. A staircase with a magnificent banister ran up along one side of the room, leading to a short balcony. Having never held a sword, he couldn't resist touching them. Both were shiny, relatively sharp and delicate with short hilt and cross guards. Nothing extraordinary. The Pennaeth kept his best weaponry with him at his country home. Purely for display, this pair stood with a precarious balance that Ford's light caress undid. Down they came with a clatter upon the floor at his feet. He froze. The sound died away, and nothing happened. That decided it for him. There was no one here, except perhaps his mother and she would likely be in the servants' quarters. A quick search of the other rooms turned up nothing. They were less furnished than the great hall and appeared to be mostly bedchambers.

The only place left unchecked was the door at the back of the house with the strange smell. He tried, but still, it would not open. It had a handle, but no lock, so Ford felt sure it must be barred from within. Having run with thieves in his youth, he had some knowledge of how to get around these things and began searching the house for something to flip the latch or bar on the other side of the door. Something thin was needed. He had been shown how to do it using a knife, but the kitchen had been quite stripped of cutlery. An idea occurred to him, and he went to the great hall to fetch one of the swords.

"Yes," he murmured when he was able to slide its thin blade into the narrow gap between the door and frame, digging grooves into the wood accidentally with his clumsy initial stabs before he had it. Lifting and holding the bar by the tip of the blade, he eased the door open with a curious lack of noise, and then, as the bar slid away on its fall to the floor, he snatched it up just before it hit the ground. Beyond the door, all was darkness. A light would be needed if he wanted to go on.

Back in the kitchen once more, it was clear the lord's cook had taken most of his favored implements, yet everything needed to start a fire was at hand. Although there were no lamps or lanterns to be found, Ford did happen upon a few rushlights left behind in a cupboard. He lit one, and on his way back he heard a voice approaching the servants' entrance door. His heart and breath seized up. Loud and angry, it sounded like someone telling off his friend. Stocky apparently had been caught loitering where he shouldn't. Taking quite possibly his only chance, Ford slipped through the door, snatched up the sword he had propped beside it and closed the door behind him.

Casting his minuscule light into the void revealed a staircase disappearing below. Ford took the first step with great caution, and although sound was more subdued in the cramped stairwell, the time-weakened wood wailed under his weight. He took the next steps with a delicacy that seemed farcical even to himself, but still the steps protested.

All the warnings going off in his head told him he shouldn't be here doing this, but he knew what he had seen, and he would follow through with it. He had not traveled all those miles to the city and lived in its squalor only to give up just when he was closest to finally finding her.

He ignored the stairs heralding his arrival and halfway down came to a landing that formed a turn in the stairwell. Another door loomed out of the darkness below. Taking the last few steps by twos with a quickening heartbeat, he stole up to the door, listened, heard nothing, and pulled gently on the handle with no luck. He pushed on it. Nothing. Like the one above, it too was barred from within. The sour smell was strong here.

"What if it's not her?" mumbled from his lips as he dropped his backside down on the stairs. If he opened that door and she wasn't on the other side, if she wasn't anywhere to be found within the house, he was sure his heart would rip itself in half. For a moment he saw the merit in never finding out. On the other hand, if he got up and left and didn't take the chance, he would never know for certain, and that was definitely worse.

One pat of his pocket and he leapt up, jabbed the sword in between the door and its frame, and found a latch on the first try. Flipping it up, he shoved the door open and was struck by a bright light and that sour stench, now pungent and foul. The light came from only two lanterns, but they were far stronger than what he had become accustomed to with his little rushlight.

His eyes adjusted quickly though and the slender form of a woman came into focus standing on the far side of a table in a fairly small, square room with walls of the rough stone finish of the house's foundation. It was her, the image of his mother as he imagined her: warm eyes and warm smile framed and half covered in long dark hair. One of his legs buckled as a fainting spell threatened to drop him. That queer hazy feeling—like an invasive delving or uninvited cohabitation of his mind—that had come over him out in the street returned to stir his swirling thoughts and perceptions like softening ingredients in a soup. But then she smiled, and he smiled back, an idiot's smile, he knew, one that stretched his face almost painfully, but he didn't care. His mind raced on and on now unchecked, propelled by adrenaline and nearly unstoppable in its boundless joy, a joy that blew through his body and threw off the faint feeling completely. He had so many questions, so many things he wanted to ask her, but more than that, he just wanted to hold her and be held by her.

The single word "Mother," tumbled nerve-racked from his lips as he lurched toward her and caught a glint of steel out of the corner of his eye as a blade slid past his neck, just missing its mark because of his long strides into the room. Spinning around to confront his blindside attacker, he found himself looking into a face of pallid skin spotted by patches of pink and streaked by veins of scarlet and blue, as if the skin had been turned inside out or stripped away and scarred by fire. The skin about its head gathered in folds that mimicked hair. Two slits on the end of a barely raised bump made do for a nose. No irises enlivened its white, translucent eyes. Shoeless, with one gloved hand and a billowing tunic, it appeared half-dressed, as if Ford had caught the host unprepared for a visitor. Its naked hand held a dagger longer than any Ford had ever seen. He staggered back into the table, driving it across the room and pinning what he had taken to be his mother against the far wall. A quick glance showed plainly that she was not his mother, nor even human. Where once had been long, lustrous hair now appeared those hideous folds of skin, and that warm, inviting face had disintegrated into a scarred nightmare with flaring white eyes at its center. She struggled to free herself while Ford turned back to the other, who was coming at him with an overhand stab meant to drive the dagger deep into his chest. Ford threw up his hand in a clumsy, instinctual defense and found he still held the sword. Its blade collided with his attacker's hand. A gut-wrenching animal screech pierced Ford's ears as finger fragments flipped through the air.

Behind him, fire from a toppled lantern was engulfing the table and the strange idol upon it. The female creature squirmed free while screeching something incomprehensible at her stunned counterpart, who stood transfixed by the clear liquid spouting from its mangled hand. Before it could react, Ford kicked it backward over a barrel and some crates. He stumbled away from both creatures into the torso of a flayed corpse hanging from the ceiling in a dark corner. Jerking away, he tripped over some bedding, regained his balance and awaited an attack amongst a pile of clothes covered in dried blood. The fire spread over the table and gained in fury. The female darted to a set of drapes hanging against the opposite wall and pulled it aside. Behind it appeared a wood panel door that she slid back, revealing a concealed passage through which the two disappeared. At first Ford dove for the passage, but stopped just short of the entrance and drove his sword into the darkness and around the corner of the wall. It connected with nothing, and after a few swipes with the blade, he peered into a black hollowness. Nothing could be seen, but he heard footsteps fading away.

He could see no gain in following them into a secret passage that they knew and he did not. Behind him the room glowed as the fire spread to the floor, and he turned to face it. The table was a loss, but he tore down the drapery, got to his knees and smothered as much as he could there. Amongst all the carnage and the flames now licking at the smoking ceiling, near his hand he saw the severed fingers. As he'd done after the beheading of Barky the warghadoc, he took the fingers and placed them in his pocket, figuring no one would believe this story without proof.

Nothing he did would stop the fire, so he crouched low to keep out of the smoke and made his way to the stairs. On the way out, his blood was still up and his pulse racing, but by the time he reached the back door the thrill subsided and his whole being deflated as the realization that he had not found his mother, after all, came flooding over him.

Outside the back door, he was met by blindingly bright sunlight as well as a man from the day watch and a pair of large brutes wielding clubs.

"Drop the weapon!" commanded the watchman. Ford looked into his face and hoped to recognize him, but didn't.

"Give me that sword," commanded one of the brutes. They were the Pennaeth's hired muscle.

"You there, stop!" cried a smaller, graying man just coming from the back door. He was dressed in servant's livery of the House of Brastersceatt and was the caretaker of the house when the master was away. Behind him emerged another of the day watch. "Arrest him!" the caretaker demanded of the watchmen. Even if Ford felt up to it, he doubted he could have fought them all off. Feeling low and somewhat dazed by what he had just gone through, he merely dropped the sword and gave himself up. "Bring him to the Hold!"

CHAPTER 17
REVELATIONS AND RESOLUTIONS

"You can't get yourself enough of the place, can you?" laughed the cripple from the kitchen upon seeing Ford at Stanrocc Hold once more. Recognizing a familiar face made him open up to the returning inmate. They spoke like old friends, and Ford learned that the man worked as the Hold's pantler, seeing to their pantry's bread. This time they met in the Jailor's chambers at the door to an adjacent common cell shared by the few remaining prisoners that couldn't pay their fines or whose crimes were considered too egregious to let them go. Ford sat on a bench unaware he was shoulder-to-shoulder with a murderer and a rapist. Grins and nudges accompanied their jesting upon his size, and he took it with as much good humor as his mood would allow.

One of Stanrocc Hold's errand boys, who had gone to get Ford's bondsman, returned quite soon, but without Stocky. Where his friend had disappeared to and where he was now was anybody's guess. In his stead, his eldest daughter Wylla crept into the room. The sight of her disconcerted Ford. However, she was so overawed by being in the Hold for the first time in her life that flirtation was the last thing on her mind. Her wide eyes grew wider still and wandered about the room. A center of administration for the Hold, it included an open filing cabinet stuffed with more bits of paper, set on finer tables than she had ever seen in her life or likely ever would. Her attention lingered over a brass-bound chest, and she started when the Jailor strolled into the room and fired a half-dozen questions at her.

The expectant runner's spirits plummeted when it came out that Wylla did not have the bail, nor a single coin on her at all. The little boy swore and stomped off to rejoin his comrades in the cells below to play in the water with the floating barrels and boxes. Bursts of their distant laughter echoed in the corridors from time to time.

Once given leave to speak with Ford, Wylla explained that she did not know where her father was. "We thought he was with you! That's what he said. And when that little wretch came to the door to fetch him, well, Mumma didn't know what to make of it, but she cursed a good deal and said if Puppa wasn't at work, for he lost his job don't you know, and if he wasn't with you as he said he was, well, Mumma cursed him for a whoremonger—" The girl tried to swallow her own words, but seeing as they were already out, she elaborated. "He will spend a shiny silver or two as we don't have at them *houses*, Mumma says." The other inmates, who had already tossed some bawdy remarks toward the girl, were really enjoying this and Ford's regret at having Wylla here returned.

"Why don't you go back home and see if you can find him? He maybe came back since."

Wylla seemed relieved to be released from her duties, and Ford was happy to see her go. Though he regarded her as a sister of sorts, the girl was more than he wished to deal with at the moment. And yet, as embarrassing as her presence was, the notion that he had just sent away his only hope of being released slowly dawned on him, growing stronger the longer he waited for his missing friend.

In the eyes of the law, breaking into a lord's abode was a far greater offense than knocking down a foreigner. He didn't think it was a hanging offense, especially since he hadn't stole anything, but they could try to blame him for the fire. The fact that there were numerous other fires blazing away throughout the east side of town he thought might be in his favor. Moreover, the Brastersceatts were harboring those creatures in their cellar, and they would likely try to keep the whole affair under wraps. Perhaps he would only owe a fine. Sweetening it with a bribe might be necessary. The Hold's common cell was quite crowded now, and it seemed like the Jailor was willing to pack it beyond capacity while there was still a chance of squeezing a few more coins out of the prisoners. At the next opportunity, Ford would remind him that he hadn't actually killed anyone.

Time passed, and his spirits quickly drooped in these surroundings. His company wore on him, reports of the waters rising below rattled everyone's nerves, Stanrocc Hold staff were fleeing like rats abandoning a sinking vessel, and the distressing noises of the city coming in through the windows made all of them anxious to break free. What a great relief it was then to see a sweating Stocky trudging through the door clutching a jingling pouch to his heaving chest. It took a while before he could speak.

"I been all over town," he said between huffs and puffs. "Got here soon as I could." He had the money for the bail, and he'd even brought something to eat. On their way from the Hold, Ford unwrapped a greasy cloth that held a handful of dried beef. He wolfed it down and gratefully took a wineskin from

Stocky. The wine had been watered down to the point of losing nearly all its potency, but that suited Ford just fine.

While he ate and drank, Stocky explained how he had waited by the Pennaeth's back door, but he had been run off by the House's caretaker. Figuring what would happen to Ford, he had gone to find the bail. At this point, they were just mounting Weald Bridge, and Ford was finishing up. Feeling much more human, he thanked his friend for all he had done. He was well aware how costly his actions had been to one in Stocky's position, what with the large family he had to care for, and it troubled him to burden him so.

"I'll pay you back for all this."

"Think nothing of it," said his friend, waving a dismissive hand.

"Wylla came to say you weren't home. She let slip you're out of work, so I know this ain't nothing. I got a little something coming to me, and you'll get back every bit I owe you." Ford looked out over the thrashing river to avoid seeing Stocky's embarrassment and to say that this was the end of the discussion. Only it wasn't.

"You don't owe me nothing." Stocky threw up a hand to ward off Ford's protests. "I got it from…from your ma." Ford stumbled off the end of the bridge into the waters flooding Brastersceatt Square. Having finally said what had been weighing on his mind for far too long, Stocky babbled at length, the words tumbling from him like the waters of the river. "See, I wanted to tell you she don't live nor work there at the lord's house, but you flew off before I could say anything, and besides, she made me promise not to say anything, and I kept my promise for years now. It's just become a regular way of things, so like always, I didn't say nothing."

"How?" asked Ford, but he had so many questions tripping over one another that he wasn't sure exactly what he was asking and had to fight to impose order on his jumbled thoughts. "Where? Where is she?" Reluctant even now to admit all he knew, Stocky evaded a direct answer, making distracted, noncommittal noises "Where is she, Stocky?" asked Ford, growing redder as his impatience mounted.

"You won't like it," said Stocky turning away to look out over the river.

"I don't care. Just tell me."

"Well, she ain't no maid, I'll tell ya that much." Stocky tossed off a flippant chuckle, but sweat was beading upon his brow.

"Tell me!"

"She works out at the fortuneteller's, the oily seer who tells your future. The Seer's Door. Mokaenyn's place. She said not to say, but I know you been looking for her hard and all and it just seemed like, oh, I don't know, it's now or never."

Ford caught only bits and pieces of what he said, so focused was he on one particular point. "You saying my mother works in a...that she's a..." His indignation tripped up his tongue. He got up close to search Stocky's face for any sign of mocking. "That's a lie!"

"I'm one of her best customers," Stocky said, spreading his arms wide, palms up. He did not like being called a liar, and his answer was defiantly flippant. Ford's fist flew so fast, and Stocky flopped over on to his backside so quickly that neither seemed sure what had just happened. The blow startled Stocky more than hurt him. Ford, while mortified by what he had done, was overruled by anger. He couldn't deal with the situation in the moment, so he spun around and splashed into the square.

"Damn me for a fool," Stocky said as he wiped his nose and grunted with the effort of getting back to his feet. "Shoulda seen that coming. Ford, wait! Hold up, son!" Ford's long strides swished through the water, while Stocky floundered behind, struggling through a swirling undercurrent. "I'm sorry! I'm sorry for what I said back there. It came out all wrong. Will you listen? Just listen." Ford finally stopped, climbed atop a pile of blocks at the new Weaverite temple construction site, and sat facing away from his friend. Stocky came around and stood before him in water that was chest-high to him. When the old secrecy made him hesitate even now, he forced himself to plow on. "It was years ago. I was going in one day, and you were coming out, and she pulls me aside, shoves coin in my hand and tells me to watch after you, which I done."

Ford dropped his head into his hands. It all made sense now, how Stocky had accosted him that day some two years prior and attached himself, forced a kind of friendship upon them, even helping him get work as a porter down at the docks. Doubt crept over him in light of the facts, leaving Ford to wonder about their friendship. Stocky felt the judging eyes upon him and saw Ford looking at him like a stranger.

"I didn't know why at the start, but finally she told me, and I kept at it even after she stopped paying. Truth be told she only paid the once." He avoided mentioning that Ford's mother had given him a generous discount on her services Afterward. It didn't seem the sort of thing Ford would want to hear, he mused while rubbing the spot on his cheekbone where he had been hit. "It was what it was, but what happened after, that came from here." He patted his own chest. "I didn't have to invite you into my family. You think Wynna was happy with things at the start? No sir, but she, like me, we got to know you, and you got on with the girls. Not none of all that"—here he waved a hand in the vague direction of the Seer's Door—"mattered so much after we got to know you. You're family now. Always will be!"

Ford took all this in, and it mingled with his own reflections, with the very fact that he, himself, had guessed that his mother might have had to take up that line of work. It was, after all, the reason he had frequented every brothel in the city he could find. It would be hypocritical of him to hold this against his friend.

"I'm sorry," was all Ford could reply for fear of losing control of his voice and breaking down in front of the only man approaching a father he had left in his life. He did manage a smile of sorts and held out his hand, and that was that.

"With all what's been going on, I forgot to tell you what happened at the Pennaeth's house. You won't believe it!" Ford was happy to have a distracting topic at hand to help them forget the unpleasantness between them, and he told of his encounter with the creatures in the cellar while helping his friend through the flooded square. It was likely Stocky would not have believed the story if not for the evidence of the strange severed fingers.

"You got to show them," said Stocky, repeating it numerous times without clarifying who *them* was. Ford could only think of Whetstone in the moment, partly from an ignorance of the upper echelons of power and partly from the distraction of their surroundings. Pandemonium had taken over Brastersceatt Square. Smoke rose above the buildings. Residents and shop owners had boarded up windows and sandbagged their doors if those doors were still above water-level. People carried away possessions, some of which were their own. Two women tugged at a body floating face down. In the northeast corner of the square a group of young men were shouting down another smaller group, who backed up their own shouts with bricks and boards.

In the midst of such disarray, no one took much notice of a few more shouts mingled among the rest, so it was not until citizens in the street were scattering left and right that Ford and Stocky saw the Haunan priest and his curates running at them, robes flapping about and dragging behind like anchors in the water. A young, beardless novice had the right idea, stripping off his robe and dashing ahead of the others unencumbered.

Now Ford and Stocky could see the priests' pursuers, two men with ash-blackened faces, one brandishing a sword, the other reloading a crossbow, splashing down the street after them with the madness of the chase blazing in the whites of the their hungry eyes. Behind them, a masked rider in a long hooded cloak rode into view on a steed prancing nervously through the muddy water. The rider spurred his horse on, digging his heels into its flank and bawling commands into its ears.

Ford and Stocky stepped aside and let the priests run by in a frightened, red-faced hurry. The last of them, a lanky but determined-looking youth guarding their rear with threatening waves of a knobbed mace, fell into the water with a crossbow bolt through his neck. The rider stood tall in the saddle, thrust forward a short rod and shot at the group a quivering, clear airwave like a long, straight multi-segmented worm. It expanded in circumference to the thickness of a bull's torso as it shuddered rapidly by Ford, vibrating his eardrums with fluttering thuds that instantly nauseated him and sent harsh tingles through one of his arms. He grasped at his stomach as he spun away from it and saw Stocky collapsing beside him, his friend's shocked eyes popping from his head as he sank beneath the water. Ford fished him out, but the men pushing by in pursuit of their quarry knocked him off-balance and dunked them both under. Ford emerged to see the rider, kicking his horse into a leaping gallop, charging straight at them. Taking hold of Stocky's collar and he lifted him from the water, but slipped on the slick ground, regained his feet and yanked at his cumbersome friend, who only floated slowly over the surface like a barge for a moment before sinking again. Seeing the flurry of powerful hooves bounding through the water ever closer, Ford leapt on top of his friend and drove them both down under the water. The horse and rider leapt clear and continued on after the priests.

"What's the matter? Can't you move?" Ford begged of Stocky, struggling to hold his choking friend's head above water. "Cough it up! Come on, spit it out!" Stocky, rigid as a fencepost, spouted and sputtered the water gurgling in his throat. "Get it all out. That's it." Stocky spit out enough water to cough and gasp in a lungful of air. "Can you stand?" His friend looked him in the eye from a terror-stricken face and could do nothing more than wheeze.

Grabbing him under the arms, Ford dragged Stocky to the nearest set of stairs that wasn't submerged and tried to lug him up it. His burden was heavy and awkward, and halfway up, Ford fell on the slippery steps. Driving his elbow hard into the stone, he kicked out in pain and exasperation at his own clumsiness, collapsing part of the low stone wall that had been originally built on the outer edge of the stairway in order to keep people from accidentally stepping off. Some of the loosened stone toppled over into the water. After some grimacing, he shook it off and returned his attention to his friend.

"How do you feel?" he asked, but not a word of complaint came from Stocky. Ford tried in vain to drag him the rest of the way up the steps, but couldn't manage it without slipping. Stocky groaned a little as they sat there together. Ford tried his best to comfort him but hardly knew how and only managed a few meaningless phrases in a somewhat soothing tone, feeling so utterly foolish that he half hoped Stocky's hearing had been paralyzed as well. After a time the fear left Stocky's face, and he went emotionless as well as motionless, but for the slightest remaining hint of panic in his eyes.

"I'm sorry, I've got nothing left," said Ford. "Let me rest a bit, and we'll try again. Who knows, maybe it'll wear off. I felt a little something, numb-like in one arm, but now it's mostly gone, so maybe you'll be better in a bit, too. If not, I'll go get someone. I have a cousin, he might know what to do," he said thinking about Danny and mages in general and wondered at the use of magic against someone out in the open as bold as can be in broad daylight. "Something ain't right." His eyes passed over the chaos in the square and wandered to the Pennaeth's charred and smoking husk of a house before falling upon Stocky lain out like a board on the stone steps. "You got to be hurtin' there. I almost got my breath back. We'll try the old legs and see if we can't pull you up the rest of the way. Then we can see about getting you home, my old friend."

"Porter!" Wrapped in surprise, greedy gladness and a sneering contempt, those two simple syllables were carried across the square by a rasp all too familiar to Ford. He looked up, and there was Barker with his arms open in mock welcome as he sloshed toward him. Behind Barker, Grady threw aside the limp body he had been shaking and followed after. A woman passing between Ford and Barker with a stack of folded blankets and assorted garments balanced on her head held up to let Barker pass before her while keeping her eyes lowered in lieu of bowing her head. Catching up with his boss, Grady knocked her into the water as if she were not even there.

After the initial shock, Ford sprang to his feet and jumped down into the water. They hadn't seen Stocky lying half-submerged on the steps facing away from them, and he wanted to keep it that way. He leaned back, hefted one of the loose stones from the stairs and advanced on Barker and Grady. Keene wasn't with them, and that worried him. He would almost rather fight all three at once than be left wondering from where the probable ambush was coming and having to keep his guard up in all directions. *Keep the house to your back*, he told himself and began pivoting this way and that to keep an eye on his flanks.

"You look concerned, Porter. Where's your little band of friends?" asked Barker. "You didn't even bring your fancy club. Bet you're regretting that now." He flashed a knife and a cutting smile. "Always come prepared, Porter." Grady slipped a club from his belt and waved it back and forth while slapping its thick head with his palm. Still coming forward, Barker lunged for Ford with his knife, but only in fun and bellowed an exaggerated, sardonic laugh when Ford jumped back, nearly tumbling over into the water. Grady joined in with his thick guffaw. This was his kind of humor.

"Can't fight me on your own, Grady? Need daddy's help?" Ford taunted. That wiped the smile off the mountainous thug's face and drew Grady to him.

It was what Ford wanted, but then Grady stepped crab-wise to flank Ford, and there was nothing Ford could do about it. If he went for one or the other he would have one of them on his back, so he did the only thing he could do and gave them both a wide berth, stepping back and to the side again and again in a broad arc. It brought Barker and Grady in a position where they could see Stocky laid out on the steps if they turned to look, but as Ford hoped, they kept their eyes on him and followed his every move across the square to the construction site. He bumped into one of the huge blocks and climbed atop it in order to take advantage of the higher ground. Here he could place the stone blocks, partial walls, and pillar bases as barriers between himself and them.

"Don't run away, Porter! This fight's just getting started!" Barker laughed as if having made a hilarious joke. Ford couldn't tell if he was drunk on spirits or just the situation, what with his reckoning at hand and no one around who would stop it, not in the city's current state of insanity.

The notion to beg for more time, to tell Barker that he could get his money, hardly touched Ford's righteous core. The money Barker thought was owed him was and had always been Ford's. He had never struck a deal with Barker willingly. It was under duress that he had been forced into fixed fights, and Ford knew that this would just keep going on and on endlessly. Barker and his toadies would pressure him into fights and squeeze the purses out of him until his reputation was shot and he was all used up from taking shots to the head. There would be no end to it until he was dead or, if he were lucky, merely maimed for life.

Barker climbed on to a stone on one side of him, and Grady found another on the other side. With shuffling steps, they crept in on him until the space between them was too tight for comfort and Ford jumped off his block, plummeting neck-deep into a foundation divot where the builders hadn't yet placed blocks in an unfinished section. He kicked his feet out and struggled to climb out. An undercurrent pressed on him, and he fell backward and went under. Barker cackled away, long and loud. Grady pursued with a determined grunting as he forced his way through the water. Half swimming, Ford splashed around unsure of his feet as they twisted and searched for footing. Grady lurched at him with unexpected speed, swinging for Ford's head, once high and then too low, catching his club in a splash of water that momentarily blinded

Ford. Blinking his eyes clear, he saw Barker lunging from the side stabbing at his face, but his footing was off too, and he flopped forward and disappeared.

Ford had instinctively recoiled, pressing his back against a pillar segment and moving around it to shield himself. Grady clambered over the emerging Barker and swung wildly, cracking the club on the pillar as Ford ducked aside. Circling around, he swung again and the club connected with Ford's skull, but the damaged weapon splintered over his head into two useless pieces. Grady stared at the stump of his club in surprise, just long enough for Ford to bring his stone down on Grady's head. With his teeth clenched and all his force concentrated in his arm, Ford threw a punch as straight as he could, yet his weighted fist was just slow enough for his opponent to turn away so that the rock did little more than tear across Grady's forehead, scraping off skin and sending a stream of blood washing over his face. Grady was left dazed but standing. Ford could sense Barker close behind. He raised the stone again, unsure which way to turn. Grady swayed, blinked bleary-eyed at Ford, and then fell forward grabbing him by the neck. Ford felt a sting in the back of his arm as he and Grady tumbled together into the water. They thrashed about, increasingly desperate for air as they grappled one another. Finding footing, Ford pushed against Grady and broke free. Both burst to the surface, spitting out muddy water and sucking in deep breaths. Ford recovered, having lost his rock, and with Grady still gagging and floundering about, he turned toward Barker who was close at hand. The two men faced off with one another as Ford sidled away from Grady to put both of his enemies before him.

***

The second wind that had buoyed Ford for a time after first encountering Barker and Grady was now ebbing away. Holding every muscle taut and ready for an attack while this relentless fight went on would soon wear him out. He knew from experience that he would succumb and fall prey to a relatively simple attack if he didn't end this fast. But Barker wasn't advancing. He merely stared at Ford, seeming confused and unsure of himself. A cloth doll floated between them. Grady coughed up a slug of mud.

A renewed surge of pain stung the back of Ford's arm and his hand, instinctively going to the area, felt an odd protrusion. He lifted the arm and from it dangled Barker's knife. Gripping the bone handle, slippery with a coating of red-brown slime, he yanked it free of his flesh with only a twinge of pain, much less than he had anticipated. A fresh gush of his own blood poured from the hole in his tunic. A dizziness overtook him, and a ringing in his ears warped his hearing. Grady's noisy splashing as he lumbered ever closer sounded like far off tinkling. All the noises bombarding his ears morphed into strange vocal apparitions of their true forms. Ford even imagined he heard someone call out his name from somewhere in the distance. He shook it off and splashed the top of his head and down the back of his neck with cold water to combat the hazy feelings and oncoming nausea.

During this brief lapse in the fight, Ford's eyes had never left Barker. Now that Ford had his knife, Barker looked grim and even more determined to finish off this debtor, whose defiance had made a mockery of him and lost him one of his trusted henchmen when Keene had left and gone to work providing muscle for another boss.

Just then something caught up in the unpredictable undercurrent rolled on to the back of Ford's legs. He thought it might have been a log or maybe one of the planks off the collapsed grandstand. Yet, this was more pliant than that. He stepped backward over it and let it pass on. Barker looked distractedly down at where his feet would be as the thing bumped against his legs, and just then Ford jumped forward and whipped the knife straight up, slashing Barker's chest and chin. Barker spun away, and Ford plunged the knife into his shoulder, driving him down into the water.

Grady stood by, stunned and as helpless as a child. Barker broke the surface thrashing like an enraged serpent, twisting his arms around and scrabbling wildly about his back for the knife until he found the handle. He plucked at it, but the reach was too far and the handle too slick. Ford fell upon him and wrenched the knife free just as Grady plowed into his blindside, dragging them both under the water in a bear hug that kept Ford's arms as well as the knife under wraps. With the wind knocked out of him, air was all he thought of. His head bumped off the ground as he struggled to break the hold and fought to reach the surface. His lungs burned, his throat convulsed, and he was about to pass out, but Grady let him go and they both vaulted up to suck in air. Ford feebly lashed out blind with the knife this way and that, spinning about as he missed and connected, but with what he couldn't tell. When finally he wiped his eyes clear, there was Grady little more than an arm's length away holding up a gashed forearm to protect his face, while beside him Barker was falling back grasping at his own throat.

"Go on, you!" growled Barker grabbing Grady by the shoulder and thrusting him forward.

Ford could never be described as quick. There were smaller, lighter men who could duck and dodge him, but Grady was neither of those. He was large and ponderous. A moment later, these deficiencies were written plain in fresh slash marks across his face, chest, and arms before he sank beneath the surface of the water, to see and be seen no more.

Still holding the bloody knife wrapped tight in his shaking hand, Ford breathed heavily and felt so weak that even the weight of his soaked clothes would be enough to drag him under if he were not careful. Struck by a wave of lightheadedness, he swayed around and faced Barker. The former fighter turned sadistic impresario looked old, haggard and unsure of himself. Badly bloodied, weaponless and without his lackey, now he was the one stumbling backward over the unseen, uneven ground with an armed and merciless enemy in pursuit. Barker got clear of the temple construction site and fled splashing from the square like a wounded duck flopping about and trying to take flight from a choppy lake. Winded and too tired to keep up, Ford lagged behind and eventually gave up the chase.

He sloshed through the water with the feeling that he was dragging his legs rather than being borne along by them. His cursing and frustration mounted as he slogged along ever slower until finally he snapped and forced himself forward, leaping clear of the water in giant bounds. Skidding to a stop in front of the stairs where he had left his friend, he saw no sign of Stocky. A hope kindled within him that his friend had gotten miraculously better and decided to get up and leave, an only mildly ludicrous thought considering the state Ford was in. He jumped for the stairs, from which he might get a better view around the square and tripped on something under the water. Collapsing on to it, he splashed about until regaining balance on his hands and knees. Beneath him, just an inch under the surface was the murky image of a pale Stocky staring vacantly back at him.

Panic-stricken and fighting off a fast and inevitably sinking heart, he clamped on to soaked cloth and pliant flesh to drag his friend free of the water and up on to the top of the landing with a reserve of strength granted to him from some desperate place deep within. Sludgy water streamed away from Stocky's lifeless body. Ford collapsed alongside and shouted into his friend's face, shook him, and pounded upon his chest, not knowing what else to do, but refusing to give up hope. He cried out to the folk in the square and anyone that ventured near, but they either shied away from the frantic man shouting at them or ignored him altogether.

Though his faith was low, he prayed and thought of finding a priest. Even Will, Elle's neighbor, would do, though Ford held a grudge against him, believing that Will had turned him in to the authorities for striking down the wife-beater. Regardless, he doubted the young priest could revive a drowned man. Even if he could, Ford couldn't afford one of those rare holy men who could work such a miracle. To find a kindhearted healer so openhanded as to work for free in this flooded, burning city filled with folk in dire need was hope beyond all reasonable hope.

Like a snapping of fingers in his mind, he realized he could try Danny and see what magic might do. Gripping Stocky under the arms and hoisting him up, he slid the body back down the stairs and tried a few steps across the treacherous ground. The awkward and immense weight in his tired arms made it all but impossible. His grip began to fail, and terror seized him with thoughts of losing Stocky altogether in the murky pool that was Brastersceatt Square. All he could do was bring the body back to the steps.

"I'm sorry. I'm sorry," he repeated, throwing himself down beside Stocky and dropping his forehead upon Stocky's chest. Silent spasms bounced his head off the body of this friend who would not be dead if it weren't for him. Gradually he broke into sobs for a length of time untold to him. People passed but paid him no heed. Eventually he sat up, huddled in a crouch and hung his head, trying to calm himself, to steady his thoughts. He hadn't lost someone he loved so much in some time. What had happened to Yonn was distressing, but this was something entirely different. Why did some people, good people like Stocky, die when others, worthless sorts like himself got to carry on? He couldn't answer that. A step to the right and he would have been in the line of fire and in Stocky's position. It seemed like the unjust work of a vindictive god. The man who had been like a father to him was gone, and there seemed to be nothing left but despair and the painful pit in his stomach.

There was something left, he realized, lifting his head to stare out over the square, over the river, and to the city on its far bank. Stocky had left him his mother. He had resurrected her after Ford had all but given up the search. Now he could and would find her. This spark of joy nearly thrust him thoughtlessly to his feet. "No." He leaned back against the great house, the stairs upon which he trespassed. First he would regain his strength and carry Stocky home. "We'll get you back to your Wynna."

People rushed by sometimes shouting or screaming, the waters swirled about the square in unpredictable patterns, the smoke floated over the roofs, and all the while Ford continued to stare out over the river. At first, his gaze had only sporadically lingered upon Stanrocc Hold, but now its focus sharpened and fixated on that ancient prison that stood out more than any other structure on the far bank. There was something there, something about it that was drawing him back by the tail ends of his deepest thoughts. Eventually, he found himself nodding in affirmation of what he believed he had seen and what he now knew he must do.

"I'll look after them, the kids, Wynna, all of them, I promise," he said plucking at Stocky's sleeve, grabbing up his hand to warm it and swear on his promise. "And I will take you home, but wait for me. There's one thing that has to be done first." He rose to one knee, placed a splayed-fingered hand upon Stocky's chest, prayed, and made a silent vow to return for him. Then he got up and waded through the square on his way to Stanrocc Hold.

Back up the worn steps that curved around the smooth stones of the round towers that made up the barbican entryway of the prison, he strode through the empty corridors to the head of the stairs that led down to the cells where he had been held and stared dumbstruck at a stairwell filled with still, black water. The entire cell level below had been completely submerged.

A set determination prompted by sleep-deprived stupidity made him step down into the water as if he might stroll under the surface to his destination. Its icy chill snapped him out of it, and he pulled his foot back. If there was anyone below, they would have drowned by now. He cast about for other possibilities and ran to the Jailor's chambers, but the Jailor and his staff were gone. Only the murderer and the rapist remained in the common cell, sitting away from the gated door with wary, almost frightened eyes occasionally glancing toward a mound of filthy rags in a corner of the Jailor's office. The pile shivered. The rags revealed themselves to be a robe with a diamond pattern. Ford knelt down beside it. The soiled garment held none of its previous charm. The knotted hair covering the buried face had lost its luster. Underneath was a human that had once been far more human. Ford guessed that he had something to do with this degraded figure, maybe a great deal to do with it. Guilt seized him, bringing with it an old, childhood urge to flee the scene. Shame at his own immaturity made him stay. This wasn't a case of getting caught with your finger in a pie; this was someone's life. His hand hovered over the body and then touched a lump he took for a shoulder. There was no reaction, just constant shaking. The chilly air and cold, damp clothes sent a shiver through his own body. Pulling gently at the clothes and brushing back the hair, he could hardly believe what he was seeing.

"Addy? Adeline?" She rolled up in a tighter ball, and his hand slid over her knobby spine. He leaned back and took in her whole fragile form. "Come on, let's get you out of here," he said and lifted her into his arms with ease. She shrieked like a caged, tortured animal and lashed with flailing arms and nails that dug deep. She kicked and thrashed almost more than he could handle and nearly broke free of his hold, but he didn't let go and held her through the confusion and disorder of the streets where even amid all the turmoil there—people fleeing with their possessions to higher ground and boarding up their houses and shops–her behavior still drew peculiar looks. He held her close until at last her writhing body gave out, and she curled up within herself.

At the mercer's shop, he kicked in the door and pushed past the mercer's affronted and gawping family on his way up to Adeline's room where he laid her on the bed. She rolled over to face away from him. He wanted to apologize, thinking that even the most insignificant words of comfort would have done, but he doubted whether, in her delirium, she could hear him or would even want to. She seemed so remote, and unlike the Adeline he had known, so inhuman as to make him wonder if she would understand him. Lingering over her body—her dress was ripped in places, and even her undergarments had been torn, revealing her pale skin—he hardly believed she was the woman with whom he had been so intimate. He took a blanket from the chair and laid it over her, then went and sat on the edge of the chair and looked about the room. It was quite bare, having been stripped of some of her furnishings. Opening the window to let in light and air, he caught his reflection in the water of the basin. Scratches covered his face. A drop of blood broke the image.

"You can't leave her here! She's no better than a rabid animal," said the indignant mercer's wife meeting him at the bottom of the stairs.

"That's what I just did, and you *will* leave her here!" He leaned into the woman, almost touching noses. "She stays right here." She shrank away, gathering herself up next to her daughter, who slipped from her clinging grasp and leaned just close enough to hand Ford a clean rag.

"Hanny!" scolded her mother. Ford took it, wiped his face and hands, and tossed the soiled rag on to a neat stack of new silk, then grabbed a hunk of bread from a plate beside the mercer and bit off a mouthful. The mercer blinked uncontrollably and, though he seemed on the brink of shedding his cold reserve and possibly protesting, his bent frame withered beneath Ford's challenging glower.

"Make sure she's cared for," he said, pointing the butt-end of the loaf at the family. "Food. Clothing." He looked them over. "Now!" They hopped to and set about finding the things he demanded.

CHAPTER 18
HOPE IN THE BALANCE

Joy and sorrow played for mastery over Ford's emotions. His world had been tipped upside down, but at least he had gotten one thing right. There was also the satisfaction in having slammed the mercer's door and shattered one of his expensive glass windows. Yes, he decided, action was the thing to cleanse the mind and lift the spirits.

Buoyed by the anticipated reunion with his mother, he found strength enough in his tired legs to carry him through the mostly empty and eerily quiet Brynseht streets. Passing closed shops and shuttered houses, he went back to Weald Bridge, where he found overwrought Eastfeld folk–mostly servants of wealthy Brynseht masters–fighting to get back to their families. A motley assortment of edgy and uneasy men-at-arms, some of them the Iarl's own House Guards with a few watchmen's jerkins visible among them, held back the increasingly belligerent townsfolk while shielding a team of carpenters industriously nailing spikes into the bridge gate and laying supports to further secure the great double doors. Above them agile boys greased the top of the gate with animal fat.

Ford joined the washerwomen, nursemaids, dung carters and gutter sweeps with anxious eyes that implored and hands that gripped the guards' jerkins as if they were the last lifeline of hope. "Let me through! I have to get through!" he shouted, adding his voice to their anguish. Beyond the gate could be seen the smoke rising over the Eastfeld neighborhoods, and it drove these people mad to be held back from their loved ones.

On the opposite side of the gate, a small handful of residents from the west side of town pounded on the boards. Their initial annoyance mingled with panic at the thought of having once again to face the floods and fire behind them. However, the guards would not open the gates for them either, for fear that once open, they might never get the gates closed again.

"You can't pass! Get back, get back," snarled Sergeant Aleward of the Iarl's House Guard, whirling his barrel of a body around and pulling a sword on Ford.

Brusque at the best of times, today he was especially irritable after being kept up all night chasing after his ambitious captain without the chance to check on his own family. The sergeant pressed forward the point of his blade along with his defiant, stubby nose set in the vast space between severe, red eyes on a face as rough as his nature. Ford spread wide his empty hands and backed away.

"Master Ford!" Dillon's beaming face emerged from among those guarding the gate. They fought their way to one of the less crowded sides of the bridge and gripped each other's arms in greeting.

"By the gods, it's good to see you," said Ford. "What's happening here?"

"It's a revolt!" Dillon's excited shout topped the tumult at the gate and the roar of the roiling waters beneath them.

"What? By who?"

"They think it's Pennaeth Brastersceatt's people!"

"It is Brastersceatt," said a decisive voice behind Ford. "Glad to see you here, my boy!" Whetstone slapped Ford on the shoulder. "Lord, look at you! Got in a bit of a scrape, did we?"

Ford nodded as he greeted him and stared dumbly at the man. Overwhelmed by the chaos and with too many questions rolling about in his head to follow what was being said to him, he caught only bits and pieces about lifting the dam's gate at the lake in Down Hills to flood the canals and much of Eastfeld, the bribing of the castle guard, and a small peasant's army formed by the Pennaeth and the heads of the Weaverite religion.

"Don't you see?" said Whetstone, grabbing Ford and leaning with him over the edge of the bridge to point out the flags and banners mustered in Brastersceatt Square. Ford saw, but only superficially. Whetstone was all that he saw with any degree of understanding.

"My friend," he stammered while grabbing Whetstone about the shoulders to turn and face him. "What happened to my friend?" The past few days had been just as long and wearying for Whetstone as for Ford, and so while one shook the other and the other resisted being shook, utter incomprehension blinded Whetstone until Ford finally added in a lower voice, "My friend the thief?"

"Ah, that! We grabbed her. I had a word with the Master, and on my recommendation she's being transported. She's on one of them ships." Whetstone nodded to the distant bay in the south where all shipping, even the tiniest of fishing boats, had been removed when the river became unsafe. Sodden, leaking hulks of retired merchant vessels were moored there in their present occupation as temporary floating prisons. The guilt and worry of what Ford had done to Elle dissolved and his mind and his body released so much pent up tension that he nearly collapsed from sheer relief at hearing she was safe. Horns blared, and drums slapped and thudded from beyond the river.

"Here they come!" shouted Sergeant Aleward clearing a path with his elbows through the dissonant swarm of people. "Whetstone, rally your men and help me clear this bridge!"

"Follow me!" shouted Whetstone to Ford and Dillon before diving into the crowd to help the sergeant pull citizens away from the gate. Dillon followed willingly enough, but Ford held back. He had more important things to do than harass distraught citizens and fight crazed zealots. Maybe he couldn't cross the river here, but he could flee the city through some open gate along Brynseht's ancient city wall to the north or west; thence he might escape to the fields, where he could find another bridge upriver and come back around to the east side of the city to find his mother.

He backed away from the pandemonium at the bridge gate and there, across the river, he saw once more the oncoming flags and banners and felt the thunder of feet upon the bridge as the Pennaeth's rabble of an army came to take the city in order to mold it as they saw fit. Like a splash of cold water to the face on a hot day, his eyes opened to the hardship that would befall his mother. If the Pennaeth Brastersceatt came into power, the Weaverites would be granted the right to shut down the brothels. Although he didn't like the idea of his mother in such a place, she had depended upon it for an income all these years. And more than that, the Weaverites would go well beyond the closing down of brothels. Following their strict code of morals, their leaders would enact edicts that strove to subjugate womankind. He watched the oncoming horde, the carpenters securing the gate against them, the guards trying to push the citizens off the bridge, Whetstone and the other watchmen stowing clubs for spears, and he knew this was not all going to blow over without a fight that would determine the future of those he loved. His mother would be safe for now, out there on the far eastern edge of the city well away from the bloodshed. He didn't have to run to her now. If anything he felt a duty to stay and fight for her, to fight alongside Whetstone. He owed that much to the man who had saved Elle's life.

"Hold the bridge! We must hold the bridge!" the sergeant shouted. To Ford it sounded like they *would* hold the bridge, they *would* stop the revolt right here, they *would* win, and the way of life he cherished could go on as before. Perhaps, reunited with his mother, it might be better than ever.

Ford rushed forward through the crowd and made it to the guards just as the rolling, indistinct murmur of horns and drums exploded in a reverberating squall and the gates buckled inward. Carpenters tumbled over, scrambled to their feet and fled through a fast panicking mob. The sky darkened with a sudden hail of rocks, sticks, hammers, roper's clubs, and even pieces of the bridge itself, which flew over the gate like a mixed flock of birds. Most of the flipping projectiles thumped harmlessly on the planks, while some bounced off the helmets and armor of the House Guards, and a few came down on the cowering heads of unarmored citizens, knocking one man off the bridge and slicing open the cheek of an astonished woman.

The barrage of missiles ended, but not the ferocious din of hollering and cursing voices as the towering wooden doors shuddered with the pounding of dozens of fists and the butts of weapons. The rabid and bloodthirsty threat made the gate seem almost insubstantial with its moldy, rotting boards weakened by weather and age. It rattled, and the bridge shook as if possessed by the whims of an earthquake.

"Hold 'em, boys!" shouted the sergeant and the House Guards lowered their halberds, those spear-like poles with the murderous ax heads, and leaned their shoulders against the doors and supports. Sharp cracks and bangs like hammers and hail drummed on the planks.

"It's holding!" cried a gleeful watchman.

"Hold your tongue!" commanded the sergeant. All the House Guards and watchmen fell silent. The last of the civilians fled the bridge. The rabble beyond the gate ceased their harassing calls and began a curious cheering too strange for the sergeant to ignore. "Damn savages!" he growled, sliding back the shutter of a lookout's window slit and peering through the hole to see what the enemy was up to. A spearhead stabbed through the hole, through his eye, and into his brain. Without uttering a sound, he fell flat on his back. Whetstone dropped with him, kneeling by his side and shifting the man's head to check the damage. His hand was instantly covered in spewing blood. The gore blanched the faces of some and proved too much for a few, who turned tail and ran.

"Come back! Damn cowards!" shouted Whetstone upon seeing that they were watchmen. He pounded his fist upon the bridge planks. "Don't another one of you dare turn coward!" He defied those gathered about him with a withering glare. Vastly outnumbered and sensing death lingering just the other side of the gate, they gripped the handles of their weapons so tight as to turn their fingers white. Their eyes twitched, and their heads jerked at sudden noises, and their anxious feet edged away from the gate. "We need men who will stand together!" The fighting spirit, buried within Whetstone after long years since his last battle as a spear-wielding soldier in the Iarl's peasant ranks, rose up and infused courage into the two dozen or so guards and watchmen.

"I'll stand and fight." Whetstone looked up at Ford, the tallest of all of them there, and thanked him with grateful eyes.

"Of course we're with you!" put in one of the House Guards. None of them would be outdone in bravery by a watchman. This show of courage bolstered the confidence of the remainder.

An awful chortle from a disembodied mouth framed in the window slit sneered back at them and spat through blackened teeth, "You bitch's arse lickers!" Another, equally foul, pushed it aside to screech, "Fucking pig fuckers!"

"Shut that up!" commanded Whetstone. Ford lunged for the window. The mouths disappeared, and a spearhead shot through the hole just under his chin. It vanished back through the hole and then jabbed through again. This time Ford grabbed the shaft, yanked it free, then spun it around and jammed it back through the window, slamming into something solid. A wild shriek from the other side brought a cheer out of the House Guards and watchmen. The spear shaft rattled around in the hole, and Whetstone leapt up, shoved it back through and slid home the window's shutter. He gave Ford a nod and ducked his head as the gate buckled under the crash of an impact from the other side. A crack appeared down the length of one of the gate's boards and a support split. The cries of those around them drowned Whetstone's first shouts, but Ford heard him say, "…must have some kind of ram."

Among the hurled rocks, sticks and weapons at their feet, Ford spotted a dropped club and scooped it up, but cast it aside in favor of a blacksmith's hammer, then spun about at the sound of another crash at the gate. A splintered board fell away, and the newly-sawed end of log was thrust in and pulled back, leaving a gap behind. In its place appeared a bug-eyed and oil-darkened face poking inward and spewing black flecks in the air as it spat, "You're all fuckin' dead!"

"The gate's coming down!" cried a watchman.

"We make our stand at Middlefield House! Follow me!" bellowed Whetstone. Under his direction they made for Wamb Hill, running down the bridge into the water that was washing over the embankment, past Stanrocc Hold, and into Brynseht. Residents peeked out from doors and windows to watch those few of their neighbors caught out in the otherwise deserted streets fleeing in fear before the troop of armed men stomping through their narrow lanes.

Whetstone's shortcut up winding stairs behind a spice merchant's did little to shorten the brutal run up the hill. It winded them all, and he allowed a quick stop at a well, where they gulped greedily from a bucket as if their lives depended on slurping up as much as possible. Then, for the first time, Ford noticed that one of the remaining watchmen was not a man at all, but rather Moll Turner, the lone woman from the night watch.

"Damn it," Whetstone sighed after counting heads and realizing some of his people had run off. A pulsing vein formed at his temple as he circled the well with his hands on his hips and his head down. "All right, that's enough! Let's go! Ford, lead on!" Trailing just behind the last man, Whetstone called out to individuals along the way, giving praise and encouragement, prodding when necessary, but above all making sure no one else escaped. The House Guards would stick it out, but he hoped to arrive with at least some of his watchmen.

Middlefield, the Iarl's fortified house did not stand out like some of the ponderous and overwrought guildhalls and other administrative buildings surrounding it, so it was not until they tore around the corner of Wrights' Hall that they could see the house's upper floor and roof rising above its encircling wall, a simple enclosure of precisely cut stone that stood not much taller than Ford's head. Being the first to reach its spindly gold-painted gate set in a tall granite wishbone arch, he shouted for the sentry there. "Let us in!" To the nervous sentry, Ford seemed the embodiment of the barbaric murderers the young man been told were in revolt against his dearly loved Iarl. Fumbling to bring up his halberd, he backed away and would have raised the alarm, but for his comrades the House Guards racing up behind Ford, demanding the gate be opened.

Working as a porter, Ford had passed the house several times but had never been past the gate. Once he found himself within the walls, the great house took on a modestly grand magnificence. Its two wings stretched out to either side so that it seemed one was walking into the welcoming arms of a stout grandmother. Huge stone blocks set its foundation, finer blocks made up its first story and topping this was a lofty garrisoned second story of a dark wood trimmed in brown. Its swirling oak leaf gingerbread moldings all along the eaves added an airier touch that still managed to maintain an appropriate dignity in keeping with religious standards. The solid lower level was more defense-oriented with the infrequent windows closest to the ground too thin for anyone to squeeze through, while the upper level held vast rectangular grids of enormous glass panes like inquisitive eyes. All around the foundation, beds of flowers bloomed in an array of colors. It gave a more lively look to the otherwise drab grounds largely covered by a gray flagstone courtyard and surrounded by the undecorated outer wall, at the base of which the house's gardener had left behind a pile of weeds in a barrow from an unfinished job.

The courtyard would have been spacious enough but for the gathered men and a type of wagon that amazed Ford. Unlike the open carts and ox-drawn wagons he knew, it had a large box with a little door and window, very much like a tiny house. A pale, but determined-looking driver sat atop it and held the reins to a pair of strong and steady horses.

"It's the Iarl's carriage," said Whetstone coming up to stand next to Ford and following his awe-struck gaze. He was about to say more, but just then some of the House Guards came from behind the house where they were trying the servant's entrance door.

"Locked," reported one of them. He didn't direct this to Whetstone, but rather said it to the assembly in general. Now that the House Guards were back on their own turf they no longer felt bound to Whetstone. There was no malevolence to it, perhaps pride, but the fact was that they took orders from their captain. If there was pride, Ford could not blame them, he, himself, would have been proud to wear one of their bright blue tunics with the Iarl's heraldic symbols of a fish and sheaf of wheat upon a sail over a mail shirt, all gathered in with a wide leather belt. If it came to a fight, he was glad at least to be on their side.

From the tall double doors of the main entrance strode the Captain of the House Guards, a man of spare build, but whose impressive bearing that exuded evident command. No one questioned the man with the sharp chin that pointed wherever he was going and the intense eyebrows framing a penetrating gaze that withered larger men. Captain Hartfield knew his business. All of the handpicked men who served under Hartfield could have dominated him physically, yet each respected his honest, direct nature and sound judgment to such an extent that they never dreamed of challenging him.

Ford was surprised to see the Jailor of Stanrocc Hold reluctantly trailing after him. For his part, the Jailor was just as surprised to be there. More than a dozen other officials had managed to concoct excuses or otherwise elude their duty, yet somehow he had been reluctantly roped into this mess. Very irregular it was, in his opinion. However, in an emergency such as this Hartfield wielded authority over him.

The Jailor was not a man who instilled confidence in Hartfield, but he would have to do. They had been speaking of arrangements for the defense of the house, and when the Jailor answered the captain back in a low mumble that he would rather no one else heard, the captain hacked through the hitherto cordial conversation. "You *will* stay and hold this position! That is a command!" The Jailor, already out of his element and highly distraught, recoiled, turned a sickly shade of yellow and began to sweat. The Captain regained a measure of calm and went on in a more conciliatory tone, one meant not to be overheard. The guards and watchmen, putting on a ludicrous act of disinterest, nevertheless caught his every word. "There is no one of rank left but you, so defend the gate as long as possible and then, if need be, fall back and defend from within the house. Just give us some time. Every moment counts. The further I can get the Iarl away, the better."

Whether he expected a reply or not, he received none from the Jailor and moved on to relay instructions to the carriage-driver. A signal was given. Both doors of the gate were flung open, the driver snapped the reins, and the horses took off, dragging the carriage through the gateway and veering away left out of sight.

"So she's gone and left us?" wondered Ford aloud, causing the House Guards to grin.

"It's what Captain calls a *diversion*," said the one standing nearest. "A decoy like, so as maybe them savages'll chase after that great heap."

"If they catch him…" mused Whetstone and let the thought trail off. "He's a brave boy."

"He is, sir, that he is."

Ford noticed an old man who had joined them in the courtyard. The robed and bent graybeard stood by the house's main entrance with a slim, middle-aged woman partially hidden behind him. He was the Iarl's personal sage, one of the more learned men of the city. She was Shyna Pond, a lady's attendant and cousin to the Iarl, who assisted the sage by carrying two jars for him. The moment Captain Hartfield spotted them, he presented himself to them so that they might get on with their appointed tasks. The sage took one of the two jars from Pond, dabbed the ointment it contained on his fingers and then smeared it upon the captain's cheeks and forehead.

"There isn't much left," said the sage. "You will have to keep your hands and as much of yourself as possible under wraps."

Pond took pinches of a chalky, white powder from the other jar and sprinkled it into the captain's dark hair, giving it hints of gray here and there. Before she finished, the sage's ointment was almost completely absorbed by the captain's skin.

"Where is she?" he asked while they worked on him.

"Here! I'm here!" said a woman flying from the front door in a blur of shiny hair and peach-skinned beauty that came to attention before the sage and her lady's attendant. While they smeared and sprinkled her, the Iarl Middlefield remained, for the most part, a picture of calm before those assembled in the courtyard. One would hardly guess that an army was out for her blood, judging by the self-possessed glint in her eye.

"Sorry," she said, avoiding the sage's fingers by speaking from the side of her mouth to Hartfield. Her generously submissive apology added a flush of embarrassment to the captain's impatience over these delays. They should have been off long before this. But still, his mistress should not be apologizing to him. A pair of gangly ghost-white boys, pages of about twelve, came out of the house with their arms loaded and gave Hartfield a welcome distraction, as he moved off to instruct them.

While the Iarl was being attended to, Whetstone pointed toward Ford's groin and asked, "Are you wounded?" Now that his clothes had had time to dry, a dark stain was visible around his pocket. Though he had forgotten all about the severed fingers, Ford's jolt of recollection was nothing to Whetstone's startled staggering back at the sight of the ball of flesh and bone encrusted in bizarre translucent blood, one of the fingers stretching out in a hideous come-hither curl.

"I–I found them, that is, I got them from...under the Pennaeth's house," said Ford.

"You what?"

Ford retold the story of how he entered the lord's house and fought the creatures that had changed their appearance, after which Whetstone looked no less amazed. "Oh my son, if that tale holds an ounce of truth, you'd best tell them." He nodded and nudged Ford toward the group gathered about the Iarl.

"No, I..." When Ford shook his head, Whetstone dragged him across the courtyard.

"Ma'am! Sir! This fellow here has something urgent to tell you." The Iarl and her people turned to them, some annoyed and some expectant. "Show them!" Ford held out to them the crumpled fingers in an open palm. They all leaned back and stared aghast at the fingers and then at him as if he might be some cannibalistic heathen.

"What is this all about, Whetstone?" demanded Hartfield. "A macabre display designed to frighten the ladies?"

"Tell them," Whetstone urged Ford. He did as ordered, but truncated the story to its barest essentials so that he might say it in the fewest words possible and be done with this uncomfortable situation.

"Well now," Hartfield said through a scowling grimace, "that is something indeed. Gruesome stuff. And you say you found them at Pennaeth Brastersceatt's?" Ford nodded and was greatly relieved when no one inquired into his reasons for being inside the house. The Jailor eyed him curiously, but the rest were much more interested in the fingers.

"May I?" asked the sage, pushing back the sleeves of his fine robe and taking the fingers from Ford to hold up to his aging eyes for a closer examination. "Yes," he muttered. "Yes, yes." He held them out to the Captain. "Does this smell familiar?" The Captain leaned in for a sniff.

"That's the horrid stuff," he said covering his nose. "Looks like we've found our culprit."

"Yes, most likely. You see," said the sage, tearing his attention from the fingers and addressing the curious faces gathering about him, "these come from an ychwangu, a creature that can change its form. In the case of these beings, to something pleasing to the recipient's mind. Although, 'victim' would be a more precise term, since assassination is their stock-in-trade." The sage had spent some time studying transformation, even transfiguration, in his early years and it all came back to him in a rising tide of joy at seeing his first sample in the flesh, albeit putrefying flesh.

"Are you saying these"—the Iarl made an attempt at the name and gave it up—"these creatures are to blame for…?" She trailed off and stifled a venomous indignation rising within her.

"For many, if not all of the recent murders, yes."

"That's proof enough for me that Brastersceatt has been harboring assassins. No doubt whatsoever," said Hartfield. Ford thought he appeared suddenly aged and far more care-worn by the discovery than one would have imagined possible. After all, it was what he had suspected, and the slap he gave to Ford's shoulder showed how pleased he was by the news. "Good man. We'll deal with this when we can, but now we *must* be off!"

While the Captain urged on the Iarl, the sage turned and spoke to Ford confidentially.

"Might I keep these? You see, they are quite rare, and I would like to study…what's this?" Flipping over the fingers for the first time, the sage noticed the pieces of flower stuck to them by blood. "Is this…? Yes, it's Larkwine's Rue, if I'm not mistaken." He peeled off the bits of the sprig and held them up to the light. "Two rarities in one find. Quite the day!"

"May I keep that, sir?" said Ford reaching out for the rue. "You can have the fingers, only the flower is a sort of good-luck charm to me."

"Luck? I've heard of it instilling a certain amount of hope in some, but never *luck*. And even so, you would need great vats of the stuff rendered down to make an ounce worth of its essence before it had any real effect on a person. No, this is or was nothing more than a pretty flower." He handed it over, nonetheless, and was so delighted in his finger fragments that he completely missed the signs of Ford's disappointment, as his body sagged at hearing that his magical flower held no magic at all.

The page boys with their burdens had been rocking rapidly back and forth on the balls of their feet and were fit to crawl out of their skin if they had to wait any longer. Finally, the Iarl and Captain Hartfield took from them dusty cloaks, gray mantles, yellowing shawls, and burlap sacks. Hartfield exchanged his House Guards' tunic for these worn cloths and hoisted a sack. The Iarl threw the shawl over her plain peasant's dress.

"Thank you," the Iarl said softly while bestowing a fragile smile upon the boys meant to convey her gratitude and affection while looking at each in turn and uttering their names before bidding them farewell. "Go home," she commanded after a hasty, but tender hug. Anxious to get back to their families and torn by the knowledge that this might be the last time they would ever see the woman they affectionately called Grand Aunt, they fled the courtyard in tears, scampered through the gate and were gone.

Dressing in shabby clothes seemed to have aged the Iarl and the captain by decades. Their cheeks sagged, and wrinkles had formed upon their foreheads and at the corners of their eyes.

"Magic's an amazing thing," muttered Dillon, coming to stand by Ford and Whetstone, and looking at each of them closely to see if they saw what he did.

"Another diversion," said Whetstone with an appreciative smile.

The Iarl turned her gaze upon the armed guards and gave them a nod that finished in a bow. "I ask, but do not demand, that some of you stay behind," she said quite clearly and without wavering. "Those who do not wish to stay may go now." While everyone's attention fell on Hartfield as he checked the Jailor's motion toward the gate, one of Whetstone's men bolted. "Let him go," the Iarl said, silencing both the Captain and Whetstone.

The urge to run rose up in Ford. Here was a chance to escape what was looking more and more like suicide, a chance given freely by the very person with the power to release him, and yet to his own astonishment, he wasn't taking it. By now, he truly felt he was here because he wanted to be, and so he fought down the urge.

No one else moved, and for a heartbeat no one breathed, as the horns and drums of the Pennaeth's army met their ears, growing suddenly wilder and more distinct as the rabble neared. If they hadn't stopped along the way to burn buildings owned by the Iarl or her sympathizers, they might already have arrived.

"We must go now!" the Captain insisted, shouldering the sack and steering the Iarl by an elbow. He was not happy about leaving his men behind, but his plan to fight alongside them had fallen apart when other city leaders disregarded their duty. Someone dependable had to see the Iarl to safety, and there was no one she depended on more than him.

A multitude of raucous voices, mingling with the oncoming horns and drums, lifted to the tops of the surrounding buildings. Hartfield took the Iarl by the arm and made for the gate. She turned back and called out, "You will not be forgotten!" As they passed under the arch, they bent themselves nearly double, linked arms, and looking very much like an aged peasant couple deserting a city under siege with a few of their possessions, they disappeared into the labyrinthine streets of Port Morton.

The sentry slammed the gate shut, and everyone turned to the Jailor, who was helping the sage back into the house. Though the lady's attendant Pond was more than capable of assisting the old man, the Jailor insisted, and once they were all inside, he closed the door behind them, leaving all the guards and watchmen dumbstruck. One of them tried the door.

"It's locked! He's locked us out!"

"And himself in," Whetstone observed, and without waiting a moment longer, he faced those assembled in the courtyard. "He wasn't going to amount to much in a fight anyhow, was he?" That quelled their grumbling. Whetstone had no speech in him for a moment like this, and he was saved from having to concoct one when the enemy's flags and banners appeared over the wall. "Ready yourselves! To the gate!"

The raging mob tore around the corner into view and plowed into the frail gate. The House Guards met them and pressed back against the bars with their halberds. Ford and the other watchmen leaned on the guards' backs to add support. The enemy first to the gate were crushed into the bars by their comrades from behind, for the army had grown in number and now hundreds clamored to be the one that cut the Iarl's throat. The gate sagged dangerously inward but held, and with the mass of bodies blocking the way, the enemy could not ram it down. Now Captain Hartfield's training showed, as those House Guards at the back leveled their weapons as one and drove the spearhead points between or over their fellows. So began the slaughter of the immobile and lightly armored enemy. Their leather jerkins and farmer's smocks were torn to shreds with each disemboweling lunge. One after another they screamed as shrilly as swine and slumped lifelessly, but none fell. They couldn't fall, not until those in the second and third ranks understood their peril and began forcing the crowd back. Then bodies began dropping at the gate into a widening pool of blood. The pile mounted, and the enemy backed away in horror. The defenders, mostly watchmen thinking they had won the battle, cheered like a party of drunken fools. Whetstone yelled at them to stay alert.

"There!" called Ford, spotting hands and arms reaching over the wall to one side. He and Dillon raced over and began pushing them back. Ford brought his hammer down on a hand that quickly vanished back over the wall. An emerging head ducked away from Dillon's stabbing spear. One man had a leg over and was straddling the wall when Moll Turner appeared and heaved him back by his foot. With a few more blows from Ford's hammer and stabs from Dillon's spear, they cleared that section of the wall.

"Here! To me!" Whetstone bellowed, and they ran to join him where the enemy was scaling the wall on the far side of the courtyard. They had no sooner repelled the oncoming horde there when, back on the other side, more hands and heads were showing themselves at the top of the wall. "Stay here! I'll take care of them!" Whetstone gathered another watchman and a House Guard to deal with those breaching the far wall. Fewer were now guarding the gate, and those that remained were being bloodied by the blades of a resurgent enemy sneaking through the bars.

Though the defenders were stretched to their limit, they seemed to be holding steady. Then a hail of rocks and weapons hurtled over the wall from one side. Heavy cobblestones pried up from surrounding streets flew lazily into the air; some crashed straight back down, but others toppled into the courtyard.

"Get away from the wall!" someone shouted, but one watchman had already fallen to his knees and was clutching the side of his head. The others retreated to the center of the courtyard, and this gave the enemy time to scale the walls. The sight of so many of them flooding over into the courtyard, screaming their bloodthirsty cries and blasting their shrieking horns caused some of the defenders to panic; one of them ran to the gardener's barrow, leapt upon it, got hold of the top of the wall and dragged himself up, where he was pulled over the other side and into the merciless arms of the enemy.

A triumphant pitchfork-wielding Weaverite standing atop the wall took a crossbow bolt to the chest and fell backward. From a second-story window she had kicked open, Shyna Pond fought frantically to reload a crossbow. After getting off two more shots, she disappeared as a volley of projectiles disintegrated the window.

Across the courtyard, Ford watched Whetstone gather about him a small group of watchmen and House Guards into a defensive circle from which they fought with their backs to one another. In this way they kept at bay the growing horde fast closing in on them.

"Dillon! Moll! Backs to me!" called Ford. Though neither had seen much fighting, they got his meaning and mimicked Whetstone's small force as a triangle that soon turned into a diamond when a man from the day watch joined them. But some fanatical devotee of the Pennaeth shot past their new comrade's spear point and drove a knife into him again and again with a fiendish glee. Ford beat on the man's back, then connected with the back of his head and knocked him out, but now they were three again.

Dillon and Moll's spears fended off the enemy's sporadic attacks well, but Ford couldn't swing his hammer with much effect. The crowded courtyard had the claustrophobic feel of Baldy's. Ford even felt his ears throb just as they used to during those fights in the dank cellar. Then that old familiar thrill welled up within, and he strode forward, swinging his short-handled hammer like a punch that threatened to crush skulls. But a carpenter's mallet pounded into his lower back and sent him reeling off balance. He twisted about, dodged the next blow, and caught the impression of a pinched face well below him just as the mallet-wielder yelped in agony from a jab to the ribs from Moll's spear. Ford caught a farmer's pitchfork lunging past him just before it plunged into her side, pulled it down and whipped his hammer around to catch the ducking man in the shoulder. The farmer tripped backward and disappeared into a sea of his own comrades, their tunics and smocks paint-smeared with the Pennaeth's colors. Ford jumped back into his defensive triangle before it was flanked again.

At the gate, two of the House Guards had fallen, while a third was on his hands and knees holding in his gutted stomach and screaming at the ground. Only three remained pressing their halberds against the bars to keep the gate from collapsing inward under the weight of the Pennaeth's rabid zealots.

More came over the wall unchecked, some weaponless or holding knives between their teeth. From the swarm of persistent foes already within the courtyard, a one-eyed man flew at Dillon, who planted himself and thrust his spear forward. The man screeched and danced at the end of the shaft. The cleaver he was ready to bring down on Dillon's head flipped away to the ground while his hands flapped in nervous spasms trying to rip out the spearhead stuck in his cheek. Ford pivoted about, trying to defend all angles, and dodged a screaming woman. The wind of some gleaming blade whistled by his ear. He plowed his shoulder into her, throwing her hard to the ground.

A thin scarlet-cheeked youth with an exuberant eye standing atop the wall waved one of the Pennaeth's flags back and forth, cheering as if it were a holiday parade. He had much to cheer about. The brief moment when the defenders looked like they might hold their ground was over and, after a running start, the mangled gate was rammed down as its loosened hinges finally gave out.

Two House Guards were pinned underneath and trampled as the enemy poured in. After a quick clash of weapons and armor, a thrashing forest of wood, leather, and steel, the defenders fell back against the house; Ford and Whetstone's groups merged and defended themselves in an ever contracting sphere that bought them a little more time.

The fight eroded into threats and taunts as the attackers played like cats with mice, throwing a rock here, jabbing with a spear there, or merely hurling insults. The rapid-fire chirps of a particularly shrill horn quieted both sides and drew their attention to the gate, where the Weaverite orator Dab Yankin stood with a foot upon the mound of dead like a conquering hero. He took the horn from his lips and stepped aside. Behind him, picking his way through the carnage with a pleased pride swelling his chest was Tintot Song adorned in piecemeal dress-armor meant for a child.

"Halt!" he snapped out in his high, piping voice. One of the Pennaeth's own House Guards supported him by the elbow, helping him clamber over the bodies in the gateway. Ford was astonished to find this man leading their army, and though he wasn't sorry he had stopped Dunn from beating him to death, he did regret not beating some sense into this little blowhard himself. He supposed it didn't matter who led the revolt because the Pennaeth could find any number of toadies willing to do his grunt work. Still, Ford was confused as to why Song would back someone like Brastersceatt, whose abhorrence of Song's secret desires could have gotten him sentenced to death by the very man he was serving. For his part, Song saw no connection between the kinds of brothels he frequented and the ones that supplied women as the commodity. To his mind it was women who were the problem; they were the ones who needed putting in place. The Weaverites would see to that, and the Pennaeth would help them.

"A message from Bowen Dome!" shouted Song, holding aloft a piece of paper and giving it a triumphant wave. "Lord Brastersceatt has taken the castle!" The new castellan had simply handed over the castle, but the Pennaeth's men cheered wildly anyway. "He has installed himself there upon his throne, and we shall receive further instruction soon. For now, we follow through with our orders and take the house and the Iarl with it!" Another cheer. "But remember, the Pennaeth wants the House undamaged." He had to raise his voice over the celebratory hollering and hooting of looters in the surrounding neighborhood. "Nothing is to be taken, nothing touched!"

"The door is locked, sir!" shouted the scarlet-cheeked, flag-bearing youth, quite indignant that they should be thwarted in this way.

"Well then, ram it down!" said Song with an offhanded giddiness. While the ram was fetched, Yankin gestured to the handful of remaining defenders who were still herded together with their weapons drooping from their weary hands.

"What's to be done with these scum?" he asked.

Song scanned the line of downtrodden defenders. Doubling back, his eyes locked onto Ford's and his eyebrows leapt. Recognition of the man who stood a foot taller than most others in the courtyard was instantaneous. Song abruptly spun away and then stalked off with his hands clasped behind his back. He made a show of inspecting the aftermath of the battle, took a turn about the courtyard and finally came back.

"Disarm them. Perhaps they will be ransomed or hanged. I do not know, nor do I care, but for now, they are our prisoners. What's to become of them is for a higher power to decide."

Ford could not relax, and the hammer had to be torn from his grasp. They had lost, and it was just sinking in that he was not going to be killed, not yet anyway. Any future at all seemed doubtful up until then, but at least there was one, and perhaps it might be one he could live with. If their meager defense of the house had bought the Iarl enough time to escape and possibly to return in force once day, then there was hope that their sacrifice was not in vain.

"The Iarl has been captured!" shouted a joyous messenger boy in a broad wicker hat as he leapt over the bodies at the gate and came skipping into the courtyard. "The Iarl has been captured!"

"Is this true, Pate? Has she truly been caught?" asked Song taking the boy by the shoulders and searching his face for the truth.

"Yes! Her carriage was spotted heading for Rall's Gate, and we've taken that one already, so they must've caught her by now! I was told to deliver the news to you immediately!"

Her carriage. Ford's heart lifted. Hope remained.

Note From The Author

Word-of-mouth is crucial for any author to succeed. If you enjoyed the book, please leave a review online—anywhere you are able. Even if it's just a sentence or two. It would make all the difference and would be very much appreciated.

Thanks!
Jason

About the Author

Author Jason R. Koivu created the Barlow fantasy series out of his love for *Dungeons & Dragons* and a desire to finally use his college degree. Born, raised and schooled in New England, he now lives in California with his wife and no kids, though they did briefly own a cat. They miss that cat…

Thank you so much for reading one of our **Fantasy** novels.

If you enjoyed our book, please check out our recommended for your next great read!

War of the Staffs by Steve Stephenson & Kathryn M. Tedrick

"Offers an enjoyable romp for high fantasy fans."

-KIRKUS REVIEWS

View other Black Rose Writing titles at
www.blackrosewriting.com/books and use promo code
PRINT to receive a **20% discount** when purchasing.

www.ingramcontent.com/pod-product-compliance
Lightning Source LLC
Chambersburg PA
CBHW011132100726
47898CB00009B/2947

9781684334360